Murder Had a Little Lamb

A Reigning Cats & Dogs Mystery

Cynthia Baxter

BANTAM BOOKS
NEW YORK

Murder Had a Little Lamb is a work of fiction. Names, characters, places, and incidents either are the product of the author's imagination or are used fictitiously. Any resemblance to actual persons, living or dead, events, or locales is entirely coincidental.

A Bantam Books Mass Market Original

Copyright © 2009 by Cynthia Baxter

Published in the United States by Bantam Books, an imprint of The Random House Publishing Group, a division of Random House, Inc., New York.

BANTAM BOOKS and the rooster colophon are registered trademarks of Random House, Inc.

ISBN 978-0-553-59237-5

Cover illustration: Bob Guisti

Printed in the United States of America

www.bantamdell.com

2 4 6 8 9 7 5 3 1

To Fabienne Bouler,
mon amie en France

Murder Had a
Little Lamb

Chapter 1

"The greatest fear dogs know is the fear that you will not come back when you go out the door without them."

—Stanley Coren, dog psychologist

D o you, Jessica, take this man, Nicholas, to be your lawfully wedded husband..."

Every woman wants her wedding day to be perfect, and so far mine had been exactly that.

The setting couldn't have been lovelier—a sprawling estate on Long Island's North Fork that had been the home of a prosperous sea captain back in the 1800s. These days, it was available for private events, which meant that today Nick and I had the charming three-story Victorian mansion, the expansive lawn, and the exquisite gardens all to ourselves.

The day couldn't have been more pleasant, either. The delightfully warm June sun shone down on my soon-to-be husband and me as we stood beneath a graceful wooden archway decorated with gauzy white fabric and colorful wildflowers. Behind us, more than a hundred friends and family members looked on. Off to the left was a large white tent set up for the wedding feast, complete with a three-tier cake.

And I was certainly dressed like the heroine in a storybook, the type that ends "and they lived happily ever after." My wedding dress was straight out of a fairy tale, made from flowing ivory silk and cut in a flattering empire style. One of my closest friends, Suzanne Fox, had applied my makeup in a way that made me look as if I were glowing. She'd also twisted my straight, dark blond hair into an elaborate updo, leaving a few loose strands to frame my face. The finishing touch was the cluster of white flowers she'd fastened to one side of my head.

As for the groom, he looked positively debonair, thanks to a well-cut tuxedo that made him look as if he were dashing off to the Academy Awards. And while I'd grown used to the lock of dark brown hair that was constantly falling into Nick's eyes, for this special occasion he'd apparently used some magic potion to tame it.

True, a few butterflies had been doing the hokey-pokey in my stomach before the ceremony. Yet everything was going exactly as planned until the moment I found myself standing in front of the judge.

I could feel the eyes of my guests boring into me as I clutched a bouquet of the same white flowers as my hair ornament. At the moment, I desperately hoped the profusion of petals hid the fact that my hands were trembling.

"...For better or for worse, to love and to cherish..."

Not that I had any doubts about marrying Nick.

Not at this point. He was the love of my life, and looking back over the years we'd been together, I realized that even though we'd had our share of ups and downs—or possibly *more* than our share—I'd never stopped feeling that he and I simply *belonged* together.

It was just that there was something so momentous about actually uttering those two words—*I do*. While I could picture myself being married to Nick, I was still having trouble getting over that one last hurdle...

"From this day forward," the judge intoned, "for as long as you both shall live...?"

It was time. This was it. So I opened my mouth, prepared to say those life-changing syllables, when the peaceful scene was shattered by a piercing scream.

"*A-a-a-ah!*"

Instantly, everyone froze.

Nick turned to me, wearing a puzzled look. "Jess?" he asked questioningly.

It seemed he just assumed that the desperate cry for help had come from me.

"*A-a-a-ah!*" we all heard again, the horrible cry cutting through the warm June day like a bolt of lightning. "No! *No!*"

Maybe it's because as a veterinarian I'm used to handling emergencies, but before I had a chance to mentally form the phrase "ruining your own wedding," I whirled around, hiked up my long skirt, and raced back down the aisle. I was only vaguely aware of the chaos erupting around me as guests rose from their seats, glancing around with worried looks.

"It's coming from the house," I said to Nick.

The fact that he was right beside me, racing toward

the house so speedily that his tux could have been made of Spandex, assured me that I was doing the right thing. "It sounds like somewhere on the first floor," he said breathlessly.

Even though I was wearing heels, I managed to reach the front door just seconds after Nick. The two of us rushed inside, exchanging a look of concern over the unmistakable sound of gasps and sobs.

"The kitchen!" I cried, sprinting down the hall.

I wondered if I'd be able to move faster if I kicked off my silly Barbie shoes, especially since I was now dealing with polished hardwood floors instead of the back lawn's velvety-green grass. But I didn't want to waste any time. Instead, I skidded around the corner toward the kitchen doorway, not knowing what I'd find.

I certainly didn't expect it to be a man lying completely still on the tile floor with what looked like an extremely sharp knife sticking out of his chest. And from the pallor of his skin and the dullness of his eyes, he appeared to be dead.

My first thought was that he couldn't have been part of the catering staff, since he wasn't wearing black pants and a white shirt the way the food preparers and waiters were.

In fact, from the way he was dressed—a blue-and-white-striped seersucker suit, a lemon-yellow necktie, and white patent-leather loafers—I concluded that he had to be a guest. But he certainly wasn't anyone I'd told my future mother-in-law, Dorothy, to add to the list of invitees.

"Do you know who he is?" I asked Nick, my voice a near-whisper.

He shook his head. "I never saw this man before in my life."

It was only at that point that I realized someone else was in the room. A young woman was cowering a few feet away from Nick and me, the expression on her face one of complete shock. Her shiny black hair was pulled back into a neat ponytail and she was dressed like a penguin, leading me to the conclusion that unlike the man on the floor, she did work for the caterer.

I also assumed she was the screamer.

"What happened?" I asked her.

"I—I don't know!" she gasped. "I went downstairs to the wine cellar for about ten minutes. I guess I was the only person in the house, since it looks as if everybody else sneaked outside to watch the ceremony. We're not supposed to, but whenever it's time for the bride and groom to say 'I do' we can't help it. Anyway, when I came upstairs just now, this is what I found!"

She paused to take a deep breath before whispering, "Do you think he's dead?"

"It looks that way," I replied gently.

Her expression still stricken, she pulled a cellphone out of the pocket of the tailored black pants she wore under a crisp white apron emblazoned with the caterer's logo. As she punched in three numbers, she stepped away to a back corner of the kitchen. That left Nick and me with the unfortunate dead man.

"Who *is* he?" I asked, my head spinning as I tried to make sense out of what I was seeing. "From his clothes, he doesn't look as if he works for the caterer.

Besides, if he did, the woman who found him would have recognized him. I don't think he's affiliated with the estate, either, since when I booked it someone would have mentioned that he'd—"

I stopped midsentence. I'd just become aware of the sharp clicking of high heels, the uneven rhythm making it sound as if they were worn by someone who wasn't used to teetering around on them.

Which meant my future mother-in-law had joined us.

"What's going on in here?" Dorothy Burby demanded. Distractedly, she smoothed the fabric of the ill-fitting blue-gray dress she'd chosen to wear on this lovely summer day on which her son was getting married. I was hoping she'd thought wearing such a drab dress was the embodiment of sophistication—even though part of me feared she was in mourning over her son's choice of a mate.

"For goodness' sake, Jessica," she added shrilly, "you can't just leave your guests sitting out there in the hot sun! This is supposed to be a wedding, so I don't understand why—"

She gasped, then slapped her hands against her cheeks.

"Good heavens!" she cried. "What happened to Cousin Nathaniel?"

"Cousin Nathaniel?" Nick and I repeated in unison.

"That's right." Dorothy fumbled inside the small rhinestone-studded clutch she was carrying and pulled out a pair of what I assumed were reading glasses. She planted them at the end of her nose, then leaned over the ill-fated man's body and peered closely at his face.

"That's Cousin Nathaniel, all right," she declared. Sighing loudly, she said, "I'm the one who invited him. I had to. He's family."

"You mean I'm related to this guy?" Nick asked, amazed.

"Of course," Dorothy sniffed. "He's Ruthie's son. You know, Gladys's sister's boy. But goodness, just look at poor Cousin Nathaniel *now*!"

From the confused look on Nick's face, I got the impression he didn't know any more about who Ruthie or Gladys were than he did about the man I was now thinking of as Poor Cousin Nathaniel.

"Who's Ruthie—and who's Gladys?" he asked, blinking.

"Ruthie was my first cousin—which makes Nathaniel my first cousin once removed," Dorothy replied, still staring at the dead man. "I never knew Ruthie all that well. I knew her sister, Gladys, a little better, since she was a lot closer to my age. Of course, both Ruthie and Gladys are gone now. In fact, Nathaniel's the only one left from that branch of the family."

A vague memory was surfacing from one of our endless phone conversations about the guest list: Dorothy mentioning that she felt obligated to invite some distant relative she hadn't seen in ages. At the time, I remembered thinking something trite like, "The more the merrier."

With a sigh, she added, "It's been so long since he's

had any contact with our part of the family that I never really expected him to show up."

I bet he wishes he hadn't, I thought grimly.

It was at that point that I realized it would be more appropriate for me to use the past tense when referring to Poor Cousin Nathaniel.

"I'll be darned," Dorothy went on, shaking her head in wonderment as she continued studying the lifeless body lying in front of us. "He looks good. I mean, better than I would have expected. I haven't seen him in—I don't even know how long it's been. But it's so like Ruthie's side of the family to ruin somebody's wedding. I bet the egotistical so-and-so didn't even bother to bring a present!"

The fact that this particular guest might not have increased my ever-growing collection of small appliances didn't seem to matter much given the fact that he wouldn't even be around to eat a piece of wedding cake.

"But who could possibly have done this?" Nick cried. "Surely it couldn't have been one of our guests!"

"I'm pretty sure everyone we invited was sitting out there on the folding chairs," I said, mentally running through the guest list.

Dorothy nodded. "While I was waiting for the ceremony to start, I counted heads to see if everyone who'd said they were coming had actually shown up." Frowning, she said, "I couldn't figure out why I came up one short, but now I know. Nathaniel must have come into the house for some reason."

That meant that every one of the people Nick and I

had invited to our wedding had an alibi. I was relieved, since the idea that one of our friends or family members could possibly have had anything to do with this was too horrible to contemplate.

I'd barely had a chance to digest that thought before people began rushing at us from all directions. The rest of the catering staff crowded into the room first. Only seconds afterward the guests began streaming inside, their furrowed foreheads and clouded eyes completely out of sync with the bright flowered sundresses and pastel-colored sports shirts they wore.

I was about to tell them all to calm down and to back away from what was now a crime scene when Dorothy grabbed my arm. She yanked me over to a granite counter at the back of the kitchen. I couldn't help noticing that it was covered with tiny quiches and scallops wrapped in bacon, neatly arranged on silver trays.

"Will you look at this?" Dorothy cried mournfully.

I blinked. "The hors d'oeuvres?"

"Of course not!" she sputtered. "*This!* It's started already, and the cops aren't even on the scene!"

"*What's* started already?" I asked. Not only was I completely bewildered, I could practically feel a black-and-blue mark forming where Dorothy's fingers were clamped around my flesh.

"The—the chaos, of course!" she sputtered. "The craziness. And the newspapers and TV stations haven't even gotten wind of this yet!"

"I can imagine how you must feel," I said sympathetically. "Losing a relative in such a horrible way, even though it sounds as if you hardly knew him—"

"I was thinking of how bad this looks," she interrupted. "I mean, what kind of people have someone in their own families murdered? Certainly not respectable people!"

I was still trying to process Dorothy Burby's obvious lack of a sympathy gene when Nick emerged from the crowd, his expression grave. Even amid all the chaos, I couldn't help noticing how handsome he looked. I also realized that I actually preferred the usual version of Nick to this polished one—that is, the one wearing jeans and a T-shirt and distractedly pushing back that renegade lock of hair.

Standing alongside him was his father, a tall, lean man with a full head of white hair and a gaunt face. Like Nick, Henry Burby wore a tuxedo. But his hung loosely on his gangly frame.

I was normally struck by how much Henry looked like his son. This time, however, what I noticed most was that the expression on the older man's face was one of complete bewilderment.

"Has someone called the police?" Henry asked, his voice edged with panic. "Dorothy? What should we do?"

"The police are on their way, Dad," Nick assured his father along with the rest of us. "And I think I've managed to convince everyone to start moving away from the area. People are already going back outside."

Turning to me, he grimly asked, "What about us? What happens now?"

"I don't think we can go on with the ceremony," I replied softly. "Do you really want to get married with

Poor Cousin Nathaniel lying dead mere feet away from our wedding cake?"

"I knew I shouldn't have invited him," Dorothy grumbled. "Even as I was addressing the envelope, I had a bad feeling. Of course, at that point I was merely afraid he'd drink too much champagne and insist on making some inappropriate speech or . . . or that he'd scarf down so many hors d'oeuvres that there wouldn't be any left for the other guests. Even as a child, he was always so . . . trying."

Tossing her head, she added, "If you want *my* opinion, I think we should go ahead and just get this over with. The best thing to do would be to have that maid of honor of yours get everyone back in their seats so we can finish up before this place charges us for overtime. Suzanne—isn't that her name?—she's pushy enough that she shouldn't have any trouble getting these people to behave."

Fortunately, that same pushy individual, the one person in the world who seemed able to take on Dorothy Burby and actually prevail, chose that moment to step in and work her magic. Wrapped around her wrist were two leashes, since her responsibilities as maid of honor included taking care of the only two canines who'd been invited to my wedding.

As usual, my tailless Westie, Max, looked as if he were posing for the Milk-Bone box, with his teddy bear face and his fluffy snow-white fur. In honor of the occasion, a satin ribbon the same color was tied jauntily around his neck. As for my Dalmatian, Lou, he already looked as if he'd been partying a little too hard. His white ribbon had come untied, and the frayed ends flopped forlornly against his chest. Of course, the fact that he only has one eye always makes him look a bit bedraggled.

"No can do," my friend Suzanne countered, wagging one finger at Dorothy.

Suzanne Fox and I went back more than fifteen years, when we'd met during our freshman year at Bryn Mawr College. We'd immediately had a common bond, since we were both biology majors who dreamed of pursuing a veterinary career.

Four years later, when she went off to Purdue University's veterinary college in her home state of Indiana and I went upstate to Cornell, we lost touch. But we'd reconnected one summer, when I'd gotten involved with a charity dog show in the upscale area of Long Island known as the Bromptons and discovered Suzanne had been living there for years after opening a small animal clinic in West Brompton Beach.

Somehow, over the years, Suzanne had managed to take on the characteristics of some of her patients. The bulldogs, for example.

"Dorothy, a man is *dead*," she snapped, standing nose to nose with Nick's mother. "The unfortunate soul was murdered, and now he's lying in the middle of the kitchen with a knife sticking out of him as if he were a—a giant baked ham. And if that wasn't bad enough, the poor guy was related to Nick—not to mention related to you!"

She grabbed my hand, then reached for Nick's. "And an occasion that was supposed to be one of the most wonderful events in Jessie and Nick's life has been ruined! Think about how *they* must feel! They must be devastated." Glowering at Dorothy, she added, "What part of this aren't you getting?"

"But the bride and groom didn't even *know* Nathaniel!" Dorothy cried. "And Henry only met him once or twice, so I'm sure he's not all that upset, either. Isn't that right, Henry?"

Henry's sheepish shrug made it clear that he'd learned long ago that arguing with his wife simply wasn't worth it.

"In fact, none of us thought he'd even show up!" Dorothy continued, wagging her finger right back at Suzanne. "The only reason I sent him an invitation in the first place was that I thought it wouldn't look right if we left one of our blood relatives off the guest list." Lowering her voice so that she seemed to be talking to herself rather than to us, she added, "Even if he was the black sheep of the family."

"The black sheep?" I repeated. "What do you mean by—?"

"Surely even *you* don't expect your son to get married with a bunch of cop cars cluttering up the lawn!" Suzanne exclaimed. By this point, her rounded cheeks were almost as bright as her fiery red hair. "Not to mention all those lights from the ambulance flashing a few feet behind the tent!"

"In that case, we'll just wait until the police go back to the station or wherever it is they go when they're not driving around," Dorothy replied, folding her arms firmly across her chest. "Do you have any idea how much work I put into planning this—"

"Ladies, be gentlemen!"

I turned, relieved to see that another positive force

in my life had just stepped in: Betty Vandervoort, looking as dignified as a queen in a pale-yellow silk dress with a matching jacket.

"No matter what each one of us thinks about this situation," she said in a soft, even voice, "it's up to Jessica and Nick to decide."

Throwing her arms around me in a gigantic bear hug, she half-whispered, "Jessica, I'm so sorry that today has turned out this way."

Thank goodness for Betty, I thought for about the millionth time in my life. Somehow, the fact that our ages were quite a few decades apart never seemed to get in the way. Not only was she my landlady, she was also one of my closest friends. She also served as sort of a surrogate parent, since I'd lost both of mine in a car accident several years before.

I cast her a look of gratitude. Then I looked at Nick as if to say, "Okay, this one's your call." After all, it was true that his mother had put a humongous amount of effort into planning my wedding. More than I deemed appropriate or desirable, in fact, since in addition to calling me countless times to talk about the guest list, for weeks she'd tormented me with questions about every single aspect of the evening— everything from what kind of place cards we should have to whether the ice sculpture she insisted was a "must" should be shaped like two lovebirds or two swans with their necks intertwined.

My guests had put a lot of effort into making this day special, too, getting all gussied up and then driving out to the eastern end of Long Island. Not that it was much of a hardship, especially on a perfect weekend like this one. While this wonderful old mansion wasn't what anyone could consider conveniently located, it was smack-dab in the middle of one of the most scenic areas that surrounded New York City. One of the most peaceful, as well.

Given the events of the day, however, the word "peaceful" hardly applied.

And as far as I was concerned, the fact that there was a dead man lying in the middle of the kitchen was a darn good reason to postpone tying the proverbial knot.

Yet while I was inclined to send everyone home with a promise that we'd reschedule, I didn't want to be the one to make the call. Not when all along I'd had a few, shall we say, commitment issues.

So I told Nick, "I'll go along with whatever you want to do."

"I think we have no choice but to cancel the wedding," he said, frowning. "Suzanne is right. I don't want our wedding photos to have police cars in the background."

"Good call," Suzanne said heartily.

Striding toward the group of dazed-looking wedding guests who still stood around, she announced, "Okay, people. The wedding is off. But it would probably be a good idea for all of you to remain on the property until after the police get here in case they want to question any of us.

"Sorry all of you had to waste a shower and a long drive," she continued, "but maybe on your way home you can save the day by hitting a few farm stands.

Even better, a few wineries, as long as someone in your party agrees to be the designated driver."

Clapping her hands loudly, she added, "Let's move it out!"

She then demonstrated a level of sensitivity I would never have dreamed she possessed by turning to me and asking, "What about you, Jess? Are you okay?"

I opened my mouth to reply. But for the second time that day, I didn't have any idea what I was going to say.

• • •

Talk about a letdown, I thought as I tottered into my cottage in my satin heels, wrapping the skirt of my wedding dress around me to keep the folds of ivory silk from getting snagged on the door frame.

My two dogs squeezed past me, loping inside with so much energy that it was obvious that they, at least, were happy to be home. As Max headed for his water bowl and Lou zeroed in on a tennis ball, I tossed my bouquet onto the couch and scanned the living room with dismay.

Nick and I had decided to delay our honeymoon until August, after he'd finished his summer internship at a Long Island law firm. That meant we'd planned on coming straight to the cottage after the reception. To make our homecoming a little more romantic, I'd draped white crepe paper streamers over the dining area, then hung one of those wonderfully tacky 3-D paper wedding bells in the center. Two champagne flutes stood side by side on the large table that did double duty for dinner plates and laptops. The glasses were supposed to go with the bottle of champagne I'd left chilling in the refrigerator.

As I surveyed the pathetic display, my two cats came into the room. Tinkerbell, who had both the coloring and the personality of a tiger, bounded in from the bedroom, ready for a cuddle. Catherine the Great, my older and wiser feline who I'd nicknamed Cat, made a much grander entrance from the kitchen. I noticed that the gray fur on her cheek was askew, a sign that she'd been easing her arthritis by lying in front of the refrigerator, basking in its warmth.

"Who's the pretty birdy?" Prometheus immediately chimed in, strutting from side to side on his perch with the skill and grace of a seasoned vaudevillian. My blue-and-gold macaw waited only a second before answering his own question: "Prometheus is the pretty birdy. Apple, *awk*! I want apple!"

My animals all struck me as inappropriately cheerful, given my own somber mood. Only Leilani, the Jackson's Chameleon Nick and I had brought back from a trip to Maui, seemed sufficiently somber. She blinked at me from her glass tank, where she rested on one of the small tree branches strewn along the bottom.

Even though I always gave each and every one of them a warm greeting, today I just wasn't up to it.

I turned to Nick. "This isn't quite the way I envisioned our homecoming," I said sadly.

"Me, either," Nick agreed, sounding as gloomy as I did. "But I think we were right about not going ahead with the ceremony. How could we, when we'd always associate our wedding day with such a terrible event?"

I nodded. I hadn't doubted for a moment that we'd made the right decision. But that didn't mean I could stop myself from thinking about all the flowers and lovely food just sitting there, completely wasted. I was also picturing our guests as the police finally allowed them to head back to their cars, some shuffling along like zombies and others half-jogging as if they couldn't wait to get away.

I jumped when my cellphone rang. I couldn't imagine who would be insensitive enough to call me at a time like this.

Then I glanced at the caller ID screen.

"Hello, Dorothy," I said, surprising myself by how calm I sounded. I cast Nick a glance that reflected how I really felt about my almost-but-not-quite-yet-mother-in-law's interruption. He rolled his eyes, then disappeared into the bedroom.

Which left me to deal with my almost-mother-in-law by myself.

"Nick and I just got home," I told her. "We've barely—"

"What an embarrassment!" Dorothy cut in, not even bothering to say hello, much less asking how I was. "Jessica, I'm beside myself!"

"It was a terrible day," I agreed. "I can imagine how upset you must be."

"Of course I'm upset!" she spat back. "This is completely unacceptable, and I want this horrid thing to go away as quickly as possible."

"We all do," I assured her. When it comes to dealing with the woman who gave birth to the man I love,

I always tread carefully. "But I'm sure the police will do everything they possibly can to—"

"And as *quietly* as possible," she continued, as if she hadn't heard a word I'd said. "Which is why I decided that *you* have to do something about this."

"*Me?*" I squawked. "What do you want *me* to do?"

"Find out who did this disgusting thing, of course!"

It took me a few seconds to get over my shock. "*Excuse* me?" I finally said.

"Solve the murder!" Dorothy insisted shrilly. "Find out who killed poor Cousin Nathaniel as fast as you can so we can all move on! That *is* what you do, isn't it? When you're not doing that—that *job* of yours, riding around in that ridiculous bus treating cats and dogs and Lord only knows what else? Solving crimes is your hobby, isn't it? You do it the way some people do needlepoint or—or collect porcelain dolls or Wedgwood."

It was hard to imagine anyone placing investigating murders and displaying dolls in the same category. Then again, this wasn't the first time Dorothy and I failed to see things the same way.

"Solving homicide cases is the police department's job," I pointed out.

"Hmph!" she snorted. "Who knows how competent *they* are?"

She had me there. But I wasn't about to go down that road.

I tried to be diplomatic. "It's true that in the past, I've gotten involved in solving a few crimes. But it's not exactly what you'd call a hobby. In fact, it's—"

"Yes, but it's something you're good at, isn't it?"

she persisted. "You have a knack for it. The way *I* happen to be good with people."

I wasn't going to touch *that* one with a ten-foot pole.

"I'd help," Dorothy went on, "but I have to get back to Florida. In fact, we're about to check out of our hotel. Not that I haven't thought about extending our trip. Even Henry agreed that it might make sense for us to stay on Long Island until this nastiness is cleared up."

I suspected that "Henry agreed" meant that, as usual, Henry felt that asserting his will was an uphill battle so demanding that it would have left Sir Edmund Hillary gasping for air.

"But I've decided to go back home, just as we'd planned," Dorothy continued. "Otherwise, the senior center where Henry and I play Bingo every day would simply fall apart. Goodness, you'd think figuring out the rules of the game was rocket science."

"I understand that you're upset about what happened to Nathaniel," I said, trying a different tack. "And of course you're concerned. Anyone would be. But that doesn't mean—"

"Jessica, I've made up my mind," Dorothy said firmly. "You're going to solve this crime. Besides, what else do you have to do with all your free time?"

I was still struggling to come up with an answer to that when she continued, "Now that that's settled, I suppose I should tell you everything I know about Nathaniel Stibbins. If you're going to figure out who committed this unseemly crime before the newspapers turn it into a circus, you're going to need all the help you can get."

I sighed. Somehow, having this conversation while I

was still wearing my wedding gown just seemed *wrong*. But before I had a chance to suggest gently that maybe this wasn't the best time for a briefing on the dearly departed, Dorothy said, "After college, he spent a few years trying to figure out what he wanted to be when he grew up—as if he wasn't grown up already. He had some crazy idea that he was meant to be a great artist or something.

"At any rate, he finally got a job teaching art, which was much more practical. He ended up staying at the same school for—let's see, he was probably in his late thirties, so it must have been something like ten years. Anyway, he spent all that time teaching at a very posh girls' school in the Bromptons. It's called the Worth School."

I must admit, I was surprised. I'd heard of the Worth School, of course. In fact, one or two of my clients out on the South Fork sent their children there. But I didn't know much about it, aside from the fact that its student body was reputed to consist mainly of the offspring of some of the biggest movers and shakers in the country, parents who'd made megabucks in the movie industry, the recording industry, the fashion industry, and just about every other lucrative industry you could think of.

Its atypical student body was a result of the school's location. The cluster of idyllic beach communities on Long Island's South Fork was close enough to New York City that it had served as a popular summer community for the wealthy for decades. In more recent years, some of the summer residents began making it their year-round home after deciding that small-town life was a better place to raise children than the big city. But I was pretty sure that Worth was a boarding school, as well as a day school. That meant its students could come from anywhere—as long as Mom or Dad were able to pay for both the hefty tuition and campus housing.

"Start your investigation at the Worth School," Dorothy instructed. "Oh, I know you probably have your own ideas about the best way to jump in, but I assume the police will manage to do an adequate job of checking out all the more obvious possibilities. Nathaniel's personal life, for one, although I don't think he was married or even closely attached. After all, when he RSVP'd he said he'd be coming alone. Of course, I don't really know anything about his social activities. I don't think anyone in the family does, since none of us made much of an effort to keep in touch with him.

"At any rate," she continued, "the only information I was able to get out of any of my relatives was about his current job. And if I were you, I'd begin by taking a close look at what was going on at that snooty school. People of privilege always seem to think they're better than the rest of us, and I wouldn't be surprised if somehow Nathaniel's association with that place is what finally caught up with him.

"Besides," Dorothy went on, barely stopping to take a breath, "when I sent Nathaniel his wedding invitation, I mailed it to the school. Since no one has been in touch with him, I wasn't sure the home address I had for him was current, so sending it to his workplace seemed like the most sensible thing to do.

And whoever did this—this *thing* to him clearly knew exactly where he was going to be today. If you ask me, somebody at that school saw the invitation and decided that your wedding was the perfect time and place to pounce. They probably figured that no one at a stranger's wedding was likely to notice them, much less be able to identify them if they were spotted."

Dorothy had clearly given this a great deal of thought. And I had to admit she had a point. That did indeed strike me as a likely scenario—especially since the wedding guests were all accounted for, clearing them of suspicion.

Of course, the catering staff offered another possibility. Yet I instantly realized that it was unlikely that one of them was the killer. After all, that meant someone would have had to have signed on as an employee after learning that Nathaniel was going to be attending the Popper-Burby event—which struck me as an impossibly convoluted scenario.

Another explanation was that Nathaniel had walked in on someone doing something he or she shouldn't have been doing—or that for some other reason a fight had broken out in the kitchen while the ceremony was starting up. But it would have had to have been quite an altercation to have resulted in such a devastating outcome. And if that had been the case, the rest of us would have heard shouting or some other sign of a commotion inside the house. After all, it was just a few paces away from the spot where the ceremony was taking place.

Besides, the young woman from the catering company had said that all the other employees had been outside. As for her alibi, being in the wine cellar, I supposed the forensic evidence the police uncovered would determine whether or not she was telling the truth.

At this point, my suspicion was that Dorothy was right: Someone who didn't like Nathaniel had learned that he was going to be there today—and had decided to take advantage of the occasion by sneaking onto the property to do him harm.

In other words, Nathaniel's murder was most likely premeditated.

"I've never thought much of that school," Dorothy said shrilly, making me lose my train of thought. "It's filled with snobbish rich kids, with their horses and their European vacations and their sense of entitlement. I never understood why on earth Ruthie's boy would want to work at a place like that. Then again, Nathaniel Stibbins always was the black sheep of the family."

There it was again: *black sheep*. That same expression she'd used before.

"Dorothy," I said, "you keep referring to Nathaniel as the black sheep of the family. What exactly do you mean by that?"

She let out a deep sigh. "It all started back when he was a small boy. Even then he was unusually self-centered. I remember that practically from the time he was born, he simply refused to share any of his toys. And whenever the whole family got together, he insisted on getting the first hot dog off the grill or grabbing the best seat in front of the TV. I can still picture him in short pants, literally climbing over the legs of the other children to get to the front of the line at one of those dreadful family barbecues one of my great-aunts insisted on having every summer. Of course, she's gone now..."

"Is that all?" I asked. Being greedy for hot dogs might not have been the most admirable trait in the world, but I didn't quite understand how it could cause someone to be branded "the black sheep of the family" for life.

In fact, I was about to ask what else Poor Cousin Nathaniel had done to earn him that distinction when I heard Dorothy say, "Not there, Henry. I said it was in the big suitcase, not the small one. It's underneath your blue shirt, exactly where I put it—"

"Dorothy?" I said, trying to reel her back into our conversation.

"Jessica, I have to go," Dorothy said tartly. "Henry needs me. But if I were you, I'd see what I could find out about the goings-on at that snobbish school. And don't worry, I promise I'll call you as often as I can to see how things are going."

Great, I thought miserably. Not only has Dorothy just ordered me to solve the mystery of her long-lost relative's murder, she also intends to plague me with questions and advice every step of the way.

"What did my mother want?" Nick asked a few seconds later, coming out of the bedroom dressed in jeans and his favorite T-shirt. It was the one I always pictured him wearing whenever I thought about him, the dingy white one that sported the faded image of Led Zeppelin, his favorite classic rock band.

"She wanted to give me a directive," I replied, still trying to grasp what had just happened.

Grinning, he said, "Don't tell me she's already planning our do-over wedding."

I cast him a look of despair. "She wants me to find out who killed Cousin Nathaniel."

"*What?*"

With a shrug, I explained, "She insists that having someone in the family murdered looks bad, and she wants it cleared up as soon as possible."

Dorothy Burby was the only person I knew who was capable of making a murder sound like a spilled glass of milk.

"Good old Mom." Nick let out a deep sigh. "What did you tell her?"

"I didn't have a chance to tell her anything!" I cried. "She never even *asked* me if I was going to do it! She just *told* me I was. She even dictated where I should begin."

"Where?"

"Apparently Nathaniel was a teacher at a fancy girls' school on the East End. It's one of those exclusive enclaves of the rich and snobbish. Dorothy thinks that's the obvious place to start."

Nick thought for a few seconds before saying, "Jess, you know I'm never crazy about you getting involved in something as dangerous as a murder investigation. But I also know that it's something you're really good at."

"Thanks," I replied, surprised by this unexpected show of support. To say that Nick didn't like me poking my nose into places where it usually didn't belong—

especially if those places were likely to have a murderer lurking in them—was an understatement. I didn't blame him for worrying, of course. It was just that I never seemed to have much choice in the matter, and having him on my side was something I'd have always welcomed.

"I also know how hard it is to say no to my mother," he continued. "Once she's made up her mind, there's no going back."

"Y'think?"

He laughed. "Look, maybe I can even be of some help. I'll feel a lot better when this long lost relative's murder is cleared up, too. But for now, I'm going to take the dogs out for a run. I could use some exercise."

Max and Lou immediately perked up. Sometimes I think they're fully conversant in English and they just pretend they don't understand most of what we say. The same goes for my cats, although it's much more likely that they're fluent in several languages.

As for me, I didn't blame Nick one bit for wanting to get out of the house.

After he was gone, I climbed out of my wedding dress and carefully hung it up.

"I'll put you to use yet," I told it as I closed the closet door.

I slipped into an outfit that was almost identical to Nick's. But with my jeans I wore a T-shirt printed with a picture of a Max clone and the words, "My Westie Is Smarter Than Your Honors Student." Then I braced myself for my next chore: putting the champagne glasses back on the kitchen shelf and pulling down the paper decorations.

Once I'd returned the place to a state that was more or less normal, I sat down at the dining room table and pulled my laptop toward me.

Might as well jump right in, I thought, scooping up Cat and dropping my sweet pussycat into my lap. I'm certainly in no mood to break into that bottle of champagne.

As I pressed the power button, I could feel the rest of the world slipping away. Even though my computer hadn't yet booted up, I was already plotting a strategy for how to proceed.

Like it or not, I suddenly found myself embroiled in another murder investigation.

Chapter 2

"What kills a skunk is the publicity it gives itself."
—Abraham Lincoln

The Worth School," I muttered as I typed the words into the Google search box. I used the fingers on one hand so I could fondle Cat's furry ear with the other hand. "W—O—R..."

I wasn't surprised that the first website listed was www.theworthschool.com. I clicked on the link, noticing that my heart immediately began to beat faster.

The home page came up, filling the screen with a photograph of elegant wrought-iron gates that opened onto a long winding driveway. Set into the metal was a gold plaque with what looked like the school emblem.

And then a bright blue headline emerged from cyberspace: WELCOME TO THE WORTH SCHOOL, WHERE EVERY STUDENT LEARNS HER WORTH!

One photograph after another began popping up. Each was a picture of a different girl who I supposed was absorbed in the process of learning her worth.

One gazed at a test tube, one had her nose buried in a book, and one played an instrument that looked like a xylophone. Others appeared to be taking a less academic route to self-discovery: laughing with friends, studying a computer screen, and—my favorite—sitting under a tree, staring off into space and undoubtedly thinking great thoughts.

Even though so far I'd seen nothing but stock photos, I was considerably more impressed by the slideshow that followed.

The photograph of the gate dissolved into one shot after another, each one showing off a different part of the campus. The Worth School's buildings and grounds made it look like a university rather than a high school. An amazingly well-endowed university, not to mention one that definitely leaned toward the avant-garde.

Most of the buildings scattered over an impressively large stretch of land were modern, incorporating architecture that ranged from fairly unusual to totally out there. The library, for example, which from the front resembled a gigantic row of books. On either side was a pair of friendly-looking lions that were clearly meant to look like bookends. The imagery of the arts building wasn't as specific. The white, free-form building looked like a linen napkin that had been dropped on the ground by some careless giant.

Not all the buildings seemed suitable for the cover of *Architectural Digest,* however. Administration, for example, was a standard multistory redbrick building that appeared sturdy enough that no amount of huffing and puffing could blow it down. And the school's small white chapel looked as if someone had snatched it off the village green of some quaint New England town. It even had a steeple towering high above the gray shingled roof.

The grounds were just as spectacular. Every square inch appeared to be carefully landscaped, some areas with startlingly large beds of colorful flowers, others with outdoor sculpture that ranged from your run-of-the-mill classic Greek gods and goddesses to a bouquet of twisted metal rods that reached up high into the sky. The facilities included two Olympic-size pools, one indoor and one outdoor; an ice-skating rink; and separate courts or fields for tennis, soccer, handball, the Italian game of *bocce,* and a half-dozen other sports I didn't have any idea how to play.

"This is not your ordinary school," I mumbled, clicking one more time to enter the website.

"Welcome to the Worth School," the text began, "a private school for young women in which every one of our 350 students is considered the center of her own private universe."

Oh, boy, I thought.

"The Worth School's educational philosophy is that no subject can be taught in a vacuum. We are strong proponents of a fully integrated curriculum. For example, the study of literature must mesh with the study of music in order for students to comprehend how words and melody interface with each other. To fully understand art, students must also learn history so they understand the context in which each work was created.

"And from the time students enter in the sixth

grade, rather than imposing letter or number grades on students, the Worth School awards three levels of evaluation: Above and Beyond, Good Job, and Persist in the Challenge.

"In short, we strive to think beyond the usual constraints of most schools. Books, CDs, and DVDs are housed in the Hall of Ideas, rather than in a simple library, and students study art, music, film, dance and creative movement, and yoga in the Center for Creative Self-Expression.

"The Worth School is located on 125 acres in East Brompton, on Long Island's East End. In addition to the traditional college preparatory classes that are offered during the Spring and Fall semesters, we offer a more experimental curriculum during our eight-week Summer School, which enables our students to explore additional disciplines they might not be able to fit into their schedule during the academic year."

Summer school! I thought. I wished cats were capable of doing the high five.

"The school was founded by Eleanor Phipps Worth," I read, "a strong, independent woman who was born and raised in East Brompton, then spent her life fighting for women's rights, including the right to vote. Upon her death in 1958, her wish to turn her estate into a progressive school for young women was realized.

"Today, the Worth School prides itself on the diversity of its student body, which we maintain by extending generous scholarships to deserving students from all over the New York metropolitan area. While we provide housing for the majority of our students in our on-campus dormitories, approximately twenty percent of the student body consists of young women who live close enough to attend the school as day students."

A yellow oval at the bottom of the page invited me to click my way to a list of courses the school offered. I wasn't that surprised to find Basic Japanese, Understanding Global Warming, or History and Politics of the Middle East. But I couldn't say the same for Zen Buddhism, Beginning Neon Sculpture, the Poetry of e.e. cummings, and the Art and Science of the Leaf. My favorite was the History of China, which included a three-week field trip. African Drumming, in which students actually studied in Africa, was a close second.

My next click brought me to a letter from the headmistress, Dr. Elspeth Goodfellow. I skimmed it and found the same public relations gobbledygook about an integrated curriculum and the importance of freeing each student's inner spirit. As for Dr. Goodfellow, she had an impressive background that included degrees from Harvard, the Sorbonne, and someplace called the School for Spiritual Intellectualism. Unfortunately, there was no photo, so I had no indication of which of those three institutions had influenced her most.

Next I clicked on the Faculty webpage, then located the listing for Nathaniel Stibbins. I clicked again, and his now-familiar face came up. I had to admit that he looked considerably better than the last time I'd seen him.

I began to read. "Our distinguished art teacher,

Nathaniel Stibbins, has been on the faculty since 1995. An accomplished artist, he works in a wide variety of media, including oils, acrylics, watercolor, vegetable dyes, and found objects."

"Found objects?" I mumbled to Cat. She looked as confused as I was. Then I realized what that term meant: other people's trash.

I read on. "Mr. Stibbins is a graduate of the Delormé School of Art in Baltimore. His work has appeared in prestigious galleries all over the world..."

I was still absorbed by the details of the murder victim's life when my cellphone rang. I was so distracted that when I grabbed it I didn't bother to check the caller ID.

"Hello?" I said, my eyes still glued to my computer screen.

"Popper, it just never ends with you, does it?"

Instantly I froze. I knew that voice, all right. It belonged to Forrester Sloan—a *Newsday* reporter and a friend. Of sorts.

About half a second after I realized *who* was calling, I realized *why.*

Forrester covered the crime beat.

"Forrester," I told him crossly, "I can assure you that this time it's simply some kind of weird coincidence."

"Coincidence?" he repeated with a hearty laugh. "I don't think so. I think you're just someone who attracts trouble."

"Which would explain why *you're* calling," I shot back.

"Actually, I'm calling in a professional capacity,"

he replied. From his voice, I could tell he was grinning. "Otherwise, I'd never bother you at a time when I'm sure you have much better things to do."

"Don't tell me," I countered. "You're covering the Stibbins murder."

"With great enthusiasm. And I need a quote for the article I'm writing—a quote from the bride who was in the middle of her wedding when the horrible event occurred."

The wheels in my head were turning. And it wasn't because I was trying to come up with a good sound bite.

"Forrester, I'm really glad it's you who's covering the story," I said sweetly.

"Really?" He sounded pleased. "Because you know I'll do such a great job?"

"Uh, that, too. But mainly because I have a huge favor to ask you."

"A favor, huh?"

I knew that by now the wheels in *his* head were turning—mainly because the word "favor" had prompted him to try to find a way to extract something from me in return. Except while my interest in him was purely professional, Forrester had let it be known on more than one occasion that his interest in me went far beyond the printed word.

Which in this case I hoped would increase the likelihood that he'd help me out.

I took a deep breath. "Forrester, is there any way I could get you to keep my name out of this?"

I took advantage of his silence to argue my case.

"Not only would it violate my privacy on a personal level," I explained, "it would also be bad for my practice. I mean, I could lose clients over this, people so put off by the idea of their veterinarian being associated with such a terrible event that they'd go looking for a new doctor for their pets."

Even though I'd been thinking about my promise to Dorothy to investigate the murder of her first cousin once removed, I realized as I said the words that it was actually a possibility—especially since from the looks of things, Nathaniel's murder was going to be splashed all over the headlines, until something more unsavory took its place.

"Popper, it's pretty likely that sooner or later, your name is going to come out," Forrester warned.

"In that case, I'd prefer later to sooner." I bit my lip. "Please, Forrester? It would really mean a lot to me."

I was about ready to resort to the "pretty-please-with-sugar-on-it" plea when he sighed and said, "You know I can never say no to you, Popper."

"Thank you!" I cried, with a touch of guilt. Without thinking, I added, "I owe you."

"I know you do," he said. I could tell he was grinning again. "And I promise that sooner or later, I'll think of a way to collect."

I decided that I'd worry about that whenever it came up.

At the moment, I was too gleeful that my cover wasn't going to be blown—at least not yet. Hopefully, that would give me plenty of time to snoop around the

Worth School, exactly as my demanding future-mother-in-law had insisted.

I got off the phone as quickly as I could, then turned back to the Worth website.

Okay, I thought, so now I know a bit more about Cousin Nathaniel. Unfortunately, it's not exactly enough to point a finger at a likely killer.

Still, while I hadn't discovered anything new about the black sheep of Nick's family, I had learned that the place where he'd worked for the past decade and a half wasn't your average high school. And I had to agree with Dorothy that it was a very good place to begin my investigation. Fortunately, I'd already come up with an idea of how to accomplish exactly that.

It may be June, rather than September, I thought ruefully. But it looks as if I'm going back to school.

• • •

Early Monday afternoon found me driving my 26-foot clinic-on-wheels down a tree-lined lane with gated mansions on both sides, a sure sign that I'd arrived in Long Island's famous Bromptons.

I was no stranger to the area, since one of the best things about working out of a van instead of an office was that I spent my days tooling around all of Long Island. I had a number of clients here on the South Fork, including both summer and year-round residents—and thanks to some juggling, I was able to combine a last-minute meeting with the headmistress of the Worth School with a bunch of house calls.

As for that juggling, I had Sunny McGee to thank. I'd met Sunny while I was a temporary cast member in the theater group Betty Vandervoort belonged to, the Port Players. Her real name was Sunflower, but the spunky twenty-year-old couldn't bring herself to use it. She was much too firmly rooted in the twenty-first century to see herself the way her parents, former flower children, had envisioned their daughter.

When we first met, Sunny had a job with a cleaning company whose clients included Theater One, the theater in which the Port Players performed. But after we struck up a friendship that became even stronger when she helped both save my life and catch a killer, she came up with the idea of becoming my assistant.

We agreed that we'd try it out for a while. But it didn't take me long to realize what an asset she was. When I'd met her, she'd dressed only in black, had a bright blue streak in her spiky dark hair, and wore so many studs in her left ear that I suspected she had to steer clear of magnets. On her first day of work, however, she showed up looking like a recent graduate of the Harvard Business School, complete with tailored blazer and metal-free ears.

But her appearance didn't matter to me. What did matter was the fact that she was a whirlwind when it came to organization. During a down period, the woman actually alphabetized my spices. She was also good with clients, animals, and a boss who sometimes went off in too many directions.

In other words, Sunny was a gem.

I'd called her the evening before and asked if she'd mind rescheduling my appointments so that I had a block of time Monday afternoon. She'd worked her magic, within half an hour accomplishing exactly what I'd asked. Giving her the afternoon off so I could spend part of it trying to wangle my way onto the faculty of the Worth School seemed like a suitable reward.

So far the rest of my plan had been going just as smoothly. Dr. Goodfellow's assistant, Ms. Greer, had sounded interested in having a real, live veterinarian teach a summer school class in animal care. Especially when I mentioned that I'd do it for free. In fact, when I told her I'd be in the area that afternoon and would be happy to stop in so the headmistress could interview me, she was more than eager to give me a two o'clock appointment.

I made one more turn, which took me off the wide residential street and onto what looked like a driveway. Sure enough, the stately gate I'd seen on the school's website immediately came into view. It even had the school emblem on it, just as it had in the photo.

I was glad that combining house calls with this visit enabled me to show up in my van. The folks at the Worth School clearly kept track of who came onto their campus, since passing through that imposing gate required checking in with a uniformed guard who poked his head out of a tiny kiosk. Somehow, I hadn't noticed him in the photo on the home page. Besides, I figured that arriving in my office-on-wheels was guaranteed to lend credibility to the story I'd told when I'd called the school's administrative offices first thing that morning: that I wanted nothing more in life than the opportunity to teach Paris Hilton wannabes about animal care.

My van was not only the source of my livelihood, it was also my pride and joy. While most other veterinarians work out of offices, I'd decided early on that I much preferred to treat dogs, cats, and whatever other types of animals needed medical care from a mobile services unit. In other words, a clinic-on-wheels. My van had everything I needed, from an examining table to an X-ray machine to a cabinet stocked with every medication imaginable. Stenciled on the door in blue letters were the words:

REIGNING CATS & DOGS
Mobile Veterinary Services
Large and Small Animals
631-555-PETS

Even though I'd had it for years, I still felt a little thrill every time I saw the big white monster waiting for me to climb in and do my Dr. Dolittle thing.

At the moment, however, I had other things to think about besides my satisfying career choice. In five minutes, I was due to meet the Worth School's headmistress. And that word—*headmistress*—conjured up a frightening image of the stereotypical prim educator, a dour woman with a drab suit, a pair of glasses swinging from a chain around her neck, and an eternally disapproving expression on her pinched face.

I had to admit that the physical appearance of the headmistress's assistant, Ms. Greer, wasn't far off from my fantasy. Not only did she wear her gray-streaked brown hair in a tight bun, she actually kept her glasses on a chain, as if they had a history of running away.

Yet while Ms. Greer fit the part, as soon as she walked me into her boss's office I saw that Dr. Elspeth Goodfellow didn't come close to matching any of my preconceived notions of what the headmistress of a girls' school looked like.

The tall, willowy woman who stood up to greet me was probably in her early forties, with a head of thick, wavy red hair she wore drawn up into a loose topknot. The fact that more than a few strands had escaped made her look like a cross between a Victorian lady and an aging hippie. That same peculiar combination was also reflected in her makeup—none except a slash of bright red lipstick. Her dark red suit would have looked conservative if it weren't for the gauzy Indian shawl splashed with bright reds and golds draped around her neck.

I was pretty sure I could see signs of Harvard, the Sorbonne, *and* the School for Spiritual Intellectualism.

Dr. Goodfellow's office was just as much of a surprise. The room had a traditional Old School look, with dark, heavy furniture, thick Oriental carpets, and floor-to-ceiling bookshelves stuffed with old leather-covered tomes. But superimposed over it were a few overtly modern touches—especially the artwork. The pieces hanging on the wood-paneled wall included an Andy Warhol that looked positively stodgy next to the tremendous paintings of swirls and globs beside it. In one corner was a gigantic marble sculpture of what, to me, looked like drops of water the size of bowling balls.

"Good morning, Dr. Goodfellow," I said pleasantly as I reached across her desk to shake her hand. "Thank you for agreeing to see me."

"Not at all, Dr. Popper," she replied in a voice that quivered slightly. "Thank *you* for coming in. Please, take a seat."

I sank into a red velvet chair that threatened to swallow me up.

"I understand you're interested in teaching a course here at the Worth School," she began. As she spoke, her fingers fluttered like hummingbirds. I got the feeling she noticed that *I* noticed, since she immediately picked up a pen and began fiddling with it. Meanwhile, her eyes darted around the room, as if she was having trouble focusing on just one thing. "Something about animal first aid?"

"All aspects of animal care, actually," I corrected her. I surprised myself by how confident I sounded. Almost as if I were the center of my own private universe. "I would cover first aid, but also day-to-day care, including basics like feeding and exercise. My goal is to help your students take the best possible care of the animals they love."

"It sounds interesting," Dr. Goodfellow said, still tapping her pen. "Here at the Worth School, we try to expose our girls to as many different subjects as possible. Our student body is so wonderfully diverse, and we do our best to make our curriculum reflect that same variety. We have students from all types of backgrounds, in terms of financial status, ethnicity, and, well, life experience. They all have their own style of learning, too. Some of them sail right through, barely needing to study. But others are getting through high school within their own time frame." With a wan smile, she added, "Which I suppose is my way of telling you that a class like the one you're proposing would fit right in with the philosophy we espouse here at Worth."

Her mouth quickly turned downward. "But I must tell you up front that we don't really have a budget for that kind of thing."

I couldn't help glancing around her office, taking in the mahogany paneling, the Warhol print, the ornate Oriental carpet so faded that it had to be an antique, and what looked like a rare-book collection—at least if the amount of dust on each volume was any indication. The idea that the woman who ran this elite educational empire couldn't scrape up a few bucks to round out her students' education struck me as highly unlikely.

"Actually," I said, "I'm willing to teach the course for free."

For the first time since I'd come in, she stopped tapping. Apparently even in a place like this, "free" was a magic word.

"I thought Ms. Greer said something about that," she said. Frowning, she added, "Usually, she's completely on top of things. In fact, I'm always telling people that she's the one who really runs this place. But I was certain that this was one of those rare times she'd misunderstood."

"It's my way of giving back to the community."

Even though it's a far cry from putting in a few hours a week at a soup kitchen, I thought wryly.

"It's quite a generous offer," Dr. Goodfellow said, looking pleased. "And I like that you're interested in serving your community. The concept of community involvement is something we take very seriously here at Worth. In fact, right now we're gearing up for an outreach program we're all hoping will be a great success. It's a Blessing of the Animals that our school chaplain will be overseeing. Come to think of it, that's something you might want to participate in."

"Definitely," I said, nodding fervently. After all, I thought, the more contact with anything at all related to this school, the better.

Still doing my best to sell my volunteer services, I said, "I'd be happy to provide you with references. And while I've never actually taught a course like this, since last fall I've been doing a fifteen-minute spot every Friday on cable television..."

"I know. I catch your TV show whenever I can. I'm a big fan."

"So you're a pet owner," I said. I was starting to relax, since with each passing moment, it looked more and more like I was getting this gig. "What kind?" I was genuinely curious, since I can often tell a lot about a person by the kind of animal he or she chooses to live with.

"Oh, I'm a cat person," Dr. Goodfellow said. "I have three right now, and they're all completely different. The one I've had the longest is Seamus, a black-and-white tuxedo cat. I always tell people his middle name is Trouble, since that's what he's always getting himself into. He even knows that 'timeout' means he's misbehaved and has to go into his room with the door closed.

"Seamus's transgressions usually involve bullying his sister, Chloe, a gray and white tabby," she continued. "She's the sweetest cat in the world and she's absolutely terrified of him. She's always jumping up to get away, so she's constantly knocking things over. My other cat, Lizzy, is a white and orange tabby. There's nothing she likes to do more than look out the window at the birds. The other day, a robin landed on the windowsill and stayed there for a while. She was in heaven. It was the closest she ever got to a bird."

As she described her cats to me—first physically, but then their idiosyncrasies—I could practically feel her relaxing. I've noticed that inviting people to talk about the animals in their lives never fails as a way of getting them to open up.

In fact, by this point I was ninety-nine percent certain I had my foot lodged firmly in the door of the Worth School. Which made this a good time to take a chance.

"I might even be able to mention that I'm teaching here at the Worth School on the air," I said casually. Studying her face so I could gauge her reaction, I added, "That might be good for Worth School from a public relations perspective. I understand that one of your teachers recently suffered a personal misfortune."

All traces of her smile faded.

"Ye-e-es," Dr. Goodfellow replied. "There was

that rather...unfortunate incident involving our art teacher, Mr. Stibbins."

"I'm so sorry," I told her. "I read about it in the paper."

Dr. Goodfellow's red lips twisted downward. "Frankly, I'm worried that we might lose students over it. So many of the parents here are concerned with how something like that looks. They seem to see it as a personal affront, rather than the tragedy it truly is."

Sounds like somebody I know, I thought, picturing Dorothy's disgusted scowl as she'd contemplated how an untidy murder might reflect on the family's reputation.

At the moment, however, it was Dr. Goodfellow who was my concern. I held my breath, hoping she might say something revealing, like "Too bad old Mr. Witherspoon, the geology teacher, never got over the fact that Mr. Stibbins won the potato sack race at the annual school picnic."

Instead, her face tensed into a stricken expression. "For those of us at the school, it really was personal," she said in a pinched voice. "Nathaniel—Mr. Stibbins—was a rising star here at Worth. He was extremely talented, but it was his passion for his art that set him apart. I don't think I'd be exaggerating if I said that many people in the art world considered him nothing short of brilliant."

Her eyes glazed with tears as she added, "It's a terrible loss. For all of us, I mean."

"Of course it is," I said sympathetically.

She leaned back in her chair, folded her hands in her lap, and in a much crisper voice said, "I'm very interested in your proposition, Dr. Popper. But there's one tiny wrinkle."

"What's that?" My optimism was already flagging.

"Our summer semester has already started. In fact, it started today."

I was still thinking, "Is *that* all?" when she added, "Would you be able to start soon? Most of our students have already chosen their summer courses, although we do encourage self-direction by allowing them to make changes at any time."

"How soon?" I asked.

"Tomorrow."

Tomorrow?

"The nine o'clock time slot would be best," Dr. Goodfellow added. "If that works for you, I'll send out an email immediately, announcing that we've added a new summer class..."

She didn't seem to notice that her new volunteer was suddenly having difficulty breathing.

Up until this point, the idea of standing up in front of a classroom had been a mere abstraction, a mission orchestrated by the woman who would eventually become my mother-in-law. Suddenly, it was becoming real. Frighteningly real.

I thought about Dorothy again, this time remembering her characterization of the students at the Worth School.

"All those snobbish rich kids," she had sniffed, "with their horses and their European vacations and their sense of entitlement..."

Still, a promise was a promise. And while I could live with Dorothy Burby's disdain for the spoiled daughters of the privileged class, I couldn't say the same for the possibility of her feeling the same way about her future daughter-in-law.

Chapter 3

"The great pleasure of a dog is that you may make a fool of yourself with him and not only will he not scold you, but he will make a fool of himself too."

—Samuel Butler

I used to believe that only kindergarten students got first-day-of-school jitters, but I definitely had that familiar why-can't-I-just-go-home-and-crawl-back-into-bed feeling the next day as I once again drove my van through the imposing gates of the Worth School.

Worse, even, since this time around I was the one in charge.

Early that morning, Nick had been amused by the way I'd agonized over what to wear.

"You're not trying to get these girls to vote for you for class president," he teased as I stood in front of the bedroom mirror, holding one shirt after another up to my chest.

"I just want to look like an authority figure," I'd explained, squinting at an apple-green linen Liz Claiborne blouse and wondering if it was too matronly. While it had looked fine in the store, it now struck me as something Dorothy Burby would wear.

It was true that I wanted to look like the person running the show, of course. But I also found myself grappling with some old insecurities I hadn't even realized I still possessed.

Back in high school, I hadn't exactly been what anyone could call popular. Sure, I'd had friends, a small group who, like me, studied hard and loved science and reading and a few other egghead pastimes. But even then I'd preferred spending my free time volunteering at a local animal shelter or hanging out with my own pets.

The idea of being tossed in with a bunch of hormonally challenged teenage girls was, in my eyes, tantamount to being thrown to the proverbial pack of wolves. And at least wolves don't make fun of your clothes.

I finally stuck my tongue out at my reflection, deciding once and for all to stop worrying about what the students might think of my underdeveloped fashion sense. Instead, I told myself it was time to start worrying about the real reason I was living out everyone's nightmare of returning to high school: investigating a murder. Instead of even attempting to dress to impress, I'd simply wear what I always wore when plying my trade: comfortable jeans, a pair of chukka boots, and a dark green polo shirt embroidered with the words, "Jessica Popper, D.V.M."

In fact, dressing as the real Jessie Popper gave my confidence a boost as I strode across the Worth School campus. So did knowing where I was going. Ms. Greer, the headmistress's assistant, had done a thorough job of orienting me. First she'd given me a tour of the administration building, pointing out such highlights as the faculty mailboxes, the copying machine, and the coffeepot. Then she gave me a map and an overview of the campus that included a description of what each building was used for.

My nine o'clock class was scheduled to take place in the Planet Earth building. While another school might have called such a place the Science Building, the folks at the Worth School were much too clever for anything that ordinary. From its name, I expected it to be a big blue sphere. Instead, it was a fairly ordinary two-story structure. At least it had been constructed from various products from the planet that was its namesake, including wood, bamboo, and several different varieties of stone.

In the entryway was an exhibit of student projects that gave a newcomer like me a good understanding of what went on in this building. From the assortment of terrariums, dioramas about ecology, and indecipherable formulas neatly copied onto homemade posters, it looked as if it was biology, chemistry, physics, astronomy, and geology, as well as math that helped all those other disciplines make sense.

When I located my classroom, I headed toward the door. I figured I'd take advantage of the few minutes before the students started arriving to look over the notes I'd made the night before. Based on the response to her previous day's email, Dr. Goodfellow had had

Ms. Greer put together a class list that had each student's name, year, and even some personal information, including her home address. I wanted to look it over so I could start to learn who everyone was.

Instead, as I sailed through the doorway, I discovered that most of the fifteen or so desks were already occupied.

My mouth went dry as I surveyed the group I was going to have to both educate and entertain for the next hour. At this point, it was nearly impossible to distinguish one from another. They all seemed about the same age, somewhere in the late-teenage range. And they were dressed pretty much the same as any other girls their age, except for the fact that just one of their pocketbooks probably cost more than my entire wardrobe.

I wonder if I'll ever be able to tell them all apart, I thought morosely.

Yet I already couldn't help noticing one student in particular: a wiry girl with straight, dark brown hair and a peculiar mismatched outfit that included a short yellow skirt and black-and-white-checked high-tops. The reason she stood out was that she had an unusually loud giggle. High-pitched, too. And from the looks of things, she was the energetic, talkative type who invariably found lots to giggle about.

I glanced at the clock in the back of the room and saw it was one minute after nine. I took a deep breath and reminded myself that I'd done a lot of things that were much more difficult than this—even though at the moment I couldn't think of a single one.

"Since most of you are here, we might as well get

started," I began, glancing around the room and making eye contact with as many of the girls as I could. "My name is Jessica Popper, and—"

"You're new, aren't you?" one of the girls interrupted. When I looked over at her, I saw she was the giggler.

"It's true that I'm new to the school," I told her. "But I'm not exactly new to my field, which is veterinary medicine. I've been practicing for about ten years now—"

"But you're not, like, a real teacher, right?" she persisted.

"I've never taught in a school like this one, if that's what you mean," I replied calmly.

One of the others girls raised her hand, then without waiting to be called on demanded, "Aren't you on TV?"

"As a matter of fact I am," I replied, pleased that one of my students actually recognized me. "I have a fifteen-minute show called *Pet People* that's on every Friday."

"It's on one of those *local* cable stations, isn't it?" she said, her voice oozing with disdain. "I mean, it's not exactly CNN."

"That's right," I said, staring her down. "Channel 14, the station that's broadcast all over Long Island."

I never claimed to be Oprah, I thought crossly.

But a less secure voice in my head demanded, *Did you really think you could earn these girls' respect— or even their cooperation—simply by showing up?*

"Do you take care of, like, lions and tigers?" one of the other girls asked eagerly.

"I rarely work with exotics. Most of the time I stick to dogs and cats." Smiling at her as warmly as I could, I added, "Since I suspect that a lot more of you have dogs and cats as pets, I'm sure you'll be—"

"Fiona has llamas," another girl called out. "That's pretty exotic."

"But they're not here," another girl, presumably Fiona, insisted. "They're at our house in Ibiza." Fixing her gaze on me, she pointedly added, "That's an island off Spain."

"I know where Ibiza is," I assured her, gritting my teeth.

I was wondering how much worse this could get when one more girl sashayed through the doorway. Something about the way she carried herself told me she was used to having the room grow silent whenever she made an entrance, with all eyes focusing on her.

Which is pretty much what happened.

It was true that she was striking. For one thing, she was tall and slender, but with the stick figure–like boniness that models have—and teenage girls worship. She also had long, silky, blond hair and big blue eyes framed by thick lashes. She wore low-slung jeans that revealed a pair of protruding hipbones and a short gauzy peach-colored shirt that kept slipping off her shoulder, no doubt because it had been designed to do precisely that.

As she floated past me, I said, "Thanks for joining us," in what was supposed to be a teasing tone.

She glanced in my direction just long enough to roll her eyes. "What-ever."

A few of the other students in the class tittered, but

I made a point of ignoring them. I had a feeling I'd just encountered one of those girls whose peers had elevated her to nearly supernatural status, albeit for reasons that were beyond the rest of us.

Which meant that if I lost her, I'd no doubt lose the entire class.

My heart pounded as I waited for her to find a seat. She chose one in back, right next to the giggler. Actually, it was more like she perched on the edge, allowing less than three inches of her butt to settle on the chair. I got the feeling this pose was one she'd carefully rehearsed, since positioning herself that way made her legs look about six feet long.

But instead of focusing on her, my eyes swept over the entire class. "Okay, everyone," I said, mustering up as much self-confidence as I could, "I'd like to start off by going around the room and—"

"Don't tell me we're all supposed to do something lame like tell the rest of the class something interesting about ourselves," the latecomer interjected. She let out a loud sigh, just in case there was any doubt about how bored she already was.

"Actually," I said, careful not to let my impatience show, "I was going to ask each girl to tell us about her pet."

Her face lit up like the sky on the Fourth of July. "Oooh, I'll start!" she cried. "Is that okay? If I go first, I mean?"

A feeling of triumph swelled in me. I felt the way Alexander the Great must have felt when he conquered Persia.

"You're more than welcome to start," I told her,

careful not to let my relief show. "Why don't you begin by telling me your name, so I can learn who each of you are?"

"I'm Campbell Atwater," she said breezily, "and I have the cutest little Maltese in the world. I named her Snowflake because she's white and fluffy and she weighs something like five pounds. Do you believe she's that *tiny*? She's so small I can fit her in my purse. Not one of those adorable Chanel purses that hold, like, a lipstick and a hundred dollar bill. But it's worth carrying something a teensy bit bigger just so I can bring her with me wherever I go. And she's *so* smart. She knows, like, twenty words. When I'm home, she sleeps with me every night, and I hate to be away from her for even a *minute*—"

"Don't you have pictures of her?" the giggler prompted.

"*Oh,* my gosh!" Campbell cried, dipping into her purse and pulling out her iPhone. "Beanie, you are so brilliant. I *do* have pictures!"

Her announcement elicited squeals of glee from many of the other girls, those who, like her buddy Beanie, had appeared to find her dramatic and disruptive entrance so amusing. They acted as if the chance to see actual photos of Campbell's beloved pooch was as exciting as learning that Johnny Depp had just entered the building.

As the other girls peered at the tiny screen, Campbell gushed about Snowflake's unparalleled cuteness, intelligence, and all those other qualities that animal lovers invariably attribute to the four-legged creatures they adore—myself included.

"Thank you, Campbell," I finally said as a way of calling the class back to order. "I can see you're really devoted to Snowflake. I'm sure it'll be useful to learn some practical skills to help you take better care of her. First aid, for example."

Her big blue eyes widened. "But if anything bad ever happened to Snowflake, I'd just send Daddy a text message and he'd have a veterinarian helicoptered in!"

I managed to regain my composure with amazing speed.

"But what if there wasn't time?" I asked. "For example, what if Snowflake was choking?"

Campbell was silent, as if it took her a long time to process that new idea. She finally said, "Wow. I never thought of that. I'm not used to having anything bad happen to me. But you're right. I guess something awful like that really could happen to my sweet little Snowflake!"

She sat up straighter and fixed her eyes on me intently, as if she'd just decided that maybe taking this class wasn't such a bad idea.

Inwardly, I smiled. I was amazed at how easy teaching these girls was turning out to be.

"Can I go next?" the giggler—Beanie—asked, throwing her arm up into the air with the enthusiasm of a Laker Girl. "I have the cutest pug in the entire world, Esmeralda. But she isn't only gorgeous; she's smart, too. And really funny. She can do this amazing trick . . ."

The rest of the hour flew right by as one by one each girl gave a short presentation about her pet, in many cases passing around photos of the animals they clearly adored. Most had either a dog or a cat, and several had horses. A few other types of animals were represented, as well: rabbits, exotic birds, and of course, Fiona's llamas.

As each one lovingly told the others about the animals in her life, I saw a new side of them. Beneath the makeup and designer accessories, they still maintained the sweetness of little girls who treasured their pets more than just about anything else in the world.

"That's all the time we have," I finally said.

My announcement was greeted with groans.

"But I have a short assignment for you to do before class tomorrow," I announced. Despite a few more groans, I continued, "I'd like each one of you to write down five things you think are important for every pet to have."

"A diamond collar!" one called out.

"A heated bed!" another added.

"We'll go over your lists tomorrow," I told them. "But right now, I've got to get to work—and you've got to get to your next class."

I certainly didn't want to keep the Zen Buddhism teacher or whoever else was next on the schedule waiting.

As the girls filed out, their excited chatter filled the classroom. I was about to congratulate myself on having survived my first class when I saw that Campbell was taking a path that led right past my desk. Her sidekick, Beanie, was just a step or two behind.

"That was actually kind of fun," Campbell commented as she breezed by me. Pausing to look me up and down appraisingly, she added, "You turned out to be a lot better at this than I thought you'd be."

I was too stunned to come up with a response. I just watched her as she took a few steps toward the door, then leaned over to whisper some comment to Beanie that caused her friend to burst into hysterical laughter.

Silently seething, I grabbed my class list and forced myself to study it. I was marveling over how many of the names I could already attach to faces when I realized that not all the girls had left. One last student was hovering near my desk.

She was probably the quietest girl in my class, one who'd chosen to sit at the very back of the classroom and to say nothing aside from a few words about her cat, Babalu. Vondra Garcia's name had actually been one of the easier ones to learn, since it was the only Spanish one on my class roster.

But it was even easier to remember her face, since she also stood out from the rest of the class physically. While she had Campbell's fine bones and regal carriage, Vondra's skin was the color of freshly brewed espresso.

But her ethnic background was only one reason she'd stood out. At least as noticeable was the different way she dressed. Everything she wore was white: her flowing skirt, her cotton blouse, even the thick white headband that helped hold her smoothed-back hair in place. The only color in her outfit was in the row of bracelets running up one arm. They were made of tiny green and black beads—not exactly the kind of thing any of the other girls were wearing.

As I smiled at her, I could feel my cheeks burning. I

hadn't realized that anyone had witnessed me being the target of Campbell's mastery of the veiled insult.

"You're Vondra, right?" I said cheerfully, trying to cover up my embarrassment.

"That's right," she said, looking pleased that I remembered her name.

After a couple of moments of silence, I asked, "Is there something I can help you with?"

"I just wanted to tell you not to mind them," she said quietly.

"Excuse me?" I said, caught completely off guard by her remark.

"Those obnoxious girls, like Campbell and Beanie," she said. Now that she was speaking more loudly, I could hear that her voice was tinged with bitterness. "They're so full of themselves, even though the only thing they've ever accomplished in their entire lives is having the luck to be born into ridiculously wealthy families."

With an angry little laugh, Vondra continued, "And it's not as if they're that great. Campbell, especially. She's so flaky that I'm not surprised she's bounced around from one school to another. But ever since she showed up here at Worth a few months ago, it was clear that she didn't care one bit about getting through high school—or doing anything well, for that matter. I'm sure she's got a nice trust fund somewhere with her name on it."

I was still trying to come up with a diplomatic way to address her comments when she added, "Not me. I'm here on scholarship. And believe me, it's something girls like that never let me forget. You'd think having parents who aren't multigazillionaires was a federal offense."

"I guess it can be tough, being at a school with such a diverse group of students," I commented.

"For everyone," she said, nodding, "including the teachers. Right now, they're testing you. But don't worry. You did just fine."

With that, she turned and walked out of the room. As I watched her leave, it occurred to me that while the school's website had made the student body sound like one big happy family, the dynamics here at Worth seemed to be a lot more complicated.

• • •

It wasn't until a few minutes later, as I stood in front of the faculty mailboxes, that I realized how exhausted I was. I had just let out a loud sigh when I heard a footstep that told me someone had come up behind me.

"Rough day?" asked a friendly voice.

I turned and saw that the person who'd spoken was a trim middle-aged man who wasn't much taller than I was. He was nice-looking, with hazel eyes that smiled at me from behind a pair of glasses and a fringe of gray hair circling an otherwise bald head. Even though he was dressed casually in a sports jacket and khaki-colored pants, he had an exceptionally neat, well-groomed appearance.

"I guess first days are always rough," I replied.

"My experience exactly," he agreed. "Fortunately, the second day is always much easier. Most of the ones that follow, too." He extended his hand. "Richard Evans."

"I'm Jessica Popper," I told him as we shook hands.

"Oh, I know exactly who you are," he assured me with twinkling eyes. "The Worth School is like a small town. No matter how discreet anyone tries to be, everybody ends up knowing everybody else's business."

I wondered if that was true even in Nathaniel Stibbins's case.

"Since I'm still new, I'm afraid I haven't learned enough to know who *you* are," I told him apologetically.

"I'm the school chaplain. Here at Worth, we believe that even teenage girls are capable of developing a moral compass—at least, with enough prompting."

I laughed.

"So I guess I should call you Reverend Evans," I observed.

He shrugged. "Richard works, too. Whatever you're comfortable with is fine with me."

"In that case, I think I'll stick with Reverend Evans," I told him. "But please feel free to call me Jessie."

"Jessie it is," he replied. "By the way, I couldn't help noticing your van out in the parking lot. It is yours, isn't it?"

"It's mine, all right. It's actually a clinic on wheels."

"Really? You mean you treat animals right in your vehicle?" A look of delight crossed Reverend Evans's face. "What a clever concept!"

"A lot of people find it useful," I agreed. "My

clients are generally people who are really busy—or for various reasons have a hard time getting out of the house. It's also a great option if an animal is seriously ill and would be traumatized by getting in a car and traveling to a regular vet's office."

He nodded. "I can think of a long list of scenarios in which your services would be just the ticket. I take it you have everything you need right in the van?"

"That's right. An examining table, medications, you name it. I even have an assistant who travels around with me some of the time."

"In that case, could I impose upon you to take a look at my dog, Chach?" Reverend Evans asked. "He's a shih tzu and he's been limping a bit. At first, I assumed he'd stepped on something sharp, and that it would heal on its own. But it's been almost a week now, and I've been thinking that I should really have it looked at."

"Have you examined his paw?" I asked, frowning with concern.

"I tried, but he kept yelping and pulling it away. I was afraid of hurting him, so I just left it alone."

"So you haven't had a chance to see if he's got a cut."

"I'm afraid not."

"You should probably have him looked at as soon as possible," I said. "I'd be happy to do it—the sooner, the better."

"How about tomorrow after your class?"

"Tomorrow's great. Why don't we shoot for around ten forty-five?"

"Perfect."

His forehead tensed as he said, "Now I feel bad that I waited so long. It's just that this has been such a crazy week."

"I'm sure you've had your hands full," I said, "counseling the girls and all. After that terrible thing happened to their art teacher, I mean."

Reverend Evans shook his head. "Such a tragedy. I do hope the police catch Mr. Stibbins's killer before long."

The police... or anyone else who's been given the challenge, I thought grimly.

Aloud, I said, "I take it Mr. Stibbins was extremely well liked here at the school."

Reverend Evans looked startled by my comment. "Well, he'd certainly been here for a long time. He was kind of a fixture."

"You must have known him pretty well," I ventured.

"Not really." Thoughtfully, he added, "Certainly not as well as someone like Claude Molter. He's our music teacher."

"Were the two of them close?"

He hesitated before saying, "They certainly had a lot in common."

"Like what?"

Thoughtfully, Reverend Evans replied, "Even though Nathaniel and Claude were in entirely different fields—art and music—they were both extremely accomplished. Claude is a world-renowned violinist. He began his career as a child prodigy in Belgium, where he was born. But he went on to perform with some of the greatest orchestras in the world."

"Wow," I said, sincerely impressed.

"I understand he's also a count."

"A count?" I'd never run into a count before. That is, aside from Count Dracula, Count Chocula, and the Count on *Sesame Street*. And none of them was real.

I was about to ask Reverend Evans as diplomatically as I could how a count who was a music prodigy ended up teaching in a private girls' school on Long Island. But before I had a chance, he changed the subject by saying, "I'll be sure to bring Chach to school with me tomorrow. While I'm tied up with school business, he can stay in his carrying case." Chuckling, he added, "I'm not saying he'll like it, just that he'll do it."

"Then I'll see you both tomorrow," I said.

I hadn't bothered to check my schedule. Even if I didn't have a slot available right after my class, I knew that having the chance to talk to Reverend Evans again was worth shifting a few appointments around.

After all, the chaplain's job was helping things at the school run smoothly. That undoubtedly entailed finding out as much as he could about the intrigues lurking beneath the surface—which meant that he and I already had a lot in common, too.

• • •

As I drove away from the Worth School, I was buoyed by the good start my investigation was off to. I was also encouraged by my teaching debut.

But it was time for me to shift gears, to throw myself into the role in which I felt most comfortable. Fortunately, my first call of the day was going to be a happy one, since instead of treating an ailing pet I was paying a kitten a well-visit call.

Smokey's owners, Deborah and Jeff West, were first-time cat owners who lived nearby in Brompton Hills. This morning, only Deb was at home. In fact, as I pulled up in front of her house, a charming white saltbox that I suspected had been built in the eighteen hundreds or even earlier, she came out of the house with the dark gray kitten in her arms.

"Hey, Dr. Popper," she greeted me. Just like the last time I'd stopped by, she was dressed in jeans and a T-shirt, and her dark blond hair was clipped back loosely so the wavy strands hung around her face. She wasn't much older than I was, yet unlike me, was new to the world of animal ownership.

"Hi, gorgeous," I greeted Smokey as Deb stepped up into my van. "Wow, she got really big!"

"We've already had her for two months," Deb said proudly. "She's really grown. She's frisky, too."

Since Sunny wasn't spending her mornings with me while I was teaching at Worth, I asked Deb to hold Smokey as I took her temperature. Next I weighed her, commenting, "Last time she was three point six pounds, and now she's at four point six—up a whole pound. How did she do after the last vaccine?"

"Fine."

"That's great. How's her health in general? Any vomiting? Coughing or sneezing? Diarrhea?"

Smokey appeared to be in great shape. In fact, she reminded me of Cat back in her spunky days of kitten-hood. Not only was their coloring nearly identical, so was the wise look in their eyes.

"This might sound like a strange question," Deb said, "but do people bathe cats?"

"It depends on who you ask," I replied. "I don't, since most cats need to be sedated in order to be bathed. But they pretty much groom themselves, so unless they run into a mud puddle or get skunked, they should be fine."

I answered a few more of Deb's questions, then said, "I'm going to give Smokey her second and final upper respiratory vaccine. I'll give it between her shoulder blades. It may be tender in that area. The next shot is rabies, in about two weeks. Then I'll start the leukemia vaccines, a series of two."

Her owner watched anxiously as I injected Smokey with a one ml solution of FVR vaccine, the common term for the Feline Rhinotracheitis-Calici-Panleukopenia Vaccine. I noticed that Deb flinched, but Smokey hardly did at all.

Still, this was the kind of visit I most enjoyed. Smokey was healthy and starting out her life with people who treasured her. As for the Wests, I knew they were going to have years of happiness with the new addition to their family. And the fact that I could play even a minor role in that amazingly rewarding relationship was what my job was all about.

• • •

At the end of the day, as I climbed back into the driver's seat of my van one last time, I was pretty wiped out. As I turned the key in the ignition, I was picturing the evening ahead, relaxing with Nick and my animals. In fact, when my cellphone rang, I just assumed it would be him.

But when I glanced at the caller ID screen, I saw the caller was someone else I knew: Patti Ardsley, the producer of my weekly TV show, *Pet People*.

"Hi, Jessie!" she greeted me. As usual, she sounded as bubbly as a glass of champagne. "I know that every week I start bugging you around now about what your topic for the next show is going to be, but for this week, I came up with an idea of my own."

"Great!" The truth was that I'd been so busy over the past few days, first with my ill-fated wedding and then with taking on the role of teacher of the rich and famous in the name of investigating a murder, that I hadn't given a single thought to Friday's TV spot. In fact, I was relieved that Patti had come up with an idea, since the last time I'd checked the index cards in my brain, they'd all been blank. "What have you got?"

"It's going to be terrific!" Patti exclaimed. "A friend of mine has a *bzzz bzzz bzzz...*"

I assumed she was saying actual words, but thanks to the flawed technology that cellphone users are forced to put up with, she sounded more like a bee than a human.

"You're breaking up!" I shouted into the phone. "*What* did you say your friend has?"

"*Bzzz, bzzz, bzzz,*" came the reply. Or at least something that sounded a lot like that.

By that point, I was desperate to start the drive home. And since talking on cellphones while driving is against the law, that meant I had to find a way to end this call.

"I'm sure it'll be fine," I assured her. "I'll just show up on Friday morning and assume that you've taken care of the rest. Thanks, Patti!"

I hung up, figuring that whatever she had in mind, I could wing it. I'd certainly done *that* before.

In fact, these days winging it seemed to be something I was getting better and better at in pretty much every area of my life.

• • •

Half an hour later, as my van bumped along the long driveway that led to my home sweet home, I was lost in thought, imagining the evening ahead. I pictured myself stretched out on the couch with Cat lying on my chest, Lou sprawling on the floor next to me, and Nick telling me all about his day.

As I neared the cottage, I expanded my fantasy to include Chinese takeout and a pint of Ben & Jerry's. I was practically in a daze by then.

But as I turned into my driveway, I let out a yelp, slamming on the brakes just in time to keep from hitting someone foolish enough to be standing smack in the middle of it.

Chapter 4

"Diamonds are a girl's best friend and dogs are a man's best friend. Now you know which sex has more sense."

—Zsa Zsa Gabor

Forrester Sloan!" I yelled as I jerked my van to a halt, threw open the door, and jumped out. "What is wrong with you? You scared the living daylights out of me!"

"Anything to get a reaction," he replied breezily. "You know I love it when you get an adrenaline rush and your cheeks turn pink and those green eyes of yours get all shiny—"

"For heaven's sake, I almost ran you over!"

"I noticed." Smirking, he added, "For the second time, no less. You may recall that that's the way you and I first met. In fact, this might be a good time to use that tired old phrase, 'We have to stop meeting like this.' "

It was true that my vehicle and Forrester Sloan's person had come *this* close to making contact once before. I'd been on my way to treat a polo pony on an estate in the ridiculously affluent community of Old Brookbury when he'd darted in front of me. At the time, he was covering the murder of a dashing young polo player. Before I knew what was happening, he had roped me into helping him.

"At any rate," I asked impatiently, "what are you doing here?"

"This is actually a social call," he replied, grinning. "I came to express my condolences—in person."

"Over Nathaniel?" I asked, blinking.

"Over your wedding getting called off."

"Thank you—"

"I didn't find that out until this morning," Forrester continued. "When you and I spoke on Saturday, I just assumed you'd finally tied the knot. Especially since you neglected to mention that you hadn't."

"We *almost* tied the knot," I said quietly.

"But once I thought about it," he went on, "I wasn't all that surprised that when it came time for the Jessie Popper I know to say 'I do,' instead she said, 'I don't think so.' "

"But—but—that's completely wrong!" I sputtered. "I mean, that's not at all what happened!"

"No? You mean your wedding *didn't* get called off at the eleventh hour?"

"It did, but that's not the reason!" I insisted.

I sounded like a four-year-old, trying to convince a grown-up that she wasn't the one who'd gobbled down all the cookies. But Forrester always had that effect on me. Not that I found him the least bit attractive. Sure, he had intense gray-blue eyes, thick blond hair that softened into curls at the back of his neck, and a definite preppy look that some women might find engaging.

But not me.

"For heaven's sake, a man was murdered!"

"I know," he replied. "I've already written several articles about it, remember? But you have to admit that it was pretty convenient." Forrester leaned against his car casually, still grinning at me in a way that made my blood boil. "For someone who was looking for an excuse not to get married, I mean."

My mouth dropped open so wide that a butterfly could have flown in. I quickly snapped it shut.

"Not that this is any of your business," I told him through gnashed teeth, "but Nathaniel Stibbins's murder precipitated a family crisis. I can't begin to tell you how distraught my future mother-in-law is. In fact, she wants nothing more than for this heinous crime to be solved so we can all get on with our lives—"

"Wait a minute," he said, his eyes narrowing. "You're investigating this case, aren't you? That's the real reason you didn't want your name in the paper. It had nothing to do with violating your personal privacy or losing clients!"

"Both those reasons are completely legitimate!" I protested.

He didn't appear to be listening. "I should have figured that out," he said, shaking his head slowly. "After all, the guy *is* related to you."

"Not quite," I corrected him. It wasn't until I'd said those words that I realized the correct thing to have said would have been not *yet*. "But yes, you're right. I have been taking a few steps to see if I can help figure out what happened. At my future-mother-in-law's insistence."

"I get it," Forrester said. "Who has time to pick out new flower arrangements when she's investigating a murder? Of course, multitasking *is* in style. Unless, of course, there's some relief mixed in there with all the grief..."

"Forrester, I think you'd better leave. As in right now."

He laughed. "I don't blame you for being embarrassed, Popper. Not only did you bail out of your own wedding, you didn't even have the common decency to invite me to the ceremony. Still, I've decided to forgive you for your faux pas—"

"I don't *care* if you forgive me!" I cried. "I don't *want* you to forgive me! I just want you to get out of here before Nick comes back and—"

"Ah. So the lucky man, as we used to call him, isn't home." Forrester's gaze shifted over my shoulder, toward my empty cottage. "You know, some people might offer an unexpected visitor a cup of coffee. Especially if that visitor took time out of his busy schedule to drop by."

"Forrester, you're not only unexpected, you're also unwelcome. So please—"

"Or better yet, how about you and me going out? I was thinking dinner, but I'd also be up for a long walk along an isolated beach..."

"No, Forrester!"

"Why not?" he asked, looking baffled. "It's not as if you're married!"

"I'm still engaged!"

"Are you?"

"I most certainly am!"

He just cast me a skeptical look.

"Look, Forrester," I said in a low, even voice, "it's been a long day. If you don't mind, I'd really like you to—"

We both froze at the sound of tires crunching against gravel.

Nick? I thought, not knowing whether to feel relieved or guilty.

When a car I recognized as Sunny McGee's pulled around the bend, I was thrilled we were being interrupted.

I had to admit that I was also glad that it wasn't Nick who was pulling into the driveway. I didn't want to have to deal with him finding me here with Forrester, as innocent as our little tête-à-tête may have been.

At least in my eyes.

"Sunny!" I cried, dashing over to her sporty little car as she turned off the ignition. "I'm so happy to see you!"

"Hi—i—i," she replied, clearly confused by my unusually enthusiastic greeting.

"I hope you remembered that we have some important business to attend to," I said, casting what I hoped was a meaningful look at my assistant.

"We do?" Sunny repeated, sounding surprised. But she was a pretty smart cookie. "Ohmygosh, Jessie. I almost forgot. You're absolutely right. If we don't get that done by tonight, I don't know what's going to happen!"

Forrester glanced from me to Sunny and back to me. I could tell by the look on his face that he didn't buy our little act for a second. Still, even he knew that three's a crowd.

"In that case," he said, his eyes burning into mine, "I'll leave you two to meet your deadline. I wouldn't want to stand in the way of—what is it you're in such a hurry to do?"

"None of your business," Sunny snapped.

She immediately glanced at me, her anxious look saying she wasn't sure if she'd just overstepped a boundary. I put her fears to rest with an approving smile.

"Well put, Sunny," I said. "Anyway, it was great talking to you, Forrester. I'm sure our paths will cross again."

"No doubt." He suddenly made a big show of checking his watch. "Whoa, it's later than I thought. I was just on my way to meet with your friend and mine, Lieutenant Anthony Falcone. I thought you might like to join me, but I can see you're too busy."

"You are?" I sputtered. "You did?"

Forrester had certainly captured my interest. And from the smug look on his face, I could see that he was perfectly aware of just how great that interest was likely to be.

I would have given anything—well, almost anything—for the chance to hear what Falcone had to say about this case. And having Forrester there as a buffer would have been the way to do it. After all, I'd butted heads with Anthony Falcone on more than one occasion. For some strange reason, the Norfolk County Chief of Homicide was never thrilled with the idea of someone like me—that is, someone who had no training, no expertise, and no official reason for being involved in a homicide investigation—doing exactly that.

The fact that at times I'd proven to be better at it than he was hadn't helped.

"Yup, Falcone's expecting me," Forrester continued. "Too bad the timing doesn't work for you. Maybe next time."

"Forrester," I protested, "you know perfectly well that—"

"In fact, I'll leave you two alone," he went on. "But hey, if you're ever interested in hearing some of the details of the case, don't hesitate to give me a call." He made that annoying gesture of extending two fingers in what was supposed to look like a telephone and holding his hand up to his ear. "I think you know the number."

His car had barely left the driveway when Sunny commented, "That guy definitely has the hots for you."

"He does not!" I shot back.

"Whatever." Sunny gave a little shrug. "So you're investigating another murder," she added, sounding impressed. "Listen, Jessie, if there's anything I can do to help, just let me know. You don't even have to pay me. I mean, I'd be happy to do whatever you needed on my own time." Her eyes were bright as she added, "That is just so cool."

"Thanks," I said. "I may take you up on that."

"In the meantime," Sunny said, "I really did have something I wanted to talk to you about. I found this cool new program for keeping track of your finances. I'd like to show you how it works so you can think about whether you want us to switch over."

Once again, I was struck by how lucky I was to have Sunny helping me run the show.

But as we went inside, it wasn't Sunny I was thinking about. It was Forrester—and the fact that he had an inside track on information about Nathaniel Stibbins's murder. Through the chief of homicide, no less. Which meant that as much as I would have liked to banish Forrester Sloan from my life, chances were good that I was going to have to put up with him just a little bit longer.

• • •

Sunny and I wasted no time in sitting down at my combination dining room table and desk with our laptops side by side so she could demonstrate the advantages of the new accounting system she'd found. She was showing me how much easier the spreadsheets were to read when my cellphone rang.

I glanced at the caller ID and saw it was Nick's mother.

"I'd better take this," I told Sunny, grimacing. Speaking into the phone, I said, "Hello, Dorothy. How are—?"

"Jessica!" Dorothy's voice was so loud that I feared for the future of my left eardrum. "I'm calling to see if you've figured out who did that terrible thing to Cousin Nathaniel yet."

Hell-*o*, I thought crossly. I've only been undercover at the Worth School for a *day*. It even took Jessica Fletcher longer than that to solve crimes on *Murder She Wrote*. And she wasn't running a veterinary practice on the side.

"Not yet," I replied calmly. I rolled my eyes at Sunny, who thanks to Dorothy's inability to modulate her voice could undoubtedly hear every word my mother-in-law-to-be said.

"It's been three days since it happened," Dorothy pointed out. "That's seventy-two hours. Isn't there some saying in the crime business that if the murderer isn't caught within the first forty-eight hours, he's not likely to be caught at all?"

"You'd know better than I would," I said dryly. "You clearly watch more crime shows than I do." I grabbed a piece of scrap paper, scribbled, "Ring the doorbell!" and thrust it at Sunny.

"The clock is ticking, Jessica!" Dorothy exclaimed. I could picture her making that annoying gesture of tapping her wrist with her finger. "I understand there were articles in the newspaper about Nathaniel's murder Sunday, Monday, and today. Some idiot reporter insists on splashing our family business all over *Newsday*."

And to think that idiot reporter was just here, I thought grimly.

Still, at least Forrester had offered to help me with the investigation—a fact I wasn't ready to share with Nick's mother.

"I'm working on it," I assured her.

"*How* are you working on it?" Dorothy demanded. "Have you been to Nathaniel's house yet?"

"His house?" I repeated. "But I thought you said the best place to learn about Nathaniel's life was the Worth School. In fact, I volunteered—"

"Of course that's important. But don't you think you should also go into his place of residence and see what you can find?"

Right, I thought crossly. It's that simple. Especially when Anthony Falcone would undoubtedly be thrilled to catch me in the act of breaking and entering.

"At any rate," Dorothy continued, "I think you owe me a full accounting of your time. I need to know everything you're doing—"

Ding-dong.

"Oh, dear, the doorbell is ringing," I told Dorothy, meanwhile giving Sunny a thumbs-up. "I'm afraid I have to run."

"Call me back as soon as you can!" Dorothy insisted. "If I don't hear from you, I'll give you a buzz back. I really—"

I hung up.

"Thanks," I said to Sunny, once again wondering how I'd ever let myself get involved in all this in the first place.

I was still pondering that question as I turned back to our matching pair of laptops. Within five minutes, Sunny had sold me on the new program. We were talking about making the switch when the doorbell rang again. Only this time, it was for real.

"Hello, Betty," I greeted my friend and landlady as I flung open the door.

She was not alone. Tucked under one arm, football-style, was Frederick, the darling wire-haired dachshund that Winston had brought to their relationship. Betty's stepdog, as I liked to think of him.

As usual, the energetic fawn-and-tan fur ball was beside himself with glee over paying a social call. He craned his neck toward me eagerly, meanwhile wagging his tail so hard that his entire body wriggled beneath Betty's iron grip. His eyes were bright, his wet nose pulsed wildly, and he made throaty noises that made it clear he was experiencing an almost intolerable amount of joy.

Of course, it wasn't only me he was happy to see. I knew the real root of his uncontrollable ecstasy was his reunion with Max and Lou, the other two-thirds of a triumvirate that often seemed like the canine version of the Three Stooges. My two doggies had zoomed over to the front door as soon as they realized their beloved playmate had come to call, and at the moment were both doing their darnedest to get to him by knocking over the only thing standing in their way—which would be me.

"I see you're busy," Betty said, glancing inside as she bent down and released her crazed captive. Frederick, lacking his owner's social skills, immediately vaulted himself through the doorway and joined Max and Lou in the most enthusiastic sniff-and-romp fest this side of the Rockies.

"Nothing that can't be interrupted," I assured her, moving over to let her in.

"In that case . . ." Once Betty was inside, she smiled at my trusty assistant. "Hello, Sunny. I thought that was your car parked outside."

"Hi, Betty!" Sunny said with a little wave. "Nice to see you again!"

"Nice to see you—and nice to see both of you, too!" Betty leaned over to give Max and Lou a warm greeting. They were only too happy to take a moment out of their rhapsodic cavorting with Frederick to say hello back.

"This isn't an actual visit," she said once she stood up. "It's more like an invitation. You haven't started making dinner yet, have you, Jessica?"

"Nope," I assured her.

"I know this is short notice," Betty went on, "but I wondered if you and Nick would like to join Winston and me for dinner this evening. Sunny, you're certainly invited to join us as well, if you'd like."

"Thanks, Betty, but I've got other plans," Sunny replied. "Maybe next time."

"I'd love to have dinner with you and Winston," I said. "Nick's not home yet, but I'm sure he'll be on board. What time should we come over?"

The prospect of dinner with Betty and Winston instantly banished the visions of spring rolls and Garlic Triple Crown that had been dancing in my head. While I truly love good food, I love spending time with good friends even more.

I wasn't the least bit surprised that Nick felt the same way.

• • •

"It was thoughtful of Betty and Winston to invite us over," Nick commented later that evening as the two of us strolled across the lawn to the Big House. "We're lucky to have them as our next-door neighbors."

I'd come to that conclusion myself a long time ago. Years earlier, in fact, pretty much as soon as I'd met my new landlady. And my first impression had been exactly right. Not only had she turned into the great friend I'd anticipated; she was also a tremendous role model.

Betty Vandervoort was one of the few people I'd met along the way who'd actually had the courage to take a stab at her lifelong dream. When she was still very young, she bought herself a one-way bus ticket to New York City, investing an entire summer's earnings from waitressing at the Paper Plate Diner in Altoona, Pennsylvania. It wasn't long before she'd taken Broadway by storm, dancing in musicals like *South Pacific* and *Oklahoma!*

Somewhere along the line, she'd also fallen in love with a man named Charles Vandervoort, who she'd considered the love of her life. Sadly, he'd been taken from her all too soon. Still, her first husband had left her comfortable enough to lead a fabulous life, meeting fascinating people and traveling around the world and eventually landing on this estate in the idyllic community of Joshua's Hollow.

As for her husband of just a few weeks, Winston Farnsworth, he was a relative newcomer on the scene. Their paths had first crossed when I was investigating the polo player's murder—around the same time I met Forrester Sloan. In their case, so many sparks had flown from the moment they met that I'd wondered if I should start carrying a fire extinguisher in my purse.

"Come in!" Betty welcomed us both as she flung open the front door.

Even though I'd expected a casual evening, as soon as we stepped inside I saw that Betty had gone all out. Her dining room table, long enough to seat fourteen, was beautifully set with her best china and crystal—at least, four seats at one end of it. In the middle of the table was a huge bouquet of yellow roses. It was framed by two matching candelabras, each with six yellow tapers that flickered in the darkened room.

"All this for us?" I asked as we all took our seats at the table.

"Betty insisted," Winston said in a jovial voice colored by a lovely English accent as he poured the wine. "She wanted to use her best things for her best friends, and I don't blame her."

I glanced at Nick and gave a little shrug. "I feel like this is a special occasion."

"Actually, I wanted it to be at least a little bit special," Betty said as she arranged a cream-colored linen napkin in her lap. "There's a reason I wanted the chance to sit down and chat with the two of you."

My ears pricked up like Max's and Lou's when somebody says the words "ball," "out," or "ride."

Still, it wasn't necessarily a good thing. Something about the way she said those words gave me the uncomfortable feeling that whatever she had to tell us was going to make me a lot less happy than my dogs were whenever they had a chance to play, romp, or travel.

"I know how anxious the two of you must be to reschedule your wedding," Betty went on. "And Winston and I would like to offer you our house and gardens, for whatever date you choose."

"Thanks, Betty!" Nick exclaimed. "Wow, that's really generous of you." Turning to me, he said, "Isn't that great?"

Before I had a chance to force words through a mouth that was suddenly extremely dry, Betty said, "I realize I should have offered the first time around. But before I had a chance, Jessica was so excited about having found the perfect spot on the North Fork. Besides, I figured the two of you wouldn't want your wedding to be so similar to ours."

"Your wedding was spectacular," Nick commented.

Winston reached across the table and took Betty's hand. "We thought so, too. The same goes for the weeks and months that have followed."

Betty gave his hand a squeeze, then said, "But given what happened at your first wedding, I thought I'd at least extend the offer. It's completely up to you whether or not you want to accept."

"Jess?" Nick asked, turning to me once again.

"I—I don't know what to say," I stuttered. "Can we think about it?" Not wanting to hurt Betty and Winston's feelings, I quickly added, "It's not that I'm not grateful. It's just that—well, I guess I'm still reeling from Saturday."

"Of course you are!" Betty agreed.

"It's only been a few days," Winston added.

"And it was so disruptive!" Betty cried. "Imagine,

the police making everyone at your wedding wait around while they took down all their names and addresses. I know they didn't really suspect any of them, but still..."

"You'd think with all the progress they've made with forensics they'd be able to catch the killer in no time," Winston grumbled. "That's how it always works on the telly. But now the papers are saying it'll take days to see if they can find a match for the prints they found on the knife, assuming the killer left any..."

"Take your time, Jessica," Betty said soothingly. "My offer stands. Just let me know what the two of you decide."

I'm not normally claustrophobic, but I was starting to feel as if I was in one of those horror movies in which the walls of the room start closing in on someone.

So I was extremely grateful when Winston changed the subject by booming, "Now, who needs more wine?"

●　●　●

"That was thoughtful of Betty and Winston, wasn't it?" Nick asked as the two of us strolled across the lawn, back to the cottage, following the exact same route we'd taken two hours earlier.

"Very nice," I said stiffly.

"And now that they've brought up the subject of planning a redo wedding," he continued, "we should probably start thinking about the details—like picking a date."

We'd reached the front door by then. As soon as I unlocked it and stepped inside, Max and Lou exploded into their usual welcome dance, snorting and sneezing and skittering around the wooden floor and generally acting as if Nick and I had just circumnavigated the globe instead of stepping out for a couple of hours to have dinner a hundred feet away.

"Hey, Maxi-Max! Hello, Louie-Lou." I lavished what I believed was an appropriate amount of love and attention on them, then let them out.

"So what about it, Jess?" Nick asked, turning to me as I watched my Westie and my Dalmatian race across the lawn in a state of ecstasy.

"What about *what*?" I replied nervously.

"Picking a new date." His voice was tinged with irritation as he added, "For our wedding?"

Maybe it was because I suddenly found myself inside a small enclosed space after being outside in the fresh air, but for the second time that evening I felt as if the walls were closing in on me.

"But I thought we'd agreed at Betty's that it was too soon," I said. "Besides, I've been totally distracted by this murder investigation your mother got me involved in. In fact, I just found out today that Cousin Nathaniel had a really close friend at the school—a count, no less—and I really need to—"

"Am I imagining things or are you trying to change the subject?" Nick asked, the same edge still in his voice.

"I'm doing no such thing!" I replied indignantly, sinking into a chair. "It's just that I realize that I haven't been keeping you updated on everything I've been finding out about your poor deceased relative. Dorothy, either. I should probably call her back. I didn't have a chance before, but this is probably a good time to—"

"Jessie!" Nick interrupted. "You're doing it again! Actually, it's more like you're doing it *still*. I'm trying to pick a date for us to finally get married, and you suddenly have to make a phone call!"

"Sorry." I hung my head like Lou when he's been caught gnawing on something that wasn't meant to be a chew toy, like my good shoes or one of Nick's law books. "Look, you're so much better at organizing this kind of thing than I am. Why don't you just pick a date and I'll adjust my schedule to make sure it fits?"

"Because picking a date to get married strikes me as something both members of the couple should do together," he said dryly.

"Okay, then let's get out a calendar."

Even though I'm generally a pretty energetic person, for some reason the idea of getting up out of my chair seemed overwhelming. "Or we could do it tomorrow, if that's better for you. It's been a long day for both of us, and—"

"You know what? Just forget it!" Nick stomped across the room, toward the bedroom. "Sometimes I wonder if we're ever going to get married!"

"But I already walked down the aisle once!" I called after him. "I had on the long white dress and—and the uncomfortable shoes and the bouquet and everything else that goes along with being a bride! Can I help it if some crazy person chose that particular time and place to murder someone—a member of *your* family, I might add?"

He didn't respond. In fact, Nick didn't say a single word for the rest of the evening.

Late that night, as he and I lay side by side in bed without talking, touching, or giving any other indication that each other was in the room, I heard Forrester's words echoing through my head.

Pretty convenient, he'd said about Nathaniel's murder dropping the curtain on my wedding. *For someone who was looking for an excuse not to get married, I mean.*

Is it possible Forrester was right? I wondered, staring at the pattern on the ceiling made by the tree branches outside the window. Was I secretly pleased that something interrupted the ceremony, an event that was completely out of my control but which nevertheless turned out to be a good excuse to keep Nick and me from sealing the deal?

Perhaps more important, did my willingness to cancel my own wedding mean I'd never have the guts to commit to a do-over?

Chapter 5

"Animals are reliable, many full of love, true in their affections, predictable in their actions, grateful and loyal. Difficult standards for people to live up to."

—Alfred A. Montapert

As I climbed into my van to drive to the Bromptons early the next morning, I felt as if a dark cloud had settled inside the vehicle. And I couldn't make it go away simply by opening a window or turning on the AC.

It wasn't only the tension between Nick and me that was responsible. True, the last twelve hours had been draining. The night had seemed endless, with both of us sleeping as close to the opposite edges of the bed as we could without falling out. Breakfast was no picnic, either, given the fact that we didn't say a single word to each other.

But I knew that I was fooling myself by pretending I was angry at him. It was *me* I was angry at. Me and my inability to keep from hurting Nick, who I really, truly loved. And it was all because of my own stupid fears.

I was in such a foul mood that when my cellphone rang, I answered without bothering to glance at the caller ID.

"Jessie? It's Suzanne."

I immediately wished I'd checked first. Not that I wasn't in the mood to talk to Suzanne. It was more like I wasn't in the mood to discuss my love life—which I suspected was exactly what she had called to talk about.

"Hi, Suzanne," I greeted her halfheartedly.

"I called to see how you're doing," she said anxiously. "What a bummer, having to cancel your wedding just when you got to the best part, the part when you both say, 'I do.' Because of a murder, no less! You and Nick must be totally freaked out."

"Freaked out definitely describes how I'm feeling right now." I sounded as grim as that cloud still hovering in my van.

"So when are you going to do it?" she gurgled. "Get married for real, I mean?"

Is there anyone in the universe who isn't dying to know exactly that? I wondered.

Aloud, I said, "We haven't picked a new date yet."

"Well, what are you waiting for?" Suzanne demanded.

"Suzanne, I promise that you'll be the first to know," I replied. "But right now, I have to get on the road or I'm going to be late for my first appointment. I'll talk to you soon!"

"But—"

I hung up, feeling bad that I hadn't told Suzanne about my new gig at the Worth School—or the reason why I'd suddenly taken an interest in shaping young minds. Or was at least pretending to.

With that thought in mind, I turned the key in the ignition. I resolved to spend the entire drive out east thinking about how to make my class run smoothly, instead of agonizing over the deplorable state of my love life—and the fact that all of it was my own darn fault.

It turned out that the prospect of returning to a classroom full of giggly teenagers wasn't much less frightening on the second day than it had been on the first. Still, as I hurried down the hall in the Planet Earth building, I reminded myself that after a slightly rocky beginning, my initial foray into the world of molding minds had actually gone pretty well.

Think positive thoughts, I told myself as I breezed into the classroom, hoping that acting confident would make me confident.

"Morning, Dr. Popper!" someone greeted me.

"Hi, Dr. Popper!" piped up a second voice.

Another girl wandered into the classroom right behind me, cooing, "Hey, Dr. P!"

I instantly relaxed. What a difference a day makes, I thought, pleased that as one girl after another straggled in, they all greeted me and gave me a big smile.

They'd barely had a chance to sit down before one of them, a tiny girl named Annie who I remembered had two cats and a German shepherd, raised her hand.

"Dr. Popper?" she asked in a high-pitched voice.

"Before we start reading our lists of the five things every pet needs, first can I ask you a question?"

I held my breath, momentarily afraid that my worst nightmare was about to come true after all: that one of my students was finally going to broach the sensitive subject of my fashion statement.

"Of course," I said coolly.

"I wanted to ask you about feeding people food to dogs," she went on with the same eagerness. "Is it really as dangerous as I've heard?"

"That's a very good question, Annie," I replied, greatly relieved. "There's been a lot written about that very subject, since it's near and dear to animal lovers' hearts. Offhand, I can name a few that are especially dangerous: chocolate, grapes, raisins, walnuts and macadamia nuts, salt . . .

"I've seen really comprehensive lists of dangerous foods on some of the better animal care websites, like the Humane Society's," I went on. "They're generally in books on pet care, too. I'll stop at the library the first chance I get and give you girls a full list. But for now, let's talk about some of the foods you may have given your pets in the past and whether they're safe."

We were off. It was hard to remember how excruciatingly slowly the beginning of the first class had passed. On day two, the time whizzed by.

Before I knew it, class was over. As the girls began putting away their notesbooks and laptops, I came up with another homework assignment: writing a one-page essay titled "What I Love Most About My Pet."

I'm getting pretty good at this, I thought with pride as the girls headed out of the classroom in twos and threes, with a few of them stopping at my desk to chat about their pets.

I felt so good about how the class had gone, in fact, that I had to remind myself of the real reason why I was here at the Worth School in the first place.

As well as the mission I'd laid out for myself for that day.

Ever since Reverend Evans had mentioned Nathaniel's close friendship with Claude Molter, the school's music teacher, I'd racked my brain for an excuse to talk to him. After all, chances were good that someone who had known Nathaniel well would be able to provide me with some insight into who his other friends were, who his enemies were, and who in either of those two categories might have wanted him dead.

As I made my way over to the arts building, better known as the Center for Creative Self-Expression, I also looked forward to meeting someone as accomplished as Claude Molter. After all, Reverend Evans had positively raved about both his talent and the success he'd had in the world of classical music, which I knew to be highly competitive.

I was also intrigued by the fact that he was a count.

The arts building, as I couldn't help thinking of it, was even more dramatic in real life than it had looked on the school's website. It still reminded me of a gigantic linen napkin, loosely crumpled on the ground. But once I got up close, I saw that the white concrete that comprised the wavy exterior was covered in bas-relief sculptures of people doing artsy things, like painting, playing instruments, and dancing. Some raised their voices in song, while others raised their arms to the sky.

I couldn't wait to see what it looked like inside.

I wasn't disappointed. The same flowing effect had been created by rounded but uneven doorways, curved walls, and free-form rooms and open spaces. The effect was disconcerting at first. I'd never been in an earthquake, but I had a feeling the experience wasn't that different.

I followed the signs to the Music Wing, hoping I'd also encounter a few signs or even a roster that would help me locate Claude Molter's office.

It turned out I didn't need either. Not when music spoke louder than words.

It was violin music, so complicated and at the same time so passionate that I was drawn to the sound the way the sailors in *The Odyssey* were drawn to the song of the Sirens. The honeyed melody wafted through a closed door at the end of a hall that was in-set with a narrow rectangular window.

When I drew near, I peered inside and saw the back of a slightly built man who wasn't much taller than I was. His unusually small size made him look incapable of producing such a tremendous sound.

I hesitated before knocking, not wanting to disturb him. But then I reminded myself that holding back wasn't going to do a thing to help me solve Nathaniel's murder.

I rapped my knuckles against the door as gently as I could, braced for the likelihood that the interruption wasn't going to be particularly welcome.

Sure enough, when the man turned around, he was

scowling. His surly expression didn't do much to improve a face that wasn't particularly attractive in the first place. It was exceptionally long and narrow, its strange shape highlighted by piercing cheekbones, thin lips, and a pointed nose that could best be described as beaky. His hair, black but strewn with gray, was a wild mane that gave the impression he'd been overly influenced by photographs of Beethoven.

Even though it was a warm summer day, he was dressed in a meticulously tailored gray suit. With it he wore a dark blue tie held in place by a gold tie tack in the shape of a musical note. In his hand he held a shiny, deep-red violin and a slender bow.

"Yes?" he asked impatiently after I took the liberty of opening the door and sticking my head in. "What is it?"

"What was that piece of music you were playing?" I asked.

"Tchaikovsky, of course." His chin jutted upward in a haughty manner. "The first movement of the violin concerto."

"It was absolutely beautiful," I told him sincerely.

"I would expect my performance to be nothing less than perfect," he replied. "After all, I first performed it with the Prague Symphony Orchestra at the age of fourteen."

Excu-u-use me, I thought.

Aloud, I said, "I've heard it before, of course, but it never sounded quite as magical."

Flattery was getting me nowhere. "Is there a good reason you interrupted me," he demanded, "or was it simply that you couldn't resist the opportunity to educate yourself about the name of the *oeuvre* I was playing?"

I was tempted to counter with an equally caustic comment. But I did have a reason for interrupting him, one that dictated that I be as conciliatory as possible.

"I'm so sorry," I gushed. "I can imagine that even someone as talented as you must require complete concentration in order to create something so amazing."

He finally seemed to soften. I figured the reason was that while I'd lavished flattery on him since I'd opened the door, I hadn't lavished enough. At least until this point.

"My name is Jessica Popper. I'm teaching a summer school class here." I took a deep breath before continuing. "Some of the girls who studied with Mr. Stibbins were quite fond of him, and they asked me to look into the possibility of the school holding a memorial service. I offered to speak to you about whether you'd be interested in providing the music."

"Why, of course," he said without hesitation. "I'd do so for anyone who's affiliated with the school, but I would definitely want to be included in this instance. Nathaniel and I were the best of friends."

"Yes, that's what I heard," I said. "And I'd like to offer you my condolences."

"Thank you." His expression darkened. "It's a terrible thing. I only hope it doesn't affect our students too negatively. They're so young...so innocent!

There are far too many things that happen in their lives that force them to grow up too quickly."

I hadn't really thought about that before. He was absolutely right. At the moment, however, it was Nathaniel who I was most interested in.

"It seems a little surprising that the two of you became friends," I commented, hoping to draw him out. "Since you were both in different fields and all. After all, he was an artist and you're a musician."

"I see no inconsistencies there," he insisted. "Especially in a place like this."

"Like this—as in the Worth School?"

"Like this as in the United States." With an irritated sniff, he said, "This part of the world is populated with so few true intellectuals. So few artists. But it was clear from the start that Nathaniel and I were simpatico. We had so much in common."

"I suppose you were both lucky to have met each other, then," I said. Doing my best to keep all traces of sarcasm out of my voice, I added, "Given the fact that you both found yourselves in such a cultural wasteland and all."

"We did our best," he replied with a sigh. "Nathaniel and I traveled into New York every chance we could to avail ourselves of the city's meager cultural resources."

Ri-i-ight, I thought. Meager cultural resources like the Metropolitan Museum of Art, the Museum of Modern Art, the Cooper-Hewitt, the Guggenheim, the Whitney...not to mention the New York Philharmonic, the Metropolitan Opera, the New York City Ballet...

I had to remind myself that I wasn't here on behalf of the New York City tourism bureau. I was trying to investigate a murder.

"Then you must be devastated," I said.

"Yes," he said simply. "Of course."

I was struck by the overt lack of feeling—not to mention sincerity—behind his words when he added, "I must say, the timing was absolutely tragic. The man was so talented, yet he went unrecognized for so long. It's horribly ironic that just when he was about to get the attention he deserved—"

My ears pricked up. "In what way?" I asked.

"The Mildred Judsen Gallery was about to put his latest works on exhibit. Surely you've heard of the Mildred Judsen." Claude peered at me over his beak, acting as if I were such an imbecile that I barely deserved the breath it took for him to speak to me.

"Uh, I'm not really as *au courant* on the art scene as I should be," I told him, purposely using a French phrase to show him I was at least semiliterate.

"He worked like a fiend these last few months, getting ready," Claude said. "Of course, Nathaniel always worked like a fiend. He spent every moment he wasn't teaching standing at an easel, either at his studio at home or the one the school provided him with here on campus."

I made a mental note about Nathaniel having had an art studio on campus, wondering if it could possibly provide any clues.

"And this upcoming exhibition was a real *coup*," he added, interjecting a French word of his own. "The gallery is one of New York's top venues, at least for artists who have yet to make a real splash. It specializes in having the artists right on-site while it's open, so they can personally discuss their work with whoever comes in to view it. They're extremely strict about their policy of only representing the work of living artists. And apparently they couldn't wait to launch Nathaniel's career, something he'd wanted for ages. The day he shipped his paintings off to the gallery, I thought he was going to burst with joy."

"I guess they had to take him off the schedule, then," I said, thinking out loud.

"Sadly, they had no choice but to do exactly that. In fact, the last I heard, they were about to ship every last piece of his work back to his studio."

"That's awful!" I cried. "To think that he was on the verge of—of greatness, perhaps. And now..."

"It's quite tragic," Claude agreed in the same matter-of-fact tone. He hesitated for only a moment before adding, "Is there anything else?"

His crisp tone of voice jolted me back into the moment. "Excuse me?"

"I'd like to get back to my music," he said. "That is, if you have no further reason to keep me from doing so."

"Oh. No, that's all I wanted to ask you."

"Fine. You'll let me know when the memorial is?"

He turned his back on me, placed his violin under his chin, and lifted his bow. Before I had a chance to say thank you or goodbye, he was completely absorbed by Tchaikovsky.

As I closed the door of the practice room gently

behind me, I contemplated Claude Molter's cool reaction to Nathaniel's death.

Maybe it's because he's a count, I thought.

What I found even more interesting was Claude's claim that Nathaniel Stibbins's career as an artist was on the verge of taking off. According to him, the artist's murder had occurred right before the opening of an exhibit at a New York City art gallery that was likely to get him the acclaim he'd undoubtedly striven for during most of his life.

I couldn't help but wonder if the timing was merely a coincidence—or if the fact that he may have been on the verge of unprecedented success was the reason why some nasty soul had decided it was a good time for him to be dead.

• • •

As I ambled out of the arts building—somehow, I still couldn't bring myself to call it the Center for Creative Self-Expression—I continued to ponder the conversation I'd just had with the school's music teacher. I was so lost in thought that I nearly collided with someone who reached the door at the main entrance the same time I did. My heartbeat quickened when I recognized her as one of my students. Of course, it was hard not to, since as usual she was dressed completely in white. The same row of bracelets, made of green and black beads, ran up her arm.

"Vondra?" I exclaimed.

She stepped back, looking surprised. "Dr. Popper!" she said. "I didn't realize it was you. Sorry about that."

"No, it was my fault. I was daydreaming, as usual." As the two of us started out along the path together, I asked, "How's that cat of yours?"

She hesitated before replying, "He's fine."

"I didn't get to find out much about Babalu," I said, doing my best to keep the conversation going. "That is, aside from his unusual name."

With a little shrug, she said, "I'm not as outgoing as those other girls. I guess I'm kind of a private person."

"You don't have to talk about your pets in order to benefit from the class," I assured her as we headed toward the center of campus. "All I care about is teaching my students enough that they can be good caretakers for their pets for the rest of their lives. And I hope you all continue to make animals a part of your family. I don't know about you, but I can't imagine living without a whole bunch of furry or feathered friends around me. I even have a pet chameleon."

Vondra smiled. "So you have animals around you both at work and at home."

"I wouldn't have it any other way."

"Well, it's really nice of you to come to the school to teach," Vondra said, suddenly shy. "Especially since you're doing it for free."

My eyebrows shot up. "How did you know that?"

With a little shrug, she replied, "Around this place, nothing stays a secret for long."

If only, I thought. True, I'd only been here for two days. But my suspicion was that this place was crawling with secrets. The trick was to become part of the pipeline. Either that, or find a way to ferret them out myself.

"It certainly seems as if the students know a lot about one another," I commented.

"*Oh*, yeah." Her voice edged with bitterness, she added, "And what they don't know, they make up."

Even though I would have loved to find out more about what she meant, something about her closed-off demeanor kept me from pursuing it.

"High school isn't easy for anyone," I told her. "I'm sure that it's just like at every other school—plenty of cliques and rivalries and all kinds of social intricacies." I hesitated before adding, "In fact, I bet that at a place like this, it's even worse than at most schools."

"Especially for the scholarship kids," Vondra said, still sounding bitter. I'm a day student, meaning I don't live in the fancy dorms like Campbell and Beanie and all those other rich girls."

"You mean you commute every day from home?"

"That's right."

"How far is it?"

"I live in Wyandogue. To get here, I take the Long Island Railroad, then a bus."

"Wow! That's quite a commute."

She cast me a wary glance. "It takes me more than an hour and a half each way. Which means I get up at five thirty every morning."

"That must be incredibly tough," I said. "But look at the bright side. At least you get to live at home, with your family. These girls who live in the dorms might be able to sleep later, but they don't have their parents or siblings around."

"Or their pets," Vondra volunteered.

I laughed. "That's a biggie. Think how lucky you are that the first face you see every morning is a furry one. Am I right about that?"

"You bet," she said, smiling. "Especially since I swear Babalu can tell time. He's the one who gets me out of bed every morning."

"I can't think of a better alarm clock," I said. "Do you have any brothers or sisters?"

Vondra shook her head. "It's just my mom and me."

"She must be thrilled that you're going to a great school like this," I commented.

"She is," Vondra agreed. Thoughtfully, she added, "My mom has actually had a pretty tough life. And being a single mother is only part of it. It's not like we have a lot of money or anything. She runs a small shop, so even though we manage to pay our bills, there's never much money left over for any extras.

"Even so, when it comes to her little girl, she wants only the best. That's why she was so determined that I come to school here at Worth. She never even came close to having an opportunity like this."

She was silent for a few moments, and the only sound was the chirping of birds and the soft thud of our shoes against the walkway. "I can't talk to her about the stuff that goes on here. It would hurt her to know everything isn't as perfect for me as she wants it to be."

"What kind of stuff?" I asked, surprised. It wasn't until after I'd asked that I wondered if she'd think it wasn't any of my business.

"Just the usual," she replied with a little shrug. "The stuff you mentioned before. The cliques and all." Her voice became thick as she explained, "Some of the rich girls like Campbell and her ladies-in-waiting, as I think of them, have no greater pleasure in life than making things difficult for the less advantaged kids."

"You mean the scholarship kids," I observed.

"Yeah," she agreed sullenly.

"Campbell does seem kind of..." I tried to think of a way to characterize her that wouldn't sound too condemning. "She strikes me as someone with a strong sense of entitlement."

"If by that you mean she thinks she has a right to own the entire universe and everyone in it, I agree with you completely," Vondra said with a wry smile. "The fact that she's famous doesn't help, either."

"Famous?" I repeated, surprised.

"Maybe not famous, exactly," she corrected herself. "More like on the verge of becoming famous. Just a few weeks ago, she went to some party in the city and the next day had her name in Page Six. You know, that gossip column in the *New York Post* that's always writing about celebrities and politicians and people like that?"

"I've heard of it," I said. "But why would a gossip columnist be interested in Campbell Atwater?"

"Because of her father," Vondra replied matter-of-factly. "He's an incredibly rich businessman. Powerful, too. He's one of those self-made men that the newspapers love to write about. Rags to riches and all that." She laughed coldly. "I've also heard he's one of the meanest, most ruthless people in the world, which I suppose is how he managed to be so successful."

"Vondra, if Campbell or anyone else is doing anything that's really hurtful, there must be some recourse," I told her. "Does Dr. Goodfellow know about the tensions between the kids from wealthy families and the students on scholarship?"

"It's nothing illegal or anything like that," Vondra insisted. "It's just that they do everything they can to keep me from forgetting that they're who they are and I'm who I am."

"A bunch of snobby rich girls," I muttered without thinking. Dorothy's take on the students at the Worth School, I realized.

I also realized I shouldn't have voiced that characterization out loud.

"I'm sorry," I said quickly. "I shouldn't have said that."

But Vondra was grinning. "I couldn't have said it better myself."

"Still, I shouldn't go around—"

"Don't worry," Vondra assured me, still smiling. "I won't breathe a word to anybody. And you know, it kind of makes me feel better to know I'm not the only one who thinks of them that way."

By that point, we'd reached the administration building.

"I have to stop in here to check my mail," I told her. "But it'll only take me a minute. If you don't have any other classes today, I could give you a ride somewhere. I'm scheduled to meet with someone later this morning, but I certainly have time to drop you at the train station beforehand."

"That's okay," Vondra replied quickly. "I am on my way home, but the bus should come in about five minutes. I actually look forward to the twenty-minute ride. It gives me a chance to get started on my assignments. By the time I get off the train, I've usually made a pretty good dent in my homework.

"But thanks for the offer, Dr. Popper," she said, turning off in another direction. Glancing back, she added, "And thanks for listening."

I watched her hurry off to her bus stop, berating myself for being so careless.

Yet maybe my carelessness wasn't such a bad thing, I thought.

After all, while my slip of the tongue had been in no way intentional, I realized it had helped me make a friend.

•　•　•

As I stepped into the administration building, I was struck once again by how elegantly appointed it was. Everything about the dignified edifice screamed wealth and privilege, from the lustrous dark wood paneling to the Oriental rugs to the artwork hanging on the walls.

And to think it's one of the few buildings on campus that's actually named for what it really is, I thought with amusement.

I smiled at Ms. Greer, who was sitting in her usual spot near the front door. As I did, a lightbulb suddenly went off in my head.

"Ms. Greer," I said, edging over to her desk, "there's something I've been curious about." I tried to sound friendly enough to break through her icy exterior. "And you seem like the best person to ask, since Dr. Goodfellow told me herself that you're the one who really runs things around here."

She cast me a wary glance. "I'm afraid Dr. Goodfellow has been known to exaggerate on occasion." I could already see those defenses of hers snapping into place, which gave me the feeling this was one of those instances in which flattery wasn't going to get me anywhere.

I forged ahead anyway. "I understand Mr. Stibbins had an art studio on campus. I've heard so much about how talented he was that I'd love to see some of his artwork. Would it be possible for me to—?"

"I'm afraid not," she replied tartly. "That room has always been off-limits to everyone except Mr. Stibbins himself. Here at the Worth School we have the greatest respect for the creative process, and that includes preserving an artist's privacy. And now, after what happened, I've been given strict instructions to keep it under lock and key until further notice."

As she said those last words, I noticed that her eyes involuntarily traveled to the desk drawer on her right.

And I bet I know exactly where that key is kept, I thought.

But I simply replied, "I see. Well, thanks anyway.

Maybe I'll have some other opportunity to see Mr. Stibbins's artwork."

With that, I turned and wandered over to the grid of wooden mailboxes. I was surprised to find several pieces of paper stuck into mine. Most were notices, including one instructing the faculty to park only in designated spots and one reminding everyone that descriptions of classes for the fall term were due in another week.

I've only been here a couple of days, I marveled, and I'm already on the junk-mail list.

But the last one actually looked interesting.

"Just a reminder," the headline on the single sheet of pink paper read. "Parent-Teacher Association Meeting, Thursday night. All faculty members are required to attend. 8:00 P.M. in the Main Dining Hall, with Social Time commencing at 7:30. Refreshments will be served. Please be prompt!"

Social Time? I wondered what that was about. Probably a chance for the teachers to gush to the parents about how wonderful their children were, and vice versa.

Still, I wanted to go, since attending a shindig that included both the teachers and the parents who were connected to Nathaniel's school would give me a chance to do some sleuthing. With refreshments, no less. In fact, I desperately hoped the term "all faculty members" included *moi*, a mere volunteer.

But even if it didn't, at least the notice gave me an excuse to talk to Dr. Goodfellow again, something I was anxious to do. The other time she and I had spoken, I'd gotten the feeling that in her eyes, Nathaniel Stibbins wasn't just another teacher—mainly because she'd told me herself that losing him was "personal."

I was hopeful that this time, I'd be able to find out just *how* personal.

Chapter 6

"The greatness of a nation can be judged by the way its animals are treated."

—Mohandas Gandhi

I didn't waste any time before sidling up to Ms. Greer's desk once more.

"Sorry to bother you again," I said, "but do you think it might be possible for me to talk to Dr. Goodfellow?"

This time, it took the gaunt-faced woman a second or two to drag her eyes away from her computer screen. "Dr. Goodfellow is all alone now."

She'd barely gotten the words out before a stricken look crossed her face. "Oh, my," she sputtered. "What I should have said is that Dr. Goodfellow is alone in her office. In other words, she's not in conference with anybody. So she could probably see you. Right now, I mean."

"Okay," I said, hiding my confusion over what had just transpired. "In that case, should I go ahead and knock on her door?"

She nodded, still looking distressed.

What was *that* all about? I wondered as I knocked on the headmistress's partially open door, meanwhile peering into the room. The headmistress's assistant clearly thought she'd put her foot in her mouth. As for why, I didn't have a clue.

I guess I didn't knock loudly enough. Either that or Elspeth Goodfellow was so lost in her own world that she couldn't hear anything going on in the one the rest of us inhabited.

And lost in her own world was exactly how she appeared. Dr. Goodfellow stood next to the window, gazing out at what, to me, looked like nothing but an empty field. She was dressed in a flowing forest green dress made of silky fabric. It had huge puffy sleeves and a full skirt. Her hair hung down loosely around her shoulders, making her look younger than I'd thought she was the first time I met her.

With one hand, she clasped a single white rose to her chest.

Between her pose, the faraway look in her eye, and the rose, she reminded me of the heroine in a Victorian novel.

"Dr. Goodfellow?" I said softly, not wanting to startle her.

I didn't succeed. She turned to me, wearing a deer-in-the-headlights expression.

"Dr. Popper!" she cried. "I didn't hear you come in."

"Sorry to disturb you," I said, stepping into the room. "Ms. Greer said it would be all right."

"Of course," she said, still flustered.

It was at that point that I noticed that in her other hand, she was holding a tiny stemmed glass that had been hidden by her skirt. In it was a clear, golden liquid.

Brandy, I figured. Or sherry. Or something otherwise alcoholic, since no one drinks apple cider out of such a tiny glass.

She regained her composure instantly, sweeping across the room and sinking into her desk chair. She gently placed the glass next to her pencil mug, acting as if hitting the sherry before lunch was part of every educator's daily routine.

"I'm always available to the members of the faculty," she informed me, sounding as if she was reciting a sentence she'd memorized. "It's part of a headmistress's duties. Please, have a seat, Dr. Popper."

"Thank you." I lowered myself into the same red velvet chair I'd sat in when I'd had my interview.

"How can I help you?" she asked.

"I just checked my mailbox," I replied, "and I found a notice about tomorrow night's PTA meeting."

"We hold them once a month." Dr. Goodfellow waved her hand dramatically. "It's a policy I instituted when I first came to the Worth School. I feel it's so important for parents and teachers, both of whom are the significant influences on any young person's life, to be in constant communication. How else can they work together to nurture our students, sculpting their brains into strong, vital organs that will continue to think and pulse and probe throughout their adult lives?"

Once again, she seemed to be reciting a speech. In

fact, for a minute there I felt as if she was reading to me from the school's website.

"I was going to ask if you wanted me to attend," I said, "but it sounds as if you think it's important for every faculty member to be there." After all, I was one of those people charged with all that sculpting and nurturing.

"But of course." Looking surprised, she added, "Don't you *want* to be there?"

"Definitely!" I told her truthfully. "As a matter of fact, I'm looking forward to it."

Especially since it'll give me a chance to check out some of the other faculty members, I thought, not to mention some of the parents. And hopefully to throw out a few carefully worded sentences designed to give me a better idea of who might have recently dropped Nathaniel Stibbins from their A-list.

"Oh, but you're just a volunteer!" Dr. Goodfellow said, as if the thought had just occurred to her. "I forgot all about that. You probably don't want to give up one of your evenings to—"

"No, it's fine!" I insisted. "I, uh, think meeting the parents of some of the students in my class will help me do a better job. I agree with you one hundred percent that it's important for me to work with the parents so I can do a better job of, uh, sculpting brains."

Somehow, that had sounded so much better when she'd said it. But at the moment I was more concerned with finding a way of bringing Poor Cousin Nathaniel into the conversation when she said, "You're certainly welcome to come, then."

"Thank you. I'll be there."

Wistfully, she said, "I have to apologize. For seeming so distracted, I mean. Normally, I'm completely on top of things. But I'm afraid I haven't been myself since Nathaniel..." Her voice became too choked for her to continue.

"I'm sure it's been difficult," I told her sympathetically. "I remember you mentioning that he was one of the Worth School's finest teachers—"

"Nathaniel was more than that," Dr. Goodfellow interrupted with an irritated edge to her voice. "*Much* more."

Her statement left me speechless. In fact, I was still trying to decide if I was completely misreading her when she added, "I might as well tell you myself, Dr. Popper, since if I don't someone else is sure to."

"Tell me what?" I asked hesitantly.

Her eyes drifted over to the window as in a faraway voice she said, "Nathaniel and I were lovers."

"Oh!"

At least that's what I intended to say. Instead, the single syllable came out somewhere between a gasp and a hiccup.

Her directness had caught me completely off guard. Normally I would have classified a confession like that as too much information. But instead, I was thrilled by her willingness to talk about the man whose demise had brought me to the school in the first place.

Especially since her admission that the two of them had been linked romantically opened up so many questions about her possible role in Nathaniel's murder.

Her revelation also clued me in to her assistant's embarrassment over her comment that the good doctor was now alone. As soon as Ms. Greer had said the words "Dr. Goodfellow is all alone now," they'd struck her as a bit too close for comfort.

"Nathaniel and I tried to keep it a secret, of course," Dr. Goodfellow went on. She paused to sniff the rose she'd dropped into her lap. Once again staring out the window, into the great beyond, she continued, "It's so difficult when two people work in the same institution. But of course we couldn't pretend for long. Our feelings for each other were so strong that it was inevitable that others would notice."

Turning away from the window and finally looking me in the eye, she said, "Schools are like small towns. Everyone knows everyone else's business. Especially when it comes to matters of the heart."

"I'm sure everyone feels terrible about your loss," I said.

She didn't act as if she'd heard me. "Not that there weren't plenty of people who were disapproving," she went on, bitterness creeping into her voice. "I'm no fool. I knew some of the faculty thought it was unseemly for a headmistress and one of the teachers to share such affection. And perhaps they could have been right, under other circumstances."

Her eyes drifted back to that unknown point outside the window. "But with Nathaniel and me, it was different," she said wistfully. "Our love for each other was great, one of those grand passions that people these days are rarely lucky enough to encounter. We were soul mates, and the fact that we both came to this school was like some cosmic imperative that knew we were meant for each other."

I cleared my throat, just in case she'd forgotten someone else was in the room. As glad as I was to be getting some insight into how Nathaniel had spent his days at the Worth School, her raw honesty made me uncomfortable. Especially since I was someone she shouldn't have been pouring her heart out to.

But even my loud "a-hem" didn't bring her back to the moment. "You would think that given the depth of our feelings for each other," she continued, "despite our roles here at the school, the others around us would have understood. Welcomed the opportunity to be amid such strong feelings, even."

I mumbled, "It's possible that they didn't really—"

"But no!" she cried, turning to me so abruptly I practically fell out of my chair. "There was jealousy! There was mistrust!" Narrowing her eyes, she added, "There was even suspicion. As if dear Nathaniel could have been guided by anything aside from the force and purity of his feelings for me!"

I was starting to grow really uneasy. What had started out as a heartfelt confession—albeit an inappropriate one—was starting to sound kind of creepy.

"So we did what we had to to keep away from prying eyes," Dr. Goodfellow continued. "Nathaniel and I met clandestinely. Whenever we were in public, we acted as if the two of us were nothing more than headmistress and art teacher. A polite hello at a faculty meeting, a nod of the head when we passed each other in the hallway..."

By this point, Dr. Goodfellow herself had started getting kind of creepy. *Really* creepy, in fact.

"Dr. Goodfellow," I said firmly, "I'm so sorry for

taking up so much of your time. I really just wanted to ask you about the PTA meeting."

"I have nothing to hide," she announced, raising her chin and peering down at me in a way that reminded me of a queen. Or at least someone trying to act like a queen. "Especially not now, with Nathaniel... gone. Besides, given the way people talk, Dr. Popper, you would have heard about this sooner or later."

Maybe not in such detail, I thought. Or with such melodrama.

Yet once I was backing out the door, profusely thanking her for her time and watching her eyes take on that dreamy look once again as she held the white rose against her cheek, it was all I could do to keep from jumping up and down with glee.

It was true that having had a chance to peek at Elspeth Goodfellow's softer side had given me the heebie-jeebies. But it seemed worth it, since I now had a better perspective on some of the intrigues at the Worth School.

Especially the ones that involved Nathaniel Stibbins.

• • •

I was still mulling over Elspeth Goodfellow's bizarre and totally unexpected confession as I headed out of the administration building, toward the parking lot.

"Dr. Popper?" I heard a male voice call.

Stopping in my tracks, I turned and saw Richard Evans, the school chaplain, striding toward me. In his arms he cradled a bundle of black-and-white fur.

"Hi, Reverend!" I called back, waving.

As he drew closer, I got a better look at Chach. The shih tzu was a particularly cute one, even though I must admit I've never met one that wasn't cute.

"I see you've brought your friend," I observed when he and his alert, sweet-faced buddy reached me.

"That's right. Thanks again for your kind offer to take a look at Chach's foot."

"No problem," I assured him, thinking, *Especially since I'm hoping that while I'm treating Chach, you'll treat me to a little inside information on Nathaniel Stibbins.*

"So this is the famous Chach," I said, giving the compact bundle of energy a good scratching behind the ear. He wagged his tail enthusiastically, no doubt appreciating the fact that ear-scratching was a skill I prided myself on having perfected over the years.

I've always found the shih tzu's history fascinating. While they're believed to have originated in Tibet, the Chinese bred them to look like lions, a symbol of Buddhism. In fact, the name means "lion dog." But there weren't a lot of lions in China, so breeders had to rely on sculptors' versions, which weren't entirely accurate. That's where the round, protruding eyes, the flattened muzzles, and the supposedly ferocious expressions came from.

The spunky lapdog was a favorite with China's royalty. Then, in the 1930s, importation to Western Europe began. Some twenty years later, a British dog enthusiast who wasn't satisfied with the shih tzu's look bred one to a Pekingese, beginning the process of modifying the breed to look the way it does today.

I bent my knees so the shih tzu and I were eye to

eye. "Tell me, Chach. How did you ever get such an unusual name?"

As usual, his owner stepped up to the plate, answering on his dog's behalf. "It's kind of a cute story," Reverend Evans told me. "My wife, whose family is originally from Panama, came from a large family. Eleven children, in fact. Needless to say, we have quite a lot of nephews and nieces. When we decided to get a dog, it happened to be early November. We thought it would be fun to charge the group of them with coming up with a name. So once the whole family was gathered around the table on Thanksgiving, we asked all the children to come up with a name and told them we'd pull one out of a hat." With a little shrug, he added, "The name we picked was Chach. One of the kids thought of it because it sounded Spanish, and she wanted to name the dog in honor of my wife."

I chuckled. "I'm sure your wife was tickled."

"She and this dog are inseparable," he admitted. "Chach is smart enough to know who's in charge of feeding him, so that's where his loyalty lies."

"I don't blame you one bit," I said to Chach. "In fact, you're a dog after my own heart.

"Now let's make sure you're in the best shape you can be," I continued. Gesturing toward the parking lot, I said, "My van is right over there. I bring it to school so I can start making house calls right after class."

"I envy your freedom," Reverend Evans commented as the three of us made our way over to my van. "It must be nice, not having to work in a stuffy office."

"Freedom is the exact word I would use," I agreed. "And stuffy offices are the very reason I decided to take the plunge and buy the van in the first place. Sometimes I think that old song 'Don't Fence Me In' was written with me in mind."

Laughing, he noted, "Except that it was written long before you were born."

"True. So I guess I'm not the only one who feels that way. What about you? What's it like, being a minister at a girls' school?"

"Well, it's a challenge, I assure you," he replied with a smile. "Serving as a moral compass for a gaggle of teenagers is not exactly easy."

"I can imagine!" I replied. "Especially since the students here seem so diverse. In fact, that's one of the things that really struck me on my first day here. This place is a strange mixture of rich girls, if you'll excuse the expression, and those who aren't even close to being in that category."

"That's exactly right." Reverend Evans sighed. "I applaud the school's commitment to a diverse student body. Both the parents and the alumnae are quite generous, which helps us maintain a very strong scholarship program."

Frowning, he added, "Still, you're right about the fact that that creates certain . . . tensions. Anyone who thinks girls are kinder than boys clearly never went to high school. Those years are difficult for everyone, and all the cliques and competitiveness create an environment that can be very difficult for everyone to deal with, from the students to the teachers to the administration. And the fact that the wealthy students at

Worth are *so* wealthy—and the underprivileged students are *so* underprivileged—makes it even tougher."

"I'm sure that's true," I commented sincerely.

What Reverend Evans was saying completely supported not only my impressions about the dynamics among the students, but also what Vondra had told me. I couldn't help wondering if the climate of the school had anything to do with Nathaniel's murder.

"By the way," I continued, anxious to pick Reverend Evans's brain even further, "I ran into Claude Molter this morning and had a chance to talk to him about Nathaniel Stibbins."

"I'm sure he gave you an earful," Reverend Evans said with a wry smile.

His reaction surprised me. "I thought you told me Claude and Nathaniel were friends."

"They *were* friends." He hesitated before adding, "At least, for a while."

"You mean they had a falling out?"

He was silent for such a long time that I glanced over to see if he'd heard me. His tight expression told me that he'd heard me, all right. He just wasn't in a hurry to respond.

"I've already said too much," he said in a strained voice. "I'm not one to gossip. It's true that Claude was someone who knew Nathaniel well, and they did indeed have their differences along the way. But I think I'll just leave it at that."

I was thoughtful as we neared the parking lot. Claude Molter had claimed that he and Nathaniel had been friends.

Maybe he simply didn't want to speak ill of the

dead, I thought. Still, the fact that he hadn't told me the whole story nagged at me.

We'd reached my van by then, which meant it was time to change the subject to something more timely: mainly, Reverand Evans's ailing shih tzu.

"Thanks again for agreeing to look at Chach," he said. "Hopefully, it'll turn out to be nothing more serious than a cut."

Once we were inside the van, I took the tense little dog into my arms and brought him over to my examining table.

"Tell me more about Chach's general health lately," I said as I checked the dog's eyes and ears. "Any coughing or sneezing?"

"Not that I've noticed."

"Any vomiting or diarrhea?"

"No. As far as I know, the limp is the only problem."

"Everything seems fine here," I observed as I palpated the dog's organs.

Something about being touched that way spooked poor Chach. His sturdy body started to twitch, and his paws skittered across the stainless steel surface of my examining table.

"Hold on there, fella," I commanded. Glancing up at Reverend Evans, I said, "It might not be a bad idea for you to hold him. Not only will it help me, it will also make him feel more secure."

As he did, I continued checking Chach's organs, admitting, "I've gotten spoiled lately. I hired an assistant who comes with me on most of my house calls. She's terrific, and having a second pair of arms really makes the job easier. But she only works part-time, and it doesn't make sense for her to come with me the mornings I teach." Focusing on my patient again, I asked, "Now, which foot has the problem?"

"The front one, on the right."

"This is what a normal leg feels like," I said as I checked it. But when I got to the foot pad, Chach let out a yelp.

"It's really sensitive in this area," I noted. "The toe looks swollen, but the nail bed is intact . . . I'm thinking he may have a broken toe."

Reverend Evans frowned. "I hadn't thought of that."

"We could get an X-ray, but that's usually pretty difficult," I continued. "We can put on a Medi-splint to allow it a chance to heal, but I usually just leave it and recommend a strict rest period of three weeks. I can also give Chach a nonsteroid anti-inflammatory. I'll give you some tablets of Rimadyl, which he needs to take once a day with food. The downside is that his foot can feel so much better that he'll want to walk on it, so you'll have to watch and limit him."

"Definitely," he said, looking relieved. "You're so good with dogs. Do you have any of your own?"

"Two," I replied. "A Dalmatian named Lou and a Westie named Max. I also have two cats, a bird, and a chameleon."

Reverend Evans grinned. "I envy you! It must be wonderful, having all those animals in your household."

"It's pretty cool," I said, pausing for a moment to think about how much they added to my life.

"I'd love to meet all of them one of these days," Reverend Evans commented. "Especially that Westie of yours. I have a feeling Chach and Max would really hit it off."

"I think you're right," I agreed. "I'd like to see Chach again in two weeks. If it isn't any better, we can try the splint I mentioned. It's a piece of plastic that takes the weight off, which helps the toe heal faster. In the meantime, keep him off the stairs, and only let him outside to go to the bathroom."

"That reminds me of a cute story," Reverend Evans said as he lifted the dog off the table. "When Chach was just a puppy, I took him with me on a trip to Arizona. When it was time for him to go for a walk, he walked up to a cactus and lifted his right leg. Let me tell you, he got some pretty serious needles in a very tender area. Now he only lifts his left leg to pee—or else he just squats."

"Poor little guy!" I said, chuckling as I smoothed his silky ears.

"I can tell you really care about your patients," Reverend Evans commented.

"I do," I replied simply.

"It's great that you volunteered to teach an animal-care class. And I don't just mean because of the value of teaching the girls something so practical."

"What do you mean?" I asked.

He sighed. "Some of our girls come from backgrounds that aren't exactly—well, let's just say their families aren't all quite as stable as one would wish. They need as many positive role models as possible, young women like you who've done something really positive and productive with their lives."

"I've actually been enjoying it," I replied.

As I said the words, I realized how true they were. Even though an ulterior motive had brought me to the school, it was turning out to be fun getting to know the girls and sharing what I knew about animals with them.

After we completed some paperwork, Reverend Evans turned to leave. But when he reached the door of the van, he turned back and said, "I almost forgot. There's an event coming up that I'd like to invite you to. Of course, I have an ulterior motive."

His use of a phrase that had run through my own mind just a few minutes earlier startled me. But it only took me a second to realize that whatever *his* ulterior motive was, chances were good that it wasn't the same as mine.

"As part of the school's community outreach program, we're holding our first Blessing of the Animals ceremony here at the school chapel a week from Saturday."

"Yes, I heard about that," I told him. "Dr. Goodfellow mentioned it to me."

"So you're familiar with them?"

"Sure," I replied, "although I've only seen them on TV."

"For the school, it's a chance for us to invite members of the community to get to know us better," Reverend Evans explained. "Anyone is welcome to bring their dogs or cats—or any other animals, for that matter—to be blessed. Afterward, we're having a big reception out on the lawn. A lot of the girls have volunteered to help shepherd people around. Since we've never done it before, we're still working out some of the details. In fact, the logistics will be one of the topics under discussion at tomorrow's PTA meeting, if you're planning to come."

"As a matter of fact, I am."

"If you don't mind, I'll introduce you to the parents and the rest of the faculty," he said. "We've never been fortunate enough to have a veterinarian in attendance at the blessing before. Your presence isn't only a valuable addition in case one of the animals gets sick, which would be rare; it would be great if you'd be willing to answer people's questions about how best to care for their animals. You could bring that Westie of yours, too."

Frankly, the event didn't sound like Max's thing. The sight of one dog usually sent him into a state of near-hysteria, so I couldn't imagine how he'd do if he were surrounded by dozens of them—not to mention cats and other assorted animals. But I'd decided to go the minute Dr. Goodfellow had mentioned it.

"I'd love to come," I told him.

Reverend Evans looked surprised. "And here I thought I'd have to persuade you to give up your Saturday. Especially since you're already doing so much for the school."

"It sounds like fun," I insisted. "And I'm happy that I can be of assistance."

I meant it, too. Being part of the event would give

me one more chance to peek at the inner workings of the Worth School. And the more people I talked to, the more apparent it became that Nathaniel had been ensconced in this place, leading me to believe that Dorothy's suspicion that the reason behind his murder was rooted here was correct.

Chapter 7

"If you don't own a dog, at least one, there is not necessarily anything wrong with you, but there may be something wrong with your life."
—Roger Caras

Thursday morning, right after class, I decided to pop into the school library before dashing off to my first appointment of the day. It was the first chance I'd gotten to check the stacks and see what else I could find about feeding people food to animals. The topic had really piqued my students' interest, and while I was starting to get comfortable in front of a classroom, I still wanted to make sure I came to each class with enough information to fill the hour.

Even though the photograph of the library—or the Hall of Ideas, as it was called at the Worth School—on the school's website had been enough to make me do a double take, it didn't quite capture the drama of the building.

The picture on the Internet had made it clear that the exterior looked like a row of tremendous white books, lined up on a shelf. It wasn't until I was up close, however, that I saw that each gigantic volume had a title carved into its spine: *For Whom the Bell Tolls, Ulysses, The Great Gatsby, An American Tragedy.*

My eyes lit on that last one for a few seconds. After all, Theodore Dreiser's great novel centered around a man whose goal of achieving the American dream was cut short when he was accused of murder.

I was still pondering that irony as I headed inside the building, and then I was struck by another. As I entered through a doorway that looked as if it had been cut from the spine of a book, I glanced up. This book was *The Divine Comedy,* according to the sculpted letters high above my head.

Interesting choice, I thought, amused by the architect's obvious sense of humor. I remembered from my Intro to Literature class my freshman year at Bryn Mawr that one of the most famous lines from Dante's epic poem had been carved above the gates of Purgatory: "All hope abandon, ye who enter here."

Yet there was nothing the least bit forbidding inside. Instead, I found myself in a large, airy entryway, with tremendous floor-to-ceiling windows and walls and carpets the same blinding white as the building's exterior. And rather than the boiling blood and black snow that Dante had envisioned, I saw an espresso bar and half a dozen leather massage chairs. I doubted that either of those could be found in anyone's vision of hell.

I moved farther inside, glancing around at the

stacks of books, the rows of computers, and long tables framed by comfy-looking chairs. I was about to seek out a reference librarian in the name of saving time when the sight of a familiar face stopped me cold.

Beanie was sitting at a large table, her narrow shoulders tense as she hunched over something I couldn't quite see. Her posture caused her lank black hair to hang down along the sides of her face, nearly hiding it from view. I could just see the tip of her pointed nose sticking out from behind her veil. In fact, I might not have even recognized her if it wasn't for the same bright red T-shirt she'd worn in class earlier that day.

But what interested me as I grew closer was the book lying open in front of her, a thick volume with large, glossy pages. Even from a distance, I could see that they were printed in rich color. I could also see that she appeared to be totally absorbed by what she was looking at.

I wandered over, trying to look lost in thought. As I walked by her, I glanced in her direction casually, then put on a surprised expression.

"Beanie!" I cried. "I thought that was you!"

She glanced up, then stared at me for a few seconds, as if she was having trouble placing me.

"Oh!" she finally exclaimed. "Dr. Popper! Sorry. I was in a daze."

"So I see." I drifted over to her side. "Doing homework?"

"Not really," she said with a shrug. "I was just looking at this art history book. Every time I come in here, I can't resist."

Peering over her shoulder, I commented, "I recognize that painting. It's by Botticelli, isn't it?"

"That's right," she said, her brown eyes widening.

"Don't tell me: *The Birth of Venus*."

"Wow, you know about art, too, Dr. Popper!" Beanie exclaimed, sounding impressed. "And here I would have thought that since you're a veterinarian, all you knew about was science."

Just don't ask me anything about African drumming, I thought.

"It's a pretty cool painting, don't you think?" Beanie asked, still staring at the page.

"Very cool," I agreed, not mentioning that she and I weren't exactly the only ones who thought so.

"It's supposed to show Venus, the goddess of love, emerging from the sea," she added. "A lot of art historians believe that the model was a beautiful woman who was the mistress of a really important man. A member of the Medici family, the famous art patrons who lived in Florence in the fourteen hundreds. It seems Botticelli was in love with her, too."

"You certainly know a lot about art," I commented.

"Not really," she said. "I took Mr. Stibbins's class last semester, Introduction to Art History. That's how I met Campbell, in fact, since she signed up for it when she got here. We took another class with him, too, a studio art class. We were both crazy about him. What a great teacher!"

"I see," I said simply.

"But let me show you my favorite painting," Beanie insisted, growing excited again as she flipped through the pages of the book until she found the plate she was looking for. "Here it is!"

I glanced over the shoulder at two colorful plates placed side by side. Both pictured a woman reclining on white pillows in the exact same pose.

"As you can see, there are actually two paintings," she noted. "They're both by the famous Spanish painter Goya. Have you ever heard of him?"

"Yes, I know a little about him, too," I told her. "I must confess that I took art history, too, back when I was in college."

"Both paintings are of the same woman," she explained. "They're identical, except that in one she's naked and in the other she's clothed. They're called *The Nude Maja* and *The Clothed Maja*. Nobody knows for sure who the woman in the painting was, but people think that she was the Duchess of Alba, a woman Goya was having an affair with."

"I've heard of these paintings," I said, studying them. "But I don't remember the story behind them."

Probably because I was too busy studying for my bio exams to spend as much time as I should have on my art history assignments, I thought grimly.

"Mr. Stibbins told us why this one, *The Nude Maja*, was so important," Beanie continued, pointing. "He said it was the first painting of a naked lady in Western art that wasn't supposed to be of some mythical character. Goya had a special way of hanging the two paintings so that he could display one of them to people who he wanted to see the nude and the other when he wanted to show the one of the woman with her clothes on."

"Interesting," I remarked. "It sounds as if Mr. Stibbins really knew his stuff."

"He sure did," Beanie said sadly. "I'm going to miss hearing his lectures."

"And it seems like you really enjoy learning about art," I added. I tried to hide my surprise that a young woman like Beanie, one who seemed more concerned with making sure she'd input all her friends' cellphone numbers into her BlackBerry than with culture, would find classical paintings the least bit interesting. Nathaniel had clearly been an effective teacher.

"I wasn't interested in art at all before I came to Worth," Beanie said. "Whenever my family traveled, my mom was always dragging me to museums. The Louvre in Paris, the Prado in Madrid...and this past spring, she took me to Russia for my seventeenth birthday and we spent *hours* at the Hermitage in St. Petersburg. I was bored out of my skull, but she wouldn't take no for an answer." Rolling her eyes, she added, "You know how moms can be."

It was hard for me to feel sorry for someone who was being forced to stroll through the world's great art museums. The best I could do was to let out a non-committal grunt.

"But then I took Mr. Stibbins's course," she continued. "It totally changed the way I look at things. Especially paintings. Now I can see what makes certain ones great."

"That's wonderful."

I had to admit that I was pretty impressed by the fine job Poor Cousin Nathaniel had done of getting someone like Beanie to appreciate art. That led me to wonder about the other teachers at Worth. The music teacher, for example, especially given Reverend Evans's comment about the friction between Beanie's beloved art teacher and Claude Molter.

"It's great that coming to Worth gave birth to what I'm sure will be a lifelong appreciation for art," I commented. "What about music? I understand the music teacher here—Mr. Molter, I think his name is—is a really accomplished violinist."

"I guess," Beanie mumbled with a shrug.

Her lack of enthusiasm about the man prompted me to add, "I understand he was a child prodigy and that he performed all over the world." When that didn't get much of a reaction, I tried, "I also heard that he's a real live count."

More eye rolling. "That's the rumor. Frankly, I've always wondered if he just made that up. You know, to advance his career or something."

Interesting idea, I thought, resolving to talk to Claude again the first chance I got.

One more thing to add to my to-do list, I told myself, resisting the urge to do a little eye rolling of my own.

Thinking about how full my schedule was reminded me that today was no exception.

"I enjoyed talking to you," I told Beanie, "but I'm afraid I have to run. I want to look for some books about nutrition to bring to class tomorrow—and then I have to go practice a little medicine."

She brightened. "You're so lucky! You have the best job in the world!"

"One of them anyway," I agreed.

"I bet taking care of animals is a lot more fun than teaching." Grimacing, she added, "Reading those essays you assigned yesterday, for example. It is summer school, you know, so you don't really have to give us homework. A lot of the other teachers don't."

"I thought it would be kind of fun for you to write about your pets," I explained.

Beanie made another face. "Homework is always a drag, no matter what it is."

"I'll keep that in mind," I promised.

I moved to the section of the library in which I thought I'd find the books on animal care I was looking for. But once I was out of view, I couldn't resist sitting down and peeking at the essays I'd collected at the end of class. I riffled through them until I found Beanie's, then skimmed it.

It wasn't half bad. She'd written that she loved the way her pug, Esmeralda, was always so happy to see her. Since she boarded at Worth, she only saw her beloved pooch on the weekends and vacations when she went home to New York City. She said that even though she missed a lot of things about home, including her own room and her own refrigerator, being reunited with her dog was always the best part.

Given Beanie's antihomework sentiments, I thought with surprise, that was actually a pretty nice little essay.

Curious to see how some of the other girls had approached the assignment, I skimmed through a few more.

I stopped, puzzled, when I started reading the fifth or sixth essay in the pile. Something about it struck me as familiar. The words that were used, the way the sentences were constructed, even the same word, "receive," misspelled the same way. Puzzled, I looked back at the others I'd read, trying to put two and two together.

It didn't take me long to figure out that this essay, which had Campbell Atwater's name at the top, had been written by Beanie—or vice versa.

One of these two girls is doing the other's homework, I realized with irritation. And I have a feeling I know who's doing whose work.

Vondra was right, I thought angrily. Campbell really does have an exceptional sense of entitlement.

Still, given the real reason why I was at the Worth School, I didn't plan to make an issue of it. In fact, I decided that I might follow Beanie's advice and stop giving out homework assignments altogether.

But I was still irked by the fact that cheating was going on in my class. Once again, I thought back to Dorothy's assessment of the students at Worth. I hated to admit that the woman was right about anything, but this was one more time that I had no choice but to agree with her.

•   •   •

I'd barely climbed into my van before my cellphone rang. When I glanced at the caller ID and saw who was calling, I debated whether to answer for about two seconds. That was how long it took me to remember that, my personal feelings aside, I was trying to investigate a murder.

"Forrester, I'm on my way to a house call," I

greeted my caller. "Unless it's important, I really don't have time right now."

"This is definitely in the 'important' category," he assured me. "In fact, I'm about to make you an offer you can't refuse."

"Forrester, will you give it up?" I said, exasperated. "I thought I made it clear that I'm not interested in any—"

"You're not interested in Nathaniel Stibbins's murder?" he interrupted, feigning surprise. "Sorry, I guess I misunderstood. I'll just leave you to—"

"All right," I said huffily. "You know perfectly well you just said the magic words. Tell me: What have you got?"

"How about a trip to the dearly departed's place of residence?"

I gasped. "Nathaniel's house?"

"I suppose that's a simpler way of putting it," he replied. "Much less intriguing, however. I always enjoy a well-turned phrase—"

"Are you going to the murder victim's house or not?" I demanded.

"Not only *to* it, but also *inside* it."

"And how do you intend to pull *that* off?"

"Hey, it's just a question of knowing the right people," he replied breezily.

"Falcone." It was a statement, not a question. "When can we go?" I asked, my heart pounding so fast and so hard that I was afraid he could hear it through the phone. Poking around the Worth School, seeking out the people who had known Nathaniel and asking as many questions as I could—largely about one another—was certainly valuable. But Dorothy had been right about the value of actually getting to see where he lived...Who knew what that might yield? "Should I meet you there, or do you want to drive over together?"

"Whoa. Not so fast," Forrester insisted. "I never said this generous offer came without any strings attached."

Of course, I thought irritably. I should have known.

"Okay, Forrester," I said, not even trying to hide my exasperation. "What do you want from me?"

"You should know better than to ask any self-respecting male a question like that," he replied. He sounded so amused that I wished I'd had the presence of mind to phrase my question differently. "But here's what I'll settle for: dinner."

"That's all?"

"At your place."

I hesitated for a couple of seconds before saying, "I'm sure Nick would go along with that. In fact, we could invite some other people, too, so that you—"

"I'm not interested in a party," Forrester insisted. "I want dinner at that cozy little cottage of yours with nobody home but you."

"But—but that's ridiculous!" I cried.

"Why? Or are you going to pull out that tired old line for the millionth time about how you're engaged?"

"I *am* engaged!"

"Then what harm could it possibly be to entertain an old friend for the evening?"

Forrester Sloan certainly wasn't an *old* friend. In

fact, I wouldn't necessarily consider him a *friend*. But I wasn't going to argue about semantics. Not when I was still trying to get him to include me in his expedition to the Stibbins residence.

"Let me ask you something, Forrester," I said. "Given the fact that I'm engaged—and given the fact that you and I tried going on something that vaguely resembled a date once before—what on earth could you possibly hope to gain by having dinner with me at my house?"

"You may recall that that date of ours was kind of a disaster," he pointed out.

"I won't argue about that," I agreed.

He took a deep breath before saying, "Actually, I believe the main reason it went so badly was that there was simply too much going on at that restaurant I brought you to. It turned out that half the people there knew me."

"And ninety percent of them wanted you to do them a favor," I added. I shuddered at the memory of the countless number of times we'd been interrupted by people who were lobbying for an article in the newspaper about themselves, their organization, or their cause.

Still, that had been only part of the problem. The real reason our date was such a fiasco was that I was too much in love with Nick to want to waste time with anyone else.

But Forrester seemed to have forgotten about that part. Either that or it had never really sunk in.

Besides, this wouldn't even be close to a date. This was a deal. A *business* deal.

At least from my perspective. As for Forrester, I still didn't understand what he expected to get out of it.

"You still haven't told me why you want to have dinner with me—alone," I pointed out.

"Simple," he replied lightly. "I'm hoping that an evening with just the two of us will enable me to showcase my charms."

I assumed he was joking. In fact, I was about to burst out laughing to demonstrate just how much I appreciated his quirky sense of humor. But the long silence that followed told me he meant exactly what he'd said.

Yet there was absolutely no doubt in my mind that I was fully capable of resisting Forrester Sloan's self-proclaimed charms, be it in my tiny, empty cottage or at Madison Square Garden. So I quickly said, "Okay, Forrester. Dinner at my house, just the two of us. But you have to let me pick the evening."

"Done." He sounded so pleased with himself that for a second there I truly regretted saying yes.

But as soon as I reminded myself what I was getting out of it, I decided that slurping up some Chinese take-out food with Forrester was a small price to pay for the chance to visit Nathaniel's home. Heck, I wouldn't even serve dessert.

"So how soon can you meet me? Stibbins lived in Elmdale."

Like the Bromptons, the town was also on Long Island's south shore, about ten miles from the Worth School. Not far, by Long Islanders' standards, even one like Nathaniel, who'd had to make the trip five days a week.

Still, I hadn't realized this field trip would be scheduled so soon.

"I can be there in fifteen minutes," I told him, doing a quick calculation in my head. "No, wait, make that twenty. Give me the full address."

"It'll be easier if you meet me at the Elmdale train station," he replied. "We can drive over together."

"Fine."

As soon as I hung up, I began scrolling through my list of numbers so I could call Sunny and ask her to rearrange the rest of my morning. So what if I had to work late, possibly right up to that night's PTA meeting? I knew a stroke of luck when I saw it, even if its source was Forrester Sloan—and it came with a rather hefty price tag.

Chapter 8

"The cat is a dilettante in fur."
—Theophile Gautier

As soon as I'd talked to Sunny and she assured me she'd start freeing up my morning right away, I headed out to Elmdale.

I'd driven by the village's Long Island Railroad station countless times before, so it was easy to find. The small, quaint building with a peaked roof and gingerbread trim looked like the basis for one of those miniatures that model train aficionados collect—or that people lucky enough to possess the Martha Stewart gene put underneath their Christmas trees.

As I pulled into the parking lot, I spotted Forrester's dark green SUV idling behind the station. I could see him watching me as I climbed out of my van and headed toward his car.

"Glad you could make it, Popper," Forrester greeted me through his open window with a wide grin. "Seeing you always adds a little extra sunshine to my day."

"Please, spare me," I insisted, scowling as I slid into the front seat next to him. "I already said I'd have dinner with you. Isn't that enough?"

"It'll never be enough," he replied with a laugh.

After heading out of the parking lot, we traveled east on Wintauk Highway, driving past one housing development after another. We'd just breezed by our fifth when I demanded, "Where exactly are we going?"

"Surely you didn't expect that an *artiste* would have lived in just any old cookie-cutter house, did you?" he asked, glancing over at me with an annoying look of amusement in his eyes.

I was still wondering what the mystery was all about when Forrester veered off the highway and onto the Norfolk University campus.

Could Nathaniel possibly have lived in campus housing? I mused. A faculty apartment—or a dorm?

But I kept silent, staring out the window as we wound along the curving roads of what had to be one of the most beautiful college campuses in the world. The school was located on the former estate of one of the world's most famous industrialists, a man who had made his fortune in railroads, shipping, and steel.

When the property was first converted to a college more than half a century earlier, most of the buildings had been left intact. The former mansion now housed classrooms, while outbuildings had been converted into such facilities as a gym, a field house, and a greenhouse that had to be every serious botany student's dream come true. In more recent decades, a smattering of houses had also been constructed on the land, but those were self-contained little communities on discreet cul-de-sacs that had been carved out at the same time.

Forrester drove past all that, heading toward the back of the property. I was relieved when he finally pulled off to the side of the road and switched off the ignition.

Not that I was any less confused. He'd stopped in front of a low redbrick building that jutted up three or four stories in the middle. The small piece of land it occupied was surrounded by a low hedge, the shield of dense green foliage enlivened by carefully maintained flower beds bursting with pink and yellow impatiens.

"We're here," he announced.

I blinked. "This looks like some kind of tower."

"It *is* a tower. A clock tower."

I still wasn't getting any of this. "Nathaniel lived in a clock tower?"

"Nope, somebody else lives there. He lived behind it. Come on."

Still puzzled, I climbed out of the car and followed him through a redbrick archway off to the left. The fact that the opening was too narrow for cars was probably just as well, since the walkway that passed under it and continued beyond was paved in uneven cobblestones.

I was silent as we walked, still half-convinced that Forrester was playing a trick on me. But then he stopped in front of a row of single-story buildings. At least that's what they appeared to be at first glance. As I studied them more closely, I realized they were actually even shorter than one story, with roofs no more than eight or nine feet high.

"What *is* this place?" I asked, widening my eyes.

"Chicken coops," he replied with a grin. "A whole row of them. At least that's what they used to be."

That explained the numerous doorways, as well as the tiny boxy windows placed at regular intervals and sealed up with wooden shutters.

Poor Cousin Nathaniel lived in farm animals' quarters? I thought. No wonder Dorothy considered him the black sheep of the family!

I was still contemplating this irony when I saw that we weren't alone. A slight man with a build that might be described as scrawny, and sleek black hair that looked as if it had been dripped in olive oil, was lurking in front of the one-time chicken coops.

The sight of Lieutenant Anthony Falcone, Norfolk County's one and only chief of homicide, made my heart sink.

"How ya doin', Forrester?" he greeted my companion, striding over on short, spindly legs and giving him a hearty handshake that actually involved using both hands.

"I'm great, Lieutenant Falcone," he replied, shaking back with at least as much fervor.

I was thinking about the fact that there was entirely too much testosterone floating around for my comfort level when Falcone turned to me.

"So we meet again, Dr. Popper," he said with a smirk.

Actually, given his heavy New York accent, what he

actually called me was "Docta Poppa." But by this point I was used to that.

What I *wasn't* used to—and couldn't seem to get used to—was his condescending manner. At least as far as I was concerned. When it came to Forrester, the man seemed to have no trouble at all treating him as an equal.

"Small world," I commented, forcing myself to smile.

Falcone's smirk tightened into something more along the lines of a frown. "I heard it was somethin' more than that. Rumor has it you were related to Nathaniel Stibbins."

"*Almost* related," Forrester corrected him, casting me a meaningful look.

"What's that supposed to mean?" Falcone looked annoyed that somebody else knew something he didn't know.

"It's kind of a long story," I answered quickly. "One I'm sure you're much too busy to listen to."

"It's true that I got a lot more important things to do than standin' around and shootin' the breeze," he agreed, jutting his chin into the air.

I can imagine, I thought. Admiring your reflection in the mirror, thinking up creative new ways of getting your name and your picture in the paper, stocking up on hair goo that I believe was once referred to as "greasy kid stuff"...

At the moment, however, I wasn't about to antagonize the man—that is, any more than I did simply by reminding him of my existence on the planet. Not when I'd been presented with a golden opportunity to pick his brain, such as it was.

"Forrester tells me you've made some serious progress on the investigation," I said boldly.

Not surprisingly, Forrester cast me a scathing look.

"He did, did he?" Falcone squirmed just enough that the highly padded shoulders of his shiny polyester suit gleamed in the summer sunlight. "We're workin' on it."

"How about those fingerprints?" I said, using the same intonation as if I'd said, "How about those Mets?" "You know, the ones that were left on the murder weapon...?"

He narrowed his eyes. "Like I said, we're workin' on it."

So there *were* prints on the knife that was used to kill Nathaniel, I thought, translating Falcone's words and body language. But the cops haven't been able to find a match for them, most likely because the killer had no previous police record.

"And the guests at my wedding—including the members of Nathaniel's family?" I was still doing my best to sound knowledgeable without threatening a man whose ego was as fragile as a butterfly's wing.

"None of them ever made it to the suspect list, if that's what you mean," he replied.

"Boy, you guys sure are covering a lot of ground," I said. "I'm really impressed."

Falcone cocked his head as if he couldn't figure out if I was being sarcastic or sincere. Actually, all I wanted was for him to keep trying not to look bad in front of another member of the male persuasion.

"From what I can tell," I said casually, deciding not to mention my conversation with Dr. Goodfellow, "Nathaniel didn't have much of a social life."

The only response I got was a slight twitch in Falcone's left eye. "What makes you think that?"

"You mean he did have a social life?" I asked. My heartbeat quickened over the fact that I was about to be handed some additional information.

"Stibbins was actually quite the ladies' man. He had one girlfriend after another." Frowning, he added, "However, the last five women he'd been seeing all had rock-solid alibis."

Five? I thought. It sounds as if the man was as terrified of commitment as I am.

"That must have been a disappointment, at least in terms of the investigation," I said. "I mean, the spouse or love interest is usually the first person the cops consider, right?"

"That's right," he replied. "We didn't find indications of any love triangles, either, in case that's where you're going with this."

"Then it sounds as if checking into his workplace is the obvious next step," I said.

"We're in the process of talking to several people at the Worth School where he taught," Falcone sounded as if he'd rehearsed that line for the press. In front of a mirror, no doubt.

Hey, me, too! But I kept that thought to myself.

Instead, I looked toward the front door of Nathaniel's house hungrily. Now that I'd wrested the information I'd wanted from Falcone about how the homicide pros were doing with their investigation, I was anxious to learn what I could about the place where the victim hung his hat. Or his beret.

"Well, I'm sure you have to get going," I hinted. "Forrester and I also happen to be pressed for time, so we should probably get on with this."

"Thanks for letting us take a look around," Forrester said.

"Hey, I always do whatever I can to cooperate with *Newsday*," Falcone said.

No doubt, I thought. This is a man who would do just about anything to get his name in the paper. Especially if his picture ran with it.

He turned back to me. "As for you, Dr. Popper, I hope you'll remember this favor." His dark brown eyes bore into mine as he added, "I'm kinda puttin' myself on the line here by lettin' somebody like you walk around the victim's house. It's a biggie."

"Almost as much of a biggie as all those murders I helped solve in the past?" I countered, returning his icy look.

He drew back slightly. It was only an inch or so, but that was more than enough for me to feel a surge of satisfaction.

"So you got lucky once or twice," he grumbled.

"Who knows? Maybe I'll get lucky again." I lifted my own chin a little higher into the air. "Especially since the deceased and I were almost related and all."

He just glared at me for a few seconds. I got the feeling he was trying to think up a snappy comeback. But that wasn't about to happen since he'd obviously used up whatever limited brain power he possessed.

Instead, he pulled out a key and unlocked one of

the many doors lined up in front of us, the one with the brass knocker on it.

He pushed it open and stepped aside. "I got one rule for the both of you, and it's a hard-and-fast rule. Don't touch anything, y'hear me?"

Forrester and I both nodded like dutiful children.

"Okay," Falcone said, eyeing us warily. "Aside from that, just make sure you pull the door shut tight when you leave."

"Thanks again," Forrester called after him.

We watched in silence as Falcone hurried off. I noticed that the extra-thick heels on his shiny black shoes clacked against the cobblestones.

As soon as he was out of earshot, Forrester commented, "I don't know why you insist on antagonizing him, Popper."

"He started it!" I cried, not even caring that this was another one of those times when I sounded like a four-year-old.

Forrester just laughed.

But I forgot all about Falcone the moment I followed Forrester inside. I braced myself for what I was likely to find, assuming from the appearance of the building's exterior that I'd be confronted by splintery wood and lots of straw.

Boy, was I wrong.

Nathaniel had converted the long, flat building into a fantasy land.

The interior was pretty much one long narrow room, no doubt the way it had been back in the days when fowl had called this place home. But the furniture was arranged to create various types of living space, with the walls of each segment painted a different color.

A *bright* color. The living room area was sunshine yellow, the dining area to the right of it a fiery orange, the kitchen just beyond a deep turquoise. Next came the part of the house used for the bedroom. Its walls were painted a deep purple that was the exact color and texture as a shiny eggplant.

Superimposed over each of the shockingly brilliant colors was another paint job, no doubt Nathaniel's handiwork. The living room walls were splashed with gigantic flowers. Some reached up to the ceiling on spindly stems, while others were lush blossoms the size of a couch, painted in brilliant pinks and lavenders. Fantastical animals gathered around the dining room table. Friendly-looking behemoths that were a cross between elephants and hippos romped with big green and yellow cats that had both the stripes of a tiger and the spots of a leopard. The walls of the kitchen were splashed with food: a tremendous stalk of celery, a bunch of bananas, a strawberry ice cream cone as big as the refrigerator.

Amid all this visual chaos, there was one oasis. The space just beyond the bedroom had walls that were painted a stark white. I walked over to that area, taking care not to touch anything or even to brush against the furniture.

Once I reached this final section of the house, I saw that no fewer than three skylights had been cut into the low ceiling. The glaring light shining through practically made the walls luminescent.

I would have recognized the space as Nathaniel's

studio even without the smell of turpentine still linger-
ing in the air. Another clue was the huge canvases
leaning against the walls, three and four deep, their
backs facing outward.

In the center, set up directly below one of the skylights, stood a wooden easel. Despite my intention not
to touch anything, I couldn't resist pulling up the
paint-splattered white cloth draped over it.

I peered at the large canvas, which was smeared
with several blobs of color superimposed over a pale
blue background. Frankly, it was hard to know if it
was a painting that Nathaniel had barely started or
something abstract that he'd nearly completed.

As I stood there studying what for all I knew had
been Nathaniel's last creative endeavor, Forrester
came up behind me.

"Hey, we're not supposed to touch—what's this?"
Forrester's mouth twisted into a thoughtful frown as
he, too, examined the canvas. "Was Stibbins dabbling
in expressionistic art?"

"Either that or it's unfinished."

Squinting at the canvas, Forrester said, "I may not
know much about art, but if you ask me, that baby's a
long way from being finished. And frankly, the way he
started doesn't make it look too promising."

"Oil paintings are created by putting layer after
layer of paint on a canvas," I explained. "Artists start
by blocking out the different sections of the canvas
with big areas of color. Then they keep adding to it.
Subtracting, too, by painting over what's already
there. That flexibility is why oil paints have been such
a favorite medium for so long."

Forrester stuck both hands in his pants pockets and gently rocked back and forth. "I'm impressed," he said. But he was looking at me, not the painting.

"Gee, you've just made my day," I replied sarcastically.

But while I usually enjoyed insulting Forrester, this time my heart wasn't in it. I was too busy contemplating the canvas.

I had to admit that there was something exciting about seeing a work-in-progress, especially one being created by an artist who was apparently on the verge of greatness. I felt a tingle over getting a behind-the-scenes peek at how real artwork is made.

But seeing something that Nathaniel had left undone also saddened me. The unfinished painting was a sad reminder that a man of talent would never have a chance to see his dreams of finally achieving fame and fortune come true.

But I didn't have time to relish either the sadness or the momentousness of the occasion.

"Hey, check this out!" Forrester exclaimed, stepping across the room.

He pulled back another paint-splattered cloth, revealing a tall, narrow bookcase lined with videos. Unlabeled videos, their edges nothing more than plain, black plastic spines.

Illegal tapes? I thought, glancing at him questioningly.

I went over and pulled one off the shelf, swallowing hard. I immediately saw a hand-printed label stuck on it. I held my breath as I focused on the words.

METROPOLITAN MUSEUM OF ART, NEW YORK, 2001: RUBENS EXHIBIT.

Not what I'd been expecting. But I still wasn't sure if it was time to start breathing again.

I pulled out another. TATE GALLERY, LONDON, TEN NEW ARTISTS TO WATCH, 2003.

I checked four or five more of the tapes, pulling them off the shelf one by one. All of them were variations on the same theme.

These were illegal tapes, all right. But they were nothing more onerous than videos of art exhibitions.

I'd started breathing normally again, relieved that the only crime I'd discovered Nathaniel to be guilty of was sneaking a video camera into the world's greatest art museums.

At least, so far.

I started in on a lower shelf, just to be sure. They, too, appeared to be bootlegged, since they also lacked a box and bore only a handmade label.

But these turned out to be professionally produced movies. *Paradise Found* (Life of Gauguin). *Vincent and Theo* (Life of van Gogh). *Pollock*—the film in which Ed Harris played Jackson Pollock. *Camille Claudel,* which I knew was a biography of the accomplished but underappreciated French sculptor who was also Auguste Rodin's lover.

From the looks of things, all Nathaniel had cared about was art.

Forrester seemed to read my thoughts. "Looks like the guy had a one-track mind," he commented.

"He was clearly passionate about art," I agreed. Given the fact that it seemed to be all he cared about,

I couldn't help wondering if in some way his dedication to art had gotten him killed.

"Seen enough?" Forrester asked, glancing at his watch and frowning. "This isn't the only story I'm working on today."

I shook my head. "I haven't looked around his bedroom yet." Anxious to alleviate his impatience, I added, "That is where most people keep their really personal stuff, isn't it?"

I was relieved that he laughed. Not that I was trying to flirt with him. It was more like I was trying to buy myself more time.

"Good point," he agreed.

He followed me back to the section of the house that had clearly been Nathaniel's bedroom. It contained a king-size bed flanked by two small tables and a large dresser. Built into the back wall was a closet.

"I wonder how thoroughly the police checked this place out," I mused, running my eyes around the room.

Even though I was speaking more to myself than to Forrester, he answered anyway. "I'm sure they did the usual search."

"Yes, but I still can't help thinking it's possible they missed something."

I was disappointed to see that the room contained few personal touches. No framed photographs, no enticing diaries left behind on one of the night tables, not even any books or CDs that might provide any hints about the man who had lived here.

Even the murals Nathaniel had painted didn't reveal a thing. He had copied some of the most familiar images from the greatest works of art, integrating them in an amusing way. Matisse's circle of joyful nudes danced amid the strange-looking beasts from Rousseau's jungle paintings, while Gauguin's Tahitian natives mingled with Seurat's refined French folk relaxing in the park, a famous painting that I recalled was actually titled *Sunday Afternoon on the Island of La Grande Jatte*.

The lack of any obvious clues didn't discourage me in the least.

Instead, I was determined to do some searching of my own. Just because the police had already gone through this room didn't mean they'd necessarily caught every possible piece of evidence.

I started with the closet. But before pulling open the handle, I stuck my hand under the bottom of my shirt, using the fabric like a potholder to keep from leaving behind any fingerprints. Once the door was open, I scanned the row of shirts and jackets in front of me and the pairs of shoes tucked beneath them.

"If Falcone finds out that you're going through the guy's things, we're both gonna be in trouble," Forrester commented. But I guess he realized his words weren't likely to have any effect on me since he immediately added, "What exactly are you looking for anyway?"

"I won't know until I find it," I replied.

I studied the top of the closet, disappointed that I didn't spot anything out of the ordinary. I considered taking down the shoe boxes stacked on the shelf and looking inside, but decided that that was pushing things a bit too far.

Instead, I turned to the long, low dresser pushed up against the wall opposite the king-size bed. The first drawer I opened was filled with T-shirts. The next one contained sweaters. I was already getting discouraged when I tried one more drawer and found socks, boxer shorts, and undershirts stuffed inside haphazardly.

"We should probably get going," Forrester said, pointedly checking his watch again.

"Two more minutes."

I continued scrutinizing the contents of the murder victim's underwear drawer, sensing that something was wrong but unable to zero in on what it was. A few seconds later, it struck me: Everything in it was either black, white, or brown—or some variation on that color scheme—except for a single pale blue item that peeked out from the bottom.

I'd almost missed it, since it was made of stretchy fabric that was just like the cotton knit of Nathaniel's undershirt collection. Yet something about the tiny patch of color caught my attention.

Gingerly I pulled it out of the drawer, still shielding my fingertips with my shirt. Socks and boxers scattered to the side as I freed the mysterious item from the disheveled pile.

"What have you got there?" Forrester asked, stepping over. "Have you just discovered Nathaniel Stibbins's softer side?"

"I'm not sure," I replied, doing my best to lay the garment across the top of the dresser. "Whatever it is, it didn't seem to fit in with everything else in the drawer."

"Maybe it was a gift from someone who didn't know his taste," Forrester commented.

"Or his size." Now that I was able to get a better look at the stretchy pale blue shirt, I could see just how narrow it was. I could also see *what* it was: a skimpy tank top with the familiar Worth School emblem embroidered over the left breast.

I shifted my gaze to the label, then glanced at Forrester. "His gender, either."

"It does look kind of feminine," he agreed.

"Check out the label," I said, pointing. "See what it says? 'Women's Small.' "

I watched Forrester's expression change from curious to stricken. "There's no way this belonged to Nathaniel, is there?"

"Nope," I replied. "More like one of his students."

"Which meant he did some entertaining at home," Forrester said quietly.

"Entertainment that involved removing articles of clothing," I added. "At least on his guest's part."

For a few seconds, we just looked at each other. I didn't know what was going through Forrester's mind until he said, "We'd better tell Falcone."

Great, I thought, my shock over what we'd just discovered instantly shifting to an entirely different concern. Not only is Falcone going to find out that I disobeyed the only rule he laid out by touching the contents of the murder victim's apartment. What's even worse is that once again, I'm turning out to be doing a better job than he and his posse are doing.

But even that paled beside the fact that we'd just

uncovered an entirely new dimension of the murder victim's life.

I knew that, technically, Nathaniel might not have been doing anything wrong. After all, in New York the age of sexual consent is 17. But he was 38, nearly twenty years older than the seniors at Worth. Even more important, he was their teacher. That meant whatever relationships he might have had with the girls weren't exactly fair and balanced.

It also meant that I'd stumbled upon a veritable minefield of reasons why someone might have been mighty upset with the man. The cause could have been a girl's anger over the feeling that she was being used—or another girl's jealousy over the latest object of Nathaniel's affections. It could even have been the result of one of the parents' fury upon learning about the art teacher's fondness for younger women.

Which meant that this discovery didn't do much to help me pin down either the murderer or the motive. In fact, all it *had* done was make the list of suspects even longer.

• • •

As soon as Forrester closed the door of Nathaniel's house firmly behind him, he turned to me and said, "Okay, Popper. I held up my end of the deal. Now it's your turn."

I just stared at him, still so lost in thought about what I'd learned from being inside Nathaniel's house that I didn't have the foggiest notion what he was talking about.

"Oh, that's right," I finally said. "I owe you dinner at my house."

"Dinner for *two* at your house," he corrected me. "And *only* two. So when is it going to happen?"

I pictured a calendar, hoping one of the squares would be filled in with a commitment Nick had made. Sure enough, I remembered that the law firm at which he was spending the summer interning was holding an all-day retreat on Sunday that was scheduled to run late.

"How about Sunday?" I suggested.

"Sunday it is," he agreed.

"But it has to be early," I warned. "Like six."

That way, I thought, I can have him out of there by eight—meaning Nick will never even have to know I've been trading moo shu pork for inside information.

"You're on," Forrester replied, sounding a little too happy. "I'll even bring dessert!"

There wasn't supposed to *be* any dessert, I thought sullenly.

But I'd already come up with a strategy for keeping the evening as short as humanly possible: eating really, really fast.

Chapter 9

"I like pigs. Dogs look up to us. Cats look down on us. Pigs treat us as equals."
—Sir Winston Churchill

The discovery I'd made at Nathaniel's house faded into the back of my mind as I rushed off to my first house call of the day. Bosco, a sweet-tempered German short-haired pointer, had been a patient of mine for a long time. Her owner, Mike Monahan, worked from home, doing something mysterious with computers. Mike was also a runner. A tall, lean man in his early thirties, he spent his free time training for marathons, usually with Bosco loping along beside him.

"Hey, Bosco!" I cried, stooping over to scratch her ears when she and Mike came out to my van. She was such a pretty dog, with an alert expression, almond-shaped eyes, and smooth brown fur I think of as the color of milk chocolate but which breeders insist on referring to as "liver."

Simply from talking to Mike on the phone, I was

pretty sure I knew the cause of the skin infection he was concerned about.

Bosco suffered from OCD—obsessive compulsive disorder. While most people have heard of humans having OCD, few realize that it also occurs in animals. It's especially common in German shepherds, who tend to chase their tails, and Dobermans, who often gnaw at their flanks. With bull terriers, it's frequently manifested as compulsive spinning.

But it can turn up in any dog that's bored or under stress. Dogs might dig obsessively, bark for no reason, attack inanimate objects such as their own food dish—or like Bosco, lick themselves. And even though some of the manifestations might seem humorous, the animal can be dangerous to people—or to herself, as in Bosco's case.

"When did you first notice her skin problems?" I asked Mike after covering the usual questions about Bosco's general health, weighing her, and taking her temperature.

"About two weeks ago," Mike replied. "It's mainly on her belly."

I bent down to check the area. "Is she taking any medications?"

When Mike shook his head, I added, "Has anything changed in the household, like carpet cleaners or shampoo?"

"Nope."

I reached into a cabinet and took out a few slides. "I see a spot I'd like to do a cytology on."

I did an impression smear by picking at a scab with the corner of a slide and pressing it against the skin.

Next, I applied some stain and looked at the slide under the microscope.

"There's a bit more bacteria than usual," I told Mike, who was looking on nervously. "It's hard to put on a topical, since she'll just lick it off. So I'd like to put her on antibiotics. She weighs sixty-eight pounds, so I'll put her on 750 milligrams of Cephalexin twice a day for two weeks."

"It's because of the OCD, isn't it?" Mike asked.

"That's what it looks like," I replied. "I know we've talked about this before, but once again I'm going to suggest that you keep Bosco's exercise up. OCD is related to anxiety, and getting her to move around as much as possible should offer her some relief."

Mike grinned. "Good thing I've got another race coming up in a few weeks. I'll make sure Bosco's in as good a shape as I am."

As soon as I wrapped up my last call of the day, I headed back to the Worth School for the PTA meeting. As I drove east toward the Bromptons, I experienced a mixture of anticipation and anxiety.

While I was excited about having the opportunity to interact with some of the parents, I was also nervous about whether or not the evening ahead would actually help me further my investigation. And with Dorothy plaguing me with phone calls, I was getting antsy about drawing this episode to a close.

As I drove through the imposing wrought-iron gates at 7:20, I noticed how different the Worth School campus looked at this hour. The sun was easing lower and lower in the sky, casting an oblique light that made the buildings appear to glow. The trees looked positively mystical, as if somehow the leaves and branches were lit from within.

There's truly something special about the light on Long Island's East End. In fact, for over a century, its uniqueness has been a major attraction for artists, starting in the late 1800s when a group called the Tile Club popularized it. About thirty of the best-known painters, sculptors, and architects in New York, including William Merritt Chase, Winslow Homer, and Stanford White, had been meeting regularly to paint tiles and promote American art. When they took a field trip out to the South Fork, they were immediately taken with the area's beauty, including its distinctive light. They were inspired to create numerous drawings and paintings that were published in a popular magazine. Before long, hordes of people started converging on the area, turning it into a summer resort.

At this hour, the buildings and manicured grounds weren't the only things that had changed. So had the parking lot.

Whenever I'd parked my van during the day, most of the other spaces had been filled with ordinary vehicles, the kind that had basically been designed to get people to and from work. Middle-of-the-line Toyotas and Nissans, mainly, along with a fair number of American cars. Many of them looked kind of tired, as if they couldn't wait for the day they'd be traded in and could finally go to that giant parking lot in the sky.

Tonight, however, I felt as if I'd stumbled into a

dealership in Saudi Arabia. Each car was more luxurious than the one parked next to it: BMWs, Mercedeses, Porsches, Ferraris. A few hybrids, including a dark gray Prius and a sleek silver Lexus. I even spotted a couple of Bentleys and, parked off to the side as if to minimize the chance of getting an unsightly scratch or dent, a gleaming white Rolls-Royce.

I actually felt sorry for my trusty but unstylish van. It wasn't used to being left in such intimidating company.

But I had much more important things on my mind as I headed for the Student Life Community Center, where tonight's meeting was taking place. Just like everything else at the Worth School, the building was completely over the top. It was made almost entirely of glass, making it look like a giant ice sculpture—or to be more accurate, a sky-high pile of ice cubes that had tumbled out of a multistory drinking glass.

I'd already learned enough about Worth that I wasn't the least bit surprised to discover that the dining hall wasn't exactly your average school cafeteria. Rather than being furnished with Formica tables and metal chairs, the expansive room was outfitted with long, solid wood tables and matching chairs that reminded me of photos I'd seen of the dining room at Hearst Castle. The floors weren't covered in linoleum, either, but tiles. From where I stood, they looked hand-painted.

And the walls weren't decorated with bulletin boards plastered with the day's menu or notices about upcoming school activities. Instead, framed paintings decorated the large, airy space, although they didn't appear to be of quite the same caliber as those in the administration building. I supposed that was because of the slim possibility that a rogue dollop of ketchup might fly over and mar the surface.

Even though it was barely seven thirty, the room was already filled with well-dressed people. They stood in groups of three or four, sipping the bright red drinks they held in their hands. If I hadn't known better, I would have thought I'd stumbled upon a cocktail party.

A very exclusive cocktail party, given the number of fancy labels in full view. Many of the men and women wore meticulously tailored business suits, as if they'd come directly from work. But those who were dressed more casually were also decked out in designer duds. In fact, in just the group standing closest to me, I spotted the logos of Chanel, Armani, Fendi, and Prada.

The woman sitting at the table placed right inside the door, however, was dressed in an outfit that looked more like what I had on: the same plain black jeans I'd worn all day and a somewhat wrinkled blue linen blouse I'd thrown over my dark green "Jessica Popper, D.V.M." polo shirt.

"Thanks for coming out tonight," she greeted me with a big smile. "Please make yourself a name tag. Oh, and be sure to write your daughter's name underneath yours to help the other parents identify you."

"I'm actually one of the teachers," I explained.

"In that case, just write 'faculty.' " Still smiling, she added, "Help yourself to some refreshments. And don't forget to mingle. Dr. Goodfellow always encourages faculty members to mingle."

Precisely why I came, I thought.

Once I was inside the dining room, I glanced around nervously. I was hoping to spot a familiar face, someone I could chat with so I wouldn't have to stand there all alone. When I didn't see anyone I knew, I instead zeroed in on the long table pushed against the back wall and covered with a tremendous spread. I wandered over, expecting to find something along the lines of caviar and lobster salad.

So I was surprised to see plates piled high with ragged-edged cookies and brownies cut at slightly irregular angles.

These don't exactly look like parents who spend their Saturday afternoons baking, I mused.

But I was willing to be open-minded. I reached for a chocolate chip cookie lopsided enough that it screamed homemade and bit into it.

"Hey, this is really good!" I remarked to no one in particular.

The woman standing next to me, wearing a chic black pantsuit and carrying a large purse in Burberry's signature brown plaid, beamed.

"Thank you!" she cooed. "I brought them. They're homemade!"

"My compliments to the chef," I said, holding up the cookie.

Still smiling proudly, she replied, "I'll be sure to pass your comments on to my housekeeper. I'm so lucky to have someone who's such a star in the kitchen!"

I grabbed a couple more cookies, then picked up one of the pre-poured glasses of red fruit punch. Not surprisingly, the glasses were made of real glass, not plastic. Once I was armed with something that would hopefully keep me from looking as if I was just standing around awkwardly, I moved away from the table, meanwhile doing my best to listen in on other people's conversations.

"Of course the south of France used to be a great vacation spot," a woman in wrinkle-free linen commented in an irritatingly high-pitched voice. "But these days it's so crowded. I'm so glad Thomas bought that sweet little island off the British Virgin Islands..."

"I just got rid of my Hummer," a businessman in a pinstriped suit told a similarly dressed man. "I was starting to get nervous, with gas prices acting so crazy. So I decided to dump it." Shrugging, he added, "Frankly, I figured I'd get slammed, but would you believe I actually *made* money on the sale?"

"I really liked what they were doing over at DuralTech," a man dressed in jeans and a sports jacket told a slender woman in a flowered wrap dress. "So I bought the company."

The idea that I would ever be able to carry on a conversation with any of these people was seeming increasingly remote. So I was relieved when I heard someone say, "Dr. Popper?"

I turned and found Claude Molter standing next to me, cupping a glass of punch. His head was drawn back just enough that he could look down at me over his beaky nose.

Once again, he was impeccably dressed in a suit and tie, complete with a music-themed tie tack. This one was in the shape of a G clef. I wondered with amusement if his students gave them to him as gifts—and he felt obligated to wear them. Then again, Claude didn't impress me as someone who felt obligated to do *anything* he didn't want to do.

"Mr. Molter! How nice to see you again," I exclaimed. Not only was I glad I'd finally found someone to talk to, the fact that at one time he'd been a close friend of Nathaniel's doubled my pleasure. After all, I was still hopeful that he'd provide me with some insight into the murder victim's life, if not some hard information. "It looks as if everyone from the faculty turned out tonight."

Grimacing, he said, "This is what's known as a command performance."

"Still, it must be kind of fun, getting to meet your students' parents," I commented. "I've been trying to figure out who's who, but the name tags people are wearing are kind of small."

"I'd be happy to help you out," Claude drawled, "except that interacting with the girls' parents has never been one of my top priorities. I'm completely committed to doing whatever is best for the students at Worth. I'd do anything for those girls! However, one thing my dedication does not include is making mindless small talk with their self-centered mommies and daddies."

I was about to change the subject to one I found to be of major interest, meaning Nathaniel Stibbins, when Claude did it for me.

"So tell me, Dr. Popper: Is there anything new on the plans for Nathaniel's memorial service?" he asked.

"Not yet," I replied.

He frowned. "I've mentioned the service to several other people, and no one else seems to know anything about it."

"That's because it's still very hush-hush," I explained. Thinking fast on my feet, I fibbed, "We haven't had a chance to clear it with his family, so we want to hold off on telling anyone about it until it's more definite."

"I see."

"But I'm sure it'll be an event that reflects how well loved he was here at the Worth School," I said. "And in his personal life, too, of course."

Claude simply raised his eyebrows.

"At least that's been my impression," I continued, speaking quickly. "Even though I've only been here for a few days, I'm already finding that everyone speaks of him highly. Dr. Goodfellow, for example."

"Hah!"

I had been expecting agreement, not a reaction like that. In fact, for a second there, I wondered if perhaps some punch had gone down the wrong pipe.

I guess my puzzlement showed, because he volunteered, "I suppose you don't know, being new and all."

Once again, I was struck by how little I seemed to know—and how much Claude *did* seem to know.

"Know what?" I asked, holding my breath.

"Dr. Goodfellow has had a crush on him since day one," he explained with a self-satisfied smile.

"Really?" I said, not letting on that I'd gotten that impression myself. "Are you saying that the two of them were...close?"

He smiled condescendingly. "I said she had a crush on Nathaniel. I never said it was reciprocated."

"Oh!" I didn't mean to show how surprised I was, but somehow that single syllable just jumped out.

"Poor Dr. Goodfellow," I commented, this time speaking in my normal voice. "To have had feelings for someone that weren't returned."

"Now, that's what's called an understatement." With a smug look, Claude added, "Nathaniel basically couldn't stand the woman. Oh, at one point I believe they had a harmless little fling. But it meant nothing to him. He did that kind of thing all the time. He was actually quite the womanizer. But from his perspective, the entire episode wasn't anything more than an amusing little dalliance."

Claude's assessment of Nathaniel's social life was consistent with what I'd gotten out of Falcone. But rather than letting on, I commented, "I didn't know him, of course, but I didn't realize Nathaniel was such a ladies' man."

"Oh, yes," Claude insisted. "Don't be fooled by those foppish suits he was so fond of. Perhaps he looked like a gentleman, but there was another side to him. A side that was, shall we say, very much the party animal, to use a despicable American expression. And Nathaniel could be quite the charmer, when he wanted to. He was extremely skilled at getting what he wanted."

Including a "harmless little fling" with Elspeth Goodfellow, I reflected.

Then again, given how smitten she appeared to be, Nathaniel probably hadn't had a very difficult time arranging a few romantic tête-à-têtes with her. Even if he'd been looking for nothing more than a good time.

But all that assumed that Claude was telling the truth, I realized. Maybe he had it wrong. Maybe Nathaniel and Elspeth really did have feelings for each other and Claude simply didn't know—or didn't want to admit it.

The question of which one of them was being honest made me determined to find out more about Elspeth's true relationship with the murder victim.

I was about to try to pin Claude down, pressing him for more details about his take on their association, when one of the parents tapped Claude on the shoulder. I recognized her as the woman who preferred vacationing on her own private island to mingling with the hoi polloi on that nasty French Riviera.

"You're Mr. Molter, aren't you?" she asked in the same high-pitched voice. "I'm Madison's mother. You know, Madison Fernley? The girl who plays the cello so masterfully?"

I lingered only long enough to watch Claude force a smile, something it turned out he wasn't very good at. I mouthed a few words at him, something like "I'll see you later," then wandered off to see if there were any other brains I could pick.

As I scanned the room, my eyes lit on what appeared to be the only attendee who was sitting all alone in the back corner of the room. I studied her from where I stood, noticing how her choice to remain isolated wasn't the only thing that set her apart from all the others. So did her appearance.

Even though she was seated, I could see that she was a large woman, not only full-figured but also unusually tall. She was dressed completely in white, an outfit that served as a striking contrast to her smooth, luminescent skin, which was nearly as dark as all those homemade brownies that scores of housekeepers had labored over. Her jet-black hair was neatly braided into cornrows. Clasped around each of her plump forearms was a row of bracelets similar to the ones Vondra Garcia always wore, except these were made of red and black beads.

Even from halfway across the room, I could see that her facial features bore a striking resemblance to Vondra's. But even if she hadn't looked so much like my soft-spoken student, her clothing and her jewelry would have clued me in to the fact that she had to be the girl's mother.

I was about to wander over and strike up a conversation when Dr. Goodfellow clapped her hands.

"Let's get started, everyone," she commanded. "Please wrap up the networking session and take a seat. Oh, and we'd all appreciate it if you'd turn off your cellphones, BlackBerries, and other electronics. Except for the surgeons and CEO's and anyone else who's on call, of course."

I thought she was joking. But no one laughed. In fact, I'd estimate that only about half the parents whipped out their electronics and turned them off.

"I'd like to have Reverend Evans begin the meeting tonight," Dr. Goodfellow continued. "As you all know, the big event we've been planning for some time now is only nine days away. And with the date for the school's first Blessing of the Animals so close, I'm sure you're as excited about it as I am. I know the girls are. But I'll let Reverend Evans tell you all about it. Reverend?"

I applauded along with the others as the balding man with the gray fringe and glasses strode across the floor toward the lectern. As usual, he was nicely dressed in a suit and tie.

"First, I'd like to welcome all of you and say thanks for coming out tonight," Reverend Evans began. "I've always thought that one of the great strengths of the Worth School is that the parents of our students recognize how important it is to be as much a part of their daughters' education as possible. Seeing such a fine turnout reinforces my belief.

"But without further ado, let me bring you up to speed on the school's first annual Blessing of the Animals, as Dr. Goodfellow requested. Even though the event is still over a week away—next Saturday, in case any of you have yet to enter the date into those electronics of yours—"

He paused for laughter. And wasn't disappointed.

"We're far enough along in the planning stages that I'm completely confident that the event will run smoothly," he continued. "We've even enlisted the aid of the Norfolk County Police Department, who have generously offered to lend us a few officers to make sure there are no mishaps. But the main reason I'm so sure it's going to be a great success is your daughters' enthusiasm. They're all excited, and a lot of our boarders have told me they've arranged to bring their pets to campus for the day.

"Even more important, many of the girls have volunteered their time for this special day. We posted sign-up sheets on the main bulletin board, and the girls couldn't wait to get involved in everything from the Poster Committee to the Refreshments Committee—although I will admit that there are still quite a few blanks on the sheet for the Cleanup Committee."

More laughter. I was impressed by the way Reverend Evans was working the room. Then again, he had the benefit of an audience who wanted to hear only good things about this school—and especially about their daughters.

"We also have an extra-special bonus this year," he continued. "Dr. Jessica Popper, who's a veterinarian, has been teaching some of your daughters about animal care in one of our summer school courses. Dr. Popper has agreed to come to the Blessing of the Animals, just to make sure that medical care is readily on hand for any of the participating animals that experience a problem.

"In fact," he added with a smile, "she's agreed to bring one of her own pets. She and I have already talked about setting up a playdate with her Westie and my shih tzu. In the meantime, I hope the fact that she's bringing one of her own animals to the event will encourage all of you to do the same. Dr. Popper, would you please stand up?"

I stood for a second or two, smiling and giving a little wave. But inwardly, I was groaning. When Reverend Evans had first raised the idea of me bringing Max to the blessing, I'd had my doubts about how my high-strung terrier would to react to being around all those other animals. But it now sounded as if this was one more of the school's command appearances.

"Thank you, Dr. Popper," Reverend Evans said. "Now let me tell you a bit more about what we have planned..."

The rapt audience continued to hang on his every word as he spelled out all the details of an event designed to help merge community and school. I had to admit that it really did sound as if it would go smoothly—once they found some volunteers to wield those Hefty bags, that is.

When he was finished, he asked if there were any questions. Immediately a man's arm shot up into the air.

"My name is Ellsworth Thornton," he said, rising to his feet and glancing around the room as if he wanted to be sure everyone felt included. "My daughter, Katharine, is a senior. And I just want to commend Reverend Evans for his outstanding work in developing outreach programs throughout the year. He's done a great job of helping increase the visibility of the Worth School while making sure everyone in the community knows what a good neighbor we can be!"

He began to applaud, with everyone else immediately joining in.

No lack of school spirit here, I thought, looking

around at the parents' rapt expressions. In fact, why bother to hold pep rallies when there's already enough pep in this room to fuel five schools?

After the parents raised a few questions about the logistics of the big event, Reverend Evans took his seat. Dr. Goodfellow returned to the front of the room, this time bearing a clipboard.

"Now that Reverend Evans has brought us all up to speed about next weekend, I'd like to move on to this year's tour of Europe's great cities..."

For the next half hour I didn't pay much attention to the meeting. Most of the business discussed had nothing to do with me—or with Nathaniel. Certainly not the burning issue of whether or not additional squash courts were needed or whether the dining hall should move to one hundred percent organic produce.

Besides, I was busy scanning the audience. What I was looking for, I couldn't say.

At least until I spotted a man sitting two rows behind me. At first glance, he looked like just another successful businessman, one with the means to have his suits custom-made.

But then I zeroed in on his name tag. Leighton Atwater.

The fact that he was Campbell Atwater's father instantly pegged him as someone I'd like to get to know better. Not only had his daughter taken Nathaniel's class, but according to Beanie, Campbell had been crazy about her art history teacher.

"Let's take a short break," Dr. Goodfellow finally suggested. As members of the audience began standing up and moving around, she added, "Please help yourselves to some more refreshments! Some of you might also want to use this time to view the student art exhibit out in the hallway."

She paused before going on. "The artwork on display was done by the girls who took Nathaniel Stibbins's Creative Expression through Multiple Media class in the spring." Her voice thickened as she added, "In a way, this exhibit is a tribute to a man who was both an exceptionally talented artist and a dedicated educator—a rare combination, indeed. So I encourage you to take some time this evening to honor this remarkable individual by enjoying the creativity of the young women he inspired."

Checking out the projects the girls had worked on while taking Nathaniel's art class definitely sounded worth doing. But at the moment, I had a much more important mission to accomplish.

I headed back to the refreshment table, meanwhile keeping an eye on Leighton Atwater. As I watched him move to another part of the room, I noticed that the exotically dressed woman I thought was Vondra's mother was slipping out the door.

After grabbing another cup of punch, I sidled over to him, doing my best to look as if I just happened to be wandering in that direction.

"Oh!" I cried when I was next to him. "You're Campbell's dad!" Smiling warmly, I extended my hand. "I'm Jessica Popper. Campbell is in my animal care class."

"Ms. Popper," he said in a deep voice that oozed confidence and control. I noticed that as he shook my hand, he didn't return my smile. "Or is it Dr. Popper, as Reverend Evans referred to you?"

"I answer to either," I replied cheerfully, "just as long as you don't call me Dr. Pepper. That happens more often than you can imagine."

I did better this time, at least eliciting a wan smile.

"So," I said conversationally, "this blessing of the animals sounds like a nice way of involving the school in the community, don't you think?"

"Hmph," he replied. "Frankly, I think almost everything this school does borders on ridiculous."

"Really?" Not exactly the response I was expecting.

"In my day," he continued sternly, "students learned Latin and math and how to write a cohesive essay, not how to play the drums or—or how to decipher the poetry of a man who didn't even know enough to capitalize letters!"

"Still, you have to admit that teaching the students something about culture isn't a bad thing," I said. Casually, I added, "Take art history, for example. I've always believed that it's critical for any well-rounded person to understand art. And Dr. Goodfellow certainly seems to feel that the school's art teacher, Nathaniel Stibbins, was an asset to the school. Campbell thought so, too."

"If you ask me, the man was an appalling influence on his students," Mr. Atwater growled. "He shouldn't have been allowed to get anywhere near children."

Immediately the image of the pale blue tank top I'd

found tossed in with Nathaniel's boxer shorts flitted through my brain.

Still, I reasoned, if Nathaniel had had unseemly dealings with his students and one of the girls' fathers was aware of it, I had a feeling the father in question would be doing a lot more than muttering complaints to strangers he met at PTA meetings. Especially if he happened to be someone as powerful as Leighton Atwater.

"Why is that?" I asked, struggling to keep my tone of voice light.

"Have you seen the dirty pictures he showed the girls in his class?" Mr. Atwater demanded.

I was too shocked to speak. At least until I reminded myself that Leighton Atwater's views on art might not be the same as mine.

"What pictures are you talking about?" I asked cautiously.

"Why—why—pictures of naked women!" he exclaimed. "So what if they were done by artists who were supposedly great? If you ask me, they were nothing but a bunch of dirty old men who used the fact that they knew how to paint as an excuse to get attractive young ladies to take off their clothes!"

I was completely taken aback by what I was hearing—so much so that I wanted to be sure I understood him correctly. Thinking back to the art book Beanie had showed me, I said, "You mean dirty old men like Botticelli and Goya?"

"Exactly!" he replied. "And Renoir and Picasso and Matisse and Rembrandt..."

And just about every other famous artist you could think of, I thought wryly.

But I wasn't about to argue about the traditions of the art world. At least, not with a man who had clearly made up his mind about where he stood.

"If you have such serious reservations about the Worth School," I asked hesitantly, "may I ask why you decided to send Campbell here?"

"Two reasons," Mr. Atwater replied with a scowl. "One is that she either flunked out of or got thrown out of the last three schools she attended. I was beginning to think she'd never graduate. Then she heard about Worth and insisted that at last she'd found one that was in sync with her personality. At least, I believe that's how she put it."

"I see. And the second reason?"

"Her stepmother sided with her." With a shrug, he said, "I can fight Campbell, but I can't fight the two of them when they've ganged up on me."

"From what I've seen Campbell is doing pretty well here," I ventured. "She's certainly made a lot of friends."

"Making friends has never been difficult for my daughter," he said with a sardonic smile. "In fact, making friends is one of her main problems. It's all she wants to do. Getting her to put even the slightest bit of effort into learning something—now, *that's* a challenge."

Nodding sympathetically, I commented, "I suppose that's a widespread problem with the children of successful parents. They know they'll always have someone there to back them up."

"Unless those parents happen to have standards," he countered. Glancing around the room, he added in a scornful tone, "And I don't believe for a minute that most of the people in this room fall into that category. Especially where their children are concerned!"

I was actually relieved when a reed-thin woman with shiny dark hair worn in an asymmetrical style chose that moment to tap Mr. Atwater on the shoulder.

"Excuse me for interrupting," she gushed, "but I've been wanting to meet you for ages. I'm Cordelia Van Hooten. Beanie's mom?"

I wasn't surprised, since both mother and daughter shared the same almost supernatural ebullience.

"Our daughters are the best of friends!" she went on. "Beanie talks about Campbell endlessly. I can't believe that for months they've been—what's that expression, BFF? Best friends forever?—and yet our paths have never crossed!"

Leighton Atwater cast me a pained look. And then, with an air of resignation, he turned back to Beanie's mom.

Personally, I would have loved the chance to speak to her. After all, her daughter was another big fan of Nathaniel's.

Yet I already had the feeling that honing in on this conversation would be no easy matter. Beanie's mother had linked her arm through Campbell's dad's and was dragging him away, meanwhile chattering incessantly.

For a moment, I actually felt sorry for him. But then I thought about the fact that he seemed to be one of the few parents I'd encountered who seemed unhappy with the school.

And he seemed even *more* unhappy with the school's art teacher. As I stood alone in the center of the crowd, I wondered just how strong that dislike was.

Glancing around, I saw that many of the parents had begun wandering back to their seats. And Dr. Goodfellow was making her way toward the front of the room, stopping every few seconds to exchange pleasantries with some of the parents.

Before I dutifully returned to my seat, however, I wanted to check out the student art exhibit. I'd been curious before, but now that I'd heard Leighton Atwater's denunciation of the Worth School's art teacher, I was anxious to see exactly what kind of "creative expression" Nathaniel Stibbins had sparked.

I stepped into the adjoining hallway—and was instantly struck by the fact that "multiple media" was no exaggeration. The students' artwork incorporated every type of artistic medium I could think of.

There were more than two dozen paintings, ranging from miniatures the size of an index card to huge canvases as big as those bulletin boards that lined the corridors in most schools. They had been done in oil, watercolor, and acrylic, with some paintings incorporating more than one type of paint. There were also drawings made with crayon or colored pencil.

But there were plenty of three-dimensional works,

too. Sculptures, I supposed, even though I wasn't certain a colorful ceramic bowl shaped like a dragon or a macramé wall hanging made from yarn, string, and computer cables would fit into that category. I saw works made from papier-mâché, blown glass, Fimo clay, blocks of wood, buttons, clothespins, Tinker Toys, marbles, and Styrofoam packing peanuts.

The only medium I didn't see represented here, I realized with amusement, was found objects. But I wasn't surprised. Somehow, I couldn't picture the Worth School's students rescuing tires or egg crates from other people's trash bins.

But what struck me even more than the wide range of media the girls had used was the subject matter. Many of the works were abstract, amorphous blobs of color or quirky materials piled on top of one another to create a pleasing but meaningless design. As for the images that were recognizable, they all seemed to be either flowers, fruit, animals, landscapes, or human faces.

In other words, there were no nudes, no random body parts, nothing that even hinted at subject matter that any parent could find offensive. Even Leighton Atwater.

The exhibit strengthened my conviction that Nathaniel Stibbins had been totally professional in his dealings with the students who took both his art history and his studio art classes.

At least, in the classroom.

Yet there had clearly been other sides to the man. That pale blue tank top, size Women's Small, was proof of that.

As I headed back to the PTA meeting that was once again getting under way, I couldn't help feeling that it was *that* side—the side *other* than the passionate and dedicated individual who ate, slept, and breathed art—that had gotten him killed.

Chapter 10

"Weaseling out of things is good. It's what separates us from the other animals . . . except weasels."

—Homer Simpson, character from <u>The Simpsons</u>

By the time I turned into my driveway that night, I was completely wiped out. The day had seemed impossibly long. In fact, it was hard to believe it was only that morning that I'd visited Nathaniel's chicken-coop-turned-castle.

The thought of slipping between cool sheets and succumbing to some serious z's had never sounded more alluring.

I tiptoed into the house, assuming that Nick was already in bed—and that he'd left a light on for me out of politeness. Actually, I was kind of *hoping* that was the case. Things between us were still so frosty that there were practically snowballs in our bed.

But as I unlocked the front door and slid into the cottage as quietly as I could, given the fact that two crazed canines were acting as if I were Odysseus returning from his travels, I saw Nick sitting at the table. In front of him was a tome so thick it could only be one of his law books.

"Hi," I said tentatively, not sure of what kind of reaction I'd get. I kept my eyes away from his by leaning over to greet Max and Lou, pretending they absorbed so much of my attention that I had none left over for him. They, as usual, seemed completely oblivious to the tension around them. As far as they were concerned, life was one big tennis ball.

"Hi," Nick replied. His voice was gentle, with none of the iciness that had characterized the minimal interactions we'd had since our argument two nights before. "I waited up for you."

"That was thoughtful," I said, finally daring to make eye contact.

He hesitated before admitting, "I was going to pretend I was studying, but I figured you'd see right through that ruse."

"It is summer," I agreed, "and you're not taking any classes."

"Right." Pushing the book away, he said, "I was hoping we could talk."

"Talking is good." I crossed the room, trailed by my dogs. By that point, Tinkerbell had padded over, too. I scooped her up and sat down next to Nick with my kitty-cat in my lap.

He took a deep breath. "I'm sorry I flew off the handle the other night."

"You had good reason to," I replied, my voice thick. "I know what a pain I've been about settling on a new date."

"Still, I was wrong to take it personally," he insisted. "Having someone get murdered at your wedding would put anyone off."

We both knew he was being generous—that there was much more behind my reluctance to jump right in and start putting together a makeup wedding. That old fear of commitment of mine was rearing its ugly head once again, using the tragedy as an excuse to postpone getting married.

But I wasn't about to point that out.

"Maybe we should just agree to wait a little longer before making any definite plans," he added.

"Agreeing is good," I said, nodding. "We should at least wait until Nathaniel's killer has been found."

"So are we still friends?" Nick asked, his voice light but his eyes questioning.

"Definitely."

"More than friends?" Tentatively he reached across the table.

"Oh, yeah," I replied, grasping his hand in my mine.

"In that case, what about kissing?"

I leaned toward him. "Kissing is good," I murmured, relieved that those nasty snowballs were about to melt. "In fact, kissing is *really* good."

● ● ●

During Friday morning's class, as I talked about the best ways of treating wounds, my eyes kept drifting over to Campbell. Frankly, I was having a hard time reconciling the party girl with her straitlaced father.

Today, for example, she was wearing a clingy, low-cut halter made from an in-your-face zebra print. Her white shorts were equally tight, revealing the outline of a pair of thong underwear.

How Leighton Atwater ever let his daughter walk around in public dressed like that was beyond me.

When class ended, I stood at my desk, saying good-bye to the girls as they streamed by. When the lithe faux zebra skin–bedecked beauty passed, I said, "Campbell? Could I talk to you for a minute?"

A look of surprise crossed her face. But she quickly regained her composure, plastering on a sweet smile.

"Sure," she said, sidling over to my desk. "What's up, Dr. Popper?"

"I just wanted to mention that I had the pleasure of meeting your father at the PTA meeting last night," I told her.

"Pleasure?" she repeated with a wry smile. "That's not the word I'd use."

My confusion was sincere as I asked, "What do you mean?"

She gave one of those "whatever" shrugs she seemed to have mastered. "He's kind of stuffy, don't you think?"

My thoughts exactly. But I was more interested in her thoughts than in mine.

"I imagine most teenage girls feel that way about their parents," I observed.

"Believe me, my dad is in a class by himself," Campbell insisted, rolling her eyes. "He's got so many rules."

"I'm sure your father only wants what's best for

you," I said. "For one thing, he let you come to this school, even though it sounds as if he wasn't crazy about the idea."

Campbell's pretty, carefully-made-up face brightened. "And I love it here."

"That's the impression he gave me."

"I guess he told you I flunked out of a couple of other schools," she said, not looking the least bit upset, much less ashamed.

"He did say something about that."

"I'm in no hurry," she said with a nonchalant shrug. "I like school. It's fun."

"There are certainly plenty of great classes here," I observed. "In fact, just yesterday I ran into Beanie at the library and she was looking through a book that the art history teacher recommended. That was Mr. Stibbins, right?"

"That's right." With a little pout, she added, "He was just murdered, you know. It's, like, the most awful thing imaginable."

"I heard about that," I said lightly. "You and the other girls must have been devastated."

"Of course we were!" she cried. "Imagine something like that happening at a place like Worth! If you're not safe here, where are you safe? It made me look at the world in an entirely different way!"

Perhaps as a world in which Daddy wouldn't always be able to helicopter in assistance? I wondered.

"It's funny you should say that," I commented, "since Beanie said almost the same thing. Only she mentioned that Mr. Stibbins's class had changed the way she looks at art. I suppose he had that effect on all his students."

Campbell shrugged. Curling a silky blond strand of hair around one finger, she said, "I guess."

I tried again. "Beanie said Mr. Stibbins was a really strong influence in her life." I hesitated before adding, "She gave me the impression that you felt the same way."

Once again, Campbell rolled her eyes. "Beanie exaggerates *so* much. You have to be careful about believing anything she says."

"Campbell!" a voice suddenly snapped, making me jump. "Are you gonna be in there all day?"

I turned to see Beanie scowling at us from the doorway. In her hand was a can of soda.

"Hello, Beanie," I said as coolly as I could. I hadn't realized she was still out in the hall. I'd just assumed that she'd hurried off with all the others, heading to another class or wherever she was going next.

Was Beanie lurking in the hallway all this time, I wondered uneasily, listening in on our conversation?

"Hi, Dr. Popper," she said brusquely. Turning to Campbell, she said, "Here's the Diet Coke you asked me to get." She held it out as if she was presenting her with a valuable gift.

"In a *can*?" Campbell squealed, sounding repulsed by the very notion. "Beanie, you don't really expect me to drink out of a *can*, do you? Especially when you know I like it with tons of ice!"

"It's all I could get," Beanie insisted. "But you have to get moving or you're going to be late for our next class." She grabbed her friend's arm and started to pull her out of the classroom.

"Sorry, Dr. Popper," Campbell said, shooting me an exasperated look as she allowed herself to be dragged away.

Even so, somehow I got the feeling she enjoyed the attention as much as she enjoyed having Beanie act as her servant—even if she did sometimes forget the ice.

• • •

As I wandered out of the Planet Earth building, I glanced at my watch. It was later than I thought, a harsh reminder that I had to get moving if I was going to get to Sunshine Multimedia's television studio in time for the live broadcast of my weekly TV spot, *Pet People*.

But because it was Friday, I wanted to be sure to check my mailbox before taking off for the weekend. So before making my way to the parking lot, I stopped off in the administration building and headed toward the neat grid of wooden pigeonholes.

As usual, mine was stuffed. I expected that, also as usual, most of it would be junk mail—or at least mail that was irrelevant, given my status as a short-term volunteer.

I pulled out the wad of paper and scanned the notices about school activities that didn't affect me. Yet there was something out of the ordinary at the bottom of the pile: a sealed brown nine-by-twelve envelope.

I studied it for a few seconds, noticing there was no postage and no return address. It didn't appear to be an internal communication, either, since the Worth School's emblem wasn't imprinted anywhere.

The only thing on it, in fact, was my name: Dr. Jessica Popper. The words had been printed from a computer and taped onto the envelope.

Curious, I tore it open and pulled out what looked like a stack of black-and-white Xeroxed pages. A second later I realized they were pages from old newspapers that had been stored on microfilm.

I lowered my eyes to the bottom of the first page. It was dated February 25, 1981.

As I was puzzling over what this could possibly be—and who could have wanted to make sure I saw it—my eyes were drawn to a single word: murder.

JEAN HARRIS CONVICTED OF MURDERING THE SCARSDALE DIET DOCTOR, the bold headline at the top of the page read.

What *is* this? I wondered, my heart pounding and my mouth suddenly dry. But I began to read.

"Yesterday, a jury convicted Jean Harris of second-degree murder, ending the fourteen-week trial that began on November 21, 1980, becoming one of the longest trials in New York State history. Harris was arrested for murder of Dr. Herman Tarnower, the cardiologist who ran the Scarsdale Medical Center in Weschester County, New York, and authored the best-selling book *The Scarsdale Diet*. Harris admitted to shooting Tarnower repeatedly."

The Diet Doctor Murder. It was something I remembered hearing about, mainly because it had been an extremely high-profile case. But I had to admit that I didn't remember many of the details.

I read on.

"The trial caught national attention not only because of the high-profile victim, but also because of the case's sordid details. While Harris and Tarnower had been in a relationship for fourteen years, he frequently had affairs with other women. According to testimony, the most recent was a multiple-year relationship with his clinical assistant, a younger woman named Lynne Tryforos. Harris, 57 at the time of the shooting, concluded that Tryforos, who was 38, was going to replace her in Tarnower's life."

I don't remember that part at all, I thought, still puzzled. But the reason I was even reading this in the first place became clear as I scanned the very next paragraph.

"The accused was also considered an unusual suspect in a murder investigation," the article continued, "since the prim, Smith College–educated woman served as the headmistress of the Madeira School, an exclusive girls' school in McLean, Virginia..."

A chill ran through me as I realized what this was about. In my hand was a stack of articles about a woman who had committed murder—but not just any woman, and not just any murder.

Jean Harris had been the headmistress at an exclusive girls' school. And her victim had been her lover.

My heart was still beating crazily fast as I riffled through the rest of the Xeroxed pages, anxious to see what else was in the packet. I quickly read through one article after another, all of them about the same case.

Even though I was only skimming, I managed to

pick up on some more of the details. Tarnower had been an attentive suitor, lavishing gifts on Harris and taking her to exotic destinations for vacations. Harris had been taking medication that Tarnower had prescribed for her, allegedly to help her cope with the pressures of her job.

In the end, Harris had driven from Virginia to Tarnower's luxurious estate north of New York City with a .32-caliber revolver she claimed she intended to use to commit suicide. When she arrived, she found Tryforos's lingerie in his bedroom, which elicited an argument.

Instead of committing suicide, she had shot the man she claimed she loved four times at close range, fatally wounding him.

It was horrifyingly obvious why these articles had been left for me. Whoever had gone to all this trouble was sending me a message: that Nathaniel Stibbins's killer was right here in the administration building, sitting less than twenty feet away from where I stood.

But did the person who wanted me to draw that conclusion really know the truth? Was he or she one hundred percent certain that the headmistress of the Worth School had murdered the man she claimed to love—just like Jean Harris, the headmistress of the Madeira School?

Or did that individual, whoever it was, have some other reason for wanting to see the blame pinned on Elspeth Goodfellow—the most obvious one being that the sender was actually the guilty party?

All this meant that I hadn't really learned much at all.

Yet as I rushed out of the administration building toward my van, I suddenly realized that there *was* something I'd just learned.

And that was that somebody here at the Worth School had figured out precisely what I was up to.

Chapter 11

"Imagine if birds were tickled by feathers. You'd see a flock of birds come by, laughing hysterically!"

—Steven Wright

The realization that I'd been found out made my skin crawl.

As I strode toward the parking lot, I kept checking over my shoulder. Not that I knew who I was looking for. It was just that I half-expected to see someone watching me, peering out surreptitiously from behind a tree trunk or a window or a piece of sculpture.

Don't panic, I told myself. Just because someone at the Worth School noticed you were showing a bit too much interest in Nathaniel Stibbins isn't necessarily a bad thing. Maybe that person could even turn out to be helpful.

I knew I was whistling in the dark. But at the moment, that seemed a lot better than whimpering.

As soon as I climbed into my van and turned the

key in the ignition, another jarring thought popped into my head.

I had a television show to do—and if I didn't make it over to the studio in record time, there was going to be nothing for the folks in the viewing audience to watch but dead air.

It's amazing how one alarming thought can take precedence over another. Still, as I raced along the Long Island Expressway as fast as I dared, the fact that someone had anonymously left articles about Jean Harris in my mailbox hung over me like a rain cloud on the day of the big picnic.

Who could it be? I wondered.

Rather than giving in to those same feelings of panic that still threatened to engulf me, I decided to methodically go through the list of people I'd met at the Worth School who had known Nathaniel—and who might have had reason to want him dead.

The most obvious of those was Dr. Elspeth Goodfellow. The fact that she and Nathaniel had been lovers made her a prime suspect. The police almost always started a homicide investigation by looking at the spouse or significant other. Surely even Falcone would figure out at some point that she and Nathaniel had been involved romantically.

On top of that, I had to admit that there were disturbingly similar parallels between Elspeth Goodfellow and Jean Harris, the headmistress of another elite girls' school. If Claude's claim that the relationship had been one-sided really was accurate, that would mean both Elspeth and Jean had had strong feelings for men who hadn't exactly returned their affections in the same manner that Romeo had acted toward Juliet.

In Jean Harris's case, there had apparently been another woman lurking in the background. While at this point I didn't know if that had also been the case with Elspeth and Nathaniel, a third party would certainly have strengthened her motive—whether her relationship with the artist was genuine or existed only in her mind.

Then there was Claude. Richard Evans had told me that while the two men had once been friends, they had had some kind of falling out. Reverend Evans had been unwilling to divulge any of the details—and Claude hadn't exactly rushed to volunteer anything about what had brought about their rift. But I'd seen for myself what an arrogant, competitive man Claude Molter was, and it wasn't that difficult to imagine him becoming extremely angry with Nathaniel. Perhaps even angry enough to kill him.

As much as I hated to admit it, I couldn't avoid considering the students at Worth as possible suspects. I'd only been teaching my animal-care class for four days, so it was impossible to identify every single girl who might have disliked him. But I'd been to the murder victim's house—and I'd seen for myself that Nathaniel had had romantic entanglements with at least one of the young women at the school.

But in addition to the students, I also had to consider their parents. Campbell Atwater's father, for example. Leighton Atwater certainly didn't have anything positive to say about the Worth School—or Mr.

Stibbins. I didn't know what, if anything, had transpired between the two men. But it was possible that Atwater and Stibbins had clashed on some issue and that Atwater, a phenomenally successful businessman who was undoubtedly accustomed to being in control, had decided to take matters into his own hands.

True, he was the least likely person on my list to have stuck those articles in my mailbox. After all, he wasn't exactly a day-to-day presence on the Worth School campus. But it wasn't impossible, either. Nor was it impossible that someone else who was a fixture on campus had done it on his behalf. Ms. Greer, for example. Or, I supposed, even Richard Evans.

Of course, either one of them could also have sent me the message about Dr. Goodfellow for their own reasons...

I was starting to feel so overwhelmed by all the possible scenarios that could have been behind the package that had mysteriously appeared in my mailbox that I was actually glad I had that morning's television spot to distract me. For at least a little while, I'd have something else to think about.

With that obligation looming in front of me, I forced myself to focus on the demands that came with hosting my own television show—even though as one of my students had so thoughtfully pointed out, it was only broadcast on a local cable station. It was true that the demands weren't that great, since all that was required of me during the fifteen-minute broadcast was speaking about some topic related to animal care—and doing it without giggling, stuttering, hiccuping, drooling, or scratching. However, pulling that off still necessitated some concentration, so I tried to get myself in the right mind-set.

Arriving at the studio later than usual didn't help. As if my earlier feelings of being overwhelmed weren't bad enough, I was also feeling pretty frazzled as I jumped out of my van and dashed across the parking lot. With only five minutes left before the show aired, I didn't even have time to comb my hair, let alone to give Patti Ardsley, the show's producer, a chance to brief me.

Good thing she took care of the topic for this week, I thought, grateful for the way she'd stepped in. Given everything else that's been going on, thinking up a way to fill my spot is something I just didn't have either the time or the energy to deal with this week.

I tore through the main entrance of the Sunshine Multimedia building, flashing my ID card at the receptionist. Fortunately, she knew me by now, so getting her to buzz me in was no problem.

"Break a leg!" she called after me.

It might actually come to that, I thought, careening around the corner past the Green Room and the dressing room and heading straight into the studio.

"Made it!" I exclaimed as I burst into the small, boxy room with black walls, no windows, and a single huge camera. Not surprisingly, Patti was already there, along with her perky assistant, Marlene Fitzgerald, a surly potbellied cameraman, and a few other assorted crewmembers.

"We were beginning to wonder if you would," Patti said dryly. Usually, the young woman with the looks of a cheerleader was the epitome of bubbly optimism.

Still, she was a professional—and that meant making sure the entire production went off without a hitch. I could understand how having the star come dashing into the studio only seconds before the show began could make anyone testy.

"Sorry," I muttered. Then I gave the one excuse that, on Long Island, never fails to elicit sympathy: "Traffic."

I headed straight for the set. As I did, I remembered the receptionist's words and took special care not to knock over the camera or trip on any cables. I plopped into my seat, a tall stool behind a counter on which there was nothing but the telephone used for the call-in segment at the end of the show. Right behind was a backdrop of stuffed animals, everything from fish to zebras made of fake fur in colors as bright as the human eye could tolerate without requiring special protection. The stuffed animals might have been garish, but at least they managed to hold still through the entire show—unlike some of the live four-legged and feathered guests on past shows.

I noticed that today, there was an addition to the set: a large cardboard box on the floor, right next to my stool. I surmised that inside it was whatever animal Patti had decided would be the topic of today's show. I didn't hear any scratching, let alone any barking, mewing, or squealing.

Whatever is in that box, I thought, *I sure hope it doesn't have stage fright.*

"We've got twenty seconds," Patti informed me with a scowl.

"I'm ready," I assured her, even though ready was the last word I'd have used to describe the way I really felt. Anxious, scattered, disoriented—all of those would have been much more accurate.

"Ten seconds!" Patti barked as I settled into my seat, ran my fingers through my hair in a pathetic attempt at combing it, and looked directly at the camera.

"Five, four, three—" As always, Patti mouthed the last two numbers, meanwhile holding up the appropriate number of fingers.

"Welcome to *Pet People*," I began confidently, aware that the red light beaming at me from the camera meant we were now on the air, "the program for people who are passionate about their pets." The intro—not my creation, but Patti the Producer's—was really a mouthful. But by now I'd said it so many times I no longer tripped over all those P's.

"I'm Dr. Jessica Popper, and I'm pleased to announce that today, we have a special treat." I hoped I sounded confident enough that none of the viewers were catching on to the fact I didn't have a clue about what that special treat might be. "Actually," I added, clearing my throat, "we have a special guest."

I leaned over and opened the flaps of the box, assuming that inside I'd find something cute and furry.

"Yeow!" I yelped, jumping off my stool so abruptly that it swayed from side to side. It would have crashed to the floor if it hadn't tilted against my hip.

Writhing along the bottom of the box were two snakes.

They weren't large and they weren't particularly menacing. But they were—well, snakes.

While no one is a greater lover of animals than I am, there is one exception. And two examples of it were slithering along the bottom of the box.

It took me a few seconds to comprehend the fact that these two particular members of the *Serpentes* suborder were today's guests.

Waves of panic cascaded over me like Niagara Falls. Desperately I glanced at Patti, hoping that somehow this would turn out to be nothing but a cruel joke. Instead, she was scowling. Even though she was only in her twenties, deep grooves cut across her forehead like telephone wires, and her perfectly lipsticked mouth was suddenly drawn into an upside-down U.

She was also making a rolling gesture with one hand, using the sign language that was so popular with people in the TV business. While I wasn't fluent, even I knew she was ordering me to keep things moving.

"I'd, uh, like to tell you about today's guests—uh, or at least today's topic," I went on, my voice cracking like a twelve-year-old boy's. "It's, uh, snakes."

I swallowed hard. Just saying the word had dried out my mouth so much it was as if I were in the dentist's office with one of those little moisture-sucking hooks in my mouth.

I stared straight into the camera, pointedly ignoring the two slithering creatures I now knew were in the room.

"A lot of people enjoy keeping snakes in their homes," I went on in a pinched voice. "And, uh, for many reasons, they make really good pets. For example, you don't have to walk them."

I made the mistake of letting my eyes drift back over to Patti. By that point, her hands were on her hips and her cheeks had taken on kind of a reddish tone.

"Actually, there are *lots* of good reasons why snakes make excellent pets," I went on, doing my best to sound enthusiastic. "Uh, they don't take up a lot of room. I mean, if you have a big dog, you have to fence in your yard or at least build a special pen. But snakes live in a tank. In fact, you don't even have to take them out of it. *Ever.*"

Once again, I glanced at Patty. Much to my horror, she was mimicking taking snakes out of a box. Which meant she thought I should be doing the same.

Instead, I sat motionless, telling myself, *The show must go on, the show must go on.*

I could hear the two snakes sliding around inside the box, mere inches away from my feet, separated from me by nothing but a thin layer of cardboard . . .

While just a few seconds had passed without me saying anything, in TV time that's the equivalent of an entire century. I could feel the tension growing in the studio. The cameraman looked stricken, and Marlene was wearing a horrified look as she kept glancing from Patti to me and back to Patti.

I have to do *something*, I thought. I can't just sit here forever, talking about the benefits of not having to put pet snakes on a leash and take them for a jog around the block.

"We have two snakes here with us today," I finally

said, fixing my eyes on the camera once again. "And I'd like to show them to you."

I could feel the level of anxiety in the room drop.

"But first—"

The tension instantly returned.

"Before I do," I said, "I'd like to tell you about what's required to keep these, uh, intriguing animals in your home."

This time, I didn't look at Patti. I didn't look at anyone in the studio. Instead, with my eyes still glued to the camera, I launched into a monologue about caring for a snake. I began with the importance of choosing a tank that was the correct size, moved on to the dos and don'ts of using heat lamps and heat rocks to maintain the proper temperature, and then launched into Snake 101, including feeding them, cleaning up after them, and even determining whether the snake in question was male or female. In short, I delivered a pretty comprehensive lecture on Everything You Ever Wanted to Know about Snakes—but without *handling* an actual snake.

I hoped desperately that by the time I came up for air, I'd be out of time.

Instead, when I'd just about run out of things to say and was considering addressing the question of whether it was possible to make little articles of clothing like Santa Claus hats for one's pet snake, I checked the big clock at the back of studio. My mouth dropped open when I saw that I still had seven minutes before the call-in segment.

No reason why we can't push that up a little, I thought.

"I'm sure a lot of you have questions about snakes," I told my viewers. "After all, it's, uh, such a *fascinating* subject. So please feel free to call in—immediately—with any questions you may have. No matter how trivial your question may seem, please don't be shy. In fact, if you have questions about anything at all, like dogs or cats or horses or—or llamas, please call. Call *now*."

I didn't care that I was beginning to sound like a spokesperson in an infomercial. An extremely desperate spokesperson.

Hopefully, I stared at the lights on the phone in front of me. Yet even though I gave them the Evil Eye, they stubbornly refused to blink.

And then something that *never* happens on TV happened.

I stiffened as I noticed Patti walking toward me with a determined look on her face. I instantly understood what was happening: The producer of my show was about to join me on camera.

I was still trying to process this unexpected turn of events when I heard Patti's voice directly behind me.

"Hello, everyone!" she said cheerfully. "I'm Patti Ardsley, the producer of *Pet People*. I'm sure you've all been enjoying Dr. Popper's extremely informative talk about snakes and what rewarding pets they make. But since we're running out of time—"

Not fast enough! I thought as feelings of panic once again began to envelop me.

"...I want to make sure you have a chance to see some of these fascinating creatures," Patti continued.

"Especially viewers who aren't as familiar with them as I'm sure Dr. Popper is."

I felt her fingers grip my shoulders—*hard*—as through gritted teeth she added, "Dr. Popper, why don't you take the snakes out of the box?"

Trapped.

I tried to mumble, "Sure," but couldn't manage to get the word out. It was the same dentist-hook-in-the-mouth problem.

Still painfully aware of Patti standing behind me, I leaned over and opened the flaps of the box once again. I hoped that somehow the two snakes had disappeared. Escaped, maybe, squeezing through some tiny hole in the cardboard I hadn't noticed and hiding by blending in with the thick black cables draped across the studio floor.

No such luck.

They were still lying at the bottom of the box, intertwined with each other like two giant sausages that had been tossed into the box haphazardly.

Both of them poised and ready for their fifteen minutes of fame.

Gulping so loudly that I suspected the folks out in TV land could hear me, I reached into the box. I could feel the room starting to spin, and lights suddenly seemed to be flashing on and off around me. All the air seemed to have been sucked out of the room, too. Which no doubt explained why I was having such difficulty breathing.

You can do this, I thought. You *have* to do this.

My chest heaved as I clamped my clammy hands around one of the snakes. I told myself it was just a toy snake. Or even one of those sausages I'd been imagining.

Wincing, I forced myself to pick up the wriggling mass of muscle, trying to minimize the amount of skin that actually made contact. Far in the distance, I could hear Patti saying, "Why don't you tell us what kind of snake that is? Dr. Popper?"

"Uh, a boa constrictor," I said, amazed that this time, the words actually came out.

"And what can you tell us about boa constrictors?" Patti prompted.

They're *snakes,* I thought wildly. What else does anyone need to know?

But somehow, a calmer, more levelheaded part of my brain was activated.

"Boa constrictors come from South America, Central America, and the Caribbean," I recited in a robotic voice.

Somehow, I couldn't quite digest the fact that I was actually holding one of these creatures in my hands. It was almost as if another Jessie Popper, a clone perhaps, was doing it while the real me was merely standing by. I had never before had an experience like this, one in which my brain felt completely separate from the rest of my body.

"They can live in a variety of environments, including both the tropical rain forest and the desert," I continued. "They eat mammals, mostly rodents, but even monkeys and wild pigs. They also eat birds and lizards."

Actually, the bulk of knowledge came from a report I'd done on boas in the fifth grade. Even then, I'd found snakes horrifying, but I decided that learning about them might help me overcome my fear.

I'd done fine with the writing part. But when it came to cutting out pictures and gluing them on construction paper, I froze. I'd ended up with a C—an A for the text and an F for the pictures, since I was the only kid in the class who handed in a ten-page report composed mostly of empty pages.

"How interesting!" Patti prompted. "What else can you tell us, Dr. Popper?"

"They generally grow to be much bigger than this one, usually about ten feet long," I continued, still sounding about as animated as a wooden soldier. I wasn't moving much more than one, either. "But some have gotten even bigger. And their average weight is sixty pounds."

"My, that's big!" Patti exclaimed.

The better to strangle you, I thought morosely.

"Boa constrictors can live for thirty years," I went on, "which means anyone who's considering getting one as a pet should think about the long-term commitment they're making."

"Are they venomous?" Patti asked with inappropriate cheerfulness.

"Uh, no. But that's because the way they capture their prey is by using their powerful, muscular bodies to suffocate them. Constriction, in other words, which is how they got their name. They do have sharp teeth, but they use them for fighting and eating. There are cases of boas that people kept as pets strangling their owners. There was this one guy—"

"Fascinating," Patti interrupted. "Dr. Popper, do

you think you could hold the boa up a little higher so everyone can see it?"

Isn't the fact that I'm holding it at all enough? I thought. But I automatically did what I was told.

Something about holding the snake up high enough that I couldn't help but stare at it set off a reaction in me. While up to this point I'd felt as if I were watching what I was doing without actually being there, as soon as I stepped back and thought about this strange phenomenon, it seemed to vanish.

I was suddenly me again, with all the pieces stuck together, holding a snake in my hands.

"A-a-augh!" I cried.

Before I even realized what I was doing, I let go. I watched in horror as it dropped about two inches, hitting the counter with a gentle thud and taking off.

"Jessie!" Patti screamed. She followed with a four-letter word that I never would have dreamed she was capable of uttering.

The entire studio instantly erupted into chaos. Marlene let out a shriek, although whether it was over a snake being loose in the studio or her boss just violating one of the strictest rules of television, I couldn't say. The cameraman, meanwhile, scampered after the runaway snake, leaping over coils of cable with more agility than I ever would have expected a man who weighed 200-plus pounds to possess. The other crew-members who had been standing by in the studio also leaped into action, yelling things like "Get the snake!" or "Stop that thing!" At least one of them cried "Eeew!" which at least made me feel a little better.

"Go to commercial!" Patti commanded. "Go to commercial!"

The next thing I knew, the bright lights in the studio dimmed, a sign that we were off the air.

"Got him!" one of the crewmembers yelled, proudly holding up the captured snake for all to see.

But it was too late.

Patti turned to me, her face now as red as—oh, say the blood of one of those wild pigs boa constrictors like to eat for breakfast.

"Jessie," she demanded angrily, "may I ask what that was all about?"

"I, uh, don't like snakes," I replied with an apologetic shrug.

"So I gathered," she snapped. "Why didn't you tell me that before we went on the air?"

"I would have if you'd told me in advance that that was the topic you came up with for today's show!"

"But I did tell you!" she cried. "Early this week, when I called you—"

We didn't have a chance to continue our conversation. The doors of the studio flew open. Standing in the doorway was a man I immediately recognized, even though we'd never met. Kenneth Decker, the president of Sunshine Multimedia.

The Big Boss, in other words.

"May I have a word with you?" he said icily.

"Jessie?" Patti said, sounding just as frosty as she gave me a little push.

"Not Dr. Popper," the Big Boss said. "*You,* Patti."

Uh-oh, I thought as I watched Patti slink out the room, following him a few paces behind.

While my first reaction was relief, that feeling quickly gave way to guilt. After all, I hadn't exactly performed to the best of my ability on air.

Poor Patti, I thought as I stole away from the studio.

Still, I had a feeling all this would blow over. Patti was good at her job, and I knew how valuable she was to the station. As for me, I resolved that from now on, I'd make a point of being completely sure of my special guests' identity before going on air.

Even though I had a feeling Patti wouldn't be booking any more snakes.

• • •

As disastrous as that week's TV spot had been, at least it was out of the way. As I got back into my van to head off to my first call of the day, my mind had already drifted back to the pressing matter that had occupied me all week: identifying Nathaniel's killer.

Oddly enough, I was in the midst of muttering to myself about my future mother-in-law, the person who'd gotten me into this in the first place, when my cellphone rang. Sure enough, it was the same person I'd just been cursing.

"Jessica! It's me, Dorothy."

As if that shrill voice could belong to anyone else, I thought ruefully.

"Hello, Dorothy," I replied with my usual daughter-in-law-esque politeness. "How are you—?"

"Jessica," she interrupted, her impatience with my passion for pleasantries spewing through the phone, "this morning I realized I never got the chance to tell you the entire story of why Nathaniel was considered the black sheep of the family. I seem to recall being rudely interrupted by Henry."

That wasn't quite how I remembered it. But at this point, I was more worried about how serious Dorothy's omission would turn out to be.

Sweetly, I said, "This might be a good time to fill me in."

"The patterns he'd been exhibiting his entire life finally came to a head when he was a teenager," she said. "There was a perfectly awful incident during his freshman year of high school that really showed Nathaniel's true colors."

"What happened?" I prompted, aware that my heartbeat had quickened.

"He was fourteen or so, and he'd just enrolled at Schottsburg Academy. You've heard of it, haven't you?"

"I don't believe I have."

"It's a prep school in Pennsylvania. A boarding school. Not one of the best schools, but still highly competitive. Nathaniel didn't have the grades or the pedigree to get into one of the top schools like Choate or Andover, but Schottsburg was nothing to sneeze at." With a little sniff, Dorothy commented, "His mother always insisted on only the best for her Nathaniel. Which, I suppose, could explain why he was the way he was.

"Anyway, a few weeks after his first semester started, one of the students stole a car," she went on. "A van, actually. It belonged to the school. In fact, it was hard to miss, since it had the Schottsburg crest right on the door. Late one night, someone took the keys from the caretaker's office and went for a joy ride. Apparently the trip lasted less than a mile, since the thief didn't know how to drive and had barely gotten it off school grounds before crashing into a wall and totaling it."

"That's terrible!" I cried. "And Nathaniel was the thief?"

"That's where it gets tricky," Dorothy said somberly. "Someone—a man who lived in town, I believe—saw the van careening down the street, and noticed that the driver was wearing a red baseball cap. In those days, Nathaniel insisted on wearing that silly cap wherever he went. He practically slept in it, for heaven's sake. When the witness heard what happened with the stolen van, he came forth and told the police what he'd seen.

"Naturally, Nathaniel was immediately called into the headmaster's office and asked to explain. Even though he'd only been at the school for a few weeks, he was already well-known as the boy who never went anywhere without his cap. But instead of admitting that he was the person who'd taken the van and wrecked it, he concocted this ridiculous story about how one of the other students had borrowed his cap— coincidentally, that very night. Based on Nathaniel's story alone, the other boy was accused of the crime and thrown out of school."

"That's terrible!" I cried.

Dorothy let out a snort. "It certainly is. Of course everyone in the family knew immediately that

Nathaniel had lied. As for the boy he chose to accuse—well, that made the whole thing even worse!"

"Who was the boy?" I wondered how *much* worse this could possibly get.

"A scholarship student," Dorothy replied curtly. "Someone who'd worked his tail off to get into Schottsburg, since his family was much too poor to pay the tuition. He had an unusual name. Wilhelm or Willard...something with a W. Something that sounded German. His last name, too. Farber, maybe? At any rate, he, too, was new at the school. But instead of getting the education he'd been hoping for, he ended up being blamed for what we all knew perfectly well Nathaniel had done."

"Did the school press charges?" I asked.

"No, they decided that throwing poor Wilhelm out of school was punishment enough. They claimed the damage to the vehicle wasn't that terrible. Besides, the school's insurance apparently covered all the costs. But my theory was that they wanted to keep the entire incident hush-hush, since they didn't want the school to end up in the headlines. The last thing a place like that wants is for its students to appear to be anything less than perfect."

"So that's when Nathaniel became the black sheep of the family," I mused, thinking out loud. "What about Wilhelm? What ever happened to him?"

"I have no idea," Dorothy replied. "But that wasn't the last time Nathaniel demonstrated the kind of person he was. Over the years, he showed us again and again that he didn't have an honorable bone in his body."

So Nathaniel started making enemies at a young age, I thought grimly, then continued to follow the same pattern throughout his life. I suppose it was only a question of time before his behavior caught up with him.

Yet the fact that the man had such a long history of ruthless behavior raised the possibility that it wasn't someone at the Worth School who was responsible for his death after all. The main reason I'd pursued that path was that it been Dorothy's original theory. But that didn't mean it was correct.

I suddenly felt overwhelmed. Piecing together the story of someone's life and figuring out who their enemies might have been was a hard job. The fact that Nathaniel had apparently exhibited a lifelong pattern of stepping over people to get what he wanted made it even harder.

When it came to figuring out which person on a very long list might have wanted him dead, that was starting to strike me as downright impossible.

Chapter 12

"Did you ever notice when you blow in a dog's face he gets mad at you? But when you take him in a car he sticks his head out the window."
—Steve Bluestone

I welcomed the weekend as a chance to take a break from playing sleuth. I also saw it as a much-needed opportunity to catch up with some of the details of my day-to-day existence.

Under the best of circumstances, running my veterinary practice keeps my schedule packed—even with Sunny's help. But on top of that, over the past week I'd heaped on the additional duties of teaching at the Worth School and investigating Poor Cousin Nathaniel's murder. All that had left me with little time to breathe, much less keep up with my email, do errands, or perform any of the other eight million tasks required to maintain a life.

So after Nick and I spent Friday evening chilling with a DVD and Chinese food, on Saturday I methodically worked my way through the to-do list I composed over breakfast. It actually felt good to do laundry and restock the freezer with Ben & Jerry's instead of struggling with a puzzle that was still missing a frustrating number of pieces.

Then came Sunday, the day whose arrival I'd been dreading more and more with each passing second.

It was the day I'd begun thinking of as D-Day. Dinner Day—as in Dinner with Forrester Sloan, Who I'd Rather Not Have Dinner or Any Other Meal With, Day.

On top of that, I felt a little guilty that I'd made a point of not mentioning it to Nick. I tried telling myself that the reason was that it was such a nonevent that there was no reason to say anything about it.

"Have fun!" I cheerfully told Nick early on Sunday morning as we both stood in the doorway of the cottage, him with one foot out the door.

He grimaced. While he was enjoying his summer internship, I knew he wasn't exactly looking forward to bonding with the partners and the other lawyers at the firm—especially since the schedule included team spirit–building activities like raft construction and scavenger hunts.

"I'll try." He let out a deep sigh before adding, "Compared to this, I think passing the bar exam is going to be a breeze."

"Just turn on the old Nick Burby charm and you'll do fine." I leaned over to give him a peck on the cheek.

"Hey," he protested, "what about a real kiss?"

With that, he took me in his arms and planted a mushy, Hollywood-style wet one on my mouth. Ordinarily, I would have melted. But not today. Not with that little cloud of guilt hanging over my head.

You have nothing to feel guilty about! I told myself. So what if while Nick is putting in a grueling, emotionally-draining day trying to impress all the other lawyers with his heretofore-unknown raft-building skills, you'll be entertaining a gentleman caller?

Not, I thought.

In the first place, Forrester is no gentleman, I reminded myself as I waved goodbye, not exactly an easy feat since I was holding Max in one arm and clutching Lou's collar with the other. And in the second place, he's not paying a call. At least, not a social call. And even if it could technically be considered a social call, it's not a *welcome* social call.

At any rate, I was determined not to put the least bit of effort into making the evening ahead into anything that could remotely be considered a success. I made a point of not straightening up, not washing my hair, and not giving a single thought to what I'd serve for dinner, aside from reminding myself of where I'd stashed my collection of take-out menus.

Yet even though I had no intention of taking any action that could possibly be interpreted as gussying up, I couldn't ignore the fact that I desperately needed a shower. So fifteen minutes before Forrester was due to arrive, I peeled off my sweaty clothes and stepped into the tub.

While I loved the cottage, even I had to admit that the plumbing was not its strong point. In fact, I'd tried to come to grips with its capriciousness by thinking of it as just one more bit of the old building's historic charm. So when I grabbed the handle of the hot faucet to turn off the water and the stupid thing came off in my hand, I wasn't entirely surprised.

That didn't mean I wasn't horrified.

"Argh!" I cried. Or at least something that sounded like that. Frankly, I was too busy staring at the clump of metal in my hand, marveling at all the rust-colored crud caked onto the piece of pipe that once upon a time had kept it attached to the wall, to pay much attention to the sounds that were spewing out of my mouth.

But the chunk of metal in my hand was the least of it. What was really terrifying was the hot water that was now gushing through the wall.

"Yow!" I exclaimed.

Frantically I looked around for something to cram into the gaping hole in the tile. I grabbed a washcloth and tried stuffing it in. That lasted about two seconds.

Trying to quell the feelings of panic that were already threatening to render me even more useless than I already was, I desperately surveyed the bathroom, hoping to spot something else that might work. A bigger towel? A handful of toothbrushes?

I was considering the effectiveness of French green clay—a gooey substance that Suzanne had talked me into buying after she'd decided that pore-reducing facials were a girl's best friend—when I looked down and saw that the water in the bathtub had already risen halfway up my calves. Which meant the water was surging through the wall faster than the drain could suck it out.

Why didn't I take any plumbing courses when I was in vet school? I wondered.

The realization that I was losing the ability to think logically only accelerated the feeling of panic that at this point was almost as forceful as the deluge.

Have to stop water. Have to stop water, I thought over and over as I climbed out of the tub. I grabbed Nick's white terrycloth bathrobe off the hook on the back of the door. I pulled it on, only vaguely aware that it was inside out, as I sprinted into the living room. My feet were still very wet, causing me to slip and slide across the wooden floor.

Both my dogs and Tinkerbell interpreted my slapstick behavior as an invitation to play a thrilling new game.

"Woof, woof!" Lou barked happily, falling into step beside me and prancing along like a drum major. Max, meanwhile, grabbed his pink plastic poodle, its head half ripped off and its color badly mottled, thanks to constant exposure to dog spit. Tinkerbell leaped onto the couch to engage in some play of her own, which consisted of swatting at the loose button on one of the throw pillows.

"Not now!" I cried. Which, of course, only incited them further. Lou started leaping up, pushing his powerful legs against me as if he'd decided that knocking me over would add one more dimension of fun to this exhilarating game.

I fended him off and grabbed my cellphone. Struggling to steady my hands, I scrolled down to Betty and Winston's number. Since they're my landlords, in the best of all possible worlds, this would become their problem, not mine.

"Hello," I heard Betty say brightly.

"Betty!" I exclaimed. "You and Winston have to come over *now*! The faucet handle in the bathtub just broke off, and the entire cottage is about to flood—"

"I'm sorry," she continued in the same happy voice, "but no one is available to take your call. Please wait for the tone and then leave a—"

"Great!" I cried, hitting the button that ended the call. Staring at the phone numbers on the tiny screen, I debated about who to call next. Nick? Not the best idea, since it wouldn't look good for a lawyer-in-progress to be getting frantic phone calls from his helpless wife-to-be. Especially if he and the other members of his team were spiritedly sailing off into the sunset on *Kon-Tiki*.

It occurred to me then that a plumber would be a much better choice. Not that I had ever bothered to program the telephone numbers of any into my phone. And that was because I didn't *know* of any plumbers.

Today was also Sunday. Which meant that there probably weren't a lot of plumbers sitting around, waiting for their phone to ring so they could grab their trusty wrenches, jump into their truck, and race over to someone's house.

I dashed back into the bathroom, anxious to see how things were progressing. I hoped the water tank might be empty by now, meaning that the crisis had passed—preferably before the water level had exceeded the height of the bathtub.

No such luck. In fact, the very thing I had been hoping wouldn't happen had just happened. Water had begun sloshing onto the floor, adding insult to injury by making a horrifying slapping noise. It occurred to me that Nick's newfound ability to build rafts might turn out to be pretty darned useful.

"Argh!" I screamed again.

My animals took my cries of agony to mean that our game had simply moved to another location. Lou came trotting into the bathroom, this time with a tennis ball in his mouth. He'd clearly decided that adding sports equipment to our pickup game would be an improvement. Max was right behind him, still carrying his favorite toy in his jaws. He gave a few violent shakes of his head, causing the pink plastic poodle to squeak for mercy. Tinkerbell darted between them, with a long piece of thread that perfectly matched the color of the throw pillow partially wrapped around one leg and partially trailing behind her.

"Lou, get *out* of here!" I screeched just as his front paws made contact with the ever-growing puddle of water. I guess my tone of voice scared him, since he immediately dropped the tennis ball. Into the puddle. Which caused a surprising amount of water to splash up onto my inside-out bathrobe. At least the water wasn't hot anymore, since the limited supply of that had apparently been all used up. For once, that was a good thing.

When the sound of the doorbell abruptly cut through all the chaos, my first thought was that a plumber had magically appeared on my doorstep.

But within about two seconds I realized that someone else was much more likely to be standing on my doorstep. Forrester.

If I ignore him, I thought, maybe he'll go away. But then it dawned on me that maybe he could be of help.

So I scurried over to the front door, once again accompanied by my entire team. The three of them gamboled beside me with their favorite toys in their mouths—or in Tink's case, on their paws—acting as if they were thinking, "Boy, this game just keeps getting better and better!"

I flung open the door. Sure enough, Forrester was standing there. He was all dressed up in khaki pants and a crisp white shirt, and in his hands he clasped a bouquet of colorful wildflowers.

But the expression on his face was one of total confusion.

"Jess?" he asked, frowning. "Am I early?"

"Flood!" I cried, grabbing him by the arm and pulling him toward the back of the cottage. "In the bathroom. A pipe-fixture-whatever-you-call-it-thingy broke off, and the water won't stop coming!"

"Well, well, well," he said, actually sounding pleased. "Never in a million years did I think I'd ever see the day the confident, self-reliant Jessica Popper would be reduced to a damsel in distress!"

"Not now, Forrester," I barked, still dragging him to the bathroom. "This is a crisis!"

As he passed the coffee table, he dropped the bouquet onto it. "Then I'm glad I arrived in time to be your knight in shining armor."

"Believe me, that armor is going to get mighty rusty if we don't do something about this immediately!"

By "we," I meant "you," of course. And just as I'd hoped, once Forrester had reached the bathroom, he said, "Is *that* all. Let me turn off the main line valve. Where is it?"

I just looked at him. "I have no idea. This has never come up before."

"I'll find it," he assured me, heading back out of the bathroom. "There are only so many possibilities."

I don't know what he did or where he did it, but no more than two minutes had passed before the water stopped. Just *stopped*, as if an act of wizardry had just been performed.

"Forrester, you saved my life!" I told him when he sashayed back into the bathroom. I didn't even care that he looked positively smug.

Grinning, he replied, "That's right, Jessie, I did."

"I'll call a plumber first thing tomorrow," I said, thinking out loud. "In the meantime, I'll keep trying Betty. She probably has someone she uses all the time."

But I only had a few seconds to bask in my relief over having finally put an end to my bathroom's temporary metamorphosis into Victoria Falls. Looking down, I saw that the water was seeping toward the rest of the house.

"I've got to mop all this up," I said mournfully. "Right now."

"I'll help," he offered, pulling off his shoes.

I was already running into the kitchen. I grabbed a mop, two big sponges, a bucket, and a small pile of rags.

"Thanks, Forrester," I said sincerely when I returned. "But you don't have to—"

"I said I'll help." Glancing down at the hem of his

pants, he added, "But I'm not willing to ruin my pants."

"Then you should probably take them off."

His eyebrows shot up. "What can I wear instead?"

Looking around the bathroom, I said, "Can't you just put a towel around you?"

"That would work," he said, nodding. "But I'd better take off my shirt, too." With a sheepish smile, he added, "I got kind of dressed up for tonight."

"Go ahead," I said, already dipping both sponges into the puddle and wringing them out in the sink.

I turned to him to suggest that he use the bucket to start dumping water out the front door, then stopped.

"Whoa!" The word just popped out before I had a chance to stop myself.

Even though he'd told me exactly what he was going to do, I was still astonished by the sight of Forrester standing in front of me seemingly naked except for the big white towel wrapped around his waist. I had to admit that he had a surprisingly well-toned torso. In fact, his tanned skin, combined with his sun-bleached hair, made him look as if he were posing for a Ralph Lauren towel ad.

But instead of giving his bare chest or his muscular thighs more than a glance, I thrust the bucket at him. "Start bailing," I commanded.

It took the two of us less than fifteen minutes to clean up all the water. As I was giving the entire bathroom a final wipe down with one of the few dry towels that remained, he said, "I'm going to get something to drink. Something cold. Want anything?"

"Definitely," I said, noticing for the first time how

warm I was. And how thirsty. While earlier the balmy June day had seemed relaxing, the combination of all that spewing water and the heat generated by two bodies undergoing extensive physical exertion had converted the bathroom into a steam room. "Help yourself to whatever you find in the fridge."

When I padded out of the bathroom a minute or two later, I found Forrester lounging on the couch, still dressed in nothing but the towel. In one hand he held a champagne glass that was filled with the bubbly stuff. A second glass, also filled, sat on the coffee table with the rest of the bottle.

I realized with horror that he'd found the bottle of champagne from my almost-wedding day in the refrigerator—and opened it.

"Here, drink some of this," he instructed, picking up the second glass and half-standing so he could hand it to me. "You earned it."

I had to admit that at the moment, a glass of champagne sounded like the perfect way of calming my nerves.

"Thanks, Forrester." I accepted the glass, then plopped down on the couch next to him, taking care to wrap my bathrobe around my legs modestly. "You're a good sport."

"Are you kidding? That was fun!" he insisted.

"Cleaning up a flooded bathroom is fun?" I repeated.

"It is with you." Grinning, he clinked his glass against mine. "I propose a toast. To dates that are anything but boring."

I was about to correct him, pointing out that we

weren't actually *on* a date, when I suddenly heard the familiar sound of the front door being opened.

I froze.

"Who's that?" Forrester asked.

At the exact same moment, a single syllable emerged from my dry lips: "Nick!"

Before I had a chance to do anything—hide the champagne, change out of Nick's bathrobe, force Forrester to put on something besides the towel wrapped around his waist—Nick was standing in front of us, his eyes darting from me to Forrester to the two glasses in our hands.

The expression on his face made me shrink back so far that I practically dissolved into the couch's upholstery fabric. He looked furious, hurt, baffled, and probably a whole bunch of other emotions I couldn't identify.

Not one of them the least bit positive.

"What a surprise!" I cried, springing from the couch. "Nick, you're not going to believe what just happened!"

"You've got me there," he replied in a strained voice. "This is definitely something I'd classify as un- believable."

"But this isn't what it looks like!" I cried. "That's what's so funny about this whole situation! You see, Forrester has been helping with the murder investiga- tion your mother got me involved in, and to thank him, I—"

"Save it!" Nick growled, turning away and heading back toward the door.

"But Nick!" I cried, running after him. "A bathroom pipe broke!"

He didn't appear to have heard me. He'd run out the door too fast.

By the time I reached the driveway, he was turning the key in the ignition.

"Nick!" I cried, racing after his car even though the gravel cut into the bottoms of my bare feet.

But it was too late. He had already driven off, without once looking back.

• • •

After sending Forrester on his way, I desperately tried calling and texting Nick. In fact, over the next two hours I punched so many keys on my stupid cellphone that my fingers hurt. But I still didn't get any response.

When my phone finally buzzed, I grabbed it and answered before the first ring was over.

"Nick?" I demanded breathlessly.

"Nope. It's Suzanne—the star-crossed lover."

My heart sank. Not only wasn't it Nick, it was someone I was in absolutely no mood to talk to.

"Suzanne, this really isn't the best time—"

"Wait until you hear this, Jess," Suzanne interrupted. "You're not going to believe what's going on with Kieran and me."

I realized then that the one good thing about a conversation with Suzanne was that it usually focused on Suzanne. And at the moment, talking about her problematic love life struck me as a much better alternative to talking about mine.

Especially since I knew from experience that my main responsibility would be to listen.

"Okay, what's up?" I settled back against the couch cushions, figuring this was bound to take a while.

Suzanne let out a deep sigh. "I'm beginning to think the man has major commitment issues."

"Why?" I asked, even though I had a feeling I was opening the proverbial can of worms. Still, it was comforting to know I wasn't the only one who was finding being in love to be an overwhelmingly distressing experience.

"Because he's balking at the idea of us moving in together!" she replied crossly.

The individual in question was Kieran O'Malley—or, to be more accurate, Trooper O'Malley of the New York State Canine Unit. In addition to being what's traditionally known as a great guy, Kieran also happened to look like a model for men's cologne. He's that cute, with sandy blond hair and eyes as green as a four leaf clover—not to mention a torso so muscular that you frequently find yourself wishing a freak gust of wind would blow the man's shirt right off.

Kieran and Suzanne had met a few weeks earlier, right in my driveway, shortly after I'd signed on with the canine unit to provide medical care. The dogs lived with their human partners—which meant that at this point, the only person Kieran shared his place with was a crime-fighting German shepherd named Skittles.

"But Suzanne!" I protested. "You and Kieran have only been going out for a few weeks!"

"Exactly!" she cried, ignoring my use of the word

"only." "Which is plenty of time for two people to recognize that they belong together."

This seemed like a good time to exercise a little diplomacy. "I don't doubt that," I told her. "But that doesn't necessarily mean you two soul mates have to live under the same roof, does it?"

"Why wouldn't we want to spend every possible moment together?" she countered. "Drinking our nonfat lattes every morning, taking out the recycling, shopping for milk and laundry soap and toilet paper..."

I guess everyone has their own idea of romance, I thought.

"I'm not sure I agree with you on this, Suzanne," I said warily. "If you ask me, you're moving kind of fast."

"I know my heart," she insisted. "And I have to follow it."

I didn't bother to mention that the last time she'd followed her heart, she ended up dating an acquaintance of mine, a fellow veterinarian named Marcus Scruggs, who could best be characterized as unsavory. As a result of that heart-following episode, her heart had gotten dragged along a road that was so filled with potholes that by the time it was over, she practically needed a cardiologist to fix it.

The time before, that same heart of hers had weathered a devastating divorce. One more experience that was, for lack of a better word, heartbreaking.

"But it seems to me there are some serious logistical issues to consider, too," I pointed out. "For one thing, you and Kieran live something like thirty miles apart."

"Thirty-three point five!" she corrected me, her voice triumphant. "Which gives him and me all the more reason to live in the same place! Just think about all the problems that causes. Expenses, too. Once you start calculating the cost of gas, not to mention the wear and tear on both our cars ... Then there's the wear and tear on each of us as we travel back and forth. And another thing: Do you have any idea how complicated it is keeping my place and Kieran's stocked with two sets of makeup, two boxes of my favorite breakfast cereal, two drawers filled with sexy lingerie—"

"Suzanne!" I interrupted, not wanting to hear any more, "all I'm saying is that I think you need to slow down."

"Life is short," she replied. "Carpe diem. Live for today."

Even if that means regretting it tomorrow? I thought.

But I'd given up on arguing. Instead, I marveled over what polar opposites Suzanne and I were. She was rushing into a committed relationship with bull-headed determination. I, meanwhile, had gone so far as to don a wedding dress, have fancy invitations mailed to all my friends, and actually stand in front of a judge wearing a white dress and holding a bouquet. Yet I was *still* dragging my feet about scheduling a do-over.

And now this. Even though I was completely innocent, even though this entire situation was a comedy of errors that was even too ridiculous for a sitcom, in a way I couldn't blame Nick for thinking the worst.

After all, I hadn't done a very good job of letting him know that I was totally devoted to him.

Instead, I kept acting as if what I was *really* totally devoted to was staying commitment-free.

After what had just happened, I was beginning to wonder if I'd ever be able to convince him otherwise.

• • •

As I drove into the Worth School parking lot early the next morning, I had a strong sense of déjà vu. It had been only six days earlier that I'd been enveloped by the same feelings of doom and gloom as I'd tried to gear up to teach a class. And the reason had been exactly the same: problems in my relationship with Nick.

But there was one major difference. Last time, I was upset because Nick and I had had an argument about choosing a date for our second wedding. This time, I was a thousand times *more* upset—mainly because I might have botched things up for good.

As I headed toward the Planet Earth building, wondering if it might be possible to move to a different planet, I kept my head down. Given the way I was feeling, merely looking around at the luxurious campus, especially on such a beautiful June day, was simply too unsettling.

So it wasn't until I'd nearly reached my destination that I glanced up and noticed that a crowd had gathered outside the Student Life Community Center. Confused, I surveyed the students, teachers, and administrators who were clustered together on the grass, wondering if I'd missed the memo about a fire drill.

Then I spotted two uniformed police officers.

"What the—?" I exclaimed.

I broke into a jog, meanwhile studying the group more carefully to see if it included anyone I recognized. I spotted quite a few of the students who were taking my animal-care course, then realized that that was probably because my class was one of the few summer school offerings that met this early in the day.

The only other face I recognized was Dr. Goodfellow's. At the moment, she was deeply engrossed in her conversation with the two cops, one of whom appeared to be taking notes on what she was telling him.

As I drew near, I saw that Campbell and Beanie were also part of the group. The two of them stood at the edge, whispering to each other. I headed over to them, figuring that if anyone was likely to know what was going on, it was those two.

"What happened?" I asked them breathlessly.

"Vandalism!" Beanie sputtered.

My mouth dropped open. I don't know what kind of response I was expecting, but it certainly wasn't that.

"I know!" Beanie agreed, her voice practically a shriek. "Do you believe that something like that could go on *here,* of all places?"

"They think it happened over the weekend," Campbell added, sounding just as upset.

"What got vandalized?" My eyes traveled to the building in front of us. From the looks of things, its exterior was completely intact.

"The student art exhibit," Campbell replied

mournfully. It was only then that I noticed her face was tense and blotched with red, as if she was on the verge of bursting into tears. "Some idiot destroyed everything—including my watercolor of two bunnies! It took hours to paint! And Mr. Stibbins said it was the best thing I'd ever done!"

"What about my mixed media wall hanging?" Beanie demanded. "Whoever did this cut it to ribbons! All that work—and all that time I spent collecting beads and buttons and everything else I put on it!"

My heart had begun to pound so hard that I felt dizzy. "I'm so sorry you lost some of your artwork," I told them sincerely. "Especially since I can see you both put a lot of effort into those pieces."

Thinking out loud, I added, "But who would *do* something like that?"

Even more important, I was wondering, could this act of aggression have anything to do with the murder of Nathaniel Stibbins—the man who Dr. Goodfellow claimed the exhibit honored?

"I have no idea," Campbell replied bitterly. "But I sure hope the cops figure it out."

My eyes automatically drifted back to the two police officers, who were still conferring with Dr. Goodfellow. From where we were standing, I couldn't hear what any of them were saying. But that didn't keep me from watching them, hoping their body language might tell me something.

So my eyes were glued to the three of them as the second cop, the one who wasn't taking notes, lifted his hand. I saw that he was holding a clear plastic Ziploc bag, the kind I knew was routinely used for storing evidence.

He suddenly raised his hand higher, as if to emphasize something he was saying.

When he did, I got of glimpse of what was inside the bag: a green and black beaded bracelet.

Chapter 13

That bracelet!" I cried without thinking. "What are the police doing with it?"

Beanie looked over in the cops' direction, squinting in the early morning sunlight. A look of horror immediately spread across her face.

"Oh my gosh," she said in a low voice. "I know whose bracelet that is!"

"That's Vondra's!" Campbell exclaimed. "She's the only person at this school who'd wear anything that tacky!"

"It's not supposed to be stylish," Beanie declared. "It has something to do with that weird religion of hers."

Campbell's eyes widened. "Voodoo, right?"

"What are you girls talking about?" I demanded. I couldn't understand why we were suddenly talking about voodoo, of all things.

"Vondra's religion," Beanie replied matter-of-factly. "Santeria. It's *like* voodoo, but it's not exactly the same." Grimacing, she added, "I got stuck sitting next to her at an assembly one time and she talked my ear off about it."

I was too dumbfounded to say anything. I'd heard of Santeria, of course. But I knew practically nothing about it—including whether or not it had anything even remotely to do with voodoo.

Puzzled, I mused, "But why on earth would Vondra get involved in something like Santeria?"

"Her family originally came from Cuba," Beanie replied. "That's where that creepy religion got started in the first place. I think it was, like, hundreds of years ago." She clearly relished the role of expert witness. "Her mother lived in Miami before she moved up here. At least, that's what Vondra told me."

"I heard her mother is some kind of high priestess or something," Campbell interjected. "Isn't that the most bizarre thing you ever heard in your life?"

"I heard that, too," Beanie agreed. "And boy, if you ever saw her, you'd believe it. If you think Vondra dresses funny, you should see her mom!"

I had seen Vondra's mother, of course. And as much as I hated to admit it, she did dress in a way that made her look distinctively different from everyone else.

"Somebody told me she runs this really bizarre shop right out of her house," Beanie continued breathlessly. "She sells crazy stuff like strange herbs that are used in secret ceremonies and special candles and—

and even these doll things that sound an awful lot like voodoo dolls."

"Eww!" Campbell cried.

"Exactly," Beanie agreed, nodding. "If you ask me, the whole family is totally out there. Not to mention that it's probably also illegal to sell magic potions. Especially since we can only imagine what's in them!"

She glanced around, as if wanting to make sure no one was listening. Lowering her voice to a hoarse whisper, she added, "But I know something about Vondra's mother that's even worse."

"What?" Campbell demanded breathlessly.

"She killed somebody!"

"You can't be serious!" I exclaimed.

Beanie shrugged. "I'm just telling you what I heard. Supposedly it happened back when she still lived in Miami."

Her eyes grew as big and wide as an owl's as she said, "They say she burned the guy's house down—with him in it!"

"Beanie, that's ridiculous!" I cried. My blood was starting to boil at such an outrageous claim.

"No, it's not," Beanie insisted stubbornly. "It was part of a Santeria ritual. That crazy religion is full of them. Its followers actually worship some god of fire or something. I think Vondra's mother was making a sacrifice. A *human* sacrifice!"

With a satisfied nod, she added, "That's why she had to move up here. She was running from the law!"

"That's quite an accusation," I told her, struggling

to keep my voice even. "Especially since it doesn't sound as if it could possibly be true."

"Oh, it's true, all right," Beanie declared.

"Beanie knows everything," Campbell agreed. "She has ways of finding out all kinds of stuff."

"In that case," I said coldly, still hoping to dissuade Beanie from spreading dangerous rumors, "can you tell me anything specific? Who she allegedly killed, when it happened, what the circumstances supposedly were—"

"Like I said, all I know is that it had something to do with that creepy religion of theirs," Beanie concluded with a shrug. "Who knows? Maybe she even killed poor Mr. Stibbins!"

"Beanie, you really have to be more careful about what you go around saying about people," I warned.

"I know what I heard." Gesturing toward the police officer holding the Ziploc bag, Beanie added, "And I know what I see."

I could tell that nothing I said was going to change her mind. Besides, this was hardly the time and place to attempt to have a reasonable discussion.

So it was just as well that the note-taking police officer suddenly turned to face the crowd.

"All right, everybody, show's over," he announced. "Let's clear the area. Go on back to your classrooms or wherever you're supposed to be."

Dr. Goodfellow came up beside him. "Even though we're running late, we'll continue with our usual schedule for today," she told the crowd. "Please go to your nine o'clock classes immediately. I know you're all anxious to find out more about what happened, and I promise the school will issue a report on the status of the investigation as soon as we have more information."

That was fine with me. I suddenly wanted nothing more than to get the heck out of there as quickly as I could.

And I wasn't sure what I found more disturbing: the act of vandalism that had targeted an exhibit dedicated to the man who had recently been murdered—or the vicious comments Beanie had made about Vondra and her mother.

Those claims of hers are utterly absurd, I told myself as I walked toward the Planet Earth building with Beanie and Campbell trailing a few feet behind me, deep in conversation. Honestly, how likely is it that Vondra's mother killed someone in Miami and then ran away to New York to hide from the law? It all sounds like the fabrication of an overactive adolescent mind—or even worse, ugly rumors that a bunch of stuck-up high school students constructed as a way of making sure a girl who was just a little bit different from them would remain outside their exclusive circle.

As for the idea that Vondra had had anything to do with this senseless act of vandalism, I found that just as hard to believe.

I felt like a robot as I taught that morning's class. It was a good thing I was as familiar as I was with the day's topic—the importance of caring for a pet's teeth. To borrow a phrase from one of Nick's favorite classic rock hits, I felt as if I was running on empty. The commotion at the school, lumped on top of the horrible scene the night before that had resulted in Nick walking out on me, had reduced me to a state that was about half a rung up from complete zombie-hood.

After class, I remained in a fog as I headed toward the administration building. Before leaving campus, I wanted to check my mailbox. Even though only an hour had passed since the cops had arrived on the scene, I hoped that Dr. Goodfellow had issued a statement about the vandalism incident—hopefully, one that included information about who the real culprit had been.

As I peered into my mailbox, it appeared that all that was stuffed inside was the usual assortment of notices. I riffled through the stack, a wave of disappointment washing over me.

It wasn't until I reached the bottom of the pile that I saw the official-looking letter with the Worth School emblem on top and Elspeth Goodfellow's signature at the bottom.

So Dr. Goodfellow *did* issue something this morning, I thought, glancing at the date printed on it. I began to read, expecting the sheet of paper to contain information about the destruction of the student art exhibit.

Instead, the first sentence made me freeze.

"Effective today," it read, "Vondra Garcia has withdrawn from the Worth School."

• • •

I felt as if someone had just delivered a swift kick to my solar plexus.

Could Beanie possibly have been right about Vondra? I thought, my head spinning. And could I have been so *wrong*?

Even though my brief interactions with Vondra had made it clear that she harbored some bitter feelings toward her classmates, she had struck me as someone who was basically levelheaded. I found it impossible to imagine her doing anything as outrageous as committing an act of vandalism.

I suddenly wanted to know more about her. And the religion that appeared to be a tremendous influence in her life struck me as a very good place to start.

The moment I got into my van, I pulled out my cellphone. After scrolling through the address book, I pressed the keys required to get Sunny on the line.

After all, she'd told me herself how interested she was in helping with the murder investigation, however she could.

"Hey, Jessie," she greeted me. "I've been entering your billing for the entire year into that cool new program. I'm just finishing up March."

"That's great!" I told her. I marveled at her efficiency, especially when it came to completing tasks I dreaded so much I'd have preferred getting a Brazilian bikini wax to confronting them. "But I have something a little different that I'd like you to do. If you're willing, that is."

"Shoot."

"Remember when you offered to help me with the murder investigation I got roped into?"

"Are you kidding?" she cried. "I'll do anything! A

stakeout or going through somebody's trash or anything at all that involves a car chase..."

"I'm afraid the task I have in mind doesn't involve anything more reckless than sitting in front of a computer," I admitted.

She was silent, but only for a moment. "I'm pretty good at that," she said. "What do you want me to do?"

"I'd like you to learn whatever you can about a religion called Santeria. That's S-A-N-T-E–"

"I know how to spell it," she interrupted. "I also know enough about its reputation that you've made me really curious. Are you going to tell me what this is for?"

"Not right now," I replied, glancing at my watch. "But it's only because I've got to run if I'm going to get to my next appointment on time. But I have a feeling this assignment will be pretty easy."

It turned out I was right. I found that out as soon I took a break for lunch and called Sunny again.

"Did you have a chance to find out anything about Santeria?" I asked.

"Did I!" she replied enthusiastically. "And boy, is it interesting!"

I didn't doubt that for a moment. But I found myself hoping that "interesting" didn't translate to "sinister"—or, to use Beanie's word, "creepy."

"Santeria originated in Cuba," Sunny began. "But its roots lie in an African religion called Yoruba that was practiced by the slaves who were brought to the New World—the Caribbean, mostly—to work in the sugar plantations. It's an earth religion, meaning it centers around nature. Yoruba is the basis for religions like Candomblé, which is practiced in Brazil, and voodoo, which comes from Haiti."

My mouth was suddenly strangely dry. I'd never even heard of Candomblé. As for voodoo, I hardly knew anything about it aside from what I'd seen in the movies or read in novels. The problem was that the way in which voodoo and similar religions were usually portrayed wasn't generally in the most favorable light.

"Anyway," Sunny went on, "when slaves were brought from Africa to the Caribbean, which started in the 1500s, they were baptized as soon as they arrived. That meant they were supposed to leave their old religion behind and become Christians. But they found a way to hold on to their old beliefs. They realized there were parallels between the gods they believed in and the saints the Catholics taught them about. So they cleverly combined them so they could appear to be practicing Christianity even though they were really holding on to their old beliefs. In fact, they believed that at midnight, the Catholic saints turned into the Santeria gods."

"So they found a way to merge the two," I observed.

"Pretty much," Sunny said. "The word Santeria actually means 'the way of the saints.' Followers worship a principle god, called Olodumare or Olofin. The worship of ancestors comes next. Then come the orishas, the lesser gods that have been merged with the saints. They have names like Elegua, Yemaya, Oshun . . . Hey, there's even one named Babalu, who's Saint Lazarus's counterpart. Remember how on the TV show *I Love Lucy* Ricky Ricardo, who was Cuban, was always singing 'Ba-ba-lu'? Now I know where that comes from."

And now I know where Vondra's cat's name comes from, too, I thought. I had to admit that I found the information a bit unsettling.

"The orishas are actually pretty cool," Sunny commented. "They all have specific colors and numbers associated with them. Different herbs and foods, too. And people often set up shrines for the different orishas in their homes." She sounded as if she was reading—off a computer screen, no doubt. "For example, one of the orishas is Chango. He's the god of war and thunder and fire—"

"The god of fire?" I interrupted. Beanie's allegation about Vondra's mother killing someone by setting his house on fire was suddenly ringing in my ears. "That sounds kind of ominous."

"I guess it ties into Santeria being an earth religion," Sunny said.

I could see the connection. But that didn't do much to make the sudden gnawing in my stomach go away.

"Anyway," she continued, "Chango is based on Santa Barbara. His day of the week is Friday and his number is six. He's got some animals associated with him, too. Pigs, goats, and roosters...Also foods, like cornmeal and plantains and apples. Wait—there are plants and herbs, too. Pine, cinnamon, mugwort...

"Apparently each person who practices Santeria is guided by one particular orisha," Sunny went on.

"Someone who wants to adopt the religion has a reading that's done by elders who become that person's godparents. To do the reading, they use cowrie shells, which are used as currency in Africa. The reading tells them which orisha guards them."

"Sounds like a guardian angel," I noted.

"I was thinking that, too," Sunny agreed. "Once people know who their orisha is, they wear a special bracelet. The bracelet has a name...wait, here it is. An *eleke* or a *collares*. See, in addition to foods and animals, each orisha also has different colors associated with it. Different combinations of those colors, too, which are used in the bracelets."

"Like green and black?" I asked, immediately thinking about Vondra's choice of jewelry.

"Let's see...Here we go. Green and black are the color of Ogun—I hope I'm pronouncing that right—who's also St. Peter.

"But I found more about the way followers of Santeria dress," Sunny continued. "They usually wear the color white, which is believed to ward off evil. And even though they wear the bracelet signifying their particular orisha on their wrist, they can also wear necklaces that symbolize other orishas.

"There are some interesting ceremonies, too," she added. "A lot of them incorporate movement, especially dance, along with drumming. Cigar smoke might be blown into the air as an offering or to fight off evil spirits. Alcohol can be spat out for the same purpose. Sometimes, for extreme situations like a serious illness or death, animals—usually chickens—are sacrificed. But the priests are trained to perform the sacrifice in a humane fashion, and afterward the chicken is cooked and eaten."

Now that she mentioned it, I remembered reading about a case concerning that very subject that had been in the news in the early 1990s. The Supreme Court had ruled that laws that specifically targeted Santeria's religious practices were unconstitutional.

Still, that didn't make me any more comfortable with everything I was hearing.

"Let's see what else . . ." I could hear Sunny's fingers clicking against the keys of her laptop. "The priests are called *Santeros* and the priestesses are called *Santeras*. There are no books, so the people who follow Santeria have to learn everything they need to know orally. And apparently healing plays a large role."

"Healing?" I repeated, not sure I understood.

"That's right. Herbs and potions are used in healing rituals, along with other things like prayer beads and charms. All that stuff is sold in special stores called botanicas."

Once again, I thought back to my conversation with Beanie. She had claimed that Vondra's mother ran a shop out of her house that sounded an awful lot like one of those botanicas.

Is it possible that some of the crazy stuff Beanie said was actually correct? I wondered, still not wanting to believe it.

"There's one more interesting thing I read about," Sunny said.

"What's that?" I asked.

"Apparently secrecy plays a big part in the religion," she replied. "There's certain information about the beliefs and rituals of Santeria that no one's allowed to know about. At least, not unless they've been initiated into the religion."

More secrecy, I thought with chagrin. Just what I need.

I only hoped the veil of secrecy that surrounded Santeria wouldn't turn out to be so thick that it got in the way of me seeing the truth—and solving this mystery once and for all.

• • •

Finding Vondra's address was a simple matter of checking the class list Ms. Greer had put together, which I'd gotten in the habit of carrying with me. Next I pored over my Hagstrom map, not only locating her house but also plotting out the best way of getting there.

The Garcias lived at 49 Jefferson Road in Wyandogue, a town on the south shore that was known as one of Long Island's rougher communities. The residents were generally low-income families, a fact that was sadly reflected in the quality of the district's schools.

No wonder Mrs. Garcia was so anxious for her daughter to go to the Worth School, I thought, even though getting there every morning was a commuting nightmare.

Which made the fact that Vondra was no longer a student there all the more disturbing.

Once I reached the exit I was looking for, I turned

off the Long Island Expressway—my second home, if it's possible to think of a 70-mile road that's almost perfectly straight and almost perfectly level as anything that warm and fuzzy. Thanks to all the miles I routinely logged as part of my job, I knew the south shore as well as any other part of the island.

In fact, I was familiar with most of the streets I drove along, at least until I got closer to Wyandogue. I couldn't recall ever having had a client there. The streets I traveled on were lined with the usual Long Island tract houses, although most were on the modest side, small and boxy and nondescript, generally with only courtyard-size lawns. Still, they were maintained fairly well, aside from all the plastic tricycles, inflatable pools, and slides that seemed to have sprung up around them like garishly-colored flowers.

But when I turned onto Jefferson Road, the landscape changed dramatically. Instead of a nicely paved road, I was now driving on one that was splattered with potholes. There were no curbs, either. Instead, patchy, weed-covered grass meandered along the edge of the street, giving the landscape an unkempt appearance.

But it was the change in the houses that really struck me. Instead of each one being identical to the next, as if some enterprising developer had turned out one after another with the precision of a cookie cutter–wielding baker, here every house was different. Not that they were anywhere close to pleasing to the eye. Rather than creating an individualistic look, these tiny houses looked as if they might have been constructed, at least in part, by the homeowners themselves. Walls seemed to be at odd angles, and windows and doors were slightly off-center. Some of the porches sagged so badly they looked as if a single decent-size gust of wind could reduce them to a pile of sticks. Practically all of them could have used a coat of paint, while some even had broken windows.

"Welcome to Wyandogue," I muttered.

Number 49, Vondra's house, was located at the very end of the street. Like the others in the neighborhood, it was basically nondescript, aside from its poor state of repair. The tiny, flat-roofed bungalow was covered in shabby white shingles, and the windows were bare except for a few that had white fabric that looked like bedsheets draped over them. Whether that was to keep whoever was inside from looking out or to prevent people on the outside from looking in, I couldn't say.

Before getting out, I drove by the mailbox and checked to make sure I had the right place. Sure enough, the name Garcia had been handwritten on the pitted metal surface with what looked like a permanent marker.

I parked my van in front, then warily crossed the stubby crabgrass-covered lawn. As I knocked on the door, once again the word "creepy" popped into my head.

In fact, I found myself hoping that no one would answer the door, at least until I reminded myself why

I'd come. And that my interest in furthering my investigation of Nathaniel's death was equaled by my concern about Vondra.

I inhaled sharply when a tall, heavyset woman with smooth, flawless skin the color of rich dark chocolate answered. She was dressed completely in white, with a row of red-and-black beaded bracelets encircling one arm. I immediately recognized her as the woman I'd spotted at the PTA meeting, even though this time her hair was concealed by the white turban wrapped tightly around her head. Gliding against her leg was a large black cat, his glowing green eyes fixed on me in a most disconcerting way.

The woman folded her arms across her abundant chest. As she did, her eyes burned into mine like two coals so intense they seemed capable of raising blisters.

"Good morning!" I said brightly, flashing a smile. "You must be Mrs. Garcia. I'm looking for Vondra."

My smile wasn't returned.

"Vondra is not here," she replied, her words tinged with just a hint of an accent. Raising her chin slightly but still looking me up and down, she asked, "Who are you?"

"My name is Jessica Popper," I replied politely. I noticed that Babalu had retreated behind her long white skirt, but that he continued to peer out at me from behind its abundant folds. "I teach the animal-care class at the Worth School. That's where I met your daughter. In fact, I'm pretty sure I saw you at the PTA meeting last week."

The woman's dark eyes narrowed. "Vondra does not go to that school anymore."

Which is mainly why I'm here, I thought. But my instincts told me that this was one of those occasions when the direct approach wasn't necessarily the best.

"Yes, I know. But when Vondra was still a student there, I remember her mentioning that you were..." I faltered, searching for the right words. "...good at helping people with their problems."

Somehow, I couldn't bring myself to say, "I heard you were a Santeria priestess." At least not without feeling like an actor in a really bad horror movie.

"What kind of problems?" she demanded, eyeing me skeptically. Her arms were still folded firmly across her chest, giving me the feeling she wasn't exactly warming up to me.

I took a deep breath. "Mrs. Garcia, I'm having problems with my love life."

She reacted as if a muscle relaxant had suddenly kicked in. All the muscles in her face lost their tightness as her expression instantly changed from guarded to sympathetic. Not only did she unfold her plump arms; she extended them toward me as if she was about to smother me in a giant hug.

"We've all been there," she said in a soothing voice. "Come in, child. And please, call me Serena."

I followed her into the house, mildly dazed over the fact that I'd somehow managed to say the magic words. I guess Babalu picked up on her acceptance of me, since he trotted along beside me as if I was his new best friend.

I expected the living room to be outfitted with

the usual couch, chairs, and TV. So I was surprised to find that the only furniture was a folding bridge table with three mismatched metal chairs. The wooden floor was bare, and the windows turned out to be the ones that were draped with bedsheets. The afternoon sun peeked in through the open spaces, but instead of cheering things up, the haphazard arrangement of the fabric cast oddly shaped shadows over the room.

Long shelves that ran nearly to the ceiling lined two of the walls. But rather than containing books, they were crowded with an odd assortment of items: sticks of incense, glass jars containing feathers and colorful beads, packets of herbs, and a wide variety of small stones and seashells.

Some of the shells and stones had been fashioned into amulets. There were other necklaces, as well, some made of beads and some adorned with charms, including an anchor, a sword, and a broom. But some had more unusual shapes—like a human arm or a coffin.

There were also plenty of candles. Some were in narrow glass cylinders decorated with what looked like pictures of saints, while others were black, red, or white wax molded into the shape of a man or woman. Wooden masks, most with frightening expressions, were lined up along the back of one shelf.

I also noticed bars of different-colored soaps stacked up. A red one that was facing me had a label that said, "Come to Me Soap." A handwritten label stuck on top read, "Used to attract members of the opposite sex."

Next to those were powders, with labels reading "Money Powder" and "Lucky Lotto Powder." There were also clear plastic bottles, one filled with a green liquid billed as "Cast-Off Evil" oil and one with a bright red label that said, "Jinx Remover," complete with a picture of a scary-looking mask.

I also noticed stacks of bracelets, the exact same kind that both Vondra and Serena wore.

A Santeria botanica, I thought, just like Beanie said.

But the real focus of the room was the colorful table in the back corner of the room. It, too, was covered with an unusual collection of items. Lined up was a row of small figurines that appeared to be fairly well crafted. Some looked like Catholic saints, with golden hair, angelic expressions, and crowns or gold-flecked wings. Others looked like African gods, their dark skin ornamented with shiny jewelry.

Interspersed among the figurines were numerous candles, as well as what looked like seven glasses of water.

"What *is* all this?" I blurted out before I had a chance to compose the question in a more diplomatic way.

"A *bóveda*." Serena replied. "What you would call an altar. It honors my ancestors as well as the orishas —spirits or gods."

"What are those glasses of water for?" I asked.

"The glasses are symbols of the spirits who protect Vondra and me and all the other members of our family," she said. "You can see that there are seven of them. That's because seven is the number of Yemaya, one of the orishas —or gods—who has a close connection to the spirit world.

"Each glass of water honors someone different, someone with whom we all share the same sacred energies," she went on. "One is dedicated to our guardian angels, one to our relatives, one to our loved ones, and one to the unknown spirits. But they also honor the spirit energies of different peoples who helped create our cultural identity—namely, the Yorubas, the Kongos, and the Native Americans."

I was glad Sunny had filled me in on some of this. Otherwise, I would have been totally mystified by the words coming out of her mouth.

"And the flowers?" I asked. "Are they just decorative, or do they have a special meaning, too?"

"The flowers stand for nature and the forces of life."

"What about these figurines?" I asked. "Do they signify special people?"

"Very special," Serena replied patiently. "Each one signifies a different orisha who came from Africa hundreds of years ago and entered the souls of those who were sold into slavery."

I watched carefully as she picked up a figurine with dark skin and a red and black dress—the same colors of the beads in her bracelets. "This may look like an African woman, but it symbolizes a warrior orisha named Chango, the god of thunder and lightning—as well as the god of fire."

My eyes automatically traveled to her red-and-black bracelets as I made the connection: Chango, the god of fire, was Serena's orisha.

"This also represents a Catholic saint, Santa Barbara," Serena went on, not seeming to notice my sudden discomfort. "The crown and the sword are symbols of both Santa Barbara and Chango."

But before I had a chance to ask any more questions, Serena took my hand and said, "But I think you are most interested in what the orishas can do for you. Tell me about the problems you are having with your love life."

For a few seconds, I was tongue-tied. And it was for reasons that had nothing to do with Santeria or fire or Nathaniel Stibbins.

The pathetic state of my love life was simply the excuse I'd used to get my foot in the door. But now that she'd invited me to talk about that very subject, it turned out I had plenty to say. In fact, before I could stop myself, I was positively pouring my heart out to the woman.

As I told her my entire history with Nick, Babalu lay quietly at my feet as if he was as used to listening to people's tales of woe as Serena was. I ended mine with the sorry state our relationship was in at the moment, thanks to Nick stumbling upon Forrester and me and completely misinterpreting what he saw. I left out the part about my disastrous wedding, since I didn't see how I could possibly explain that it had gotten canceled without mentioning Nathaniel's murder.

Which, after all, was the main reason I was here.

"I see," Serena finally said once I'd finished. I was relieved that she showed absolutely no sign of judging me. "I think I know what you need to do. I'll get you everything that is required for what in Santeria is called the love magnet spell."

A love magnet spell sounds like something Suzanne would definitely be in favor of, I thought as I watched her go over to the shelves. Thoughtfully she began picking out one item after another.

"Let me see," she muttered. "Love Drawing Fragrance Coil, a candle with a love amulet, a set of male and female magnets...oh, and of course a mojo bag..."

A mojo bag? I thought, suddenly remembering where I was. What have I gotten myself into?

Fortunately, Serena decided to give me the love magnet spell supplies to go. Personally, I generally prefer casting spells in the privacy of my own home.

"I've included the instructions," she told me, handing me an ordinary plastic bag filled with everything she'd chosen for me. "Be sure to follow every step."

"I will," I assured her. For a second, I even considered actually doing it. After all, I figured, it couldn't hurt. "And thank you, Serena. I'm sure this is just what I need."

As I paid her, I realized it was getting to be time for me to make my exit—which meant I would do well to try to accomplish what I'd really come here to do.

After reaching the front door, I turned back to her. By that point, she'd picked up Babalu and was cradling him in her arms.

Studying her carefully to gauge her reaction, I said, "By the way, did you hear about the vandalism at the Worth School?"

Serena stiffened. "What are you talking about, child?" she demanded.

I hesitated. "Over the weekend, somebody broke into the Student Life Community Center and destroyed all the student artwork that was on display. The exhibit was the same one Dr. Goodfellow made an announcement about the night of the PTA meeting."

"Oh my!" she cried. "What a terrible thing! Do they have any idea who was responsible for such a monstrous thing?"

"No." I was silent for a few seconds. I hated being the bearer of bad news, but at this point it seemed I had no choice but to continue. "But it seems the police found a bracelet amid the wreckage." I took a deep breath before adding, "It was made of green and black beads, like the bracelets Vondra wears."

"Many people wear those bracelets!" she exclaimed. "Not only my daughter!"

By that point, her agitation had even upset Babalu, who leaped out of her arms and withdrew to the back corner of the room.

"Besides, it is impossible that the one found nearby was Vondra's!" Serena cried. "My daughter is not capable of doing something like that. Someone must have planted it there to make her look guilty!"

"I thought of that, too," I told her. I chose not to add that if that was the case, whoever had come up with the idea of making Vondra look like the culprit had certainly done a first-rate job. "But you should probably expect to hear from the police."

Serena's dark eyes blazed. "Just like I thought," she

said through clenched teeth. "The people at that school are vicious. I am not surprised that somebody targeted my daughter. She is different from all those other girls. And it is not only because we are not rich, like their families. It is also because of the way Vondra looks and the way she dresses and the religion she chooses to follow. I am more certain than ever that I did the right thing by taking her out of that place!"

I decided to take a chance. Choosing my words carefully, I said, "There are rumors that the vandalism might have been related to the fact that the art exhibition was in honor of the art teacher, Mr. Stibbins. The man who was murdered."

"Mr. Stibbins," Serena repeated, enunciating each syllable. Her eyes narrowed as she said, "He was the most evil of them all."

My ears perked up. "Why would you say that?"

"Because it is the truth."

"I didn't realize you knew him," I said gently.

"I did not know him, but Vondra did," she replied. "My daughter took an art class with him."

"Did she have a bad experience?"

She stared at me for what felt like a very long time before adding, "Vondra had an argument with him."

My heartbeat quickened. "What did they argue about?"

"An art exhibition," she said, her voice still venomous. "Something he was working on for a long time. I could never get her to tell me the whole story. All I know is that when they disagreed on something about the exhibition, that horrid man actually threatened her."

"Physically?" I cried. "I hope Vondra reported it to the police!"

"It was nothing like that," Serena assured me. "The man was much too clever."

I was growing increasingly uneasy. "Then how did he threaten her?"

Bitterly, she replied, "Mr. Stibbins told Vondra he would find a way to get the school to take away her scholarship."

Serena's words hit me like a slap in the face.

No! I thought as a sick feeling rushed over me like an ocean wave. Is it possible that once again Nathaniel turned his wrath on a helpless scholarship student, someone who was only able to attend a high-quality private school and get a first-rate education because of support from the school?

First Wilhelm or Willard, that scholarship student at Schottsburg Academy. And now Vondra Garcia.

"I don't blame you for being angry," I said evenly. "But if you were concerned about Vondra losing her scholarship and being unable to continue at Worth, why did you end up taking her out of the school anyway?"

The expression on Serena's face was as hard as those stones on the altar. "Because I realized that even though the education those people could provide my daughter with might have been worthwhile, the type of people they were—and the values they held—were not something I wanted her exposed to."

"Serena," I said, keeping my voice as even as I could, "when did this incident with Mr. Stibbins occur?"

"At the end of the term," she replied. "Around the first week of June." She waved her hand vaguely in the air as if the actual timing didn't matter to her.

But it mattered to me. A *lot*.

According to what Serena had just told me, the disagreement that Vondra had had with Nathaniel had occurred just days before he had been murdered.

Chapter 14

"Old age means realizing you will never own all the dogs you wanted to."

—Joe Gores

As I drove away from the Garcias' house, I agonized over the possibility that Vondra could have had something to do with Nathaniel's murder. While the notion was chilling, I realized I had to at least consider the idea that their recent argument about the upcoming art exhibition had made her angry enough to kill him.

I also couldn't completely discount the possibility that her mother might be the killer. According to Serena, there had been bad blood between Vondra and Nathaniel. When it came to protecting their children, mothers often reverted to their animal instincts, turning into lionesses the moment one of their cubs was threatened. Even though I still wasn't buying Beanie's outrageous claims about what had happened in Miami, I felt I had no choice but to add Serena Garcia to my list of suspects.

At this point I was more curious than ever to know why Vondra and the Worth School had parted ways. Had she left because her mother had insisted on pulling her out, as Serena insisted? Or was the reason more ominous? Had Vondra been thrown out—and if so, had the reason been that she'd been legitimately linked to vandalizing the art exhibition?

While I still hadn't found out why she was no longer enrolled at Worth, there was one person who was guaranteed to know. And so first thing after Tuesday morning's class, I made a beeline for the administration building.

"Can I help you?" Ms. Greer asked, peering at me over the eyeglasses roosting on the edge of her nose.

"I have to talk to Dr. Goodfellow," I said brusquely, not bothering to hide the fact that I wasn't in the mood for pleasantries.

Ms. Greer frowned. "I believe she's busy right now, but perhaps you could—"

"I need to speak with her about one of the students," I insisted. "It's an emergency."

"Oh!" A look of alarm flashed across Ms. Greer's face. "In that case, go ahead and knock on her door."

So much for being busy, I thought with irritation.

As I approached her office, I saw that the heavy wooden door was slightly ajar. But since it was only open a couple of inches, I couldn't see inside.

"Dr. Goodfellow?" I called, rapping on the door sharply. "Do you have a moment?"

"Of course," she replied from somewhere within.

Actually, it was more like she said, "Of coursh." At least, that was how it sounded to me.

I told myself I must have heard her wrong because she was inside the room and I was outside. But as soon as I stepped into her office, I realized my ears weren't deceiving me after all.

In addition to the usual pencil mug and stacks of papers, sitting on her desk was the same small crystal glass I'd seen the last time I was in the headmistress's office. And just like last time, it was half-filled with a liquid the same golden color as whatever was in the decanter right next to it.

I automatically checked my watch. It was 10:08. In the morning. The last time I'd checked, ten A.M. hadn't been recognized as the official beginning of cocktail hour.

"Dr. Goodfellow, I need to talk to you about Vondra Garcia," I said, seeing no reason to waste any time. I lowered myself into my usual seat, the red velvet chair directly opposite her desk. "I'm extremely concerned about her leaving the school."

She stared at me blankly. From the glazed look in her eyes, I realized that this morning, cocktail hour had begun way *before* ten o'clock.

I took a deep breath and squared my shoulders. "Vondra was a student in my class," I continued. "Even though I didn't have a chance to get to know her very well, I still can't help feeling involved in her education."

"I appreciate your dedication, Dr. Popper," Dr. Goodfellow said. This time, there was no mistaking the fact that she was slurring her words. She stumbled through "dedication" with as much difficulty as I suspected she'd experience if she actually tried getting up and walking. "But I can assure you that Vondra's departure had nothing to do with you."

I was trying to come up with the best way of getting her to tell me what her departure did have to do with when she picked up her glass.

Staring into it, she mumbled, "The girl had to go, and that's all there was to it."

So Vondra *was* thrown out, I thought. But even more surprising than how forthcoming Dr. Goodfellow had been in announcing this piece of news was the tone of voice in which she'd done it.

Whatever is in that tiny glass must be mighty powerful, I thought.

Dr. Goodfellow seemed to have come to that same realization the moment I did. Plastering on her professional demeanor, she said, "We cannot permit young women who have no respect for our school to remain part of the student body."

"You must be talking about the destruction of the art exhibition," I said somberly. "I understand that something of Vondra's was found at the scene."

She jerked her head up. "How did you know that?"

"I saw the police officer carrying Vondra's bracelet around in a plastic bag," I replied. "Or at least a bracelet that appeared to have been hers."

"What do you mean, 'appeared'?" she asked archly.

"Only that it might not actually have been Vondra's bracelet," I said evenly. "It could have looked like one of hers, but it might not have been identical. And even if it did belong to Vondra, someone could have planted it there. That person could have found one of her bracelets—or stolen it, for that matter. They could even have gone out and bought one, and then planted it at the scene to make Vondra look like the guilty party.

"Besides," I added, still struggling to keep the emotion out of my voice, "it seems to me that Vondra was tried and convicted with amazing speed. Yesterday I saw the cops standing outside the Community Center at nine o'clock, and by ten there were already notices in the faculty mailboxes, stating that Vondra was gone."

Dr. Goodfellow's eyes narrowed. "You have a very active imagination, Dr. Popper. But believe it or not, so do the people who run the Worth School. Don't you think we also thought of all those possibilities?"

From the way her words wavered, it sounded as if she and whoever else had been involved in passing judgment on Vondra hadn't thought of them at all—at least, not until now.

True, it could have simply been the sherry that was making her sound so uncertain. But something about the way she couldn't quite bring herself to look me in the eye, combined with the fact that the art exhibition had been dedicated to a man who had been murdered only days before it was vandalized, made me suspect that something else might be going on.

"Of course Vondra was responsible!" Dr. Goodfellow continued. She was speaking much more loudly than usual, which only emphasized how badly she was slurring her words. "I can assure you that all of us who were involved in seeing that the culprit was caught did everything that was necessary, including involving the police. We certainly shouldn't be blamed for our efficiency! We did what needed to be done. Those of us at the Worth School who are responsible for its good name must be very careful to restrict its students to those of the highest caliber, both academically and morally."

Fury rose in my chest as I listened to her tirade. How about the idea that your decision to throw Vondra out of the school had nothing to do with her character—or the vandalism? I thought angrily. What about the possibility that she knew too much?

Serena Garcia's claim that her daughter had had some kind of disagreement with Nathaniel shortly before he was murdered certainly opened up that line of reasoning. But I knew perfectly well that the more likely it was that there was something else going on between Vondra and Nathaniel—or even Vondra and the school—the less likely it was that the headmistress would give me any indication of what it might have been about.

In other words, I knew a brick wall when I saw one. I also knew that in Dr. Goodfellow's increasingly bloodshot eyes, as far as Vondra Garcia was concerned the case was closed.

Which led me to wonder if one of those aforementioned people who were involved in running the school had passed such severe judgment on Nathaniel Stibbins.

I decided it was time to take a different tack.

I took a few deep breaths, doing my best to calm myself down. And then, in an effort to appease Dr. Goodfellow, I said, "If you're convinced that Vondra was responsible, I suppose it's a good thing that she's gone. Especially since the artwork she destroyed was on display as a way of honoring poor Mr. Stibbins."

"Mr. Stibbins," Dr. Goodfellow repeated, the words coming like a hiss.

My eyebrows shot up to my hairline. True, I'd heard from Claude that the relationship with Elspeth and Nathaniel hadn't quite been the way she'd described it the first time she had spoken about him. But that didn't mean I'd expect her to admit that to me.

"The man never appreciated me," she went on, spitting out her words. "Even when I went against the entire board of directors by choosing him over Claude."

I froze.

Nathaniel had been chosen for something over Claude Molter? This new piece of information set my heart pounding like a jackhammer.

"I'm sorry, Dr. Goodfellow," I said as calmly as I could, given all the construction work going on in my chest, "but I'm afraid I don't know what you mean."

She stared at me in amazement, as if she just assumed everyone in the universe was as involved in Worth School politics as she was. I might have been irritated by her attitude if I wasn't hanging on her every word.

Just because I wasn't in the loop didn't mean I wasn't anxious to be corralled in.

"Why, the job, of course," she said, still acting surprised by my ignorance. "Director of Creativity."

I guess my blank expression made it clear that I still had no idea what she was talking about because she added, "What some schools might call the chair of the arts department."

"I see."

And why was that so desirable? I wondered.

But I'd barely had a chance to think up the question before she added, "It's one of the most highly coveted positions at the Worth School. We truly value the arts here, and so we have a tremendous budget for music and painting and all the other manifestations of the creative process. That means our Director of Creativity holds a lot of power. He makes decisions about what speakers we bring to the school, who we invite to be artists-in-residence, and even which courses we offer. The job also entails deciding which programs our students can get credit for, as well as which girls will be allowed to take advantage of them. Our semester in Florence, for example, studying the art of the Renaissance—or our summer in Vienna, in which students who are interested in music learn about the great classical composers.

"But there's more," Dr. Goodfellow continued. "The Director of Creativity is such a high-profile position here in the Bromptons that it puts whoever plays that role in touch with some of the most powerful people in the New York arts scene. The curators at museums like the Metropolitan and the Guggenheim and the Whitney. Conductors and musicians and even board members at the Metropolitan Opera and the New York City Ballet. Even people from Broadway, not only producers but also directors and actors and set designers and all those other creative minds."

I was beginning to understand. The job of Director

of Creativity not only provided the lucky individual who landed that position with an incredible amount of power within the Worth School. It was also a passport to hobnobbing with the movers and shakers in New York City's culture scene.

Which meant a person who had ambitions of his own could use the position to do some valuable networking.

"So both Nathaniel and Claude were under consideration for Director of Creativity?" I prompted.

"That's right," Dr. Goodfellow replied with a nod. "They had both been here at Worth for about the same length of time, they were both similarly accomplished . . . In the end, it was a judgment call. And even though the board felt strongly that Claude was the more qualified candidate, I dug my heels in." She was back to sounding angry as she hissed, "A lot of good that did me!"

"I'm curious," I said, still trying to sound as if my interest in the Worth School's internal workings was only casual. "How did you manage to sell Nathaniel Stibbins as the better candidate if the board members were so convinced that Claude Molter would have been the better choice?"

Once again, she looked surprised that I'd asked a question with such an obvious answer. "Why, that big New York art exhibition, naturally."

"The one that was scheduled to open in a few weeks?" I struggled to remember the name of the gallery. Fortunately, it was a factoid I'd managed to retain. "The one at the Mildred Judsen Gallery?"

"Of course." Dr. Goodfellow continued to act astonished by my ignorance. "I worked hard to make them understand that the exhibition was guaranteed to launch Nathaniel's career. In the end, they finally saw that I was right."

I was about to ask another probing question when she narrowed her eyes and added, "Not that I ever actually saw any of the paintings he planned to include in the show. No matter how much I pleaded, he simply wouldn't let me. There was a side of Nathaniel that was ridiculously secretive. Frankly, it was something I found hard to take. And it wasn't even because he and I were so...close. Even more, it was because I couldn't help wondering what kind of artist doesn't want to show his work to everyone who's willing to take the time to look at it.

"The gallery just returned them, since they won't be putting on that exhibition after all. I suppose I should take a look at them at some point, but frankly, none of that seems to matter much anymore."

My heart was back to pounding wildly. I was getting an aerobic workout and I wasn't even standing up.

"Why do you think Nathaniel was so secretive?"

Dr. Goodfellow pondered my question, meanwhile pouring herself another glass of sherry.

I watched while she downed it with alarming speed.

"I have no idea," she finally replied, keeping her eyes focused on her glass instead of on me.

After she filled it one more time, I noticed that the bottle was now empty.

"Dr. Popper," she said suddenly, "I believe our business is finished. If you don't mind, I have some important things to attend to."

Like making an emergency run to the liquor store? I wondered cynically.

But I simply nodded, then rose to my feet.

"Thank you for coming in," she said, her eyes clouded and her voice distracted. I had a feeling she was in the habit of saying that every time someone was about to leave her office—no matter what had brought that person there in the first place.

"Thank you for your time," I replied, sounding just as mechanical.

As I left Dr. Goodfellow's office, I was certain there was plenty the sherry-sipping headmistress wasn't telling me.

Yet I had to acknowledge that she'd told me quite a bit—most notably the reason for the break in Nathaniel's friendship with Claude.

Once again, Nathaniel's ambitiousness had reared its head. This time, it appeared to have been at the expense of a friend.

But while the two had suddenly found themselves embroiled in a cutthroat competition, I still didn't have a very good sense of who Claude Molter really was.

Had he been another one of Nathaniel's unfortunate victims, just like that poor scholarship student, Wilhelm or Willard or whatever his name was, who had been thrown out of Schottsburg for a crime that Nathaniel had committed?

Or was the violinist's ambition as ruthless as

Nathaniel's—so much so that it could have even driven him to kill?

* * *

I was glad that Sunny was coming over to the cottage that evening to help me in her ongoing quest to get me organized. And while my original reason for asking her to put in a few extra hours had been to help banish some of the loneliness now that Nick was gone, I now anxiously awaited her visit for another reason.

Given what I'd just learned about the rivalry between the two Worth School teachers, I was more curious about Claude Molter than ever—and she was just the person to delve into his background.

"I've got another job for you," I informed her the moment she showed up on my doorstep. "Something else related to Nathaniel's murder."

Her eyes grew as big as Oreos. "*Now* do I get to go on that stakeout?"

"Sorry. More computer work."

"Whatever," she said with a shrug, sinking into a chair at the dining room table and whipping out her laptop. "It's all for the cause, right?"

"Exactly. Sunny, I'd like you to find out whatever you can about the Worth School's music teacher. I'll tell you everything I already know about him . . ."

Once she'd written down the few facts I related, she asked, "So is this guy a suspect?"

"I'm not sure yet," I replied vaguely, not wanting to influence her research.

"Oh." Picking up on the disappointment in her

tone, I quickly added, "I forgot to mention that he's a count."

"A count? Like in romance novels? And all those movies about English history? Wow!"

"He *may* be a count," I corrected myself, glad that her enthusiasm had returned. "That's one of the things I want you to find out."

I left her to her research while I spent some quality time with my animals. I took Max and Lou outside for a romp, held a petting-fest with my two kitty-cats, and had one of the most interesting conversations I'd had all day with my blue-and-gold macaw. I also checked everyone's water dish and handed out treats like Santa Claus. For a while, at least, it was all good.

When I couldn't wait any longer, I sidled over to Sunny. She was hunched over the computer, the expression on her face anything but triumphant.

"Have you managed to find out anything about Claude Molter?" I asked anxiously.

Sunny frowned. "I thought I was good with computers, but I'm starting to wonder."

"What do you mean?" I asked, puzzled. If there was ever anyone who was meant to be part of the computer age, it was Sunny.

"I keep trying to find something—anything—about a violinist named Claude Molter, but I keep coming up dry. I even tried a bunch of different spellings. I still can't verify anything you told me about his history."

"What happens if you Google 'Claude Molter Prague Symphony Orchestra'?" I asked. Frankly, I was still having a hard time understanding why Sunny was having such difficulty tracking down information about such a prominent musician.

"Why don't I show you?" she offered.

I watched the screen of Sunny's laptop as she typed in those very words, her fingers flying across the keyboard.

"As you can see, plenty of listings come up," she pointed out. "But the only one that links Claude Molter to the Prague Symphony Orchestra is his biography on the Worth School's website."

We must be doing something wrong, I thought with confusion.

"What about Googling 'Count Claude Molter'?" I suggested.

"Same thing."

Once again, Sunny's hands flitted across the keys, and the very words I'd just uttered appeared inside the search box on the Google page. As soon as she hit ENTER, a full page of listings came up. But the only one that referred to anyone named Claude Molter as a count was the music teacher's biography on the Worth School's website—a biography that he had either written himself or someone else had written based on information about his background that he had provided.

"It's almost as if there was no such person as Claude Molter before he joined the Worth School faculty," Sunny observed.

"I don't understand," I said, more to myself than to Sunny. Yet the uncomfortable knot in the pit of my stomach told me that I actually did understand. Perfectly, in fact.

"I found something else that's kind of strange, too," Sunny went on. "There's this guy named Carl Dougherty—"

"Who's that?" I asked anxiously.

"From what I've been able to piece together by looking at different websites, he's someone who grew up in Ohio. I should probably warn you that this is so far out there that it's probably meaningless. But according to information I came across on a bunch of other websites, he sometimes went by the name Claude." Uneasily, she added, "It seems he also had a thing for some composer named Molter."

Her words tightened the knot even further.

"Let me tell you everything I learned about the guy," Sunny went on. "He graduated from high school in a small town called Delaware, the birthplace of Rutherford B. Hayes. You know, the nineteenth president of the United States?"

Personally, I wouldn't have been able to name which president Hayes had been. But he wasn't the person I was interested in at the moment.

"I found a website that was set up a few years ago by some of the school's graduates who were planning a reunion," Sunny continued. "It had a chat room, and I found a bunch of comments written by people who went to school with Carl. It seems that once he hit his junior year or so, he started asking people to call him Claude."

"How do you know that?"

"Here, I can show you." Sunny clicked keys until the chat room she'd mentioned appeared on the screen.

"Hey, does anyone know whatever happened to Carl Dougherty?" someone named CheerleaderForever had written.

A person named LoveMyHarley had written, "You mean CLAUDE Dougherty, don't you? Our junior year, he started telling everybody to stop using his real name and start calling him Claude? LOL. I heard he went to music school somewhere in the Midwest but ended up dropping out."

Someone else, ClevelandColleen, had written, "Remember his obsession with that composer nobody but him had ever heard of? Boy, that was weird. He even dressed like him for a while. I can still picture that crazy white shirt with the billowing sleeves!"

One more student from Rutherford B. Hayes High School, someone known as SoccerDad, had responded with a four-word sentence: "The composer was Molter."

The knot was on the verge of turning into an actual cramp.

"This sounds like it could be our guy," I told Sunny in a strained voice.

"That's kind of what I thought, too," she agreed. "I found out some information about Molter, if you're interested."

If I'm *interested*? I thought. But I merely said, "Sure. What did you find out?"

More flying fingers. "Johann Melchior Molter was a Baroque composer from Germany. He wrote during the 1700s, turning out orchestral music, chamber music, and concertos. He hung out with some of the biggest names from that period, including Vivaldi and

Scarlatti." She paused, meanwhile scanning the screen. "Oh, yeah, I almost forgot. The guy was an accomplished violinist, too."

So much for Sunny's claim that she's not as good with computers as she thought, I mused.

Yet while I was impressed with her skill, I was more focused on the information she'd gleaned from her laptop. In fact, it was making my head spin.

"I could show you what this Carl Dougherty dude looks like," Sunny offered. "Or at least what he looked like when he was eighteen."

"How can you do that?" I asked, growing more impressed with her abilities with every passing second.

"Once I knew where he went to high school," she replied matter-of-factly, "I went to a second website, Classmates.com, and tracked down his yearbook picture. Here, let me find it for you."

I watched as she whizzed through a few more web-pages until she finally located the one she'd been looking for.

"Here he is," she announced.

She hadn't needed to tell me. Staring back at me was what looked like a much younger version of Claude Molter. His hair was darker and shaggier and his skin was as free of creases as a freshly ironed shirt. But a few things hadn't changed at all—most notably, the fire in his eyes and the arrogant tilt of his head.

It was Claude Molter, all right. But in those days, his name had been Carl Dougherty.

And he wasn't from anywhere even close to Belgium. He was a graduate of Rutherford B. Hayes High School in Delaware, Ohio.

"Aside from the guy's yearbook picture, there's not much else here on Classmates.com," Sunny said, her fingers still skimming along the keyboard. "This website wasn't nearly as helpful as the other one. There are just a bunch of postings from people who went to high school around the same time—"

"Wait!" I cried. "Go back!"

"Wha—?" Sunny's dancing fingers had hit a key that had taken the screen away as quickly as it had flashed before my eyes. But in that second or two, I had zeroed in on a name that made my blood run cold.

"Can anybody tell me how to get in touch with the graduate of your high school who became a music teacher at a private school in the New York area?" the posting read.

It was signed Willard Faber.

Chapter 15

"Cats' names are more for human benefit. They give one a certain degree more confidence that the animal belongs to you."

—Alan Ayckbourn

My heart pounded so hard in my chest as I stared at that name on the computer screen that I was certain Sunny could hear it.

Maybe she couldn't, but I guess she could see the look on my face.

"Jessie?" she asked, frowning. "Are you okay?"

"Willard Faber," I read aloud, still peering over her shoulder. Breathlessly, I added, "I think that's him."

"That's *who*?" she demanded.

Even though I could see how puzzled Sunny was, I simply asked, "Do you know how we can we find out more about him?"

"I think so. At least I can try."

I kept my eyes on her laptop as she clicked on the keys and brought up the Google home page. Her fingers flying, she typed in W-I-L-L-A-R-D F-A-B-E-R.

She hit ENTER, and a page full of listings instantly came up.

"How about this website?" I suggested, pointing at one of the URLs that had come up. "Wait—maybe we should try that one."

"You know what?" Sunny said brightly. "Why don't I work on this while you make us both a cup of tea?"

I got the hint. So I dutifully padded into the kitchen, leaving Sunny to work by herself. After all, the last thing I wanted was to turn into Dorothy Burby.

Five minutes later, I returned, this time bearing two mugs of tea.

"Got anything yet?" I asked anxiously.

"As a matter of fact, I do," she replied. "At least I think I found his address. Willard Faber—at least *this* Willard Faber—lives on Long Island. The address I found for him is on Vanderbilt Road in Seawood."

"Wow." As usual, Sunny had worked her magic. "Let me write it down . . ."

I just hope it's the right Willard Faber, I thought the following day as I drove to Seawood. My stomach was doing flip-flops, thanks to a mixture of both apprehension and hope.

This could turn out to be another dead end, I warned myself. Chances are there's more than one Willard Faber in the world. And even if he turns out to be the same one who went to prep school with Nathaniel, that still doesn't mean he'll be able to tell me anything useful.

Or be willing to.

Still, my hopeful side won out as I turned onto the

street that the Willard Faber who Sunny found on the Internet lived on.

Given the fact that his street was named after Vanderbilt, I expected to find a row of mansions. Or at least one of those upscale condominium complexes, the kind that has a gatehouse at the entrance, complete with a living, breathing guard.

Instead, a few hundred yards ahead I spotted a cluster of one-story garden apartments that looked as if they'd seen better days. The three U-shaped buildings were made of red brick interlaced with dingy mortar. The concrete steps that led up to the front doors were cracked and chipped, making them appear to be begging for a makeover. The three courtyards all looked as if the landscaper had specialized in crabgrass and weeds.

If Willard Faber's real estate choices are any indication, life hasn't treated him all that well, I thought grimly as I knocked on his door.

When it opened, I expected to find myself face-to-face with the person who had answered. Instead, I was looking at empty space.

But not for long. It only took me a fraction of a second to realize that making eye contact required looking down.

That was because the man who'd answered the door was in a wheelchair.

It was only then that I noticed that next to the concrete steps was a wooden ramp that connected this particular apartment with the walkway.

"Mr. Faber?" I asked.

"You got 'im," he replied with a friendly smile. The

fact that he had the rounded cheeks and big blue eyes of a toddler made his greeting seem even warmer. "What can I do for you?"

I was pretty sure I detected a trace of a southern accent.

"My name is Jessica Popper," I said. "I'm looking for information about someone you once knew."

His smile flagged considerably. "Are you a cop—or a private detective? I guess what I'm really asking is, is a friend of mine in trouble?"

From what I've heard, I thought, I doubt that you'd characterize Nathaniel Stibbins as a friend.

"To be perfectly honest," I told him, "from what I know of the man's past, I don't think he's someone you were particularly fond of."

"Okay, now I'm intrigued." Willard rolled his wheelchair backward, then gestured for me to enter his apartment. "Come inside and I'll make you a cup of tea. That's what my mama taught me to do."

As I stepped inside, I commented, "From your accent, I would have thought your mama taught you to offer guests a mint julep."

He laughed. "You got me there. So much for my plan to substitute a New York accent for the one I got growing up in Georgia."

Willard Faber's openness was already making me feel relieved. If he had anything to tell me about Nathaniel, I was nearly certain he wouldn't hesitate to share it with me.

Now that I was inside his apartment, I saw that the décor was shabby but comfortable. I supposed the living room furnishings weren't that different from what any middle-aged man living alone would opt for: a large couch covered in what looked like fake brown leather, a coffee table littered with glasses and cups and newspapers, and a huge flat-screen TV.

"Have a seat," he offered. Glancing down, he said, "I hope you don't think I'm rude for sitting before you do."

I smiled as I lowered myself onto the couch. "You don't really have to make me a cup of tea, Mr. Faber. I wouldn't want you to go to any trouble."

"First, please call me Willard," he insisted. "Second, it's no trouble at all, thanks to the handicap-accessible kitchen I had installed when I first moved in here seven years ago. And third, I was about to make myself some tea anyway. Having some company just makes it that much more pleasant."

While he was in the kitchen, I did whatever snooping I could do from a sitting position. A single bedroom jutted off to one side of the living room, and through the open door I could see that the double bed was unmade and the blinds were still drawn. Once again, I wondered if I should feel sorry for this man who obviously lived by himself—or if Willard Faber was just one more single guy with the freedom to keep things exactly the way he liked them.

He certainly seemed like the picture of confidence as he rolled back in, this time bearing a tray with two cups of tea balanced on it. He handed me one and then grabbed the second for himself before finding a place for the tray on the coffee table.

"Nothing like a caffeine fix," he said as he lifted his steaming hot mug to his lips. "This is something I do every day at the same time. Since the accident, I've found that having a little routine in my life helps me get through the days."

"What happened?" I asked gently. "The accident, I mean?"

I found myself hoping desperately that Nathaniel hadn't had anything to do with it.

Gesturing at his wheelchair, he said, "I'm afraid this was the result of my own hubris. A skiing accident." With a wan smile, he added, "As an intermediate-level skier, I should have known better than to think I could handle the north slope of the mountain. Even the friends I was skiing with that day tried to convince me that the trail was too difficult for me. But I'm one of those people who never stopped trying to prove I was as good as everyone else. This time, things didn't go quite the way I'd planned."

"It sounds as if that's not the only time in your life that that's happened," I said gently.

He looked at me quizzically, remaining silent for a few seconds before asking, "Who are you?"

I waited until he had set his mug down on the table before answering. The last thing I wanted was for him to spill hot tea and burn himself.

In an even voice, I replied, "I'm trying to find out whatever I can about Nathaniel Stibbins."

Instantly the expression on his face changed. For a moment, I was afraid he might order me to leave.

Instead, in a controlled voice, he said, "May I ask why?"

I took a deep breath before telling him, "A week and a half ago, Nathaniel was murdered."

"Ah." This time, the look on his face didn't give any indication of what he was thinking—or feeling. "If you're expecting me to gasp and say something like 'How terrible!' or even 'I'm sorry,' I'm afraid that's not going to happen."

"I know about what happened when the two of you were at Schottsburg Academy," I said.

He suddenly looked deflated. "Goodness, if I'd known the conversation was going to go this way, I really would have offered to make us both mint juleps. Or something else with alcohol in it. A *lot* of alcohol."

"I'm sure it's still painful, even after all these years."

"Painful? Yes, I suppose that would be the right word."

For the first time since I'd arrived, I heard bitterness in his voice. "Getting that scholarship to Schottsburg Academy was the best thing that ever happened to me," he said. "It was my ticket out of a childhood that otherwise was guaranteed to go nowhere."

Willard shook his head slowly. "I'm not someone who likes to cast blame on others. But that incident with Nathaniel—well, there was nothing else I could do but blame him. After all, if it hadn't been for him, my whole life would have turned out differently."

"How did it turn out?" I asked. "After you left Schottsburg, I mean."

"I got shipped back to Georgia before I'd had a chance to catch my breath," he replied, still sounding angry. "This time, they didn't pay my train fare, either. I went back to my original high school, which was as crummy as the town I grew up in. The people who actually managed to get jobs worked in the mill a few miles away. The others sat on the front porch all day, feeling sorry for themselves. Do I need to mention that some of them found whatever solace they could in those famous mint juleps—or some variation on the same theme?

"At any rate, simply graduating from high school, even one of such poor quality, was a major event around there. The fact that I was both fairly smart and extremely motivated made me practically a star. My teachers were always telling me I was the best student they'd ever seen come through there. That didn't mean much at first. It wasn't until one of them—my English teacher, Mr. Marlin—encouraged me to apply to Schottsburg and I was offered a full scholarship that I realized they were right.

"And then it all ended—like that." He snapped his fingers. "One Saturday morning, I was lying in bed in my dorm room, trying to decide whether I'd spend the morning studying math or working on a history term paper, when there was this loud knock on the door. A really angry knock. I knew immediately that something was wrong, even before I opened it and found the headmaster himself standing there, looking like he was about to explode.

"What followed was like something out of the Spanish Inquisition," he went on. His eyes had taken on a faraway look, as if he was actually reliving the events he was recalling. "I was hauled into the headmaster's office, where an entire committee was waiting for me. I barely had a chance to say a word. It was more like they told me what had happened—that the night before I'd stolen the school's van, meanwhile wearing some stupid cap I'd taken from Nathaniel so I could try to pin it on him."

"It sounds as if you didn't have much of a chance to defend yourself," I interjected.

"Hah!" he barked. "No one would even listen to my alibi—which three other students were more than willing to vouch for. The four of us had spent all of Friday night playing Scrabble. The board was still set up in the first-floor community room, since it had gotten too late for us to finish our last game."

"Guilty without being tried," I said, thinking aloud. And then I asked, "Couldn't you have applied to some other prep school?"

"An incident like that has a way of following you around forever," he answered. "It's like a tattoo, something you can never get rid of. I hadn't managed to prove my innocence while I was still at Schottsburg, so there was no way I was going to be able to convince anybody else. Especially the board of admissions at some other fancy private school."

"So what did you do?" I asked softly.

"Tried to make a go of it at my old high school," he replied with a shrug. "That lasted a few months. Even though I'd only been at a real school for a short time, I was already painfully aware of the differences.

"Eventually I dropped out. I moved around the country a bit, living here and there and working at whatever jobs I could find. I did manage to earn my GED along the way. Then, when I was nineteen, I joined the army, thinking a stint as a disciplined military man might help me get my life together. Boy, was that ever a miscalculation.

"Since then," Willard continued, "I've pretty much just drifted from place to place, getting jobs that I thought might be interesting but always turned out not to be. I took some college courses, too. Turned out I did pretty well at them, too. But somehow I never figured out what I wanted to do with my life.

"And then," he said with a little shrug, "I ended up here."

His silence told me he was done with his story. And I had to admit that it hadn't added up to much. That is, aside from the fact that he saw what had happened at Schottsburg as his one chance for a better life being ripped out from under him.

Which could be a very strong motive for murder, I thought.

Except for the fact that he was in a wheelchair. I could see for myself how difficult his situation would have made it for him to sneak across the lawn at the estate on which my wedding was taking place, get into the kitchen, and stab Nathaniel with a large knife.

But there was one other loose end I hoped to tie up.

"Willard," I said hesitantly, "there's someone else I wanted to ask you about." I took a deep breath before adding, "Claude Molter—or you might know him as Carl Dougherty. He's a music teacher at the Worth School, the same school where Nathaniel taught."

All the blood drained from his face. "What do you know about that?"

"Nothing, aside from having found your posting on

the Classmates.com website, asking if anyone knew how to get in touch with him."

His eyebrows shot up to his hairline. "My, you have been sniffing around, haven't you?"

"It's kind of a long story," I said. "But I'm basically trying to find the answers to some very confusing questions."

"I only met the man once," Willard said, sounding defensive. "It was at a restaurant. Well, a bar, actually."

"Where?" I asked.

"New York City." He paused. "The Village."

From the way he was answering, I suspected that the establishment in question was in New York's West Village—meaning it was most likely a gay bar.

"Yet you tried to track him down afterward," I observed.

"That's right. As I said, we only had the one conversation. We happened to be sitting next to each other at the bar. We didn't exactly—click, if you know what I mean."

I did.

"Anyway," Willard went on, sounding resigned to telling the whole story, "he mentioned in the course of the requisite small talk that he was from a stifling small town in Ohio. He said the only thing the least bit memorable about it was that it was the birthplace of Rutherford B. Hayes. He went on to say he was now a teacher at a fancy private school somewhere in the New York area. A music teacher. He said the thing that had gotten him out of Ohio was his passion for music.

"Since we were still in the meeting and greeting phase, I made a polite comment about how it must be interesting, teaching at a private school. He said not really, since it was located in what he called a cultural wasteland. He complained that he'd only met one other person he'd connected with, an art teacher. As he talked about the friend he'd made out in the hinterlands, he referred to him as Nathaniel. I jumped on it, since there aren't that many people named Nathaniel these days. Sure enough, it turned out that the man he was talking about was Nathaniel Stibbins.

"I was so shocked that Nathaniel's name had resurfaced after all these years that I didn't know what to make of it. It wasn't until I went home and started to brood that I realized that finding the man at the bar could be a way of finding out about Nathaniel. So I decided to track him down. The problem was, he'd never told me his name. The name of the private school where he taught, either. The only thing I did know, in fact, was where he'd gone to high school."

Shrugging, he said, "So I decided to use the Internet to try to find him. Since I knew about his connection to Rutherford B. Hayes's hometown, I went onto Classmates.com and posted a query, asking if anyone could tell me how I could find him."

"But at that point, couldn't you have just Googled Nathaniel Stibbins's name and found him directly?" I asked. "I'm pretty sure his name would have come up and led you straight to the Worth School's website."

"But I wasn't simply looking for Nathaniel," Willard explained. "There was no way I was going to approach him directly. Believe me, after what happened at Schottsburg, I had no interest in talking to him. But I figured that if I could initiate a relationship—a *friendship*—with the music teacher I'd met at the bar, I'd be able to use him as a source of information. You know, find out how Nathaniel's life had turned out.

"On the surface, it looked as if he was doing just fine," he continued. "Teaching art at a fancy school and all that. But I was hoping there was more to it, that deep down he was miserable. A lifelong disease he had to live with, a history of difficult relationships, something along those lines."

He paused to let out a deep sigh. "But in the end I decided to let it go. I never even followed up with my plan to find the music teacher. There didn't seem to be any point. What's done is done, and every day I try to learn to live with it."

A look of shock suddenly crossed his face. "But you thought I might have murdered him, didn't you? You thought the terrible thing he did to me almost twenty-five years ago had finally caught up with him!"

I couldn't bring myself to lie. "It did cross my mind."

"I suppose I don't blame you," he said, the creases in his forehead deepening. "But from what I know of Nathaniel's character, he undoubtedly angered a lot of other people over the past two and a half decades. If you're trying to find out which one of them finally became furious enough to kill him, it sounds as if you've really got your work cut out for you."

I guess that's what happens with the black sheep of the family, I thought grimly. It's not only his relatives who figure out that he's someone they'd rather not have around.

"Which brings me to the question of how you even found out about me," he added. He picked up his mug once again, keeping his eyes fixed on me as he took another sip.

"A distant relative of Nathaniel's told me about what happened at Schottsburg," I told him. "She remembered your name."

Frowning, Willard asked, "But why was this distant relative even talking to you about Nathaniel in the first place?"

I hesitated before answering. Maybe I haven't always been correct in my judgments of people's character, but Willard Faber struck me as somebody who was exactly who he appeared to be. Which led me to conclude that I could be as honest with him as I believed he was being with me.

"She's my future mother-in-law," I told him. "She asked me to try to find out who killed him."

"Because she was so upset?" he asked dryly.

I cast him a sardonic smile. "Actually, it was because she was afraid having a murder in the family would look bad. She wanted me to make it all go away before too many people found out about something so shameful."

"I see. And how did you locate my address? Or even find out I lived around here?"

With a little shrug, I replied, "Just like you, I have a great appreciation for the magic of the Internet."

"I see," he said with a little smile. "So tell me more about Stibbins getting murdered. I hadn't heard about it, since I try to insulate myself by avoiding newspapers and the news on TV. Who finally gave that son of a—sorry. Who finally gave him what he deserved?"

"That's a question I can't answer," I told him honestly. "But it's precisely what I'm trying to find out."

A heavy silence fell over us both. I filled the lull in the conversation by taking another sip of tea.

As I did, another question occurred to me. "Willard," I asked abruptly, "do you have any idea why Nathaniel stole that van in the first place?"

He looked surprised by my question. "You mean you never heard that part of the story?"

I shook my head.

"To impress a girl," he said. "Not just any girl, either. Daphne Lindner was the prettiest and most popular girl in our class. She was also someone who normally wouldn't have given Stibbins the time of day. Which was all the more reason he was dying to come up with a way of impressing her." With a little shrug, he added, "Taking her on a joy ride was the idea he came up with."

"So she was in the van, too?"

"That's right. Everyone knew about that. Schottsburg was like a small town. No secrets. But after Stibbins wrecked it and was caught red-handed, Daphne's name was never brought into it." The bitterness was back in his voice as, almost as an afterthought, he muttered, "Not that that was any surprise."

"What do you mean?"

"Daphne Lindner's father was one of the school's primary benefactors," he said coldly. "The man had money beyond belief. Powerful connections, too. In fact, even though Daphne was beautiful, her social status was the real reason Stibbins was interested in her."

"You mean he was a social climber?" I asked.

"It's more like he was always determined to make himself more important than he was. He loved hobnobbing with the rich and famous and socially connected. That's why he was trying to impress Daphne in the first place. It's also why there was no way he was going to let himself get in trouble for stealing that van. Being at a place like Schottsburg simply meant too much to him. So he looked for the most obvious stool pigeon, which meant somebody who didn't have a rich father who'd go to bat for him."

"And that turned out to be you," I concluded.

With a sad smile, Willard held up his mug of tea as if he were making a toast. "And the rest, as they say, is history."

• • •

As I drove away from Willard Faber's house, the tragedy of his life filled me with sadness. It was hard to say how things would have turned out for him if that incident with Nathaniel had never occurred and he'd been able to finish his education at a prestigious prep school like Schottsburg.

And while I'd instinctively trusted the man and everything he'd told me, I knew I had to at least consider the possibility that he may have been lying. I still didn't believe he would have been capable of murdering Nathaniel, given where the stabbing had taken place. Not when he was bound to a wheelchair. But his story about his relationship with Claude Molter could have contained inaccuracies. It was something I hoped to check out.

At the moment, I was much more interested in what I'd learned about Nathaniel.

So the man yearned for recognition, especially from the rich and powerful, I thought as I eased onto the Long Island Expressway. And he was willing to go to any lengths to achieve that end—no matter who he hurt or even destroyed in the process.

Now that I knew the details of the incident at Schottsburg, my mind kept drifting back to what Dr. Goodfellow had told me about Nathaniel's recent promotion. From what I could tell, he had taken advantage of her obvious affection for him to snatch the position of Director of Creativity away from his one-time friend, Claude Molter.

I wondered if Claude might be willing to tell me anything more about it.

And so right after Thursday morning's class, I headed straight for the Center for Creative Self-Expression. Just like the last time I'd come looking for him, Claude was making magic with his violin in one of the practice rooms.

Which meant the door was closed—and that once again I was going to have to disturb his practice session.

Still, the alleged musical genius wasn't nearly as intimidating this time around. As I rapped on the door, all I had to do was remind myself that I wasn't interrupting a Belgian count who'd performed with the Prague Symphony Orchestra practically before he'd begun sprouting facial hair. I was simply trying to initiate a conversation with Carl Dougherty of Delaware, Ohio.

He jerked the door open, looking just as cross this time as he had the last time I'd come a-knocking.

"Mr. Molter," I said politely, "I know you're busy, but there's something important I'd like to talk to you about."

"Ye-e-es?" he asked, sounding skeptical about the possibility that I could possibly have anything that was even remotely important to say.

"It's information I need for the memorial service," I continued.

Even though the expression on his face made it clear he wasn't buying that, either, I took advantage of the small gap between him and the doorway to step into the practice room.

"Mind if I come in?" I asked boldly.

Since I was already in, there was nothing he could do but make that sweeping arm gesture that means "please enter."

"I won't take up much of your time," I went on, aware that I was babbling. "I'm trying to find out more about this upcoming art exhibition of Nathaniel's. The one that was scheduled to open at the Mildred Judsen Gallery soon."

When his expression didn't soften, I added, "The one you told me about, remember?" I hoped reminding him that he'd been the one who'd brought it up in the first place would give him a reason to be forthright with me this time around.

"Oh, I remember," he assured me with a cold smile. "How could I forget, when it's something I've been obsessing over ever since I heard about it?"

The word *obsessing* grabbed my interest.

"Why?" I asked, hoping he couldn't hear the thumping of my heart.

"Because Nathaniel didn't deserve it," Claude replied with a sniff. "He was good, but he wasn't *that* good, if you catch my meaning."

"But the people at the Mildred Judsen Gallery must have thought so," I insisted. "After all, they're the ones who make the decisions about which artists to showcase." Then, wondering if perhaps some subtlety of the operations of the art world eluded me, I added, "Aren't they?"

He responded with another condescending smile. Only this one was accompanied by a hard look in his eyes. "Let's just say the people at the Mildred Judsen Gallery know what sells," he said archly, "as well as what's likely to garner them the most publicity."

I frowned. "I'm sorry, but I don't understand what you mean." Maybe it's because you insist on talking in riddles, I thought impatiently.

"How could you understand?" he replied in a lofty tone. "As someone who's not familiar with the intricate workings of the art world, you would have no way of knowing that a gallery like the Mildred Judsen thrives on sensationalism. Or, to use a word that's even more accurate, exploitation."

I just stared at him for a few seconds before asking, "Are you saying there was something exploitative about the paintings Nathaniel planned on showing?"

"To be honest, I've never actually seen them," Claude replied icily. "Nathaniel always made such a big deal about his privacy, especially where his paintings were concerned. He kept them under lock and key, right here in his studio in the arts building. And frankly, that's probably where they'll stay, now that the Mildred Judsen Gallery has sent them back. That is, at least until someone finds his will and figures out what he intended to do with them after he died."

Before I had a chance to ask him about what he'd meant when he'd used words like sensationalism and exploitation, Claude suddenly said in an icy tone, "Dr. Popper, I've noticed that you seem to be unusually interested in Nathaniel Stibbins." He hesitated a few seconds before adding, "I've heard a few other people remark about it, as well."

"Really?" My voice sounded less certain than I would have liked. "I guess I'm just curious. I mean, I'd barely started working here at Worth when I found out that one of the teachers was recently—"

"But you're not working here," he interrupted me. "You volunteered."

I raised my chin higher in the air. "Yes, that's right. I wanted to share what I know about animal care."

His lips twisted into a sneer. "I've heard of do-gooders wanting to work with the underprivileged," he said, "but I must say that I've never heard of anyone going out of her way to work with the *privileged*."

I could feel my cheeks burning, a sign that by this point they were undoubtedly bright red.

I was trying to think up an excuse, some way of justifying my sudden appearance on the Worth School faculty, when he leaned closer. As his nose approached mine, I instinctively leaned back. But I quickly found out that my head was a lot closer to the wall than I'd realized.

"You know, Dr. Popper," he said, his steel-gray eyes boring into mine, "you might be better off leaving all this alone. When you go snooping around somewhere you don't belong, you don't know what you're going to find out—or who you're going to upset once you do."

A chill ran through me as I realized that Claude Molter had just threatened me.

At least I thought he had.

Or maybe he was just giving me some advice. Some *good* advice.

After all, it's possible that he knows who killed Nathaniel, I thought, still wriggling under his gaze. And he's trying to help me protect my skin.

Either that—or he's trying to protect his own.

• • •

After such an intense day, I expected to have a hard time falling asleep. Instead, as soon as I slipped between the sheets, comfortably cool in my usual oversize T-shirt and underpants, I sank deep into oblivion.

Yet at some point afterward—it could have been minutes or hours later—I felt myself being dragged out of a deep, satisfying state of unconsciousness.

While at first I drifted slowly to the surface, I suddenly snapped awake.

Something felt wrong.

My eyes flew open, but for a second or two, I remained totally disoriented. Although my bedroom was still dark, through the window I could see that the sky had begun to lighten.

Nothing looked out of the ordinary, yet something was making me afraid.

And then, in a flash, I knew why.

Dark curls of smoke filled the room, stinging my eyes and burning my nose.

Which could only mean one thing: The cottage was on fire.

Chapter 16

"Getting over a painful experience is much like crossing monkey bars. You have to let go at some point in order to move forward."

—C. S. Lewis

Instantly a deluge of adrenaline began surging through my entire body.

"Nick?" I instinctively cried, fighting feelings of panic as I threw back the covers.

It only took me a split second to remember that he wasn't in the house with me.

But my animals were.

As I leaped out of bed and my feet hit the floor, I brushed against something furry. Max, hovering next to the bed, no doubt frightened himself.

I was already in survival mode as I scooped my trembling doggie into my arms.

"It's okay, Max," I told him in a hoarse voice. "I'll get you out of here. I'll get us all out of here."

I was already scanning the room, straining to see in the shadowy darkness.

"Lou?" I cried as I looked around frantically. "Where are you?" I tried desperately to locate my Dalmatian, who I knew wouldn't be handling this well.

Sure enough, I found him cowering behind a chair.

"There you are, Lou," I said as calmly as I could. "Come on, sweetie. Let's get out of here. *Fast*."

I grabbed my shaking dog's collar and dragged him toward the door. I was glad I'd gotten into the habit of closing it before going to sleep, since doing so had kept my dogs inside the room with me. Ironically, it was a tip I'd picked up while talking to a firefighter. I'd really been struck by his claim that if a fire broke out, a closed wooden door could buy you an hour before the flames got into the room.

As I reached the door with both dogs in my grasp, I found myself remembering some of the other lessons I'd learned about how to react in a fire—but never in a million years thought I'd ever have to use.

Checking under a door before opening it, for one.

Even in the dim light from the window, I could see dark gray curls of the horrifying stuff wafting into the room. Which told me that opening it would mean letting even more smoke into the room.

Still, I had to get all of us out.

It was only then that I tuned in to the screeching that, up until this point, had been nothing more than background noise to a terrifying situation. I realized the ear-piercing noise was Prometheus's frightened squawks.

My blue-and-gold macaw wasn't the only one on the other side of that door. So were Cat and

Tinkerbell. Leilani, too, my helpless chameleon trapped in her tank.

And then I heard a loud, desperate mewing sound. One of my cats, probably Tink, begging to be let in.

Use the cat door! I thought, letting out a whimper of my own.

"I'm coming, Tink!" I cried.

Gingerly I touched the metal knob, using only my index finger.

"Ouch!" I screamed, pulling back my hand.

Lou immediately began to bark. In response, Max moaned even more loudly, his sturdy little body quaking.

Stay calm! I ordered myself. Even though my heart was pounding and my stomach was in knots, I knew the most important thing was not to panic.

Instead, I forced myself to focus on the lesson about how a hot metal knob usually means there are flames on the other side of the door.

In order to rescue the rest of my animals, I was going to have to find another way into the living room.

I whirled around and headed for the bedroom window, still carrying my quivering Westie in my arms and dragging my poor whimpering Dalmatian beside me. As I passed the small night table next to my bed, I noticed my cellphone. Balancing Max on my forearm, I grabbed it and stuck it into the elastic waistband of my underpants.

Thank goodness I live in a single-story building, I thought.

I let go of Lou's collar long enough to push up the window, which was already partially open. He was frightened enough that he stayed close to me. By resting Max on my arm once again, I managed to use both hands to pull off the screen.

"Okay, Max, out you go," I ordered. I lifted him up to the window and gently dropped him down onto the lawn. Like most terriers, he was almost as smart as a human, and he immediately raced toward Betty's house.

"You're next, Lou." I grabbed my terrified dog's butt and boosted him up to the windowsill. His long, gangly legs flailed in a dozen different directions, yet with my help he somehow managed to crawl out after Max. He dropped to the ground, then took off, heading toward the wooded area behind the Big House.

As I stood at the window, watching him for a second or two, I could still hear Prometheus's desperate squawks. I knew I had no choice but to get myself out next. I only hoped that once I did, I'd be able to figure out exactly where the fire was—and find a way to get my other animals out of the house.

Sliding through the window was easy. The dewy grass felt cool and comforting beneath my bare feet, and I realized for the first time what a relief it was to breathe in fresh air. But there was no time to waste. I ran away from the house, meanwhile dislodging my cellphone from my underwear.

Thank heaven for elastic! I thought, amazed that the phone had pretty much stayed in place.

With trembling fingers I dialed 9-1-1.

"There's a fire!" I told the dispatcher as calmly as I could. "In Joshua's Hollow. Here's the address..."

Once I'd made the call, I stood outside on the lawn,

my mind racing. I knew that another rule about fires, probably the most important one, was that no one should ever go back inside a burning building.

But I also knew that four of my animals were just a few feet inside the door.

I studied the cottage, concentrating on the smoke surging upward from one section of the roof. It looked as if it was concentrated in the area of the kitchen. That meant there was a chance I could get in through the front door, grab my animals, and still get out...

I was still debating whether or not to break that all-important rule of fire safety when I noticed some movement, two small blurs at the side of the cottage.

"Thank God!" I cried with relief as I realized those blurs were actually balls of fur, one gray and one orange. My two cats had gotten themselves out, no doubt finally figuring out that escaping through the cat door, instead of waiting for me to help, was the best idea. And now that they were outside, they were both heading away from the fire.

That still left Prometheus and Leilani inside the burning building.

My mind was on overdrive, moving almost as fast as my heart. I can't just leave them! I thought. Not when I'm ninety-nine percent sure I can dash inside, grab them, and get out.

Besides, I could see through the windows that the swirling black smoke inside the house kept growing thicker.

Even though I never actually made a conscious decision to go back inside the house, before I knew it I was running toward the front door. This time, I anticipated the metal knob being hot, so I grabbed it with the bottom of my T-shirt.

It didn't move.

It's locked! I thought, feelings of panic rising up inside me once again. Of course it's locked. I'm the one who locked it before going to bed last night.

I dashed around to the side of the house, wondering if I'd be able to fit through the cat door Cat and Tink had used to get out.

And then I heard the shriek of sirens.

I had never heard anything more beautiful in my life.

I jogged toward the driveway, waving my arms in the air to be noticed by the driver of the red fire truck that was careening along the narrow driveway, its lights flashing and its sirens screaming. I was vaguely aware that I probably looked like a crazy lady. But at the moment, that was the least of my concerns.

"Anyone inside?" one of the firefighters demanded in a loud voice as he leaped off the side of the truck.

"Two animals," I yelled back. "A parrot in a cage and a lizard in a tank. They're right inside the front door, in the living room. Look to the left, about ten feet in."

He was already dashing toward the front door, brandishing an ax.

I felt a nearly overwhelming mixture of emotions as I watched him smash the wooden door. All around him, the other firefighters were jumping off the truck, shouting to one another as they dragged thick, heavy hoses across the lawn.

I was relieved that help was here—and that in just a few seconds, my parrot and my chameleon would be rescued.

But I was also watching my home being destroyed—not only by the blows of an ax, but also by the flames that were now leaping upward through huge gashes in the roof.

"Move back!" one of the firefighters commanded, gesturing toward the huge stretch of lawn beyond the cottage.

I did as I was told, meanwhile keeping my eyes glued to the little house that I loved so dearly.

When I saw two of the firefighters emerge through the doorway, one carrying Leilani's tank and the other bearing Prometheus, fluttering around wildly inside his cage, I dropped to the ground. It was only then that I let go of the flood of tears that had been building up inside.

In fact, I suddenly found myself crying hysterically as I finally let myself feel the fear I'd been fighting off since the moment I'd awakened.

I jumped when I felt a comforting arm around my shoulders.

"My God, Jessica! Are you all right?" Betty cried breathlessly.

I raised my eyes and saw that she was kneeling beside me, dressed in a bathrobe and slippers.

"I'm okay," I assured her, swiping at the tears streaked across my cheeks. As I spoke, I could taste their saltiness on my lips.

"And the animals?"

"They're all fine," I said. "The cats and dogs are

running around the property somewhere. I pushed Max and Lou out through the bedroom window, and the cats escaped by themselves. The firefighters carried out Prometheus and Leilani."

"So everyone is safe—which is all that matters." Betty reached into the pocket of her bathrobe and pulled out a wad of tissues. "Here. Take these."

"Thanks."

Hugging me closer, she said, "It looks like they're already getting the fire under control. Why don't we go into the house?"

I just nodded, glad that I had someone there with me. The fact that Max suddenly appeared out of nowhere didn't hurt, either.

"Max!" I cried, grabbing my Westie and burying my face in his soft white fur. "I'm so sorry you had to go through such a terrible experience!"

And then Lou was there, too, nudging me with his nose. As I turned to give him a hug, I saw that Winston was standing a few feet behind us. He was carrying Frederick in his arms, as if he'd wanted to make sure not to let his beloved dachshund out of his sight.

"Let's all go inside," Betty urged. "We can look for Tink and Cat after all the chaos dies down."

Casting me a meaningful look, she added, "And trust me, Jessica. The chaos *will* die down."

• • •

An hour later, Betty, Winston, and I sat in the kitchen, sipping cups of Betty's famous whiskey-spiked tea. Max and Lou sat at my side, practically glommed onto my legs, while Tink was nestled safe and sound in my lap. Cat, meanwhile, lay on the soft rug Betty had laid on the floor next to her.

A loud knock reminded us that this wasn't your ordinary tea party.

"It looks like the police," Betty said, craning her neck to see out the window.

I dashed across the room past Prometheus's cage and Leilani's tank and opened the back door. Standing there was a balding middle-aged man with a ruddy complexion, dressed in a jacket and tie.

"I'm Detective Dan O'Reilly," he said somberly, flashing a badge. "Arson Squad."

"Arson?" I squawked. I had just assumed that the fire in the cottage was the result of faulty wiring, since the building's electrical system was probably in as bad shape as its plumbing.

"It's standard procedure for us to check out the cause of every fire," he informed me. "Are you the resident?"

After he stepped inside, we all introduced ourselves, with Betty explaining that she and Winston were the owners and I was the tenant. Once Detective O'Reilly had established that we all had a stake in the building that had just been destroyed, he said, "It's too early to give a full report, but I looked around enough to get a pretty good idea of what happened here."

From the grim expression on his face, I had a feeling he was about to confirm what I'd already concluded.

So I was braced for the worst when he said, "It looks like arson, all right. A really amateurish job, too. We found a plastic container of gasoline we're going to dust for prints. Hopefully that will help us find the person who did this."

Even so, his words sent a chill running through me.

Arson? Committed by an amateur?

Instantly the name Serena Garcia filled my head.

A sick feeling came over me as I replayed Beanie's words: "I heard she burned the guy's house down—with him in it!"

At the time, I'd found her claim impossible to believe. Even Serena's belief that the Santeria god of fire was her orisha hadn't convinced me.

Suddenly, I wasn't so sure.

As for what Serena's motive might have been, the most obvious one was that she was trying to scare me away from the investigation—the reason being that I was getting dangerously close to discovering that either she or her daughter had killed Nathaniel Stibbins.

Or perhaps she had been trying to do more than scare me. Maybe her goal had been to get rid of me—this time, for reasons that had nothing to do with any Santeria ritual.

I sat in silence, debating whether or not to say anything to Detective O'Reilly. Yet even as he handed a business card to each one of us, inviting us to call him if we had any information about the incident, I recognized the danger of bringing up Beanie's unproven claims.

Instead, I resolved to work even harder to determine the identity of the person who had committed not only murder, but also arson.

A few minutes later, I was still ruminating about what my next step should be when the crunch of tires caused me to glance out the kitchen window. As soon as I saw the familiar black Maxima pulling into my driveway, I mumbled something to Betty and Winston and flew out of the house.

Yet I didn't know what to think about Nick's arrival—even though his expression as he climbed out of the car and slammed the door behind him was one of deep concern.

"Jessie!" he cried when he spotted me. "Are you all right?"

I didn't answer. I was too busy running across the lawn. When I reached him, I threw my arms around him. He immediately enveloped me in his.

"I'm fine," I finally said, my voice breathless. "Just a little shaken up."

"And the animals?"

I pulled away just enough that he could see me nod. Between my shock over seeing him and the sudden thickness in my throat, I was having trouble speaking.

"They all got out okay," I finally said, choking out the words.

I was back to hugging him as he said, "Jessie, I felt sick when I heard." His voice was muffled by the fact that his mouth was buried in my hair. "I freaked out when Betty called to tell me what happened."

He tightened his grasp as he added, "I don't know what I'd do if anything ever happened to you."

"I feel the same way," I replied hoarsely.

Part of me said it was time to let go. But I didn't feel like doing that. Not now and not ever. In fact, at the moment, holding on to Nick for the rest of my life seemed like the only thing I wanted to do.

He was the one who finally loosened his hold. But he put both hands on my cheeks so that he was cradling my face. "It's so good to see you, Jess. I've missed you."

"I've missed you, too." I took a deep breath. "Nick, I want to apologize for everything I've ever done to hurt you. I've been so stupid."

"We don't have to do this now," he said. "Right now, we should get you someplace comfortable so we can both calm down and—"

"But I need to tell you how I feel!" I insisted. "Nick, I love you. And that ridiculous scene with Forrester the other night was all because the bathroom flooded and he helped me clean it up. You know how ancient the plumbing is, and I was just getting out of the shower when the handle of the faucet came off in my hand—"

"That's all it was?" he asked, sounding surprised.

"Of course! That's why I wasn't wearing anything besides your bathrobe. And there was so much water on the floor that Forrester was afraid he'd ruin his clothes, so he put on that stupid towel . . ."

I searched his face, anxious to see his reaction. "And the only reason he was there in the first place was because he wanted me to have dinner with him, just once, as payback for him getting me into Cousin Nathaniel's house. He had to call in some favor with Falcone. I figured ordering in some Chinese food to keep on his good side was harmless. I had no idea it would turn out this way!"

I paused to take a deep breath. "That's exactly what happened, Nick. I swear on my life!"

His eyes traveled over to our pathetic-looking cottage. "You don't have to do that," he said. "Swear on your life, I mean."

I nodded. "Okay. I just wanted you to know that I'm telling the truth."

"I believe you," he said simply. For the first time since he'd shown up, he cracked a smile. "If anybody else in the world was telling me this, I'd probably think they were making it up. But I know you—and I believe every word."

I just took his hands in mine and gave them a squeeze.

"What happens now?" I asked, sounding as somber as I felt. "The cottage is going to be uninhabitable for a long time." I was unable to keep from choking as I added, "It might even have to be razed."

"We can probably stay with Betty," Nick replied. "At least until we get a place of our own."

The fact that he used the word "we" made my heart do cartwheels.

•   •   •

"Of course you can both stay with us," Betty declared a few minutes later as the four of us sat at the kitchen table, clustered around a second pot of tea. "For as long as you want."

"We'll be happy to have the company," Winston added. Winking at the dachshund lying by his feet, he added, "I'm sure Frederick will also enjoy having an extended sleepover with Max and Lou."

"Thanks, you guys," Nick said. He reached over and put his hand over mine as he added, "I don't know what we'd do without you."

"Uh-oh," I said, suddenly distracted by some movement outside the window. Two cars had just pulled into the driveway. I recognized them immediately as Falcone's blue Crown Victoria and Forrester's dark green SUV.

"Here come Frick and Frack," I mumbled as I pushed my chair away from the table and stood up.

"Huh?" Nick asked.

"Finish your tea," I told him. "I'll deal with them."

At the moment, these two were the last people in the world I felt like dealing with. Still, it was possible Falcone might know something. Not likely, but possible.

I sauntered over to their cars, hoping they wouldn't stay long.

"Looks like you had a little trouble here," Falcone began. I couldn't tell if he was smirking or if the objectionable look on his face was simply his natural expression.

"I guess you could say that," I replied. "That is, if you consider someone's house burning down 'a little trouble.' "

I turned to Forrester. "How did you know about this?"

"Falcone gave me a call." Shaking his head slowly, he added, "Boy, it's a good thing I wasn't there."

I blinked. "Excuse me?"

"What I mean is, let's say you and I hit it off the other night, the way I was hoping we would," he went on breezily. "And let's stay that I started, you know, staying over. Regularly. For all I know, I could have been sleeping at your place last night. Which means my life would have been in danger, too."

My blood had already escalated to the near-boiling point when he said, "Speaking of which, you are all right, aren't you? You look okay. Did you get out un-scathed? And did all those pets of yours get out of the house, too?"

I just stared at him, unable to believe the things that were coming out of his mouth.

Frankly, I couldn't believe they could come out of anyone's mouth. And Forrester was someone who was supposed to care about me. At least, according to him.

"I think this would be a good time for you to leave," I said in a low, even voice. I was looking at Forrester, but I was really referring to them both.

"As soon as I have a brief word with you," Falcone said.

Actually, what he said was, "As soon as I have a brief word witcha."

I would have liked to say, "No, thank you." But I knew I really didn't have any choice in the matter, so I simply nodded.

"I just had a talk with O'Reilly from the arson squad," he told me.

"We met," I interjected.

"Naturally, he hasn't had a chance to do a real in-vestigation yet," Falcone continued. "But based on his initial look-see, he's sayin' this was the work of a real amateur. Seems to me somebody doesn't like you,

Docta Poppa." He paused, no doubt for dramatic effect, before adding, "Or that maybe somebody is even tryin' to send you a message."

"Next time, I hope they send me an email," I muttered.

He chose to ignore my great wit. "We can't be sure, but there's a good chance this fire was motivated by the fact that you've been sniffin' around the Stibbins murder."

He looked at me expectantly, as if he was waiting for me to say something. To apologize, perhaps, or even to beg for his protection.

"That thought occurred to me, too," I said noncommittally.

"Really." He looked surprised, as if it hadn't occurred to him that I might be clever enough to come to that conclusion completely on my own. "I'm glad you agree."

And then he leaned in closer, his eyes as dark and round as two black olives as they bored into mine. "I hope you also agree that the smart thing to do is to drop it. You got no business getting involved in any of this, even if this guy was a relative of yours."

An *almost* relative, I thought. But I had enough self-restraint that I didn't bother to correct him.

Still, there was something I didn't have enough self-restraint not to do: cross my fingers behind my back.

And that's because I smiled at him sweetly—or at least as sweetly as I could—and said, "You're absolutely right."

A look of surprise crossed his face. I was enjoying this little charade so much I couldn't resist adding,

"Thank you *so* much for your concern, Lieutenant Falcone. And thank you for the good advice, too."

Even though my fingers were no longer crossed, that didn't mean I wasn't thinking the exact opposite of what I was saying. And it wasn't because I didn't want somebody like Falcone telling me what to do.

It was because of my increased resolve about finding Nathaniel's killer.

Despite all the chaos, I'd also come up with a plan for how to proceed. While I knew it was possible that Serena Garcia had killed Nathaniel, I realized I wouldn't be able to figure out who was guilty until I knew *why* he'd been murdered.

In the aftermath of the fire, fragments of conversations I'd had over the past week and a half had flitted through my head like a montage in a movie. They played through my head again as I slowly walked across the lawn, back to the Big House.

"He was the most evil of them all," Serena had said of Nathaniel.

She had also explained that the argument Vondra had had with him was over the upcoming art exhibition. "All I know is that when they disagreed on something about the exhibition," she had told me, "that horrid man actually threatened her."

As for Willard Faber, he had described the murder victim by saying, "He was always determined to make himself more important than he was."

So much of what I'd learned seemed to point toward the exhibition that was scheduled at the Mildred Judsen Gallery but had been canceled because of Nathaniel's death.

I decided it was time for me to see those paintings for myself.

I was still mulling over the best way to accomplish that when I suddenly stopped in my tracks.

Something on the ground had caught my eye. It was small but shiny, its metallic surface glinting in the bright June sunlight.

Even before I bent down to pick it up, I knew exactly what it was. And simply spotting it there, lying less than fifty feet from the ash and rubble that had once been my home, was enough to send a chill running through me even on this warm summer day.

Chapter 17

"We think caged birds sing, when indeed they
cry."

—John Webster

My heart pounded wildly as I leaned over to get
a better look. When I saw that the sparkling
metal item was exactly what I'd thought it
was, I picked it up gingerly, using the edge of my shirt
as a potholder.

For a few seconds, I simply stared at the gold tie
tack in the shape of a violin.

This means one of two things, I thought, trying to
focus despite the distracting throbbing in my temples.
One is that Claude Molter sneaked onto the property
to set the fire and in the process lost his tie tack.

The other is that someone else wants me to *believe*
that's what happened.

And that person is most likely the same one who
made sure the police found that bracelet at the trashed
art exhibition, the one that looked a lot like Vondra
Garcia's.

A little voice inside my head told me to show the police what I'd found. In fact, Detective O'Reilly's business card was practically burning a hole in my pocket.

But another voice was telling me to wait, and frankly it was making a much more convincing argument. After all, I wasn't convinced that I wasn't being intentionally led astray.

Which gave me one more reason to forge ahead with my own investigation.

Both my mind and my heart raced frantically as I tried to come up with a way to sneak into Nathaniel's on-campus studio. I realized almost immediately that the ideal opportunity was only a day away. As the Worth School's biggest event of the year, the Blessing of the Animals was guaranteed to keep the faculty, staff, and students busy.

Which made it the perfect time to strike.

• • •

On Saturday morning, I made a point of getting to school early. As planned, I brought my van to the campus so I'd be able to take care of any animals that needed attention, and I wore my dark green shirt embroidered with "Jessica Popper, D.V.M.," so I could easily be identified. But I also armed myself with an excuse for showing up ahead of schedule: having a few administrative details to attend to.

I had no choice but to bring Max, since Reverend Evans had put in his request not only privately but also in public. I supposed it was possible that having a canine sidekick might actually come in handy. Still, I couldn't help worrying about how he'd respond to being in a closed space that was packed with animals of all types and temperaments.

I stuffed a Ziploc bag of Milk-Bones in my pants pocket, just in case.

The first of the vague duties that had brought me to campus early, should anyone ask, was checking my mailbox. Of course, it happened to be conveniently located just a few feet away from Ms. Greer's desk, where I was nearly positive the keys to Nathaniel's art studio were stored.

Despite the fact that I felt like a bank robber, I tried to act natural as I walked into the administration building. It had turned out to be a perfect summer day, sunny and warm with low humidity. I loped along the walkway, acting as if I actually belonged there. Max was surprisingly well behaved as he trotted alongside me on his leash, possibly because there were so many fascinating new smells that he was too busy luxuriating in a sniff-fest to make any mischief.

Just as I'd expected, the front door of the administration building was unlocked. And just as I'd hoped, no one was around. In fact, the building was eerily silent.

Even so, I scooped my Westie up into my arms, hoping to make as little noise as possible. I wanted to minimize the possibility of running into someone and actually having to use my rather lame excuse for prowling around the school's offices on a weekend.

In case someone was lurking behind some doorway, watching me, I went straight to the mailboxes, still carrying Max under my arm like a football. I actually found two pieces of mail waiting for me, one a notice about ordering school rings and one a memo reminding everyone about the summer parking rules. I left them there, however, in case I needed to prove that I'd had good reason for feeling the need to check my mail on a weekend.

After looking around a bit more—which I accomplished by pretending to massage my neck with the fingers of one hand, meanwhile stretching as I turned my head in every direction—I decided the coast really was clear. I sidled over to Ms. Greer's desk with my sidekick. Given her prim nature, I wasn't surprised that she'd left the top completely clear, aside from her computer and the requisite Worth School pencil cup to keep it company.

I quickly thought up another excuse in case anyone came by and wondered why I was rummaging around in someone else's desk.

A paper clip. I'd claim I was in desperate need of a way of attaching those two all-important notices sitting in my box.

I took a moment to mourn the fact that my formal education had lacked not only plumbing training, but also acting lessons.

But this was not the time to regret the gaps in my schooling. Instead, I sat down at her desk and plopped Max into my lap. Then I nonchalantly reached for the drawer that Ms. Greer had unconsciously glanced at when I'd brought up the subject of Nathaniel Stibbins's studio.

I hoped my intuition had been correct.

When the drawer opened without the slightest resistance, I let out a sigh of relief. But that didn't mean my mission was accomplished. Not when I had yet to determine whether the key I was looking for was inside.

It was. Or at least it *probably* was, depending on whether any of the dozens of keys on the gigantic ring lying at the bottom of the drawer was capable of unlocking the art studio.

I started to panic. There wasn't enough time in a single day to try every one of those keys, and I didn't actually *have* all day anyway...

And then I noticed the multitude of white cardboard squares surrounding all that metal. Ms. Greer's compulsion to organize had apparently extended to her duties as keeper of the keys. She'd labeled each one with the name of a building, a room number, and in some cases a descriptive name.

Keys to the keys, in other words.

Ordering my hands not to shake, I methodically began checking each label, one by one. Janitorial closet, chemistry lab, biology lab, dining room, freezer...

Freezer? I thought. They lock the *freezer*?

I wondered if this school was full of Ben & Jerry's addicts like me. But I didn't allow myself to spend much time pondering that possibility, since I still had a heck of a lot more keys to check.

It was all I could do to keep from yelling something like "Eureka!" or at least "Hooray!" when I finally found the disk labeled "Art Studio—N.S." Thanks to some persistent fumbling that caused Max to glare at me a couple of times, I managed to pull it off the ring.

I stuck it in my pants pocket with the Milk-Bones, put the other keys back, and closed the drawer.

The next step was getting myself over to the Center for Creative Self-Expression, finding the right room, and hoping that Ms. Greer's labeling system was accurate.

I used a side door to exit the administration building to minimize the risk of running into anyone. Not only was I still hoping not to have to test the effectiveness of my excuse about all those nasty administrative responsibilities, the clock was ticking, and getting drawn into a conversation, even a pleasant one, could still keep me from accomplishing my goal.

Once I was outside, I finally put Max down. As the two of us made our way across campus toward the linen napkin–shaped arts building, I tried to look as if I was in a hurry, dragging my dog away from the bushes and flower beds that kept attracting his attention. After all, a fear of being late was an excuse no one could argue with, especially with the blessing scheduled to begin in less than half an hour.

I was only a few hundred yards away when I came across two of my students strolling in the direction of the chapel. One carried a birdcage with three chirping canaries in her arms, while the other grasped the leash of a spirited Airedale who, being a terrier, was in way too much of a hurry.

Max instantly went on High Alert.

"Hi, Dr. Popper!" the dog owner called, waving with her free hand. "Aren't you excited?"

"I sure am," I replied, thinking, But you have no idea why.

In the meantime, I'd tightened my grasp on the

leash. Max was emitting a low growl, and I could see that throwing him in with so many other members of the Animal Kingdom was going to make for an especially trying day.

But I stopped worrying about what might lie ahead as soon as I reached the doors of the Center for Creative Self-Expression. I was too busy assessing the situation.

Fortunately, the building was far enough away from the chapel that no one else seemed to be in the area. Acting as if I owned the joint—or at least as if I was as entitled to creative free expression as the next guy—I pulled open the door and strode inside, my sidekick in tow.

While in the past I'd always focused on the Music Wing, this time I went in the opposite direction, following the sign that identified the Art Wing. I walked purposefully along the corridor, for the first time worrying about how I'd figure out which room was Nathaniel's art studio. But then I saw that most of the doors had the same narrow rectangular windows as the practice rooms in the Music Wing.

I peered into each room I passed. They all looked like classrooms. One was outfitted with a dozen pottery wheels, while another had huge tables with the giant squeegees used for making silk-screen prints.

The last one, located at the very end of the long hallway, had black paper covering its window.

Something told me this was the place I was looking for.

Sure enough, when I fumbled in my pocket, took out the key, and put it into the lock in the silver metal doorknob, it fit comfortably. Even though my hand was so moist that it was slippery, when I tried the knob it turned easily in my hand. Moving as stealthily as I could, I opened the door and stepped inside.

The room was unexpectedly dark, due mainly to the fact that the blinds were drawn. Yet even though Max hesitated, clearly apprehensive about venturing into a space that was not only strange but also dark, I didn't dare turn on a light. Instead, I blinked a few times, waiting for my eyes to adjust.

As they did, I gradually made out some of the big dark shapes in the room—and realized there wasn't all that much to see. The large space was basically a classroom that had done double duty as a studio. It was practically empty, aside from a couple of wooden easels and some shelves that housed a haphazard collection of paint tubes and brushes.

But it was the paintings that interested me.

I saw dozens of them, canvases of varying sizes lined up sideways in the back corner, resting on the floor. The fact that they were stashed between the shelves and the wall kept them from toppling over. I then noticed that next to them were three or four big wooden crates that from where I stood looked empty.

"Come on, Maxie-Max," I said softly, pulling him along with me as I headed over to the paintings.

Sure enough, the packing crates were empty. And the return address on them was the Mildred Judsen Gallery.

These are Nathaniel's paintings, I thought as I looped the leash through the back of a chair to free my hands. The ones that were about to go on display.

I pulled out one of the canvases. As I did, my heart

was pounding with such violence that it felt as if it had leaped out of my chest and gotten lodged in my throat.

I rotated it gently on its bottom corner so that it faced me, then stooped over slightly to get a better look.

The painting was of a woman wearing nothing but a headdress. She was draped across a couch, shown from the back but glancing at the painter over her shoulder.

I blinked. It looked oddly familiar, but at the same time jarringly different.

I immediately understood why it seemed so familiar. It took me only a few seconds to identify it, thanks to my art history class at Bryn Mawr. It was *Le Grande Odalisque*, painted by the French painter Jean-Auguste-Dominique Ingres in the early nineteenth century.

Yet even though I wasn't all that familiar with this particular work of art, I knew enough to recognize that it wasn't an exact reproduction. The face on the model was too modern. Too young, as well. And something about the look of it—the skin tones, the pose—just seemed *off* somehow.

The uncomfortable gnawing in the pit of my stomach helped me understand what I was looking at.

My mouth was dry as I hauled out a second painting, this time reaching for one of the larger canvases. I dragged it away from all the others that were lined up in the corner and leaned it against the wall.

The image was strikingly similar. This time it was a re-creation of Botticelli's *The Birth of Venus,* the same painting I'd recently seen in the art book Beanie had been leafing through in the school library—and one Nathaniel had talked about in his art history class. The painting featured a nude woman standing on a seashell at the edge of the sea.

And then I focused on Venus—especially her face.

It was Campbell Atwater's face.

The room was starting to feel very warm.

As I looked more closely, I realized the body wasn't the same as the one in the famous Botticelli painting, either. This one was taller, more slender, more youthful. And just like in the other painting, this nude woman also had different skin tones from what I remembered seeing in the original.

Which led me to conclude that it was also Campbell's body.

Oh my God! I thought, growing even warmer as my original hunch started to take shape. Nathaniel had his students pose for him in the nude! He used them as the models in his re-creations of the classic paintings he loved, substituting the faces and bodies of the girls at the school for the original ones. He might have even used the fact that they were famous classics that had earned a place among the greatest works of art in history to sell them on the idea of posing.

My hands shook as I pulled out one more of Nathaniel's paintings. I recognized this one, too. It was Goya's *Maja*—the nude version. This painting depicted a naked woman stretched across a couch lined with fluffy white pillows.

Only this Maja also looked familiar. Her face, and no doubt her body, were Vondra's.

My stomach was so tight that I felt nauseous.

Could this have been what Vondra's argument with Nathaniel was about? I wondered, my mind racing. Perhaps she posed for him, believing no one would ever see the painting, then learned he intended to put it on exhibit at a prominent New York art gallery—one that was known for its skill at garnering lots of publicity.

Hurriedly I pulled out more of Nathaniel's paintings, lining them up one by one as if they were on display at a sidewalk art sale. They were all nudes, some in the classical style, some modeled after artwork from the twentieth century. Yet all of them had a more modern look than the original on which they were based, leading me to conclude they all featured young women who had been Nathaniel's students. Even works that looked as if they'd been inspired by artists with a more abstract style, like Matisse and Picasso and even Warhol, featured models whose faces I was nearly certain I recognized. One looked a lot like a young woman in my class I'd never really gotten to know. Another was a dead ringer for someone I remembered passing on campus a couple of times.

My mind raced as I tried to digest what I was looking at—and what the implications might be. Nathaniel had been on the verge of creating a stir in the art world, all right—mainly by exploiting his female students. He had intended to exhibit these paintings of them in the nude, making a name for himself at their expense.

Until someone stopped him.

As for who that someone might have been, the gnawing in my stomach told me I'd just figured it out.

At least when I combined my gut feeling with the voice echoing through my head.

Claude Molter's voice.

"They're so young...so innocent!" he'd said the first time I met him. "There are far too many things that happen in their lives that force them to grow up too quickly."

At the PTA meeting, he'd said, "I'm completely committed to doing whatever is best for the students at Worth. I'd do anything for those girls. I see them as little flowers that need to be protected."

And then I remembered something else he'd said. His eyes had been penetrating as he'd told me, "Dr. Popper, you might be better off leaving all this alone. When you go snooping around somewhere you don't belong, you don't know what you're going to find out—or who you're going to upset once you do."

He'd clearly found out about what Nathaniel was planning to do. While he claimed he hadn't actually seen these paintings, at some point, perhaps before their falling out, Nathaniel must have told him about them.

"Let's just say the people at the Mildred Judsen Gallery know what sells," Claude had commented to me, "as well as what's likely to garner them the most publicity."

In addition to hearing his voice, I was also haunted by a disturbing image: the violin-shaped tie tack I'd found near the remains of my cottage.

It suddenly seemed clear that Claude had killed

Nathaniel—and that the reason had nothing to do with vying for the job of Director of Creativity. It was to prevent these paintings from being put on exhibit. And when he'd realized I was trying to find Nathaniel's murderer, he'd sent me a warning.

I was still marveling over how neatly everything suddenly seemed to fit together when I heard the door behind me shut softly.

Which told me I was no longer alone.

Doing my best to act calm—that is, as if I actually had a legitimate reason for being in Nathaniel Stibbins's locked art studio—I turned around. As I did, I forced myself to smile at whoever might have just caught me red-handed.

Standing in the doorway was Beanie Van Hooten.

"Beanie!" I exclaimed, relieved. "What are you doing here?"

"I saw you come in with your dog and I wanted to meet him," she replied cheerfully. "I hope you don't mind."

"Not at all," I said. "Did you bring your pug today? Her name is Esmeralda, right?"

"You remembered!" she cried. "I sure did. Right now, she's with Campbell."

She went over to Max and crouched down. "What a cutie!" she gurgled. "What's his name?"

"This is Max," I said. "He's a Westie."

Frowning, she asked, "What happened to his tail?"

"He's a rescue dog," I explained, not wanting to expose her to the whole nasty story.

As she continued to make a fuss over my dog,

scratching his ears and making affectionate cooing sounds, I glanced over at the paintings nervously. The canvases I'd pulled out were in full view.

I was still wondering what to say about them when Beanie looked up and asked, "What's with all these paintings? Did Mr. Stibbins make them?"

Her question gave me an out. "I'm not sure *who* made them," I told her.

"But this was his studio," Beanie pointed out. "I've never actually been in here before, since it was always kept locked, but I know that—"

Her voice trailed off as she focused on the painting of Campbell posed as Botticelli's *Venus*.

"Is that—is that *Campbell*?" she asked, her tone filled with disbelief.

I didn't answer. There was no need to. Not when she could see for herself that that was exactly who it was.

I, in turn, could see that all the blood had drained out of her face.

"But she's naked!" Beanie cried. "You mean Mr. Stibbins painted her without any clothes on?"

I didn't answer that question, either.

"Are people going to see this?" she demanded, her expression panicked.

"Not anymore," I said.

Sounding puzzled, she asked, "What do you mean?"

"I'm pretty sure these were the paintings that were going to be in Mr. Stibbins's upcoming exhibition," I explained. "But the gallery only exhibits the work of living artists, so they've canceled his show."

"Good thing!" Beanie cried. "Campbell would have freaked!"

Frankly, I was a little surprised by how relieved she appeared to be. "I know it might have been embarrassing for Campbell," I said, choosing my words carefully, "but from the looks of things, she did pose for him."

"But she couldn't have known that Mr. Stibbins planned to show this painting to anyone!" Beanie insisted. "Otherwise, she never would have done it. Not with *her* father!"

Startled, I asked, "Do you think he'd be that upset?"

"Upset?" She let out a loud, abrupt laugh. "*Upset?* Are you *kidding* me? I've never met anybody more straitlaced in my entire life! Mr. Atwater has incredibly high standards for Campbell. He's very clear about how he wants her to act—and how he wants other people to see her. That time she was mentioned in that gossip column in the *New York Post,* he grounded her for a month. He totally disapproves of his daughter being in the news—unless it's because she's been doing some charity work or something."

Her eyes drifted back to the canvas. "If Campbell's dad ever saw this painting of her in the nude, I bet anything he'd pull her out of this school and send her to a—a *convent.* I mean, can you imagine the way the press would have jumped on this? Not only the tabloids, but even the legitimate press? This story would have been all over the news! TV, newspapers, magazines...Everybody in the entire world would have been talking about Campbell Atwater!"

She turned back to me. "And do you know what her father would have done?"

"No," I replied.

"He would have cut her off," she said, her eyes narrowing. "Closed out her trust fund, written her out of his will, done whatever he needed to do to keep her from getting a single penny."

"But Campbell's father loves her!" I protested. "She's his daughter, for heaven's sake!"

Beanie grimaced. "You obviously don't know Mr. Atwater very well."

She was right; I didn't. But I had met him, and I'd seen for myself what a hardnose he was. Heard about it, too—for example, from Vondra Garcia, who'd characterized him as "ruthless."

So Claude Molter *was* trying to protect his students by murdering Nathaniel, I thought.

I felt as if the room was whirling around me. But I reminded myself that I wasn't alone—and that Beanie had undoubtedly seen enough.

"Goodness, it's getting late!" I said, making a big show of glancing at my watch. "I didn't realize it was so close to starting time. I'd better get going." Remembering that neither of us was supposed to be in here, I added, "In fact, we both should."

Beanie lingered in front of the painting of Campbell, her eyes still glued to it.

"Beanie?" I finally asked. "Are you coming?"

"Sorry," she said, her face reddening as she reluctantly tore herself away.

When I saw how slowly she was moving, I figured

she was still in shock. I also realized I was in too much of a hurry to wait for her.

"If you don't mind, I'm going to run ahead," I told her as I locked the door behind us. "I'll see you at the chapel."

"Okay," she said.

I left her behind as I dragged Max out of the building, then broke into a jog as soon as I hit the paved walkway. Yet the speed with which my heart was pumping had more to do with what was going on inside my head than with any physical exertion.

All the pieces had snapped into place. Not only had I finally seen Nathaniel's paintings, I'd also heard from Beanie what a devastating effect they could have had on his students' lives. I was more convinced than ever that Claude Molter had killed Nathaniel.

The next step was convincing everyone else.

Fortunately, the Blessing of the Animals provided me with the perfect opportunity. Not only would Claude be there, so would hundreds of spectators, the school's faculty and administrators, members of the press, and the police.

The trick would be figuring out a way to pull it off.

• • •

As I neared the chapel, I was struck by the festive feeling that electrified the campus on this perfect summer day. All kinds of people from tiny babies to senior citizens were streaming toward the small building, accompanied by dogs on leashes, cats in carriers, and other assorted animals in cages, tanks, or cardboard boxes. Everyone seemed to be in good spirits, laughing and chattering and taking pictures. More than a dozen Worth students were handing out programs or running the refreshment stands—two rows of folding tables that straddled the walkway leading up to the chapel's front door.

Max and I passed through the open double doors into the building. As I distractedly accepted a program, I was pleased to spot two uniformed police officers standing together just inside the front entrance.

Just as I'd anticipated, the back wall was lined with members of the press, even though the three or four reporters appeared to be more interested in chatting with one another than taking notes. The group included two videographers with gigantic cameras balanced on their shoulders, no doubt camera crews from a couple of local cable stations.

I scanned their faces, looking for Forrester's. He wasn't there.

As I scooped Max into my arms, I surveyed the interior of the chapel, a small building with white walls, wooden pews, and colorful stained-glass windows. The single room was already crowded, not only with hundreds of people but also with at least as many animals. Dogs of all shapes and sizes were either nestled in people's arms or straining at their leashes, their eyes bright and their muscular bodies quivering with excitement. Some wagged their tails and strained to sniff the other canines. Others looked tense, as if a low growl was sitting in their throats, just waiting for the right moment to come out.

At first glance, it appeared that just about every

breed imaginable was represented. At one end of the spectrum was the pair of tiny Chihuahuas checking out every four-legged being in the room from the safety of an oversize designer purse. At the other extreme was a sleek Great Dane that was almost as tall as his bearded bear-size owner, who wore a sleek leather jacket with the Harley-Davidson logo emblazoned on the back. It was hard to tell who deserved the prize for Biggest Dog, the Great Dane or the amiable-looking Saint Bernard panting contentedly, his massive body taking up half the aisle in which he sat. There were also many of the None of the Above variety, mixtures that resulted in dogs of every size, color, body type, fur type—and from the varying ways in which they were behaving, disposition.

All kinds of cats were in attendance, as well. A few were curled up in their owners' laps wearing every expression from curiosity to disdain as they eyed the proceedings. But most were in carriers. Still, even they couldn't resist peeking out, marveling over what for most of them was probably the largest congregation of fellow furry creatures they had ever seen.

Beyond the usual dogs and cats, there were birds in cages, hamsters and gerbils in tanks, quite a few rabbits, two or three lizards, a few fish in a small glass globe, and a couple of downy ducks. There was even a goat standing at the back. Tied around her neck was a pink satin ribbon as well as a rope with ragged ends.

I was actually pretty surprised at how well behaved the animals were. That included my own canine—at least, so far. I did notice one dog who appeared to be primarily wire fox terrier yapping away nonstop while his nervous-looking owner, a teenage girl, desperately clutched his collar. And there were lots of paws skittering around as dogs struggled to reach one another across the pews, over the backs of the pews, and even underneath the pews.

But while it would normally have been great fun to watch the animals' antics, at the moment I was too focused on my mission to linger. I wove through the crowd, my eyes darting around as I sought out the familiar face that I now knew belonged to Nathaniel's killer.

He's got to be here, I thought anxiously.

I still hadn't spotted Claude when Reverend Evans took his place at the podium. Chach sat next to him contentedly, tethered to his master's wrist by a bright red leash.

"Would everyone please take a seat so we can get started?" Reverend Evans boomed.

The chatter immediately died down, and the people and animals who were still milling around hastily made a beeline for one of the few empty places that still remained. It was as if someone had suddenly initiated a massive game of musical chairs. Some of the people in the aisles headed toward the front of the chapel. As for me, I scanned the back rows, looking for a seat that would enable me to survey the entire room without having to turn around every two seconds.

Fortunately, I spotted a narrow space on a pew that looked just wide enough for me to squeeze into. Unfortunately, it was smack in the middle of the row.

And it was between an elderly woman who was constantly stroking the nervous-looking Persian cat in her lap and a beefy man whose sausagelike fingers were clamped around a leash with an equally beefy English bulldog panting at the other end. While the man and the woman barely seemed to notice each other, the Persian and the bulldog couldn't keep their eyes off each other—and not in a good way, either.

Not exactly an ideal situation, I thought, hoping the two animals wouldn't suddenly decide to demonstrate that old expression about "fighting like cats and dogs"—especially when mine would have been only too happy to cheer them on.

Still carrying Max in my arms, I jockeyed my way around the knees and heads of the people and pets who were already sitting. I must have mumbled "excuse me" and "sorry" about a million times. Once I finally reached the vacant seat, somehow I managed to wedge myself into it, minimizing the amount of space Max took up by keeping him in my lap.

The chapel was so charged that it felt as if it were about to explode. So I was relieved that Reverend Evans didn't waste any time before getting the service under way.

"I'd like to begin by welcoming all the pets who came today," he began, "as well as all the humans they brought with them." He paused to smile at the audience. "As most of you know, this is the first time the Worth School has hosted this Blessing of the Animals, which we hope will become an annual event. In large part, we see it as a means of inviting to our campus all the members of the community—including those with fur, feathers, scales, and gills. But it's also an excellent time to step back and appreciate the things in life that bring us joy, especially the animals that play such an important role in our lives..."

I glanced around again, but I still didn't see Claude Molter. I was beginning to experience a sinking feeling. Was it was possible that he'd opted out—even though this was one of those "command performances" he'd mentioned?

Nervously I checked the back of the room. The reporters and photographers were still lined up—which was the perfect setup for the moment I finally figured out a way of revealing the identity of Nathaniel Stibbins's murderer.

I was still looking around when I heard a low growl emerge from Max's throat.

"Max, sh-h-h!" I whispered. But I saw that the woman sitting in front of us was holding a large cage in her lap—and inside it was a rabbit.

Terriers hate rabbits.

"Max, be quiet!" I commanded, more loudly this time.

This is the last time you play Starsky to my Hutch, I thought, glaring at my Westie.

Then I remembered that I'd brought a distraction. Squirming in my narrow seat, I somehow managed to wrest the Ziploc bag from my pocket and pull out a Milk-Bone.

I was congratulating myself on my success when I noticed that Beanie had finally come into the chapel and was lurking in the aisle. She studied the crowd, frowning. Then her face lit up and she headed across the room.

I guess Campbell saved her a seat, I thought. I sure hope Esmeralda and Snowflake are handling this better than Max is.

The seat Beanie took was just a few rows in front of me. In fact, I had a surprisingly good view of her and the back of a head of silky blond hair that did indeed look as if it belonged to her friend. Peeking over her shoulder was a snow-white Maltese. Snowflake, no doubt, the dog she'd talked about so lovingly on the very first day of class. And I could see a tan rump that I assumed belonged to Beanie's pug.

"Let's start with a hymn," Reverend Evans was saying as I tuned back in. "Please rise and join me. You'll find the words to 'All Creatures of Our God and King' printed in the program..."

Inwardly I groaned. Once everyone in the room was standing, it would be that much more difficult to maneuver my way out of the row and toward the killer.

Yet within about three seconds, all the people in attendance were on their feet, still holding the animals they had brought with them, whether they were in their arms, on a leash, or in a pet carrier. I glanced to the right and then the left, picturing how difficult it would be to get myself out of there.

And then hundreds of voices came together as one to sing, *"All creatures of our God and King, lift up your voice and with us sing...!"*

As all around me the chapel filled with the beautiful and powerful sound, I noticed that the animals calmed down a bit. The fact that everyone was now looking straight ahead, toward Reverend Evans, also gave me a good chance to study the audience—at least the backs of their heads. I ran my eyes along the rows, methodically checking each person as I searched for Claude.

"O burning sun with golden beam and silver moon with softer gleam..."

I noticed that not everyone was singing. Beanie, for example, who I saw was whispering in Campbell's ear. Even from where I sat, I could see how frantic her expression was.

She must be telling Campbell about the painting, I thought, bracing myself for her friend's reaction.

Much to my amazement, Campbell just shrugged.

My mouth dropped open. But I clamped it shut as I decided I'd simply been wrong.

She must have been telling her something else, I decided.

Yet something about their interaction nagged at me. If Beanie had just learned about that painting of her best friend in the nude only minutes ago, wouldn't it have been the first thing she would have talked to Campbell about? And when Campbell found out it had been shipped off to an art gallery in New York City, wouldn't she have become extremely upset, just as her best friend had predicted?

I was still puzzling over the scene I'd just witnessed as hundreds of voices blossomed around me.

"Hallelujah...hallelujah!"

Suddenly, a wave of heat that had nothing to do with the closeness of the tiny building passed over me.

Oh my God, I thought, my stomach wrenching. Was I wrong? Is it possible that Campbell already *knew* about Nathaniel's plan to exhibit the painting?

And given what I now know about what her father's reaction would have been, was it possible that *she* had killed Nathaniel to keep him from putting that picture in his upcoming art show?

As my mind moved faster than the speed of light, I suddenly realized what a coincidence it was that Campbell's best friend happened to walk in on me while I was in Nathaniel's art studio.

Was Beanie following me? I wondered. Has she been watching my every move?

By that point, my heart was beating so loudly that I was glad the chapel was filled with song. But my relief faded when the hymn came to an end and Reverend Evans instructed, "Everyone please be seated."

Like everyone else, I complied. But I kept my eyes fixed on the back of Campbell's head. My heart pounded like a jackhammer as I tried to decide what my next move would be.

"We are here today not only to bless our beloved animals," Reverend Evans told his rapt audience, "but also to honor Saint Francis. Even though our service today is interdenominational, I believe that there is no single individual throughout history who we've all come to associate more strongly with animals—with the possible exception of Noah."

He paused to let the laughter die down before he continued. "One of the best-known stories about Saint Francis is also one of my favorites. He once visited a town in Italy called Gubbio, which had been terrorized by a large wolf that had attacked not only animals, but also people. Saint Francis promised the townspeople he would tame the wolf.

"Because the animal was so ferocious, they begged him not to try. But he insisted, and rather than waiting for the wolf to find him, he went into the woods by himself to look for the wolf. And he found him, all right. In fact, the wolf bore down on him, his teeth bared as if he was ready to kill. But Saint Francis stood his ground, raising his arms to make the sign of the cross. When he did, the wolf stopped in his tracks, as if he was watching and listening.

"In the end, Saint Francis struck a deal with both the wolf and the townspeople. The people agreed to feed the wolf and the wolf agreed not to hurt anyone else. From that point on, the wolf walked at Saint Francis's side like a devoted pet.

"And now," Reverend Evans boomed, "with the spirit of Saint Francis in mind, I'd like to begin blessing all the dogs that are present."

All the dog owners rose to their feet, acting as if they'd attended a rehearsal, or at least done this once or twice before. As they did, they lovingly cradled their canines in their arms or patted the heads of the animals beside them. Those who were seated near the aisle stepped out, as if wanting to be sure to catch whatever positive thoughts and wishes Reverend Evans was dispersing throughout the chapel.

"Oh, Lord," Reverend Evans intoned, "for all your creatures we thank you, but especially brother dog.

Dogs fearlessly protect our homes, they selflessly safeguard our families, and they provide us with companionship throughout their lives. Every day they exhibit unwavering loyalty and infinite devotion. And in return, they ask only for our love. In the name of the Father, the Son, and the Holy Spirit..."

Everyone remained in the same spot as Reverend Evans continued with the prayer. "If the dog owners will please be seated, we'll have more room for the felines," Reverend Evans finally instructed.

Once again, the members of the audience acted as if they were doing a dance they knew well. The dog owners sat down, with those who had stepped into the aisle finding their way back into the pews. The cat owners took their place, either rising to their feet or moving into the opening between the two rows of seats.

Once the rearrangement had taken place, I glanced over in Campbell's direction and saw that she was still standing, with Snowflake cradled in her arms. In fact, she was the only dog owner in the entire room who was still on her feet.

What's going on? I wondered.

I watched, flabbergasted, as she made her way across the aisle, stepping over the feet and knees of everyone in her way.

Why is she leaving? I thought as feelings of panic rose up inside me. Something is happening here.

And then I saw that Beanie was trailing right behind her.

"Heavenly Father," Reverend Evans continued after surveying the chapel and seeing that the reshuffling had come to an end, "bless our sister cat. Cats are our steady companions, delighting us with their sharp wit and their beauty. As kittens, they charm us with their innocence and playfulness. As they grow, they continue to inspire us with their curiosity, their serenity, and their peacefulness. My Almighty God bless all cats, in the name of the Father, the Son..."

The ceremony was moving along more quickly than I'd anticipated. I suspected it wouldn't be long before Reverend Evans did one final blessing for all the other animals, the gerbils and fish and goat, then started to wrap things up.

I was aware that I had to take action, even though I still hadn't figured out what that action should be. But I had to know what was going on with those two—*before* the Blessing of the Animals came to an end and everyone dispersed.

Which meant I was running out of time.

Chapter 18

"The trouble with the rat race is that even if you win, you're still a rat."

—Lily Tomlin

On impulse, I stood up, too.

Clumsily I made my way across the pew, holding Max tightly against my chest like an oversize clutch purse. Once again I kept muttering, "Excuse me, sorry," meanwhile crunching down on more toes than I would have liked. At least I managed to keep from stepping on any paws.

Once I was in the aisle, I headed in the same direction as Campbell and Beanie. Doing so took me through a door in front of the chapel, immediately to the left of the altar.

As soon as I did, I heard their voices coming from somewhere in the back of the chapel. As I walked along the short hallway, taking care not to make any noise, I spotted a single room at the end of the short corridor. It was separated from the hallway by a small anteroom—really a pass-through with a door that I surmised opened into a closet. Stroking Max's ears in an effort to keep him calm, I peered inside and saw that it was comfortably furnished as a sort of sitting room. Probably the spot where Reverend Evans conversed with anyone seeking his counsel, I concluded.

But at the moment, Campbell and Beanie occupied the room. The slim blonde lay stretched out on the couch, a pair of sandals with impractical high heels on the floor beside her and her Maltese curled up at her feet. Beanie, meanwhile, sat on an uncomfortable-looking straight-backed chair, with Esmeralda sitting on the floor beside her.

Fortunately, neither girl had seen me. I pressed my back against the wall and noiselessly slunk into the closet, which happened to open in the direction of the hallway. That meant that if I left the door ajar, I could see into the room through the narrow space on the hinged side. The opening was just wide enough for me to see both girls reflected in the mirror hanging on the wall beside them.

I could see and hear everything. My only concern was keeping Max quiet. I buried my nose in his fur, meanwhile scratching his neck in the way he particularly liked.

"I had no idea this thing was going to be so boring," Campbell whined. "I was getting so antsy in there!"

"Campbell," Beanie said as she glanced around nervously, "we really have to—"

"If I'd known this stupid blessing was going to be like this," Campbell went on, acting as if she hadn't heard her, "I never would have come. To think I could have gone into the city this weekend instead! I'm missing some great parties. But for some reason, I thought it would be fun to bring Snowflake to this—"

"Campbell, listen to me!" Beanie insisted.

Campbell looked shocked. "Since when do you talk to me in that tone of voice?"

"Since Dr. Popper might have figured out what happened." Beanie swallowed hard. "You know. With Mr. Stibbins."

"I don't want to talk about that," Campbell insisted. "Especially since I didn't do anything wrong." Impatiently she continued, "In fact, if anyone was a victim here, it was me. No one could blame me for being so upset when all of a sudden Mr. Stibbins changed the rules. I mean, from the very start he told me and all the other girls that the paintings were just studies he was working on for his own—what was the phrase he used? Oh, that's right. 'Artistic development.' He swore up and down that no one would ever see them."

"I knew from the start that going to his house and posing for him without any clothes on wasn't a good idea," Beanie countered angrily. "I know you were flattered, just like all the other girls who posed for him."

"Of course we were flattered!" Campbell exclaimed. "Besides, it all seemed so innocent. It's not as if he ever wanted to do anything besides paint us!"

"But I still didn't trust him," Beanie said. "And I tried to talk you out of it. But as usual, nobody can tell you what to do. In fact, I wondered if me telling you it was a bad idea made you want to do it even more."

"That's ridiculous!" Campbell cried. "How was I supposed to know he was going to change the rules? I had no idea he'd decide he could get famous by exhibiting those paintings—especially the one of me! That's why *I'm* the real victim here! After all, I'm the one the press would have pounced on! I'm the prettiest and I have the best fashion sense—not to mention that my father happens to be one of the richest men in the country!"

"In that case, were you really surprised that Mr. Stibbins decided to put those paintings on display?" Beanie demanded.

"I don't know," Campbell said petulantly. "What does it matter now? What's more important is that *you* were supposed to take care of everything—like making a bunch of other people look as if *they* were the ones who killed him. Dr. Goodfellow, Vondra, her mother, Mr. Molter..."

"But I keep running into things I wasn't counting on!" Beanie shot back. "Like that nosy Dr. Popper!"

Campbell let out an exasperated sigh. "There's that crazy idea of yours again. All that nonsense about her being a private investigator—all because she happened to show up on campus a couple of days after the murder. I swear, Beanie, you watch way too much TV!"

"But it was her wedding!" Beanie cried. "Dr. Popper and Mr. Stibbins knew each other! So doesn't it strike you as an amazing coincidence that just a couple of days after he was killed she showed up at our school? And just a few minutes ago I followed her to Mr. Stibbins's art studio!"

Campbell froze. "You were in his studio? Was the painting there?"

Beanie nodded. "It's back. I saw it."

"Then why didn't you take a knife or something and rip it to shreds?" Campbell demanded in a shrill voice.

"How could I, with Dr. Popper standing there the whole time?"

"Beanie, sometimes you are just so useless!" Campbell cried.

"Don't worry, Campbell! I'll do it!" Beanie said. She sounded as if she was close to tears. "I've done everything else you asked me to do, haven't I? I left those newspaper articles in Dr. Popper's mailbox, I trashed that stupid student art exhibit...and I *really* put myself at risk by setting that fire to scare Dr. Popper away. I even went to all the trouble of making it look as if Mr. Molter was responsible!

"And before all that, I'm the one who watched Mr. Stibbins week after week. I even found out that he was going to that wedding! We never even would have known about it if I wasn't going through his mail every day!"

"Oh, go get me a Diet Coke, will you?" Campbell commanded crossly. "I'm dying of thirst."

"But Campbell, this is important!"

"In a glass, this time, not one of those stupid cans. And do you think you could remember to put ice in it?"

Beanie's face was red, although whether it was from rage or embarrassment, I couldn't say.

"I'm sorry about that. That other time I couldn't find—"

"Just hurry, will you?" Campbell insisted.

As I watched Beanie rise reluctantly from her seat, the wheels inside my head were turning. The more I thought about it, the more sense it made. Beanie was the one who had followed Nathaniel to my wedding. Campbell was used to having other people doing things for her. The very first time I'd met her, when she was forced to consider the possibility that her dog could become ill, her reaction was that her father would simply find someone to take care of her problem.

When Mr. Stibbins's decision to exhibit the paintings threatened to keep her from benefiting from her father's fortune, it seemed highly likely that she would have done the exact same thing: find someone else to make the problem go away.

Someone like Beanie.

The certainty that Beanie had killed Nathaniel at her best friend's insistence had barely formed in my head when I noticed that all the muscles in Max's body had hardened. At first, I thought he was simply reacting to my own tension. But suddenly he let out a low growl.

Glancing down, I saw that we were being watched.

Esmeralda's big, round eyes were just inches away, on the other side of the narrow opening between the door and the doorjamb. She'd been trotting after Beanie as she'd headed toward the door, but stopped when she'd gotten close to Max.

Max's growl immediately erupted into a woof. Esmeralda, in turn, started barking.

"Esmeralda, what's going on?" Beanie cried, sounding irritated.

At the same time, Campbell jerked her head up. Through the crack between the door and the jamb, I saw her cast her steely gaze in the direction of the closet.

"I have a feeling we're not alone," she said to Beanie as she rose from the couch.

She padded across the room in her bare feet. Without hesitating, she flung open the closet door.

"Dr. Popper!" Campbell cried, a look of shock crossing her face. "What are you doing here?"

Beanie's expression became stricken the instant she spotted me. "Oh my God," she said in a hoarse whisper. "You know everything, don't you?"

Turning to Campbell, she cried, "She knows about Mr. Stibbins, Campbell! I was right! She figured out that we killed him!"

"*I'm* not the one who killed him!" Campbell shrieked. "*You* are!"

"But it was your idea!" Beanie countered. "You're the one who wanted him dead!"

"I have no idea what the two of you are talking about," I insisted, holding up both hands. "I just came in here because Max was having such a hard time dealing with all those animals. Especially the rabbits—"

"She's lying!" Campbell exclaimed. "Beanie, do something!"

The dark-haired girl's eyes immediately darted

around the room. Something about their steely, calculating look told me that what she intended to do was locate a weapon—in other words, a quick, easy way to get rid of one more of Campbell's problems.

I wasn't about to let her do that. Especially when I saw her zero in on a large porcelain vase that looked as if it could inflict great harm if used correctly.

In fact, I was about to bolt. But then Campbell cried, "For God's sake, Beanie, not *here*! Not with everybody right outside!"

So Campbell's the brains of the operation, I thought. I have a feeling pulling off the Nathaniel Stibbins caper took the two of them working together.

But I didn't have much time to work out the details of exactly how these two operated.

"Run, Beanie!" Campbell added, darting across the small sitting room and grabbing her sandals. "Let's just get out of here!"

After slipping into them with amazing speed, she dashed toward the corridor with Beanie right behind. Snowflake and Esmeralda skittered after them, as if afraid they might miss out on something fun. All four of them were in such a hurry that they banged into one another, reminding me of those old Keystone Kops movies. In fact, the situation would have been funny if I wasn't dealing with two people who had conspired to commit murder.

I put Max on the ground, grabbed his leash, and ran after them. Fortunately, there was only one way out.

Through the chapel.

Where hundreds of people, including two police officers, were gathered.

Campbell and Beanie were so frantic over having been found out that they didn't have the sense to slow down and act as if everything was normal. Instead, they burst through the doorway that led back into the chapel, then suddenly stopped as they remembered that a service was taking place in the next room.

Actually, it looked as if that service had already ended. Reverend Evans no longer stood at the podium, and people had begun drifting outside onto the lawn. That meant that instead of the dogs and cats and other animals being safely tucked away in the pews, kept under control on leashes or securely held in their owners' laps, they were cluttering up the aisles and half-blocking the doorway.

But even though people and animals were milling around, that didn't mean the sudden appearance of two wild women running through the chapel didn't bring all the activity to an immediate halt.

Especially when I yelled, "Stop them! They killed Nathaniel Stibbins!"

"I didn't kill anybody!" Campbell screeched. "Beanie did it!"

The sea of shocked faces told me that most people didn't understand what was going on. Yet all that running and screaming set off a chain reaction inside the chapel—not among the humans, but with the animals. A few of the dogs began barking wildly, which motivated plenty of other dogs to join in. It seemed as if every last one of them got caught up in the moment, some leaping up and down and others straining at their leashes.

A few of the dogs, the ones whose owners hadn't been holding on tightly enough, broke free. Suddenly at least a dozen dogs of all colors, shapes, and sizes were charging around the chapel, their paws skittering against the hard tile floor.

Most of them thought they were playing a wonderful game. The hefty English bulldog who'd been sitting next to me charged across the chapel, colliding with a Jack Russell mix that had been frolicking in the aisle, acting like a typical terrier by jumping right into the fray.

But dogs weren't the only ones who took advantage of the sudden anarchy to escape from their owners. So did some of the cats.

Felines who only moments before had been curled up peacefully in their owners' laps were suddenly streaking through the chapel, some of them hissing and snarling like creatures in a horror movie.

The commotion set the birds in attendance screeching. The chapel, formerly a relatively serene setting, suddenly sounded like the jungle, with high-pitched, ear-splitting screams cutting through all the barking and growling and yelling.

But just because the chapel had erupted into chaos didn't stop the two miscreants in miniskirts from trying to make their getaway.

"It's Beanie you want!" Campbell cried.

Her voice was loud enough to be heard over the cacophony comprised of the barking, screeching, and hissing of the animals and the accompanying yelps and cries of their human counterparts. I watched in amazement as she demonstrated surprising agility by leaping over a good-size metal cage housing two dark brown Dutch rabbits that looked like chocolate bunnies come to life. "I didn't do anything!"

"You planned the whole thing!" Beanie yelled back. "I never would have done it if you hadn't insisted!"

"I never insisted!" Campbell screamed. "All I did was suggest that it would make my life a lot easier if he wasn't around!"

By this point, the two uniformed cops were in pursuit of them. At least, they were trying their best. One of them nearly tripped over a pair of dachshunds who were watching all the action with wide brown eyes, one growling and one simply looking confused. The other cop, who was taller and leaner, deftly circumvented a massive sheepdog, his eyes half-hidden by his furry bangs, who was intent on sniffing a white French poodle.

But not all the dogs were taking advantage of the melee to interact only with one another. Some of them decided to join in the chase. Four or five excited canines circled around Beanie, while a loping Doberman kept pace with Campbell. He barked excitedly as he followed her through the doorway and out onto the front lawn, which was also littered with dogs and cats and small animals in cages, as well as their baffled-looking owners.

I, too, ran after Campbell, although I wasn't nearly as fast or well coordinated as the Doberman and therefore couldn't get nearly as close. Still, it turned out she didn't get very far, thanks to those high-heeled sandals of hers. That plus the fact that she was in such a hurry that she failed to notice the goat standing in her path.

"What the—oh-h-h-h!" she shrieked as she stumbled against the hefty animal. She went down instantly, tumbling onto the grass.

Fortunately, the goat was sturdy enough that she didn't even seem to notice that she had just made contact with a projectile traveling at an unusually high speed. She just let out an annoyed bleat and went back to chomping on the stray program she'd found lying on the lawn.

Beanie was making much better time. I looked up in time to see her racing across the wide expanse of grass, heading for the parking lot.

It doesn't matter if she gets away, I thought. Sooner or later the police will track her down. I might as well let her go.

The Saint Bernard who'd come to today's blessing didn't seem to feel the same way.

Beanie had almost made it to the parking lot when the huge lumbering animal caught up with her. Despite his massive bulk, the dog jumped up high enough to press his two gigantic front paws against her back, sending her sprawling onto the ground.

"Omph!" she cried as she hit the ground, twisting around as she fell so that she landed on her back.

The well-meaning Saint Bernard wagged his long, furry tail excitedly as he straddled her, meanwhile licking her face with a tongue the size of a slice of bologna. Even though Beanie squirmed around like a worm in an attempt at escaping from his affections, she was still struggling without any success when the cops reached her.

"It wasn't my idea to kill Mr. Stibbins!" Beanie squealed. "Campbell made me do it! She said she wouldn't be my friend anymore if I didn't! It's all her fault!"

But the police officer didn't seem to be listening. He was too busy handcuffing her.

• • •

"A Saint Bernard, huh?" Nick said with a chuckle. "Do you think it's a coincidence that a dog who's named after a saint caught the murderer—at a Blessing of the Animals, no less?"

"I wonder," I replied with a smile.

I snuggled up closer, relishing the comfort of Betty's living room couch. But even more, I was enjoying a quiet moment with my fiancé. Betty and Winston had taken advantage of the warm, sunny Saturday afternoon by driving Max, Lou, and Frederick to one of the local beaches for a run. That meant we had the Big House—our home now, at least for a while—all to ourselves.

"Then again," I added, "a goat helped catch the other guilty party." I sighed deeply. "I'm just glad Nathaniel's killers were caught—no matter who was required to get the job done."

Somberly, Nick said, "When two people conspire to commit murder, the way these girls did, they're both punishable to the same extent."

"The fact that both Beanie and Campbell confessed

in front of the cops, the press, and a couple of hundred people will certainly make Falcone's job easier," I noted.

"The fact that they've been caught should make your job a lot easier, too," Nick observed. "I'm talking about the teaching part."

"That hasn't been hard at all!" I exclaimed. "I've actually been enjoying it a lot more than I expected."

Thoughtfully I added, "Of course, I won't have much of a class left anymore. Beanie and Campbell will be gone, of course. Then there's Vondra. I'm really disappointed that she's not at the Worth School anymore."

"Maybe you can have a little talk with Dr. Goodfellow and Vondra's mother," Nick suggested.

"Maybe I'll do that," I replied. "Especially now that two of the school's terrors are no longer students there."

My cellphone rang, and I glanced at the caller ID screen as I pulled it out of my pocket.

"Speaking of terrors..." I muttered.

Into the phone, I said, "Hello, Dorothy. I've got good news. Nathaniel's killer has been caught!"

"I know," she said breathlessly. "Nick already called to tell me."

I glanced over at him, aware that he could undoubtedly hear his mother even though he was standing a couple of feet away. He just grinned and shrugged.

"I knew I'd be able to help you solve that crime," Dorothy continued. "I told you from the very start that you should look at that fancy private school, didn't I? And I gave you all the clues you needed. I seem to have a real nose for the crime business!"

Hell-o, I thought irritably. Do I get any credit at all?

"I feel so much better, knowing that I helped put Nathaniel's murderer away," Dorothy continued. "In fact, I was just about to celebrate with Henry. Henry, did you figure out a way to open that champagne yet? Be careful with that thing! You're going to put your eye out!"

"So much for earning brownie points with your future mother-in-law," Nick teased after I hung up.

"That's okay," I assured him with a smile. "There's only one member of the Burby family I want to earn brownie points with, and believe me, it's not my future mother-in-law."

I was suddenly aware that his entire body tensed. "Hey, Jess?" he said casually.

"Umm?"

Without actually looking me in the eye, he said, "Speaking of the future, I just had an idea."

Something about the offhanded way he was trying to sound—and the fact that he was doing a really bad job of it—made a lightbulb go off in my head.

"What's your idea?" I asked, even though I was pretty sure I already knew the answer.

The huge grin he was wearing as he turned to me told me I was right.

"Are you thinking what I'm thinking?" I asked coyly.

"I am," he replied somberly. "The town clerk's office

is open on Saturday afternoons, and we have the blood test and the license—"

"And we have something even more important!" I cried. "We have the dress!"

• • •

"I told you I'd get around to using you one of these days," I muttered as I walked up the steps of the huge, impersonal office building that housed the town clerk's office less than two hours later.

It was only the second time in my life I could remember talking to a dress. Still, this dress deserved special treatment. Not only was it about to play a starring role in its second wedding in two weeks, it had also made it through a fire. True, it smelled a bit smoky. But that only showed how strong it was—and how determined to survive.

Kind of like my relationship with Nick.

I continued up the steps, carefully lifting the folds of ivory silk with one hand. In the other, I clutched an impromptu bouquet composed of pink, yellow, and white flowers I'd picked from Betty's garden. Even though getting hitched at Town Hall isn't supposed to be particularly romantic, I was so overcome with emotion that I was close to tears. After all, I was embarking on one of the most monumental experiences of my life.

I also expected it to be one of the most terrifying. Even though I'd already gone through a dress rehearsal, I just assumed that the butterflies that apparently reside in my stomach wouldn't be any more cooperative the second time around.

Yet this time, I was enveloped in a strange sense of calm. It was as if I just knew I was doing what was right for me.

I paused, half-turning as I waited for Nick to catch up with me. Since he'd returned his rented tuxedo long before, dressing up in his wedding finery wasn't an option. He'd offered to put on a suit and tie, but since that was what he wore to the law firm every day, I told him to wear whatever he'd feel most comfortable in. Given that directive, I wasn't all that surprised that he'd emerged from Betty and Winston's bedroom dressed in his best suit, his most conservative tie, and his favorite Led Zeppelin T-shirt, the one that was so badly faded it was nearly impossible to see the band's picture.

When he saw that I'd hesitated at the top of the stairs, he glanced up at me with a look of concern. "Are you okay, Jess?" he asked anxiously.

"I've never been better in my life," I assured him with a smile.

As soon as he reached the step I was on, I linked my arm in his, adding, "I just figured this was something we should be doing together."

He squeezed my hand. "I like the sound of that word."

A few minutes later, I stood next to him in front of the town's wedding officer. As I glanced around at my surroundings, I couldn't help noticing how different everything was compared to the last time around. No gorgeous Victorian mansion, no tuxedo, no sky-high wedding cake. Even that bottle of champagne was long gone.

But I didn't care. Marrying Nick wasn't about any of that. It was about him and me and the two of us being together for the rest of our lives.

"All set?" the wedding officer asked, smoothing the jacket of her dignified blue business suit. From the glazed look in her eyes, I got the feeling she'd done this quite a few times before.

But for me, all this was an exciting new adventure.

"Do you—uh." She glanced down at her notes. "Wait a minute. Oh, here it is. Nicholas Burby. Do you, Nicholas Burby, take this woman—?"

"I do," Nick said without waiting for her to finish.

A startled look crossed her face, then quickly vanished. I had a feeling this had happened once or twice before, too.

"Okay," she said with a curt nod. "In that case, do you—that's Jessica Popper, right?—take this man—"

"I do," I interrupted.

And I did. I absolutely, positively, definitely, completely did.

About the Author

CYNTHIA BAXTER is a native of Long Island, New York. She currently resides on the north shore, where she is at work on the next Reigning Cats & Dogs mystery, which Bantam will publish in 2010. She is also the author of the Murder Packs a Suitcase mystery series. Visit her website at www.cynthiabaxter.com.

Don't miss the next

Reigning Cats & Dogs mystery

Crossing the Lion

by Cynthia Baxter

On sale in Summer 2010